"Soul nourishment! Ginny e[ ]
compassionate insights. She ha[ ]
Wisteria REALITY fiction. Real friends. Bumpy family ride. Faith questions and yearnings. Some answered, some not. And most of all, spiritual inspiration from the only source that counts. Jesus."

— *Miriam Neff*, author, counselor, and creator of *Widow Connection*

"*Wisteria* paints a bittersweet portrait of Angela, a woman wrestling with sudden widowhood and its challenges to her family, her friendships, her faith, and her future. With a tenderness born of experience, author Ginny Graham drew me into Angela's heartaches and hopes so deeply that I found myself crying, laughing, and reading page after page to see if Angela would find her way to the other side of grief."

— **Karen Ingle**, author of *With Me in the Storm*

"Angela had all the natural emotions that came with grieving. Her established faith in God helped her navigate those emotions. Instead of removing herself from others, she became more engaged, more sensitive to others' pain."

— **Linda Gunderson**, Book Club Coordinator

Wisteria

Rekindling faith
and purpose

GINNY GRAHAM

a novel

Wisteria

Rekindling faith
and purpose

Wisteria
© 2023 Ginny Graham

This book is a work of fiction. Names, characters, places, and incidents are either the product of the author's imagination or are used fictitiously. Any resemblance to actual events, locales, business establishments, or persons, living or deceased, is entirely coincidental.

Any emphases in Scripture quotations are the author's.

Cover Design and Interior Design by J.B. Sisam | Living Lights Media

ISBN: 979-8-9882209-0-9 (Print)

23 24 25 26 27 28 | 10 9 8 7 6 5 4 3 2 1

Printed and bound in the United States of America

To Bob, whose memory I cherish

Wisteria

Rekindling faith
and purpose

1

Northgate, Minnesota—May 15th—4:30 a.m.

"Angel?" Todd's Celtic blue eyes twinkled. "What's this?"

"Bacon, eggs, hash browns." Angela smiled. "You need real food before you stop for cinnamon rolls at Toby's."

"An unavoidable detour for fishermen." Todd smiled, tucked his long legs under the kitchen breakfast counter, and picked up Angela's files spread across the countertop. "Is this why you couldn't sleep? Still worried about your business?"

Angela slumped onto a stool next to her husband, wishing she hadn't brought up the subject last night. His solution to her dilemma was simple. Close the flower shop or let her husband bail her out again. She had rankled at both notions. Was she letting pride get in the way?

But today needed to be about Todd. "It'll work out. I want you to think only about fishing for the next week. Enjoy your time with Brock and Greg."

1

Todd's perpetual frown appeared. "When I come back, how can I help?"

Angela laughed. "What is it you do again? Run a company of three hundred employees?"

"Most days it runs me." They both laughed.

Angela let Todd carry the conversation with his fishing plans. Her mind was too filled with worries about her flower shop to say much more. Wisteria. Long life. Would the name she chose for her flower shop live up to its symbolic meaning? Her accountant didn't think so. Her husband didn't think so. Her little flower shop's financial struggles must seem like chump change compared to the company merger Todd had just engineered for his employer. He gulped his breakfast, picked up his gear, kissed her good-bye, and headed for the garage.

Angela shuffled papers into their folders. A folder slipped on the edge of the counter. Catching the wayward file, her hand almost upset the travel mug Todd had forgotten.

"Oh, no." Angela raced to their garage filled with sounds sure to wake the neighbors. The loud muffler of their next-door neighbor's pickup throbbed in the driveway. Sheets of rain pelted a staccato beat against a background of thunder. Even while standing inside, wind whipped rain into her face. Nothing would keep Todd from the fishing opener tomorrow, not even a storm.

Brock's voice boomed over the thunder. "Hey Todd, your tackle box is bigger than a bait shop!" Todd's best friend always seemed to have a way with words.

Greg, their next-door neighbor, vaulted into the back of his pickup. "Same joke every year." Todd's laughter mingled with metal clinking against metal as the men rearranged fishing gear in the bed of the pickup.

"Todd, your coffee!" Angela halted at the edge of the garage opening and lifted his travel mug.

Todd bounded toward Angela. His lips brushed her cheek, leaving a wet trail from his tilted cap. Finally his frown disappeared. "Thanks, Angel. Almost forgot. 'Bye. Love you."

"Love you ..."

Todd dashed through the rain and sprang inside the cab with his buddies. The pickup's headlights swung a yellow arc across the driveway, momentarily spotlighting the late-blooming tulips before it vanished in the pre-dawn gloom.

---

9 a.m.

Angela arrived at her flower shop an hour before opening. She needed to be alone, to clear her head and think through the changes her accountant had suggested. Her stomach churned. Which employee should she let go? There must be another solution to making her business viable. How long would she need to depend on Todd's salary to help her over the bumps? A knock on the glass of the front door interrupted her concentration. She drew back into the shadows. Not opening it. Not today. The early-bird customer can come back at ten.

A calming hum from the overhead fluorescent lights helped her focus on work orders. Angela's heart twisted when she sorted through the hospital deliveries. Until a year ago, she loved making hospital deliveries. The bright bouquets bringing a cheery note of hope to the patients who received them. But now hospitals would forever carry a different connotation. How many trips to the hospital had she made with their daughter,

Bethany? How many trips to the clinic and trips all the way to Minneapolis to see a specialist?

Angela jumped at banging now on the back door. Her foot caught on a chair leg. Limping, she groped her way through the dim back room. Had one of her employees forgotten their key? She fumbled with the lock and flipped on the lights.

Two police officers stood at the door, water puddling around their feet.

"Mrs. McKinley?" A member of the Northgate City Police removed his hat and touched his nameplate. "Officer Jamaal Brown. May we come in?"

"What's wrong?"

"Please have a seat." He nodded to a chair at the break table.

The other officer scrambled to drag the chair closer.

Angela's back stiffened. "I'll stand. Why are you here?"

Brown tucked in his chin and took a deep breath. "Is your husband Todd McKinley?"

"Yes ..."

"Ma'am, I regret to say there's been an accident."

"Todd?" She stepped back.

"Your husband was in a collision heading North on Highway 53, just past Cloquet—"

"No! They left at five this morning. The fishing opener. They should be at the cabin—"

"I'm very sorry." His hands twisted the brim of his hat. "Your husband didn't survive the crash."

Angela smothered a scream.

Between gasps and sobs, she managed, "What happened?"

The young officer with him spoke up. "A logging truck—"

A stabbing glance from Brown stopped him. "Let me give

4

you the number of the officer on the scene. They'll give you the details."

A logging truck? Logs were rolling over her chest right now. She stumbled toward the break table. The officers eased her into the chair. Her shoulders shook.

The terrible truth rolled over her again and again.

2

Three days later—10 p.m.

"**A**ngel?"

Angela startled awake. "Todd?" Only Todd called her Angel.

Another dream. Todd wasn't calling her. He would never call her again.

She slid out from under the rumpled comforter, still in her day clothes, now equally rumpled. She rubbed her head, trying to dispel the fog that had settled into it since the accident. Still couldn't wrap her head around it. Todd and everyone else in the pickup had lost their lives. Next-door neighbor, Greg. Todd's college buddy, Brock. Her husband and close friends she'd assumed would be a part of her life forever.

Tears slipped unheeded as she rose and paced the length of her bedroom. The kitchen light in her next-door neighbor's house flared. Marge must be home. She grabbed her phone and texted her.

Wisteria

Is it too late? Want some company?

When Marge texted back, Angela snatched her raincoat and hurried next door. A cold May drizzle peppered her face. Three days since the accident and it was still raining. Her next-door-neighbor's open garage seemed cavernous without Greg's pickup. Marge's compact car huddled by the back door. She tapped their signal of three quick knocks and stepped inside.

Still in her nursing scrubs, Marjorie Malone looked exhausted. A coffee maker sputtered behind her. "Decaf okay?"

Angela nodded. "You worked today?"

"They were short-staffed in the OR." Marge moved through the kitchen, pulling cups from the shelf, a spoon from the drawer, using her OR precision.

So like Marge. Angela studied her stoic friend.

"The fishing opener. They go to your cabin every year. Why did Greg decide they should go in his old dilapidated pickup?" Marge clanked mugs of coffee on the table. "But he called it a souped-up classic." She sniffed. "Did they even wear seat belts? That truck's so old there were no shoulder straps."

"I know." Angela lifted the steamy mug, but her first sip stuck in her throat. How could she swallow?

"Did you hear the police report?"

"No." And she didn't want to.

"Our local police told me to call Cloquet Police Department, closest to the accident scene. Got only sketchy information. Hazardous road conditions with the storm. A fully loaded logging truck skidded over the median and struck the pickup on the driver's side shortly after seven a.m." Marge caught her breath. Her nostrils flared. "Launched it against the trees. Three men in a death trap."

"Marge, stop."

7

"Not a very good friend, am I?" Marge picked up the creamer.

Angela squeezed Marge's arm, leaned back, and stared at the ceiling. "You know, I wish I could get angry."

Marge's stout form straightened as she humphed. "It'll come. You're still in shock."

Marge drizzled cream into her cup. Angela watched the liquid explode and paint patterns in the cup before dissipating. Its fleeting movement seemed to mirror her life of the past week. The late news from the TV in the living room blared.

"And the third person killed in the tragic crash, prominent Minnesota business executive, Brock Chadway, CEO of Wood-hill Consulting—"

"Still reporting after three days? Should have turned off that TV." Marge punched the remote. "Poor Caroline, so stunned when I called her Friday."

"Why did they have to move?" Angela sighed. "I loved having them across the street. The big two-story house looks lonely without them. Caroline and Brock were like family."

"Uhumm, family." Marge's eyes clouded. "I let Greg's family help me with ..." Marge sank back in her chair and rubbed her forehead. "The arrangements."

Marge had no children to share her burden. Angela couldn't imagine how that would feel.

"Greg's service will be at Gardner's Wednesday at 10:00. Todd's at 2:00? And then we're driving to Minneapolis for Brock's service at 7:00?"

Angela nodded. "I can't believe we're calmly discussing this." She buried her head in her arms.

"Don't get me started, okay? Here, I keep the tissues handy." Marge pushed the box toward Angela. "Your aunt coming to the funeral?"

"Yes ..." Angela looked up and turned away. "Aunt Rita arrives tomorrow."

"Ouch."

"That's one way to put it." Angela had tried for decades to get past much of that history. If she hadn't had summers with her grandmother ...

"Greg's brother and his wife jumped right in to help plan the service, and I just let them." Marge folded her arms. "Why not? They're like you, you know, churchy."

Angela winced. Marge's idea about God never moved beyond that stereotype. Angela knew faith was the only thing that had carried her through the past few days. But did her actions reflect her grip on God's hand?

She glanced at Marge, unsure of how her words would sound. "I'm finding joy ... in something that may sound odd to you."

"Joy?"

"The flowers to cover Todd's casket." She smiled, remembering her plans to return to her flower shop tomorrow. "My gift to him. I know exactly how they will look."

Angela left Marge, stepped over the storm-riddled tulips along the driveway, and returned to a darkened house. Looking at the front of their home, it appeared to be a rambler with an attached garage built on a hillside. But the front door opened into a foyer that dropped into a two-story high living room, dining room, and kitchen. At the foot of the floating staircase, a view of windows reached to the top of the living room's vaulted ceiling. A house that seemed huge now. The wide hallway of the U-shaped upper floor seemed to swallow her as she hurried to her bedroom.

Her bed brought no rest. Red numbers flickered on her digital clock as midnight met the morning. Then an odd surge of excitement filled her when she recalled her plans for the blanket spray of flowers for Todd's casket.

Why not go to the flower shop now? She sat up. In the middle of the night? At least she'd have privacy.

Angela considered the freedom she felt to roam as she drove through the deserted streets. An oddly thrilling but empty freedom possessed her. No one to caution her about driving alone in the middle of the night. No one to care. Fifteen minutes later, she arrived at Wisteria Floral and Gifts. Its purple-and-white sign looked forlorn at 1:00 a.m.

Angela proceeded straight to the fresh-cut flowers. When she reached for the white calla lilies, her eyes blurred. This would be her finest creation. Honoring Todd with the work of her hands. Drawing from a bucket of deeply scented crimson roses, she extended the calla lily centerpiece. Each rose she added had to be perfect with the right drape in the long stem. Ivy filled in the gaps and curled around her fingers like an old friend. Narrow white ribbons flowed from the centerpiece and reached over the edge of the worktable. At the end of each ribbon, she tied lover's knots around tiny sprigs of baby's breath.

She gasped. Roses, ivy, streamers ending in lover's knots. Substitute white roses for the crimson, and that was her wedding bouquet.

Hot tears fell atop the roses and lilies and ivy. She wrote a tag and gently laid the spray on the top shelf in the refrigerated case. She kissed the tips of her fingers and touched them to a velvety smooth rose.

"I love you, Todd."

When she closed the glass door, its gentle swoosh lifted the paper tag into a swaying dance. Todd's name swung into sight. His name. Seeing it attached to a funeral spray cemented the awful truth. She clutched her chest. Could the crack through her heart get any wider?

3

Two days later

Angela's children filled the house again. Her three bees. That was Todd's pet name for Bethany, Benjamin, and Becca. They looked like young adults on the outside, but their eyes windowed their struggle and sorrow on the inside. Life hadn't prepared them to adjust to this kind of loss, and each seemed to be dipping into a different well in an effort to cope. Angela didn't know how to ease their pain. She was too full of her own.

Aunt Rita's arrival only compounded that pain.

"Lavender?" Aunt Rita eyed Angela's dress. "For your husband's viewing?"

"Todd bought this dress for me. He knew it was my favorite color."

Aunt Rita sniffed as she adjusted the jacket of her tight-fitting suit. "But you always looked so good in black."

Angela noted Aunt Rita's lavender painted nails with turquoise highlights and turned away, massaging her temples.

"Got a headache, honey?"

"I just need to rest a few minutes before we leave for the funeral home." Ignoring her aunt's quizzical look, Angela retreated to her bedroom.

It seemed she'd just closed her eyes when someone knocked on her bedroom door. Time to leave.

Todd's viewing with no viewing.

She stood beside the closed casket for three hours, receiving words of sympathy from friends and acquaintances. The entire town of Northgate seemed as shocked as she was. Never had a tragedy involving three well-known men happened in their small community. If anyone said a trite or well-meant-but-insensitive remark, she was too numb to notice.

Angela's children and Aunt Rita stood beside her through the visitation. Arriving home late, the family tried to eat, but gave up and drifted into the living room. Everyone except Bethany, her husband, Emerson, and their son, two-year-old Phillip. They paused at the foot of the steps leading to the entryway.

"Bethany." Angela caught her with a hug then touched her face. "You're so pale."

"That's exactly why I'm taking them back to the apartment." Emerson Dahl carried a slumping Phillip and nudged Bethany.

"Don't worry, Mom, I'll be okay." The droop in Bethany's posture belied her words.

Aunt Rita watched them climb the stairs to the entryway. "After all these years, I can't get used to your house. It's upside down. The living room and kitchen down here, the entry and front door upstairs."

"It's custom designed for this hillside," Angela said.

"Well, talk about 'sunken living room,' I guess!" Aunt Rita said.

Angela headed back into the living room. Her son, Benjamin, met her. "Mom, got some emails to catch up on. I think I'll turn in." He hugged her and headed to his former bedroom.

Her youngest daughter, Becca, glanced Angela's way. "I'm heading to bed, Mom." Suddenly, unwillingly, Angela was alone with Aunt Rita.

"I never saw so many people in my life. They just kept a-comin'." Aunt Rita stretched out in Todd's recliner.

Angela bit her lip. "Todd ... had a lot of friends. From work, school, childhood. So touching to see young adults from Todd's youth group, some with their spouses."

"Angie, honey, you've got years of memories with Todd."

Angela heard her children thumping around in their rooms. Did they need to talk? Surely any moment someone would call her away. But no one did.

Aunt Rita was on a roll, spewing family details. They steamrolled over Angela as she massaged her feet and stifled a moan.

"My husband died in the war, as you know." Aunt Rita continued without skipping a beat. "You never met him. That was a long time ago. But your dad stepped in and was there for me through that loss. What a brother. We were so close growing up. Even after your mama and he married and they settled down in Beaumont Springs not far from my house. You and Lorrie looked just like your mama. Cute little blonde girls. Maybe that made it even harder for your dad.

Everything changed when your mama died. He never got over the loss. Don't blame him for making the decisions he did."

Angela absent-mindedly twirled a lock of hair as her thoughts drifted. Another wave of loss engulfed her, this one from long past. Something close. Something she could almost touch. "I wish I could remember my mother."

"Land sakes! You were only two."

"I know." If only Angela could remember a touch, a voice, a shadow of a face.

"They were quite a couple. Your mom was outgoing. Your dad was the quiet one. He took her going hard. But, he always sent money to raise you girls. He was a good man."

Angela nodded. What could she say about the man she only remembered as stiff and formal each time she saw him?

"Then we lost him, too. What a shock to get that call," Aunt Rita said. "A heart attack, of all things. He just dropped dead. No warning. Dotty and I closed a couple of bars that night. You remember Dotty? I needed someone to talk to in the worst way."

An edge crept into Angela's voice. "I remember Lorrie and I stayed up late that night, afraid to go to bed."

Unbidden, Angela shifted into her nine-year-old self. Daddy's gone? What if Aunt Rita died, too? What would happen to them? Angela had stood at the window that night, watching for her Aunt Rita's car. Her older sister, Lorrie, had wisely called their Grandma Em. Angela could still hear her grandmother's voice even though Lorrie held the phone close. "Rita went where?"

"Oh, speaking of your sister, she's real sorry she couldn't come. No vacation time left," Rita said. "Still living in that same dinky apartment. I can't believe she never married some nice man instead of hanging out with that crowd. She never had luck with men like you did."

"It wasn't luck." Angela caught herself and softened her tone. After all, Aunt Rita meant well. "It wasn't luck with Todd and me. I believe it was God guiding our lives." Angela closed her eyes for a moment. Was she just spouting "churchy" words she'd heard? She searched her heart. "Someday I'll understand why He took Todd home."

"Angie, honey, you were always sentimental. Sounds like something Grandma Em would say." Aunt Rita invariably called her own mother Grandma Em. "By the way, might have another funeral coming up. Grandma Em's about to bury her third husband."

"Oh!" Angela's voice shook. "She didn't mention it when I called her."

"No, she wouldn't. Just takes whatever life dishes out to her." Aunt Rita droned on, but Angela didn't hear the words.

Angela inhaled sharply. "Always trusting God." Her grandmother had been the greatest influence in her life. Visions of standing in her grandmother's flower garden filled her thoughts. Every flower so tall in her little-girl mind. She brushed past peonies, heavy with perfume. But her grandmother's garden held miniature wonders, too. "Look, Angie." Her grandmother bent over until her apron touched the ground. She cupped a pansy in two fingers. "See their little fairy faces?" And Angela's love for flowers took root.

The funerals

Three funerals. Three graveside services. Wave after wave of people pressing against Angela.

Then the silence of her home.

That night, Angela lay between cold sheets, her face on a cool pillow. She closed her eyes to the haunting image of white ribbon streamers ending in lover's knots tied around sprigs of baby's breath tumbling in the wind. As though her heart was also tumbling in the wind.

4

One week later—Northgate Clinic.

An American flag whipped against the flagpole in a valiant dance. It reminded Angela of why she sat in the oncology waiting room. Courage. Patience. Perseverance.

"Wanna go home." Angela's two-year-old grandson, Phillip, whined and threw his head against her chest.

"I know. Me, too." Angela rocked him back and forth. Louis Armstrong's gravelly crooning of "What a Wonderful World" wafted overhead. She let the irony of the lyrics sink in. Phillip relaxed in her arms. Northgate Clinic should feel like a second home to him. Bethany's diagnosis of leukemia had come just after Phillip's first birthday. Angela and Todd had spent hours crying, praying, holding each other, and trying to support their daughter and her little family.

The steel clock on the wall clicked to twenty-five minutes past twelve, when a brisk movement caught Angela's eye. It was Bethany. Her eyes sparkled. "Low numbers have stabilized for the past month. The doctor said I'm definitely on maintenance now."

Angela's mouth fell open.

"Mom?" Bethany cocked her head and grinned. "The look on your face."

Angela felt a new sensation start at the tips of her toes, slowly rising until a smile burst forth. "Bethany! Such awesome news." Angela's delight bubbled forth in a laugh. Her frozen heart had forgotten there could be joy in life again.

"I didn't want to tell you last week. Well, just in case there was a relapse."

Angela squeezed Bethany with one arm until her grandson, held in the other, protested.

Bethany's beautiful smile spread even bigger as she stepped back and held out her arms to Phillip. "Let Mommy carry you?"

"No! Want Gamma." Phillip clung to Angela's neck.

"Happens every time." Bethany dropped her arms.

"Oh, Phillip." Angela laughed at his clinginess. "He'll get past it. Besides, you need to take it easy."

"Mom." Bethany lifted the all-purpose bag and an empty trail mix wrapper. "You're hovering again."

"That's what moms do." Angela held the Northgate Clinic door as sunshine flooded the entryway. "It's embedded in our DNA."

Bethany touched Phillip's springy curls. "It is."

With a spring in her step and Phillip on one hip, Angela hurried toward her car.

"Bumblebee!" Phillip squealed.

Bethany froze. "Where?"

"He sees my car. I can't believe you remembered, Phillip."

Angela opened the back door and glanced at Bethany. "That's what we named the car last summer."

Bethany eyed the yellow and black Mini Cooper. "Cute."

Angela sat Phillip in his car seat but let Bethany finish strapping him in.

"They didn't change my medication. Just monitoring it for now." Bethany's head bobbed as she buckled Phillip into his car seat. Her short blond curls lacked the luster they once had. "Remission. I'm almost afraid to say the word." A smile spread across Bethany's face. "Fear not. My new motto."

Angela started her car and waited for Bethany before swinging around to see where she was backing the car.

Bethany exhaled audibly. "Odd, the statistics."

"What statistics?"

"My doctor didn't want to give me false hope. But he said if you have leukemia, CML is the one to have."

"What?"

"Well, CML patients typically stay on chemo meds, like tyrosine kinase inhibitors, all their lives. There doesn't seem to be a cure for CML, but many patients lead a somewhat normal life." Bethany stared ahead. "He encouraged me to join an online help group."

"This is so scary for me," Angela said.

"Me, too. But I feel like God has a future for me. For us." Bethany glanced at her sleepy two-year-old. "Our family."

They had just turned onto a familiar street when Angela caught her breath and slammed on the brakes. A tall, slim man, built like her husband Todd, walked in front of her car. She waited as he rearranged cones as nonchalantly, as if stepping from an office cubicle for coffee instead of walking into a busy traffic lane.

The workman waved them on, but the image of Todd's face

remained. How ecstatic he would have been to hear Bethany's news. Angela could feel Todd's arms swoop her into a bear hug. Without meaning to, Angela's thoughts wandered to their last evening when she told Todd about her flower shop's financial troubles. He had always supported her venture, but his attitude of "maybe it's time to pull the plug" still unsettled her. He had called it her "project." Had he never understood it was her dream? She wanted to make the shop viable and do it on her own, yet she still yearned for his advice. Now she'll never have that again.

They passed Wisteria, and Bethany glanced at Angela. "So, have you been back to the shop?"

"Yes. Just a couple of times."

"Made any of those hard decisions?"

"Like who gets the axe?" Angela shook her head. "Don't want to think about it yet. I'll need both employees until I'm back to working full time."

"Come over any time, okay?"

"Thanks, I'll take you up on that."

It was a quick ride to Bethany's apartment. Phillip's eyelids fluttered when they trundled him into his bed.

Visibly drooping, Bethany forced a smile. "Would you like a cup of tea?"

"No thanks. I'll let you join Phillip for a nap."

But did Angela really want to face that empty house?

5

Would cutting one employee really save her business? Angela waited until Friday to return to her shop, not ready to face the daily challenge of her business, let alone deeper issues like how to turn the business around.

Parking her car next to the flower shop van, she noted the scuffed back door to the shop. Wisteria's lavender color scheme wasn't ideal for outdoor trim. Paint applied two years ago was toast. The back door stuck again. Giving the handle that special lift and pull, she pushed through and pasted on a wobbly smile. Both employees were busy and the phone was ringing without being answered.

Angela grabbed the call as she jotted down the phone order. "We can have them ready for you this afternoon."

Shane, a beanpole with red hair and freckles, stood next to Angela, spinning florist tape around an orchid so fast one couldn't tell when he added a fern and a bow to the corsage. He wrapped and handed it to a man Angela recognized as Todd's barber.

The barber nodded to Angela. "Sorry to hear about Todd."

"Oh," Another customer looked at Angela with wide eyes. "That was your husband, wasn't it?" Milling customers stood still, all eyes on Angela. "Such a tragedy, I'm so sorry," said another.

Others chimed in with sympathy.

"Thank you." Through a blur, she watched them nod and leave. Only the constant motion of her hands held her together.

As customers filed out, Shane printed online orders and organized them by due date. By far the more talented of her two employees, Shane had run the shop the past year while Angela focused on Bethany's needs. Angela's newest employee, Rosa, worked with hesitation on a squatty vase of chrysanthemums. Should she help Rosa find other employment? But where? Rosa, a former resident at the local women's shelter, was a single mom with little work experience.

During a lull, Angela scanned the shop. "Shane, it seems like an unusually busy day for a Friday morning."

"Must be the fifty-percent-off sign I put up this morning. Overstock on plants from Mother's Day." He pointed to a massive display of potted chrysanthemums, azaleas, and hyacinths.

"How could that have happened? Over-ordered?" Angela quieted when new customers arrived.

A middle-aged woman marched straight to the display case and frowned. "No lavender daisies with yellow centers?"

The woman behind her snorted and pointed at the flowers. "Look at all the colors they have. Robin will like whatever we send." She dropped a large purse on the counter to settle the issue.

Angela hustled to the worktable, assembled the arrangement, and rang up another sale. While she worked, the state of her business gnawed at her. Perhaps she had managed with too loose a hand, dumping everything in Shane's lap for the past year. But what else could she have done?

She recognized the woman next in line, Trudy Bauer, an acquaintance in their circle of friends.

"Angela." Trudy crossed behind the counter and hugged her. "You have my deepest sympathy."

"Thank you," Angela said.

"We've been on vacation and just heard about Todd from a neighbor. To think this could happen in a town our size, three men, all at once. I don't know how you can bear it." Without taking a breath, Trudy gushed like a torrent going over Minnehaha Falls. "We're all going to miss him so. I hope it doesn't make you sad for me to talk about him."

"No, not at all." Angela flipped a strand of hair behind her ear. Her hand trembled. "It's a comfort to talk about Todd."

Trudy's eyes narrowed into small slits. "Do you talk to him yet? You will. My dad's been gone for a year, and I talk to him every day."

Angela smiled, pricked by her words but knowing she meant well. Why would she talk to Todd? Todd's in heaven. That would almost seem like praying to him. Strange.

"Like I said, Angela—"

"Honey?" Arnie, Trudy's husband, grasped his wife's arm and pulled her to a display of greeting cards. He lifted a hand to Angela. "Sorry to hear about Todd."

"Thank you."

Trudy placed her order, and Arnie nudged her out the door as a large woman in her eighties entered.

"Hello, Mrs. Dexter. Here for your pink carnation?" Angela said.

"Yes, I am. A sweet carnation just like the first flowers Otto brought me."

Wisteria

How many times had Angela heard the story of her corsage of pink carnations? Mrs. Dexter's husband, now deceased, her first and last sweetheart. A widow. Angela's eyes smarted as she chose the biggest, freshest carnation.

"I heard about the accident." Mrs. Dexter shook her head, took the package, and patted four bills on the counter. "At least you're still young."

Angela watched her amble to the front door. Why should that be a comfort? More years without Todd?

What a contrast to her friends at church. Many mentioned a memory of Todd, or how much they missed him, or just a hug, saying nothing at all. What a comfort that was.

"Shane, can you and Rosa run the shop for the rest of the day?" Angela transferred her phone from her apron pocket to her bag and checked phone messages.

A text from Marge:

Angela and Caroline, free for dinner tonight? 6:30?

6

Marge's house—after dinner

With a tray of coffee in hand, Marjorie coaxed everyone into the living room.

Angela circled past Greg's recliner to sit next to Caroline Chadway on the sofa. Caroline's shoulder-length auburn hair danced about her face as she bent to brush a speck of lint from her dark slacks. Caroline was striking. Heads turned when she walked by. Lovely thing about Caroline, she seemed unaware of creating a stir.

"Not able to get the written accident reports yet," Marge said.

"Sorry, Marge," Angela said, puzzled. What difference will it make?

Marge continued. "Received more information over the phone, though. Remember when we heard the driver of the truck died shortly after the accident? I found out he suffered a massive heart attack. They're not sure when. Perhaps the driver was speeding, lost control, missed the curve, and that brought

26

on the heart attack. Or, the heart attack happened first and caused the crash. They lean toward the latter. The officer told me the truck driver was an independent driver, no company affiliation, no immediate family, drove an old truck, and somehow got by without insurance. The officer hinted at the uselessness of filing a lawsuit." She gritted her teeth. "As if I was interested in suing anyone." Marge sniffed and grabbed for tissues.

Everyone did the same.

In the kitchen, the refrigerator's compressor kicked on, punctuating their awkward silence.

"I can't come to terms with the fact that Todd's gone ..." Angela's last word came out in a whisper.

Caroline merely stared at the carpet. Her grief seemed to pull her into a closed room with a door that Angela couldn't open.

"Death was the furthest thing from my mind. Greg, at the height of his dreams," Marge said, "not at all like the death of a child."

"A child?" Caroline's head jerked toward Marge.

"Somehow Greg's death, seeing my mom and dad at the funeral, brought it all back," Marge said. "Never mentioned my little brother who died, did I?"

Angela looked twice at Marge. "I'm sorry, I didn't know."

"Few people do. When I was eight-years-old, I had to process it as best I could. Like an elephant in the room. Everyone knew it was there, but my mother didn't allow any of us to speak of Sam." Marge scooted her cup to the lamp table. "Still that way."

"Would it help to talk about it?" Angela said.

Marge had a faraway look in her eyes. "I guess. It's on my mind, like it happened yesterday. Memories have a way of slipping out of their assigned compartment. We tried to do it mom's way. I realize now her way didn't work. I think that's why I'm having such a hard time giving in to the grief of Greg's death. She taught me not to grieve."

Marge paused. "Sam was six years old. He'd a terrible cough all winter. One night, after a rough day of coughing and fever, my mom said we should take him to the emergency room. Dad said no, he had gone to the doctor the day before; give the antibiotics a chance to work. I can still hear him hacking. The next morning his fever rose even higher. That's when they took him to the hospital. Double pneumonia. They had sent me to school. I never saw him again." Marge's eyes were bright with unshed tears.

"Worst of all," she continued, "at the funeral, a little old lady hobbled up on her cane to my mother. She said, 'God wanted a new little angel in heaven; that's why He took your son.' I can still see my mother's eyes burning a hole in that woman's back. My mother never went to church again. Oh, she sent me, or dropped me off when the weather was bad, until I figured out ways of not going."

Caroline nodded. "I've heard people say those same words at funerals."

"But God didn't say that." Angela blurted out.

Marge's brows furrowed.

"I mean," Angela said, "why would your mother stop going to church because of what one person said?"

"I don't know." Marge shook her head. "The fact remains, that woman changed our family dynamics without ever knowing. What I can't get past is the way my mother tried to wipe out Sam's memory. Maybe she thought it would protect us from the pain. It hasn't. The pain just sits there."

"Is that the reason you became a nurse? Your little brother suffering so?" Caroline said.

Marge seemed to consider Caroline's words. "Maybe it is. I lose myself in my work now."

"Work can distract us from pain," Caroline said.

"It's hard." Angela stared at the coffee dregs at the bottom of her cup. "Where do we go from here?" Angela made eye contact with Marge, then turned to Caroline. "If only we knew other widows who could advise us ... women who have been through this."

"My aunt is a widow," Caroline said, "but she's the last person I would ask for advice."

Angela and Marge nodded. They had met Caroline's aunt.

"Our church doesn't offer a grief counseling program. Too small." Angela lifted her gaze. "But we could drive to a larger church in Minneapolis or St. Paul. It's not that long of a drive."

"I'm not sure meeting in a church is the answer for me." Marge squirmed in her chair.

"There are three of us—that makes a group." Caroline turned to Angela. "Isn't your degree in counseling?"

"That was years ago. I don't remember much about grief counseling." Angela's throat tightened. "Never had a reason to put it to use."

"I'd be more comfortable with just the three of us." Marge sipped coffee.

"Maybe." Angela hesitated. "But if we form our own group, we'd need direction."

"There must be something online," Caroline said.

"I'll look for resources." Angela made up her mind. "Shop's closed on Mondays, so how about meeting at my house this coming Monday night?"

Angela walked across the yard with the day of the accident

playing through her mind. Her hand stiffened on the doorknob. That moment of fear when facing an empty house. She steeled herself as she peeked in each room and checked behind doors, trying to get past the feeling that she was all alone. Her trek ended in the bedroom where she had slept with her protector, Todd. How long would this ritual continue?

Sleep eluded her, so she dragged herself to Todd's computer and began her search for widows' counseling resources. Tomorrow she would place a few calls. This could be a good thing. She needed Marge and Caroline, and they seemed to feel the same way. She prayed the study would give each of them closure and comfort. Just what Angela's heart ached for right now.

Still sitting at Todd's desk, she fingered the envelopes she'd received from his company. It was a notice of his final paycheck, the merger bonus, and accrued vacation. Her brows knitted. Better ask her attorney how to deposit them in her account. Quite a sum. Even after her tithe. No loan needed. Savings account intact. The deposits would carry her for a while.

She slit open her credit card statement and dropped it in shock. How had the zero balance skyrocketed to thirty thousand dollars? She and Todd had always paid their bill at the end of the month.

Of course. The funeral, related expenses. Angela threw her pen at the statement. The pen spiraled and pointed back at her, accusing her. Spending money as if she still had Todd's income to depend on. Even without the funeral expenses, her paycheck from the shop would never cover her present lifestyle. The lifestyle Todd and she had taken for granted. His last paycheck and bonus shriveled before her eyes. How was she to live? How many household expenses could she cut? How far would her savings stretch?

Angela's head jerked at a noise in the upper hallway. Her heartbeat quickened. It was late Friday evening, and she didn't expect anyone. A key turning the lock. By this time, Angela stood frozen at the bottom of the steps.

7

Angela caught her breath as the front door opened and slammed shut.

"Hi Mom, caught a ride with Amanda." Her youngest daughter, Becca, tromped toward her room, laundry bag trailing behind. "Cell's not working or I would've called. Amanda said we would drive back Sunday afternoon."

"Becca, wait." Angela almost cried with relief. She bounded up the steps and caught Becca in a hug before she reached her room. Becca wearily responded with a few light taps on Angela's back.

"So glad you're home." Angela locked an arm through Becca's.

Becca's gaze took in the lower level as if never having been in the house before. She pulled away from Angela. "Yeah, home."

"You must be starved. Let's grab a snack?" Angela watched her youngest kick her bag to the side and bump her way down the steps.

"Prepping for finals. I'm beat, Mom."

"I'm sure you are."

Becca reached the lower level, walked into the kitchen and swung open the refrigerator door, digging past jars of dressings and a jug of milk. "Where's the blueberry yogurt? Was always a pint in the fridge."

"Oh, did you like that, too?"

"Yeah, don't you remember? Dad and I used to ..."

It was Angela's turn to slump away.

"Mom? You okay?" Becca caught Angela by her arm and spun her close. "Here I'm worried about having to face the house, knowing Dad's not here. And you, you live here every day."

She allowed Becca to lead her to the sofa where she curled up and buried her face on Becca's neck. Roles reversed.

Awaking early Saturday morning, Angela prepared a huge breakfast for Becca.

"School's out next Friday?"

Becca brightened, her sunny mood the opposite of the night before. "Yes. No need to pick me up. Amanda's driving me again."

"Did you line up your job for the summer?"

"Uh-huh, same as last year, senior care."

"Our nurse of the family." Angela finished her breakfast and grabbed coffee.

"Well, nursing assistant." Becca chewed slowly.

"Which shift?"

"Three-thirty 'til midnight. Beats last summer's night shift."

Angela smiled. "It'll be nice to have you home for the summer."

"The house seems so empty without ..." Becca shook her head and carried her dishes to the sink. "When it's you and me this summer, even the bar with four stools will seem too large."

Angela looked around the large kitchen, dining room, and living room. She thought of the two bedrooms downstairs, two bedrooms upstairs. "This is ludicrous."

"What is?"

"Why am I looking for ways to economize while maintaining a home of this size? Why am I even thinking of staying in this house?"

"You would sell this house?" Becca swallowed hard.

Angela rubbed her forehead. "I don't want to."

"Wow." Becca shook her head. "Well, I'm going over to Amanda's to study."

"Before you leave, I need your help."

"Doing what?"

"Just get me started on the lawn mower. I've never used it."

"You've never mowed the lawn? Yeah, I guess dad and I always took care of that."

"Todd enjoyed yard work."

"Mom." Becca closed her eyes. "Look. I'll just do it later."

"No, I want to know how. This is another thing I'll have to learn."

"But Mom, I have a whole day of studying—"

"Becca, ten minutes. Just get me started."

Sunlight flooded the garage when Angela punched the remote to lift the creaky door.

"Dad sure knew how to pick 'em." Becca rounded the workbench to a recessed area. "It's the Cadillac of riding mowers."

It seemed the size of a road grader to Angela.

"Did dad even use it this year?"

"Yes, the week before he—" Angela's breath caught in her throat. She turned aside and rubbed her hand over the shiny fender. "Looks brand new. Todd always cleaned it after he mowed."

"See, electric start, gas tank's full, you'll be fine."

Angela scrunched her eyebrows.

"Now, watch everything I do." Becca started the mower and took the first lap around the yard. "See? Easy." She motioned for Angela to climb on.

"Give it more gas. You can do it!" Becca ran alongside like a parent teaching a child to ride a two-wheeled bike. "Don't get so close to that tree."

Angela instinctively lifted her hand and received a jagged scratch from a dead limb.

"We'll do the trimming later. Don't forget, lean into the hill going up that rise," Becca shouted.

Angela nodded. With a determined breath, she angled her wheel to overlay the previous row. The motor thundered in her ears and the tires dug into the incline. When she slowed, the mower stopped. She floored the pedal to keep moving. The hillside never looked steep before. Good heavens. What would keep the mower from turning over? What had Becca said? Lean into the hill.

The motor died. Now what? Had Becca left already? Angela jumped off and ran inside.

"Becca! Good, you're still here. Why did the motor die going up the hill?" Angela called. She ran to the bathroom to wash the blood off her arm. "I leaned to the inside just as far as I could."

"You probably leaned too far. If all your weight's on one hip, the sensor thinks you fell off. It's an automatic shut-off."

Angela winced when the water stung her arm. "I guess that's a good thing."

Becca slung her backpack over one arm. "Going to Amanda's. I'll be home late."

"Hold on a minute. Watch to make sure I get going again." Angela's voice was shaky. She headed to the stranded mower.

How did Becca say to start it? Oh, yes. The mower jumped and Angela tightened her grip. With a jerk, she took off. She soon hit a rhythm. Her neighbor appeared with a weed whacker and waved at her. She let go of one side of the wheel long enough to wave back. A weed whacker, one more machine to master? She inhaled the smell of freshly cut grass. The way Todd's clothes smelled after he mowed. Even smells conspired to remind her of Todd.

8

onday Angela kicked into grandma mode: a full
morning of caring for Phillip while Bethany rested.
After a quick lunch, she drove him home again to take his nap.

"Thanks, Mom, I'm better today. Already started dinner for tonight. Would you like to join us?"

"Thank you, but Marge and Caroline are coming over. We started a ... sort of ... grief recovery group."

Bethany's eyes filled and she wrapped her arms around Angela.

"Mommy? Cwry?" Phillip patted his mother's arm.

Bethany turned and reached out to Phillip. "It's okay, honey."

How confusing for the little guy. Tears everywhere. So hard for him to understand. Angela smiled at Phillip and hurried home, blinking back tears of her own.

Angela scooped the material for the widow's group meeting into her arms and headed to her favorite chair to review their lesson. Would this study heal the ache in her heart? Could anything do that?

It was late afternoon, and Angela still hadn't planned their meal. She kicked herself for not picking up something after leaving Bethany's. Multitasking seemed a thing of the past. Eating alone had become an ordeal for her. This would be one less meal the three women would eat alone. Even if it was take-out. Takeout would be less stress.

Less stress. That's what life was about now. Heading to the deli section at the local Save-Mor, she tried to remember Marge and Caroline's favorites. Chinese always works. Why did her mind refuse to function? She reached for Todd's yogurt out of habit and hesitated. She closed her eyes. Remembering that it was Becca's favorite too, she added it to the shopping cart. What a joy it would be to have Becca home for the summer. When she turned a corner, a man's cart tooled around the aisle, blocking her way. When he courteously backed his cart, he bumped into his wife.

"Sorry," he said to Angela. "I seem to be in the way."

"He's always in the way," the woman behind him said with a knowing smirk.

Angela took a deep breath to quell what was welling inside her. *Don't say that, my husband just died three weeks ago!* Somehow she found her way to the checkout counter before everything blurred. She paid the clerk and hurried away from the checkout.

"Excuse me?" the clerk called, "your groceries?"

"Thank you."

Angela raced to her car with tears streaming down her face, not caring that people stared at her. She slumped behind the wheel. She would never have felt Todd was in the way.

Wait. Who was she to judge? Their last night together she had bantered with Todd about her flower shop. What did she say to him? They had talked about her business, his job. Why hadn't she told him how much she loved him? How he completed her life. How much she cherished his love. She had said none of that. She thought they had tomorrow and countless tomorrows after that. Regret replaced self-righteousness. She dried her eyes and rushed home.

With time running out, Angela hustled into the shower. She stepped out and partially dried her hair. Glancing in the mirror, she remembered the care she used to take with the way she looked. Not anymore. She combed through the shoulder-length curls, grabbed the quickest thing to put on, and headed for the kitchen.

Angela unpacked bags and assembled her supplies. Before she finished warming the containers of Chinese takeout, Marge and Caroline arrived. They ate for a few minutes in silence.

"I'm sorry we weren't able to make it to your house after the funeral, Caroline." Angela picked at the tasteless food.

"I understand. It was late. There were so many people ..."

"And your new home," Marge said, "Is construction complete?"

"Everything but the yard." Caroline placed silverware squarely in the middle of her plate. "We had been living there about a month."

"I'm sure it's a beautiful home," Angela said.

"It's quite large, too large." Caroline realigned her silverware. "Going to work at your shop tomorrow, Angela?"

"For a few hours." Angela sat back. "Work is the worst place for me."

"What do you mean?" Caroline said.

Angela frowned. "People who come into the shop do more than offer a simple condolence. They give homespun 'advise' or platitudes ... that aren't helpful."

"Like what?" Caroline said.

"Such as, you're still young—as if I'm thinking of remarriage. Or, it'll get easier. Almost like, get over it."

"Humph," Marge said. "Good thing I don't work retail."

"It will become old news," Caroline said.

"After a thousand people filter through her shop." Marge snorted.

"Well, after telling you, I realize they wanted to comfort me in the only way they know. They're just being courteous."

"They are," Caroline said. "I can't tell you how many people from Northgate contacted me. Many attended the funeral even though we left two years ago."

"I guess it's the blessings of living in a small town. The Christian thing for me to do is love them for their effort." Angela rose and stacked the plates. "Thanks for listening."

Caroline followed with leftover food. "Sometimes it helps to unload."

Angela opened the fridge to store the leftovers and stopped. "What's this?" She removed a huge pitcher with tinkling ice floating on top. Angela carefully placed the pitcher on the counter, her shoulders shaking. Not from tears, but from laughter. "Guess what? I made fresh lemonade for us."

Caroline smiled.

"Can you believe I forgot?"

"Yes." Marge grinned. "Welcome to the club."

"At least I can still laugh at myself." That cleared the air for Angela. Her depression from her earlier experience disappeared.

Angela filled their glasses. "Now we'll have plenty of lemonade for the rest of the evening." She led the way to the living room and loaded a DVD.

"Workbooks?" Marge pointed to the coffee table.

"Workbooks, a lesson for each week." Angela punched the remote. "And a video to watch."

"Overwhelming." Caroline sank into the cushions next to Marge.

The video was a series of interviews with widows. Their stories touched Angela's heart. A counselor drew viewers' attention to the different ways the widows handled their grief.

When the video ended, Marge sighed. "So others know what we're going through?"

"And they survived?" Caroline shook her head as if she didn't expect that would happen.

Angela leaned her head back. "I'm not crazy?"

"Exactly what I was thinking," Marge said. "I've experienced sporadic emotions and odd responses since Greg has been gone."

Angela led the ladies through a short list of questions. Each struggled to verbalize their experience. "Is your grief harder than you imagined?" Angela said.

"You'll never know." Caroline covered her mouth.

Angela waited for her to explain but Caroline's lifted chin closed the subject.

"It's complicated," Marge said. "I have my work at the hospital. After work, I spend time at Greg's company, with a host of people looking at me, wondering if their jobs will continue. I don't have time to mourn."

"I'm surprised by the pain." Angela shook her head and turned back a page in her workbook. "Their opening struck me —permission to grieve and honestly express your emotions. You don't need to be strong. I love this verse: 'blessed are those who mourn, for they shall be comforted.'"

"Remember my background? Dropped off at church?"

Marge shifted on the sofa. "I can relate much better to the video than statements from the Bible."

"I'm sorry that happened, Marge," Angela said. "Just take what works for you. I need the two of you. I need your support."

"I'll be here," Marge said. "Our friendship is a great comfort."

"It's the only time I can be real," Caroline said.

"Maybe we could spend some uninterrupted time together. Just the three of us." Angela sat back and closed her eyes for a moment. "In fact, this is something I've been thinking about all week. I have a plan."

Marge seemed disconnected, Caroline indifferent, but Angela dropped the bomb anyway. Their reaction was much as she thought it would be.

"Go to the cabin?" Caroline sat up. "You want us to go to the cabin with you?"

"Yes, just the three of us," Angela said. "What do you think?"

"You realize we'll go past the accident scene?" Marge said.

"That occurred to me." Angela twirled a lock of hair around her finger. "Do you think it's too soon?"

Marge took a long drink of lemonade. "No, I believe I can handle it. I'd like to go with you."

"Good, how about you, Caroline?"

"I'd like to get away from ... everything. When?"

"This weekend okay?"

Caroline's gaze narrowed. "That soon?"

"Sure, why not?" Marge said. "I think I can arrange it."

"Bring your workbooks along," Angela said. "Plenty of time to finish what doesn't get done during the week."

Wisteria

"Why don't we have our session at the cabin?" Caroline said.

"No reason why we can't."

"Sure." Marge stood and peered out the window at the gloomy evening.

"What is it, Marge?" Angela said.

"It's just Greg's company."

"You have it up for sale, right?" Caroline said.

"It's in the process. Not as easy as it sounds."

9

Friday afternoon Angela inched her car through the exodus of traffic heading north for the weekend from the Twin Cities of Minneapolis and St. Paul. Marge and Caroline chatted with her nonstop for the first two hours of their northbound trek. They fell silent, their reserve of small talk spent. Traffic thinned. The dappled sunshine played hide and seek through birch and oak trees, sending splashes of light across the car. The grass was as green as June could make it.

"Let's see, forty-seven miles north of ..." Angela checked her mileage. "We should be close."

"I think I see it on the right. That stand with the broken trees and ..." Marge lowered her voice. "Plowed-up dirt everywhere."

Angela pulled to the side of the road. A fifty-foot strip of mowed-down trees marked the spot. A trio of three pines remained at the end of the leveled tract. Three broken and scarred pine trees.

Nothing told the story more graphically than witnessing

the scene. Heavy rains had cemented ruts from the truck's skidding trajectory. Grass, earth, and trees had plowed a strip across the easement that halted in a mound of dirt and scraps of metal impaled on the three pines.

"Why did I come?" Angela said. One look and she wanted to run away. Far away.

"Looks like an excavation site." Marge opened her door. "I'm going closer."

Angela and Caroline watched Marge follow the path of ruts, step over limbs, then lean against a scarred pine tree. Slowly both joined Marge.

Caroline pushed her sunglasses back. A stream of tears ran down her face.

"I'm sorry I brought you here." Angela's voice broke. "I don't know what I expected to see, but it wasn't this." She swayed against Caroline.

"Don't be so hard on yourself." Marge shifted her substantial weight. "I don't feel that way. I'm glad we came. Sometimes what you imagine is worse than reality."

Three splintered pines. Three shattered marriages. Three lives twisted and gray as the highway stretching north. A whoosh of wind from a semi whipped the loose top Marge wore and lifted Angela's hair from her forehead. Caroline was the first to turn away.

Again on the road, the landscape changed. Lakes appeared tucked behind pines. Cabins dotted shorelines. Usually a pleasant sight, but today the abodes looked desolate. Angela turned on headlights and stared at the road ahead. Eventually they left the highway and meandered through graveled lanes. Her mind drifted to the many times her family had followed this road to the cabin. Remembering Todd's smile, hearing his laughter as he teased the kids. She missed the deep companionship a husband and wife share. Her shoulders shook. It was too much, too soon.

"Want me to drive?" Marge touched her arm.

"No, I'll be fine." Angela gripped the wheel tighter. "Not much farther."

When they arrived, Angela fumbled with her keys to open the dark cabin. Inside, she stared at walls of tongue-and-groove knotty pine, a replacement for drywall. Todd had insisted they buy nothing pretentious when they purchased the cabin. Just a place to sleep, cook meals, and enjoy their children growing up.

Angela recovered and touched a fishing hat on a lamp table. "What's this?" The limp top covered with lures collapsed over the brim. "I don't remember seeing it."

Caroline shrieked, frozen in her spot. "It's Brock's."

"I'm so sorry." Angela picked up the hat. "That's right. He opened the cabin for Todd the first of May. He must have left the hat the weekend when he was here. Shall I put it in your room?"

"No." Caroline's eyes narrowed. "Just dispose of it. Please." Caroline made a wide circle around the hat in Angela's hand.

"I'll take it outside to the trash can." Marge offered.

Unloading bags and finding a place for the food was all they accomplished before heading to their bedrooms. Angela crawled in the right side. She stretched her arm to Todd's side of the bed and pulled his pillow to her face to muffle her sobs. Through the open window came the mournful call of a loon. It was too soon to come to the cabin. Her grief was too raw.

Angela awoke the next morning and listlessly padded down the hall to the kitchen. A full pot of coffee greeted her. She opened the cabinet and chose a dark green mug. It felt good to watch the coffee splash into Todd's favorite cup. Angela carried it to the deck. As she suspected, there sat Caroline.

"I hope I didn't wake you," Caroline said. "I tried to be quiet."

Caroline's eyes were puffy. A deep wrinkle spanned her forehead.

"Oh, no. I'm always up early. Usually have had my morning walk by this time."

"It's a workout at the gym for me." Caroline sipped her coffee. "I get there much later than this. I'm not sleeping well."

"You too? Sorry to hear that." Angela tried not to allow her thoughts to dwell on the fact that last year at this time she was having coffee with Todd in this same spot. "Guess it goes with being a widow."

"Perhaps." Caroline studied the scene before them.

Morning wore a green velvet dress. Angela marveled, thinking of how God must have reached down and planted every tree to achieve the unity of pines, oaks, and birches. Familiar pine trees with cinnamon-colored trunks covered in gray-green lichen receded in the shade.The private inlet held a perfect green reflection of pines in the still water. The sun warmed her face. The serenity warmed her heart.

Angela cupped the mug with both hands, feeling the rough relief of the pattern against her thumb. She caught her breath. Her fingers jerked out of the handle so quickly she slopped coffee over the side onto her bare leg.

"What–whatever is the matter?" Caroline said.

Angela jumped up, lifting her shorts away from her leg.

"The cup." She turned it so Caroline could see the mug embossed with a stand of three pine trees. "It reminds me of ... I need cold water."

Caroline followed her to the kitchen, grabbed a clean dish-cloth, and ran cold water over it.

Marge joined them at the kitchen sink. "What happened?"

"Just a little coffee spill."

"Let me see." Marge lifted the wet cloth. "Only redness, no blisters."

"Thanks, nurse-in-charge-of-coffee-burns." Angela smiled and refilled her cup.

"Any time." Marge followed them with her coffee to the deck.

"What a peaceful setting." Caroline's expression softened. "It's been hard to let go and enjoy anything."

Angela finished her coffee and stood, determined to carry on as if this were a typical morning at the lake. "Anyone hungry? Stay here. I'm a one-woman chef."

Soon the smell of frying sausages and eggs lured the others to the kitchen. Angela watched her friends relax over breakfast.

During breakfast cleanup, Angela was about to throw the paper napkins away. "The waste basket's stuffed full." She frowned at a waste can behind the table. "Oh, probably from last month when Brock opened the cabin for Todd."

Before she reached it, Caroline stopped her. "Wait, what's that?" Robin's-egg-blue paper dangled over the edge. "I would know Tiffany blue anywhere." Caroline rummaged in the trash, uncovered a box, and stopped.

"Go ahead, I'm curious," Angela said.

Wisteria

Caroline removed an empty box with flaps sticking straight up. The label prominently displayed Brock's name above the address of his company. Her hand shook when she read the packing list. "Marquise diamond pendant." Caroline dropped the empty box.

10

"Caroline, did he bring you a gift?" Angela leaned forward. "Oh, how lovely that would be."

"No, he didn't." Caroline's icy voice shook.

"Maybe it's at home somewhere. Or maybe he was saving it for a surprise, a special occasion? Your last gift from him?" Angela closed her eyes as she mentally wove a sweet love story. When she opened them, Caroline was gone. She called Caroline's name, but the only answer was Caroline's bedroom door slamming shut.

Caroline returned from her room three hours later to join them for a hurried lunch of cold cuts. After an uncomfortable silence, everyone followed Angela outside.

"Guess I should check things out," Angela said. "There's a whole winter and spring of maintenance to do around here."

Pine needles, wood chips, and natural grasses subbed as a low-maintenance option for the common yard and eliminated the need to mow grass. Downed branches littered the area. Angela stacked them near the burn pile. Marge and Caroline followed suit.

"Thanks, ladies." Angela surprised herself at her sense of accomplishment. "Anyone up for a walk?"

"Let me grab my hiking boots." Caroline raced to the cabin.

When she returned, she had replaced her sandals with worn, scratched, but well-seasoned boots.

"For a city gal, you sure look comfortable in the wilds," Marge said.

"I grew up on a farm, remember?" Caroline said. "Brock preferred the suburban life, so I played the part." She took a deep breath of fresh air, and her demeanor brightened.

Soon they were on a familiar path that paralleled the lake. They dipped into a marshy spot surrounded by ferns.

Angela searched the slope. "The lady slippers return around the first of June each year to this area. At least, they did."

"The pink lady slippers?" Marge said.

"No. They're later, around the first of July. I'm looking for the yellow ones."

"There." Caroline pointed ahead of them. "Something bright yellow."

Angela followed, careful not to step on foliage she stroked a glossy yellow pouch with twisted lateral petals.

Caroline squatted beside her. "Only one?"

Angela nodded. "This hillside should have been dotted with them."

"There's sand washed down all the way to the trail." Marge pointed to flattened stalks. "Must have been the storm."

"The storm devastated the wildflowers." Much like her once-beautiful life. Angela swallowed the lump in her throat.

She touched the bright yellow bloom with its faint purple stripes as if to say good-bye to that life.

They circled past the boathouse, then to the dock. Caroline unfastened her boots, tied them by the laces, and slung them over her shoulder. As if by mutual consent, they sat on the edge and swung their legs over the water. A fish broke the water, flipped, and smacked the surface. Ripples spread in perfect circles, rolling toward them with metered precision.

"Waves lapping against the shore," Angela said. "Such a peaceful sound."

"Peace. If I could only take some of it home with me." Marge straightened, hands resting on her thighs.

"What do you mean?" Caroline said.

"The morning Greg left, he asked me to check on the business from time to time while he was away," Marge said. "I asked him what he wanted me to do, and he just made a joke."

The putt-putt of a trolling motor announced a fishing boat on a neighbor's dock.

"His exact words were 'you know, just throw your weight around.' And he gave me a pat on the rear." She made a sound between a snort and a laugh. "I told him that shouldn't be too hard to do." She sobered. "What do I know about a machine shop? I wish he had said more."

"Have you noticed anything unusual?" Caroline adjusted her seat on the planks.

"Nothing I can put my finger on."

Their silence seemed to invite wildlife to join them. A golden eagle floated past, its wingspan casting his shadow over the lake. It landed in the dead branches of a nearby oak and quietly folded its wings, its eyes intently scanning the water. Angela sighed. How could anyone observe this scene and not be in awe of God's creation?

"Do you have people you can trust to run the business?" Angela said.

"Well, I trust Darren. He's been with us since startup. Darren's the engineer. Greg was the inventor. Darren took Greg's designs and made them work. They made a great team. It amazes me how Greg set up the company to more or less run itself so he'd be free to pursue his ideas. Of course, it may be running itself right into the ground. We've lived so many years on my salary at the hospital to supplement our income, waiting for the business to stand completely on its own. Well, that's never happened. I'm used to cutting corners. Guess I can wait it out until we find a buyer."

Marge dipped her foot and kicked upward, creating an arc of spray. The water separated into beads and fell, barely disturbing the surface.

"How about you, Angela?" Marge said.

"I'd like to be out of the public's eye, just be alone for a while longer. Becca's coming home from school this weekend. Maybe we can spend some time together. I plan to work part-time, let Shane and Rosa take care of the shop for a couple of weeks before I ... make any decisions."

"Angela!" a lone fisherman yelled, cutting his motor in the middle of the lake. "Tell Todd he doesn't know what he's missing."

Before she could answer, he waved and shoved the throttle.

"Thanks a lot, Nick." Angela glared at the V-shaped wake behind his boat.

"Blindsided, again?" Marge said.

Angela nodded. "I called some friends from the lake. I assumed they would spread the word about Todd."

Evening came quickly in the forested hideaway. The dropping temperature nudged the trio inside.

After dinner they grouped around the rough stone fireplace, now crackling with burning logs and warmed their hands.

"Nice picture." Marge nodded toward a photo taken last summer of Todd in a red-and-black plaid shirt, Angela behind his chair, arms around his neck in a mild stranglehold.

"His favorite shirt."

"How old is that shirt?" Marge said.

Angela smiled and shook her head.

Caroline pointed to a photo tucked in the back. "And here's one of the six of us." She examined the frames grouped on a mantel that was made from a hefty pine log sawn in half.

"Sometimes it hurts to look at photos. Other times, it's a comfort," Angela said.

Even in June, the fire felt good as the outside temperature lowered. Angela stretched out in a favorite chair and stared at the flames. Memories flooded over her, reminding her of a life lost forever. A spark shot up and died—dreams. A glowing ember faded—hopes. Dry wood crackled—shattered promises. Would she ever dream again? Have hope? Believe in a future?

Caroline broke into her reverie. She rubbed the checkerboard painted top of the coffee table. "Angela, you have a gift with decor."

Angela glanced around the room. "Oh, just things we picked up at garage sales and junk shops."

"Every nook and cranny blends together. Who would have thought of an old wooden sled made into a shelf draped with netting and lures?"

"I agree with Caroline," Marge said. "It's amazing the way you pull things together."

"Our home is mid-century modern." Angela smiled. "Todd liked the style. His dream home. But, here I'm free to be eclectic. Mix everything together. It's been so much fun." She sobered. "At least it was fun."

Marge nodded, a reflective look in her eyes.

"What about your workbooks?" Angela noticed each had their workbooks close at hand.

"I finished the daily work." Caroline flipped through pages.

"Finished one page," Marge said. "But let's go through it. I'll finish as we go."

They watched the video then spent the next hour in their workbooks.

Angela picked up her Bible. "I liked their reference in Isaiah."

"Read it to us." Caroline eased her head against the cushion.

"Fear not, for I have redeemed you; I have called you by name, you are mine. When you pass through the waters, I will be with you; and through the rivers, they shall not overwhelm you; when you walk through the fire you shall not be burned, and the flame shall not consume you."

"Fear not." Caroline closed her eyes for a moment. "I want to read more. Our workbooks have printed verses, but I'd like to find my Bible and start reading it again."

With a longing look, Angela said, "It helps."

Marge flexed her shoulders and stretched her neck. "Angela, we've known each other for years, and I know you're religious. Perhaps the workbook equates widowhood with passing through deep waters and walking through fire. I know I can relate to that with Greg suddenly gone from my life. But can you explain how God can allow three good men like our husbands to die? Poof! Just like that?"

A mini explosion from a burning log sent a shower of sparks upward.

"No, I can't. You fall in love, you marry, raise your family, look forward to growing old together, then—" Angela held up empty hands and dropped them. "Religious? I must confess I feel like I've failed to lay a firm foundation. I was angry with God. Bethany with cancer. How could that be? I read my Bible every day, but I suddenly realized I was doing it out of habit. Even when Bethany began to get better, it was as if I had pulled her through, not God. I can't answer your question, Marge. But I'm going to find peace. I'm going to trust Him to walk with me through this trial."

Marge stood, grabbed the poker, and pushed the broken log back into the grate. "I'm sorry to bring it up. I didn't mean to be rude."

"Don't feel that way. How can we heal if we don't voice our questions? Say what's on our hearts? We're friends."

"That's right," Caroline said. "To talk with two friends who understand, well, most of what I'm going through ..." Caroline's lips closed tight.

Angela's eyebrows lifted. What was Caroline saying behind those words?

"Agreed. It helps." Marge walked past them. "I think I'll take a shower and turn in."

Angela stood. "Please let me know if you need anything."

With Marge's shower blasting, Caroline turned to Angela in the hallway. "I'm not much of a Christian, not at all well-versed in the scriptures. But I wish Marge could find comfort where you're finding it."

"Not much of a Christian? You heard my confession. I'm a Christian still trying to find my way. As for Marge, we'll trust

God to work in her heart," Angela said. "Let's pray for her right now." They closed Angela's door and knelt beside a chair.

Later, Angela closed her eyes with wistful thoughts of her Heavenly Father. His faithfulness, His patience, His presence. He hadn't deserted her. He was ready and able to carry her through the fires and floods of the life ahead. That was head knowledge, but how to transfer it to her heart? She sighed and prayed again for Marge and Caroline.

As she drifted off to sleep, her last thought reverted to the morning. A diamond pendant? What was that about?

11

Angela returned home from the cabin late Sunday night bone-tired. When she tripped over a bag in the entryway she noticed Becca's explosion of college clutter extending down the hallway. The next day, Monday, Becca's friends ran in and out making the house shake with the loud, lived-in feeling children bring. Finally, late that evening, Angela and Becca were alone.

"Good to have you back," Angela said.

"Thanks, Mom." Becca looked tiny at one end of the sofa in the living room. She hunched her shoulders and shivered. "Gonna be hard."

"I know." Angela moved beside her and pulled her close. "But we'll make it."

"I love you, Dad." Becca's voice quavered.

Angela pulled back from Becca. Her hand flew to her heart then followed Becca's gaze to their family portrait above the fireplace. "You're speaking to dad in the portrait? Becca, you gave me a start."

Last fall. Todd looked so happy, an arm looped around

Angela, their children and their grandson surrounding them.

"I'm so glad you and dad had that taken."

Angela smiled, and for the first time no tears welled up. "So am I."

Angela lectured herself as she drove to the shop Tuesday morning. Take it slow. Decisions to make, but not yet. Not yet.

Rosa wheeled around when Angela entered the shop. "You have a voice mail from Shane."

Angela hit the message button, and Shane's voice filled the room.

"Hey, Angela! Wanted to tell you, but I wasn't sure this would pan out. Man, I'm sorry to do this, but they've offered me a job in Texas, same place my cousin works. The problem is, my cousin is going back today and offered to cart me and my stuff with him. I couldn't find your cell number." Angela closed her eyes. "So I'm leaving a message at the shop. Call me at this number if you need anything."

Anything? Some notice would have helped. Angela fought the fear making her chest constrict. Now what? She stared at the row of vibrant-colored ribbon spools. How dare they flaunt their gaiety at a time like this?

"I'm so sorry." Rosa pulled her dark curls to the back of her neck and flipped a band from her wrist.

"Thanks." Time to stay busy. Pick up the pieces of her life and press on. Angela pulled an order prepared for morning delivery and moved it to the staging area. She couldn't help but notice the arrangement seemed amateurish, no lines, not an arrangement Shane or she would have created. It looked like, well, like every other flower shop in town. She knitted her brows. The wrong person had quit.

"Why don't I make deliveries this morning?" Rosa said. "Shane sent me once."

"Only once? I asked Shane to train you in all areas."

"I think he liked to get away from the shop. He took care of deliveries."

"I see." Angela nodded. "Please, go ahead."

Rosa hustled the last plant on one hip. "Most are going to the hospital. I won't be long."

Feeling bad for sounding curt, Angela looked around the shop searching for a way to compliment Rosa. "All the orders are filled, hanging baskets displayed outside. I can tell you're an organized person."

"Thanks."

Angela wondered at Rosa's inscrutable look, almost a frown as the van pulled away. How long would it take to get to know her?

With a jolt, Angela glimpsed Todd's Cherokee coming to a stop in the back parking lot. Todd's jeep without Todd. The back door jiggled.

A half-breath later, Angela recovered. "Becca." Of course. Becca needed transportation for the summer and lending her Todd's jeep had seemed the most natural solution. Angela groaned inwardly. Why did she have these little memory lapses? Each jolt back to reality was an unwelcome shock.

"Hi, Mom."

"You were sleeping when I left," Angela said. "Doing okay?"

Becca shrugged, her petulant look back. "I'm just here to get away. Empty house."

"Looks like I'm full time. Shane quit." Angela recounted the story of his flight to Texas.

"That's going to be tough."

Rosa returned in time for a quick burst of business. Just as quickly, the shop emptied.

"Wow," Becca said. "That was intense."

"We call it the noon rush." Angela finished a sandwich, brushed crumbs from the table into her palm, and flipped them into a nearby trashcan. "People tend to spend their lunch hour running errands."

Rosa pushed the watering cart around the room while Angela donned a painting smock.

"What are you working on?" Becca followed Angela to an art table tucked against the wall.

"It's a plaque. One of the little signs we have throughout the store. They're so popular I can't keep them in stock."

"I like it." Becca leaned over Angela's shoulder reading the Bible verse she was lettering. "Now I could get into this."

"Do you mean that? Because if you do, I'll put you to work." Angela lowered her voice as Rosa circled to the front of the shop. "Wait. I need to level with you. My accountant tells me that's my biggest problem—payroll. That black hole. After Shane's exit, payroll should be manageable, but only if I keep the shop at two full-time people."

"You don't have to pay me. I want to help in the shop," Becca said. "Let's call it pay for my room and board. Besides, anything beats being home alone."

"I had hoped to employ you at least a few hours a week this summer," Angela said softly.

"It's okay. It's part of our new normal."

"That's an interesting way of putting it. I'm having a hard time remembering what normal was like," Angela said, returning to her painting. "I wish I could spend more time with you."

"This could be the answer. I'll hang out here a few mornings a week, okay?" Becca brushed away a tear and touched the plaque. "One of my favorite verses, 'I am the vine, you are the branches.' What if I added a bunch of grapes, let's say at the top left corner? Paint some vines curling down the side, add a few leaves. Have you seen my thumbprint grapes?"

Angela moved over. "Show me."

"We did this in high school art class. Red and blue to make purple, add a dollop of white." Becca dipped her thumb into the acrylic paint. "Dab of each color on your thumb and press. Needs a little more blue."

Working back and forth, she quickly formed the top of a cluster of grapes.

"My little finger for the smaller grapes at the bottom."

"Look at the texture. I love it," Angela said.

The bell at the front door announced a customer. Angela and Becca peeked over the half-wall.

"Becca! I didn't know you were working here." A young woman wearing a snug top showing a bare midriff above a curvy short skirt danced Becca's way. Her pretty face beamed.

"Hi, Molly." Becca greeted her old friend from high school. "Only a few hours a day. Come see what I'm doing."

Angela handed Becca her smock, scrubbed her hands, and sorted orders. Shrieks and chatter preceded Becca and Molly as they returned to the discount table at the front of the shop. Molly perused the table, setting aside two pots with the largest blooms.

"Mom sent me to pick up a couple of these plants on sale," Molly said as she paid Becca. "Got to run." She turned to include everyone in her jaunty wave as she whooshed out the door.

"An online order just came in for a new sign." Angela handed Becca the printed form.

"Awesome. Let's see, what does it say? 'This is the day the Lord has made, let us rejoice—'" With a wounded shriek, Becca ran out the back door.

12

The squeal of tires faded. "What happened?" Rosa said.

Angela held up the order form for a plaque. "I should've remembered. That was her father's favorite verse. It's posted all over the house." Angela picked up Becca's jacket. "I'd better run home. You'll be okay alone?"

"Sure." Rosa shrugged and cocked her head at the empty shop.

A few minutes later, Angela pulled into her driveway and punched the garage remote. No Cherokee.

"Where could she have gone?" Angela said to the empty garage. Becca could be anywhere. She didn't answer Angela's text. Picking up her phone to check messages again, she sent a text to Becca's friend, Amanda.

> Have you seen Becca?

Angela's phone rang immediately.

"What's up?" Amanda's nonchalant voice at the other end told Angela she knew nothing about Becca.

64

"Amanda, I'm sure Becca's fine, but something at the shop sparked an old memory of her dad." Angela mentioned the way she fled the shop.

"Poor Becca! I'll call the gang and see if we can find her."

"No, wait." Angela took a deep breath. "I'd rather you didn't do that. I know Becca. She'll want to keep this private. Just wondering if you had any ideas."

"No, but I'll drive around our old haunts and text you back if I find her."

"Thanks."

Angela headed to Bethany's apartment to check out all possibilities. A pale-faced Bethany answered her knock. "You okay?"

"Nausea, again." Bethany ran her fingers through her hair. "But I'll be okay. Emerson's in town. He'll be here to help with Phillip tonight." Bethany collapsed full-length on the sofa. "Forced me to do some research. According to our online help group, I should eat a carb each time before taking the medication. I'm learning."

A sleepy Phillip stumbled into the room and saw his grandmother.

"Gamma." He twined his arms around her legs.

"Wow." Bethany rolled on her side. "Short nap for you, buster. Hope you don't make a habit of this."

"I just stopped by ..." Angela picked up Phillip. "Well, Becca's having a rough time."

Angela grabbed Phillip's favorite stuffed animal and deposited them both next to Bethany.

Bethany snuggled his pony under his chin. He giggled.

"Mommy." He patted her cheek and wiggled close.

Angela tiptoed out the back door. Close call.

Becca. Where else could she look? Angela drove to the park

a mile away and snaked around through its narrow roads. She checked out the church parking lot. Realizing the futility of her search, she headed back to the shop.

An hour later, a text came from Amanda.

Found her. High school tennis courts.

Followed by a text from Becca.

Headed to work.

Before leaving for work the next day, Angela peeked into Becca's room. The soft light in her room defined Becca's delicate features and dark hair. Todd's dark hair. How Angela wanted to talk with Becca when she woke up. Instead, she wrote a note and left it on the hall table.

Opening her shop a few minutes later, Angela applied the therapy that had always worked in the past. She threw herself into her work, cleaning shelves, regrouping displays, scrubbing the floor.

Angela felt her eyes smart, blinked back the tears, and quickly repressed the thought of Becca suffering. She pulled her apron strings tight, as if that could stiffen her spine.

"Shall I make the deliveries today?" Rosa juggled the back doorknob and a peace plant.

"Yes." A wave of aversion to meeting people broke over Angela. "And if you don't mind, you can take over that job for the present."

"Sure, I enjoy it."

Angela wiped down shelves. "We'll talk when you're back."

"Oh?"

Lost in her thoughts of what could make her shop more appealing to her customers, Angela didn't reply.

Rosa returned from deliveries, glanced at Angela, then stared at the floor. "You wanted to talk?"

"I've been thinking ... we're both needed on Friday night when the shop stays open late. Would you like to take Friday mornings off so you won't have such a long day? I'll take a morning or an afternoon when things are slow."

Rosa's face lit up with a smile. "That would be perfect."

"Good. I'm going home to check on Becca after lunch. Catch her before she leaves for work.

"Before I leave ..." Angela frowned at the perfectly lined rows of gift items, dried and artificial flower arrangements in the shop. "I haven't taken a good look around for a long time. Rosa, maybe I just need a sounding board. Displays are neat and uniform. But where are the artistic angles? Where's the surprise? Something should delight the eye. Everything's spread out. It almost shouts 'low inventory'."

She swung around. "Please don't think I'm criticizing. You and Shane did the best you could while I took care of Bethany and Phillip. We made it through a long year, didn't we?"

"We did." The phone rang. Rosa rushed to the worktable. Soon another order slip was clipped to the wall.

"Look at this." Angela picked up one of her ceramic collectibles. "I thought I would have a hard time keeping them in stock. The boxes are dusty. Apparently, people don't collect anymore." She gathered the boxes. "Another display with marked-down prices should attract attention."

Her frown increased. "Todd wanted me to rent this building because of its location. It's on a main highway but twice as much space as we needed."

Rosa shook her head and continued to sort orders. "It would be such a large room if they took the divider down. I wondered ..."

"If we remove the partition that divides the rooms—" Angela peeked behind the wobbly divider that hid more shelving. "It's almost twice as big." Angela squinted. "Bigger gift shop? No, that's not going over. Maybe something for the home. Home furnishings?"

Slowly, Angela turned her back on the gift area, but an undercurrent of ideas surged as she started on new orders. She perfected an Oriental-looking creation on autopilot while her mind wandered.

"How do you do that?" Rosa said. "I've memorized every arrangement in that book we show customers, but yours have a mind of their own. Movement. Energy."

"The book? You're speaking of our display book?"

"Yes, the one on the counter."

"Well, that's a good place to start, especially if it's what the customer picks out. But your creativity needs to kick into gear." Angela turned to the catchall shelf. "Where is it?"

"What?"

Angela sorted through a stack of phone books and located a hardcover book. "Here it is. I loaned it to Shane. Vertical, horizontal, triangle, S-curves, circular, radiating. This is everything I know about arrangements."

"I thought it was Shane's book."

"Wait. Are you saying this wasn't part of your training?"

Rosa shook her head.

Angela handed the book to Rosa. "Let's get started. Pick a shape."

Rosa flipped a few pages. "An off-sided triangle looks interesting." She pulled out buckets of fresh flowers in her favorite vibrant colors.

"Which stalks are you using for your points?"

"Maybe I'll add snapdragons." Rosa turned back to the case.

"The soft pink and white will never hold its own with the deep colors you've chosen."

Rosa swapped the bucket for purple delphiniums. "I see what you mean."

Angela watched Rosa twine purple statice around anthuriums. "You have an eye for texture."

Rosa let out a long breath as though she had run a marathon. "What should I try next?"

"Off-sided triangle."

Rosa frowned. "Again?"

"Keep trying them until you can make them in your sleep."

Rosa laughed. It was a high, lilting, tinkle of a laugh. The kind of laugh you wanted to hear again.

"Becca?"

"In here."

Becca sat cross-legged in front of the TV, *Monk* reruns blaring, a half-eaten pint of ice cream in her lap.

"Mom, what are you doing home?"

"Just wanted to check on you."

Becca dropped her spoon in the carton long enough to dismiss her mom with a limp one-handed wave. "I'm okay."

"Come here." Angela dropped next to Becca, ready to take her in her arms.

Becca scowled. "Don't touch me now. You'll make me cry."

"If that's what you want."

"I don't know what I want."

"Is there more ice cream?"

"Yeah, butter pecan." A sniffled snort. "Ick."

Angela focused her gaze on the floor unable to stop the amusement that curled her mouth into a smile.

Becca glanced sideways at Angela. "Kind of pathetic, aren't I?" Becca laughed and hugged her mom.

13

After lunch the next day, Angela scanned the sparse room of Wisteria. She grabbed the keys to the van. "Can you hold down the fort? I won't be long."

"Sure," Rosa said.

That morning Angela had negotiated a loan from the bank with a balloon payment due at the end of December. She should be able to pay it off with the shop's Christmas income, which historically was more than one-third of her annual sales. "That should make my moon-shot idea doable." She reassured herself as she headed across town. Northgate offered a business called Antiques by Olaf, a combination antique, flea market, and junk shop. This had better work.

She walked behind his store where items were subject to the weather in three-sided sheds, an area Olaf called his trash pile. A battered trunk teetered on top of scrap-iron railings. She could visualize the trunk with new hardware and a dark stain to highlight the wood grain. Inside, she picked up an interesting light fixture.

"Hey, that chandelier don't work." A bony man with wiry gray hair sticking out of a grimy baseball cap pointed behind him. "I've got three in the next room that do; like to see 'em?"

"No thanks, Olaf. I want one that doesn't work. It's ... decorative."

"Humph."

"I'll take these candlesticks."

Olaf sniffed and pressed his lips together, protruding his prominent jaw. "I'll take them to the counter."

"Where's Avis today?"

"How should I know? Out gallivantin' around instead of working her afternoon shift."

Angela cocked her head. "I'll need prices on all these items."

"You'll get it."

Years ago, Olaf had doubled the size of his shop by purchasing another storefront building. Angela mounted the step that divided the two rooms and found furniture piled at one end.

"Olaf, what's this? A loveseat, chairs?"

"Yeah, not antiques. Came from an estate sale."

A new idea rattled around. "How much for the loveseat?"

Olaf scratched his head and named a price.

"What if I add this chair," Angela brushed her hand over a faded green brocade chair with lines from the '70s, "and this one?" She touched a mulberry-colored wingback.

He mumbled a dirt-cheap price.

"I'll take all three pieces."

Olaf shot her a look of disbelief mingled with regret.

"Do you have any bed headboards?"

"Sure do, maple, walnut, just got in a mahogany." He

pointed a stubby finger at her. "Now that's what you need. Do you know how rare mahogany is?"

Angela smiled.

"I suppose you want something that's ready to fall apart," he mumbled. He made his way out of the shop, stooped under a lean-to, and lifted boards. "Decorative?"

Angela stopped him when he uncovered a headboard made of an undefined wood with blistering veneer.

"You want that?"

"I do. And the matching footboard."

Angela gathered an assortment of pots, utensils, wall hangings. Olaf picked up a stubby pencil and continued writing.

"Drawers? Without a dresser to put 'em in? Big ones, dinky ones," Olaf rambled on, shaking his head.

"Here's your total." Olaf tore a page from his sales book.

He took her check, punched ornate keys, and cranked the antique cash register. "Ka-ching, the only piano I play."

"Olaf." Angela shook her head. His mood always improved with a check in hand. "How often have I heard you say that?"

"Prettiest music I know. None of that piped-in stuff going on in my place." Olaf smirked. "Is that gonna do ya? Otherwise, got a couple of burned-out engines, maybe a transmission or two out back I can sell you. You could decorate them up real pretty with flowers. 'Course, ladies that buy 'em might get a little axle grease on their dresses." He threw back his head and cackled.

Angela took a deep breath. Olaf was being Olaf. "I didn't realize you were such a gentleman to be so concerned about ladies' dresses."

Olaf flashed her a look of pure amusement. Another cackle as he followed her out the door helping her load her purchases.

In her van, Angela punched speed dial to call her landlord about removing the partitions that divided her shop. Amazingly, he said he needed the partitions at another location. He would be there first thing in the morning.

"Thank you, Lord," Angela said. But with the deficiency in her prayer life, the words felt foreign on her lips.

Returning to the flower shop, she popped her head inside. "Rosa, I need your help to unload the van."

Rosa glimpsed the back of the packed van with the doors wide open.

"En serio!" She covered her mouth but couldn't stop a giggle.

"Don't laugh, there's more to come. I need to make a second trip to Olaf's."

Rosa shook her head.

Customers, phone calls and unloading the van occupied the rest of their day.

"We did it." Angela leaned against the back wall and smiled at Rosa. "I'll try to decide what goes where. You go home and get some rest. You've worked hard today."

"You're sure you don't need me to stay?" Rosa said.

"No, but thanks for offering."

Rosa shimmied sideways out the back door. Now alone, Angela stood in the middle of the mess. Was this what it was like to be in a reality TV show? This had better work. With a soapy sponge, she scrubbed a scarred old bench, visualizing a whitewashed finish. Angela sprayed and washed and planned as visions for her shop's new direction formed in her mind. She made remarkable progress until thoughts of Todd intruded and zapped her energy. He would have hopped in his Jeep, driven over, and helped her unload. She could picture him picking up every piece, shaking his head at her ideas, but encouraging her nonetheless. How she missed him. Might as well push herself to stay and finish the job of cleaning. Becca was working. No need to hurry home. Todd ... no need to hurry home.

14

"Love bears all things, believes all things, hopes all things, endures all things. Love never fails." Pastor Bailey's Sunday morning Scripture reading bookended his sermon on God's never-failing love.

Angela could only focus on the loss of Todd's love. No shoulder bumped hers in the pew. No Todd to bear, believe, hope, endure all things with her. No longer here to share Father's Day with his children. How long would the loss assail her?

Her hands shook as she held the hymnbook. No one was there to steady it for her. Singing started. She fell apart.

Would she ever be able to sing without tears? Angela glanced down the length of the pew, trying in vain to act normal when she felt anything but that. She should be grateful the rest of her family filled the pew beside her. Becca stood next to her, then Bethany and her husband Emerson, and Benjamin with his new girlfriend, Tatum. Benjamin and Tatum had driven from St. John to Northgate to surprise Angela this morning.

Across the aisle, one row ahead, sat her accountant, Wade Carlson, all alone. His wife had left him ... how many months ago? No wife, no children. Behind Angela, no need to turn around, she could hear ladies and their children from the women's shelter. Their director, Miranda, led their singing with her sweet alto.

Distracting herself with people-watching worked. The song was over, and Angela's attention returned to the congregation gathering their Bibles and bulletins. Progress was slow as Benjamin introduced Tatum to those around him.

She shook hands with her new pastor and his wife, Susan.

"Glad your children are with you today," Susan said. "Would you like to come over for lunch soon? Maybe next Sunday?"

"Thank you. I'll let you know," Angela said. How long could she deflect the Baileys' invitations?

Angela's children followed her home for Sunday lunch. The way it used to be. Almost.

Benjamin's voice echoed down the hall. "And here's a family picture of us when I was in high school. That's my dad."

Angela snatched a tissue from the counter and blew her nose.

"Coming down with a cold?" Bethany tilted her head. "Oh."

Angela washed her hands and occupied herself in pulling pre-made concoctions from the refrigerator. Thank goodness for salads and crockpots.

Everyone shuffled from their usual positions at the dining room table to accommodate Tatum. Emerson wrangled Phillip into his booster seat. By then, only Todd's chair remained empty. Emerson hesitated and glanced at Angela.

Angela smiled. "It's Father's Day. Please, sit at the head of the table."

Bethany reached for his hand, and a tear trickled down her face.

"Todd was a wonderful dad, wasn't he?" Angela said. "Shall we pray?" She bowed her head and closed her eyes. Suddenly overcome she looked down the table. "Sorry," she whispered, "Emerson?"

"Of course." Emerson's even voice led them in prayer.

Angela took a deep breath. "Tatum, this is a very emotional day. Please forgive us for not being the best company."

"Nothing to forgive. It must be very hard," Tatum said.

"We're happy you joined us," Angela said. "What about your dad? Are you celebrating with him later?"

"No." Tatum's eyebrows lifted. "He's overseas on a business trip. Besides, my parents live in California."

"So, Tatum, how did you and Benjamin meet?" Bethany said.

"We live in the same apartment complex," Tatum said. "The landlord organized volunteers to help plant annuals for the summer and put me in charge. Benjamin was my first recruit."

"How could I say no?" Benjamin's glance lingered on Tatum. "Cute blonde asked for help? I'm glad I volunteered."

Tatum bent her head toward Benjamin and they smiled at each other. A lovely petite young woman, she wore a silky, flowing dress with a scooped neck, revealing a shoulder tattoo. Her straight blonde hair covered the tattoo when she wasn't moving, which was very little of the time. She sat next to Angela's grandson, Phillip, looked at him through the tines of her fork, made faces, and giggled along with him.

"I enjoyed the service," Tatum said putting down her fork

and looking at Angela. "It's different from our church though. There's no praise and worship band."

"Tatum is one of the worship leaders at her church," Benjamin said.

"You are?" Becca's eyes brightened. "So is my best friend from college."

Bethany whispered to Phillip and covertly slipped him a package.

Phillip's eyes twinkled, and he slyly pushed the package to Emerson. "Happy Daddy's Day."

"Whoa," Emerson said. "What's this?"

"Mug for your car."

Everyone laughed, and Phillip joined in, clapping his hands as Emerson tore into his gift.

Angela cleared her throat. "Do you know what would please me more than anything? Could each of you share your favorite memories about dad?" Angela turned to Tatum. "If you don't mind, Tatum."

"Not at all. I'll get to know Benjamin's father through his kids," Tatum said.

"Oh, Mom, I don't think you have enough Kleenexes for that." Becca's face paled, marking a stark contrast in her features. She was the only child in the family with Todd's Celtic blue eyes and dark hair.

"I think it's a great idea, Mom," Benjamin said. "Why don't I start?"

Benjamin was off, remembering his dad saving the day when the well-fed raccoons invaded the food left outside their cabin. Todd had had a talent for telling a story, and Benjamin was just like him. With his humorous twist, he had everyone laughing. It was the first time they had really laughed together since Todd's death. Everyone added a memory, and even Becca opened up, with only a sniffle or two.

While they talked, an idea came to Angela. She twirled a strand of hair. There should be a legacy for her children from their father. A tangible way for them to remember him. A way to ease the burden financially for those so young, just starting out in life. Todd's life insurance would be a tidy sum. Instead of sharing her thoughts with her children, Angela stood.

"Ready for dessert?"

Benjamin looked at Tatum, then his mom. "Sorry, gotta skip dessert, meeting friends soon."

After they left, those remaining moved outside with their dessert. It was a perfect day on the shaded patio. Bees droned nearby roses. Birds called and flitted from tree to tree. The summer sounds seemed to make everyone drowsy, including Phillip. He didn't complain as Emerson picked him up and carried him to Bethany's old room. "His room" as he now called it.

"Several things on my mind, kids," Angela said when Emerson returned. "The first is the matter of your father's clothes and personal items." She glanced at Emerson. "I'm glad you and Benjamin looked through his things and took what you wanted."

"I'm outta here. Got a long shift today." Becca ducked her head and left for her room.

Angela's eyes followed Becca. Angela would have liked to be 'outta here' as well when it came to this discussion. Determined to follow through, she straightened her shoulders.

"Your dad was tall, Bethany," Emerson said in a light tone and crowded next to Bethany. "Nice that I found a couple of his sweaters that fit."

"I know." Bethany swallowed.

Angela moved to the edge of her chair. "Kids, I'm selling the house."

Bethany and Emerson exchanged glances.

"Oh, no," Bethany said.

"Is that really necessary?" Emerson said.

"Yes, this house is huge. The expense of upkeep is too great for me alone."

"I suppose it is." Bethany's pain mirrored Angela's. "It's just a shock, Mom."

"I know." Angela blinked. "Also, I need your advice."

"We're glad to help. What do you need?" Bethany said.

"Any suggestions for a realtor?"

"We were looking at houses," Emerson said and turned to Bethany. "And we will again. So we've checked out several realtors in the area. They say go with a winning team."

"And we know who that is." Bethany smiled.

"The Andersons," Emerson said.

Angela smiled. A mental picture flashed of Mary Anderson. The energizer bunny in a blazer.

Inside again, they finished loading the dishwasher, and Angela's gaze took in the dining and seating area. "I'll miss having all of this room when you come for dinner."

"We'll adjust." Bethany walked up to her mother and linked arms. "Mom, you mentioned dad's things?"

Angela exhaled slowly. "I did."

"Well, there's no time like the present."

Today? Was she up for that? "I suppose you're right, Bethany."

"Of course I am." Bethany lifted her chin, a twitch at one side of her mouth.

"Let's start with his duffle bag in the garage. I see it each time I leave the house," Angela said. "Odd how it survived the crash."

"I'll grab it," Emerson said.

Angela led the way to the upper level and turned to her closet. "It hurts so much every time I open the door and see Todd's things."

Emerson retrieved the bag from the garage. "You'll be so glad you did this while we're here to support you."

When Emerson unzipped it, Todd's red-and-black plaid shirt popped out and sprawled across the bedroom floor. His favorite shirt. Lying there as though none of this tragedy had ever happened.

Angela covered her mouth and turned away to hide the tears.

"Go ahead and cry. We're here for you." Bethany rubbed her back.

"I'll get the trash bags." Angela retreated to the utility room. "Why?" she whispered to the ceiling.

"Mom?" Bethany had followed her. "It's too much. We'll do this. Why don't you go back downstairs and lie on the sofa?"

"Shouldn't you be the one lying down?"

"No, I'm fine."

She let Bethany guide her to the lower level. "I love you kids, but how I wish I could just go to heaven and be with Todd."

Bethany stopped in mid-stride. "Mom. Don't you mean go to heaven to be with Jesus?"

Angela rubbed her forehead. "Oh yes. Of course I do."

Later that evening, alone in her room, she picked up her Bible. Bethany, who knew nothing about the struggle in her mother's prayer life, had nailed the problem. Turning her back to the empty side of the closet, Angela knelt and tried to pray.

When had she stopped her nightly habit? When Bethany was struggling with cancer? She had prayed, but with a nagging resentment—and the question of "why our family?"

The words didn't come. She gave up and climbed into bed. Maybe if she read her Bible. It fell open to her last reading in Deuteronomy: "The eternal God is your dwelling place, and underneath are the everlasting arms." How she wanted to cling to that promise.

"Everlasting arms." She and Todd had sung the duet two weeks before Todd began his everlasting. A sob broke loose. Teardrops dampened the page of the Bible in her lap. She reached for the lamp switch but stopped. Might as well leave it. She was alone. The light wouldn't disturb anyone.

"Dear Jesus, please forgive me for putting Todd before you. I know that's wrong. He's gone. His loving arms are gone, but I have your everlasting arms. Your love which never fails. I want to see You first of all when I reach heaven."

15

Angela had the perfect opportunity to organize her shop since she closed on Mondays. She hadn't realized how much she had to accomplish to rearrange her floor space. Although Rosa and Becca had helped her place the heavy items in strategic spots, the rest of the pieces lay in jumbled stacks. Her heart sank. She needed more than a magic wand to transform the space. Trying to envision the finished displays, she pulled and stacked and stood back. Interrupted by a knock on the glass, Angela hurried to the front door and recognized Arnie, Trudy's husband. Ah yes, Trudy who speaks to her deceased father every day. Angela couldn't forget their conversation on one of her first days back in the flower shop. She unlocked the door and stepped back.

"Sorry." Arnie cocked his head. "I know you're closed today. But I forgot flowers, and it's our anniversary. Well, you know Trudy."

"Don't apologize. This happens all the time." She piloted him around a stack of boxes. "Watch out. I'm afraid it's a mess today."

"Wow. You're transforming the place." His strong, square face, framed with a neatly trimmed beard of red and gray whiskers, lit up with a smile. "This is a cool idea."

"You're the first one to say that."

"I like antiques." He stepped gingerly around a bird cage.

"That's right. You and Trudy make road trips, don't you?" Angela stopped at the sales counter. "Let's see, fresh flowers or a potted plant?"

"Not sure. Do you think she would like this?" Arnie pointed to a phlox. "She wears a lot of blue. Blue eyes." He halted, embarrassed, then laughed. "I'm afraid I'm not a romantic."

"I wouldn't say that. It doesn't take much to impress us wives."

Wives? But she was no longer a wife. Angela would have to learn an entirely new vocabulary. She ducked, coughed in her hand just to get control, and swung the phlox on the counter. "Good choice."

Angela rang up the sale and followed him to the front door, assuring him again that he had caused her no trouble. Did Trudy fully appreciate the rare man she had married?

By late afternoon, Angela had half-filled the additional space. Her back room swelled as she stored each item that needed paint or repair. She swept and cleaned and tweaked. Needing a distraction, she turned to her newly created corner. Her client's planning area, a private spot to sit with clients. She studied the cozy loveseat and chairs combination and became almost as excited about this idea as she was about staging her treasures throughout the shop. Placing brochures and binders on a shabby coffee table, she stepped back. It definitely needed special lighting. She angled a floor lamp on one side, a Victorian table lamp on the other, and marveled at the amber glow surrounding the space. Angela added a fern sitting high on a pedestal, blooming potted plants, and a cute tabletop sign from Becca's artwork.

The area appeared too visible. She wandered to the back room where a gnarly trifold screen caught her eye. Moving it on the outer edge between the planning area and the sales counter created a separate room. Perfect. Well, one spot at least.

A long day, but satisfying. And, for maybe the first time in more that a month, Angela looked forward to something, too—her and Marge meeting at Caroline's new home.

That evening, en route to Caroline's home in North Minneapolis, a garage sale caught Angela's attention.

"Marge, could we stop? My mind is still on the shop. It's lacking something."

"Sure, we have plenty of time."

Marge braked in front of a ranch-style home and glimpsed tables laden with glassware and bric-a-brac crowded into its garage. "I'm curious why anyone would have a garage sale on Monday? And in the evening?"

Angela meandered through the garage. She carefully picked up a dusty lead crystal bowl. Picking up a silver fork nearby, she tapped the bowl and received the sound of "chimes," declaring itself to be good lead crystal.

A young woman stepped through the back door. "Oh." Her eyes widened. "Forgot to close the garage door."

"Sorry," Angela said. "We'll leave."

"No. I mean, since you're here, go ahead and look around." Her shoulders slumped. "I've been at it all weekend. Hardly anyone showed up today." She looked around her chaotic garage. "Make me an offer," she announced and blew at her hair falling in her face.

"How much for the quilts?" Marge patted a stack with muted colors from many washings.

"One dollar. What can you do with such things? Doesn't fit our bed. The kids want comforters."

"Is this your collection?" Angela said.

"Heavens no. One of my dad's aunts left me everything, and it's simply not my taste. I'm ready to cart it away to recycle. Make me an offer!"

"I ... may," Angela said, picking up a magazine rack and inspecting the bottom. "Let me look around for a moment."

"Feel free." The woman dismissed Angela with a wave and disappeared through the back door.

"Maybe you should make an offer." Marge tightened her grip on a quilt and looked around. "There's so much stuff here. You could always make a second trip if needed."

Angela nodded and began stacking items in an empty corner. "I'll hurry."

"Take your time. We're ahead of schedule."

A few minutes later, Angela knocked on the back door and negotiated a deal with the harried housewife.

"We'll take what we can tonight, and I'll return in the morning with my van. Is 8 a.m. too early?"

"Don't worry. I'll be up. My husband will be happy when he can pull his car into the garage again."

Angela's mood lightened when they loaded Marge's old Corolla. "You're a good sport, Marge. This will blend in nicely. Just what the shop needed."

"Glad I could help," Marge said.

Angela rearranged a vase wrapped in a dresser scarf on the floor beside her. "How are we doing for time?"

Marge glanced at the map on her phone. "Only about ten miles to Caroline's house."

Post-World War II homes disappeared, and a new development took over.

Marge carefully followed streets that curved around palatial homes with two-acre lawns then turned into a circular drive lined with newly planted trees. Lacy textures of leaves on a uniform row of mountain ash softened the approach to the jaw-dropping, two-story brick home.

"Even when Brock and Caroline lived in Northgate, it was the nicest house in the neighborhood for Brock," Marge said.

"I always thought it was fun to have at least one friend with extravagant taste."

"Owning the smallest home in the neighborhood was all Greg and I could swing while getting the business off the ground. I can't see things changing much now." Marge murmured and stopped in front of a sweeping paved walkway. "That must have been some promotion Brock received."

"Ohhh." Angela's eyes widened when she stepped out of the car. She could see past the unfinished work to the vision that would pull it all together. "It's beautiful."

Grounds in various stages of completion ranged from sparsely planted shrubs to an apparatus sticking up, perhaps awaiting a fountain. The pristine lawn still retained faint stripes of recent sodding.

Caroline stood in the doorway. A tall Airedale beside her waited for a sign before he bounded toward them.

"Baxter." Angela reached out and the dog obediently sat before her.

Marge rubbed his ears. He quivered in appreciation, wagging his whole body.

"What happened to your car?" Caroline pointed to the

packed back seat and the trunk lid tied with a rope over a dresser.

"Angela's new inventory," Marge said. "I can't believe we packed so much in one car!"

The three laughed.

"Come in, please." Caroline ushered them into a foyer large enough to hold a tiny home or a Hurricane Katrina cottage. "Welcome to my home. At least it's my home for the present."

Caroline's shoulders slumped. Her hair hung limp. Angela touched Caroline's arm. "How are you? Really."

"Probably going through nothing more than both of you are going through. I listed the house. It upset the kids because they think I should stay here. Sidney and Dalton were ready to move in with me until I told them there's still a mortgage." Caroline impatiently flipped her hands.

"They still live in apartments. When they have homes of their own, they'll understand," Angela said.

"Where will you move?" Marge said.

"Certainly not where everyone thinks I should move." Caroline's eyes snapped as she spoke. "A condo. That's the advice I'm receiving. As if I can't mow the lawn and remove snow or hire someone to do it." Caroline rubbed her forehead. "Sorry, this is no way to behave when I have guests. What's the matter with me?"

Marge humphed. "Nonsense, after what you've been through?"

"I can understand what you're saying, Caroline," Angela said. "I enjoy my house and my gardening even after working all day in a flower shop."

"I'm glad Greg kept a plain lawn, minimum landscaping," Marge said. "Little trimming to do, and quick to mow."

"I'm seeing your house and yard in a different light, Marge.

A dream to take care of for a single woman. I'll keep that in mind." Caroline took a deep breath. "Forgive me for being emotional tonight."

Angela studied her friend. Not behaving as the old Caroline she had known. But then, none of them were the same. "Did you notice our workbook assignment?" Angela said. "No one should expect us to be rational."

Marge cocked her head. "Thanks, Teach."

"Rational?" Caroline said. "I don't remember what that was like." She seemed to rally herself to the hostess role. "Would you like to see the house?"

"I'd love to," Angela said.

Caroline led them on a tour. Baxter danced ahead. Each room competed with the next for appeal. Upstairs, small sitting areas tucked at odd angles made perfect little nests to sit or read. Back down to the main floor, the rooms flowed into another, ready for entertaining guests. The great room lived up to its name with a floor-to-vaulted-ceiling fireplace and a stately dining room beyond. The house reflected its owner, neat and pristine.

"Your piano." Angela walked into a music room not in the least crowded by a baby grand.

Caroline caressed the closed top of a glossy, blue-black Steinway. "I had to cancel my agreement to play for church and choir. Just couldn't do it. Besides, who knows where I'll be living?"

"You're not sure where you will move?" Angela said.

"Not really. I'll probably put the furniture in storage." Caroline pivoted. "What will I do with this furniture? It involved the decorator from the beginning, and the furniture is practically custom made for this house. The decorator ... but that's another story." Caroline's eyes darkened, and she hurried them through Brock's office and into the hall.

The tour ended at the brick terrace. After trips to the nearby kitchen, the shaded patio table soon overflowed with an inviting array of food. They finished eating and headed inside while Baxter retreated to the mudroom for a nap.

"Our lesson focuses on forgiveness." Angela opened her workbook. "The mourner forgiving someone who may have caused the death of a loved one. Forgiving ourselves for things we might have done, things we might have said, or things we can never take back."

"What if ..." Caroline clenched her fists. She looked around the room."What if ..."

Tears rained down her cheeks. Not the cleansing type, but angry tears. Her question remained unfinished.

Angela circled her arms around Caroline. In that safe space, her sobs broke loose like a dam bursting.

16

The next morning, Angela flung open the van's side door just as Rosa arrived for work.

Rosa jerked her head back. "Shopping again at Olaf's?"

"No, a garage sale in Minneapolis. Second trip." Angela lugged in a rattling box of glassware to the break table, then washed a couple of Tylenol down with coffee.

"You're just full of surprises, aren't you?" A smirk lifted one side of Rosa's mouth.

"What's that supposed to mean?"

Rosa backed up at her tone. "Nothing, nothing at all. Let me finish unloading for you."

"I would appreciate that." Angela knew she should change her attitude, but that took too much effort. Was she stressing out over recent purchases or just exhausted? Or both?

Becca arrived and squinted at her mother's frown. "Got one of your headaches, don't you?"

"Um hum."

Becca tiptoed around a stack of plates on the floor. "So,

where did all this junk come from? We just got the back room clean."

Angela glared. "An estate sale on my way to Caroline's last night."

"Sorry, just yanking your chain, Mom," Becca said.

Angela offered a weak smile. Maybe the Tylenol's kicking in. She softly touched Rosa's arm. "Sorry for being short with you."

"S'okay. I understand."

Shamed by Rosa's pity, Angela hugged her. "Thanks."

Between customers, Angela scrubbed glassware, polished silver, and found a new home for as many items as possible.

"So this is where our treasure hunt ended?"

Angela jumped at the voice. "Marge, I didn't hear anyone behind me."

"Who would have thought?" Marge touched brightly polished silver candlesticks and lowered her voice to a whisper. "Weren't these black last night?"

Angela nodded. "It's called elbow grease."

"You've definitely got the touch."

"Thanks." Angela glanced at Marge out of the corner of her eye. "I guess."

"Looking good." Marge ended her walk in front of the fresh flower case. "And hopefully you have a bouquet for me to take to Greg's secretary. She's been putting in extra hours."

"What do you think she'd like?"

"Pink and frilly, that's Tammy." Marge pointed to an arrangement on the second shelf.

As Marge left, Angela massaged her temples. Counting seven collectibles left on the sale table, she quickly found a new home for each of them among the antiques. She had just nestled a cherub in a soap dish when the bell over the door sounded.

"Hello, Susan." Angela met her pastor's wife at the counter.

Susan, a thirty-ish woman, light brown hair, impeccably dressed, greeted Angela without a smile to brighten her face. "How are you?"

"Fine." Angela touched a hanging basket of annuals Susan carried. "What's this you've found?"

"Would you believe there's another spot at my house to hang one? Also, I need one long-stemmed rose, please." Susan spoke in that formal way she had about her.

Rosa peered around the wall of refrigerated cases, a packing box in her hand. "Oh, does that mean there is another baby at the shelter?"

"Hello, Rosa. Yes, this is for the mom." Susan's eyes lit up then the flicker disappeared. "Remember Anastasia when you visited the center last week? She delivered a baby boy, and both are doing well."

"I'm glad. I remember her. We talked for a long time that evening. Is she still thinking adoption?"

"Yes, Anastasia seems reconciled and plans to go home to her parents. So young." Susan turned to Angela. "She was quite excited to know a Christian couple was waiting to adopt a child, and she invited them to the hospital after delivery to be the first to hold the baby."

"Brave girl." Angela exhaled shakily and wrapped up a bud vase holding a red rose surrounded by asparagus fern. Why did a whiff from the rose conjure the image of Todd's casket blanket? Why now? She handled roses every day. Ironic. A rose for a death. A rose for a birth.

Susan reached for the rose. Did her eyes mist over? She blinked. "You forgot to charge me for the rose."

"My gift. I haven't had time to volunteer since ..." how long had it been? Bethany's cancer, Todd's death. Time blurred. "Well for quite some time."

"I hear you've volunteered in the past. We need people like you. People who become involved in the lives of our residents. But, I understand, your shop must keep you busy. Just remember you are welcome at the women's shelter anytime." Susan shifted her purse strap over her shoulder. "I'd like to have you both over for coffee. Maybe this week. Could you come over before you open the shop one morning?"

"I'd love to," Rosa said.

"Thank you, Susan. I'll try to come." Angela's mind whirled to think of a reason not to go.

"How about I see you both at eight-thirty, Friday morning?"

Angela managed a weak smile as Rosa walked Susan to the door.

"She's so good at counseling the ladies at the shelter." Rosa took long strides to the workroom while she spoke. "You know, the shelter was the turning point in my life. And I'll never forget what you and Todd did for me, either."

"We prayed for you, but you did it, Rosa. You made the right choices."

"You hired me and taught me a new skill. Helped me survive and take care of my son."

Scenes of the women's shelter, appropriately named Shepherd's Fold, rushed through Angela's mind. Todd leading a Bible study, talking, praying, giving the women a picture of a godly man. "Maybe I should return to help. Just need to find the time somehow and do it."

"They always need volunteers," Rosa said.

"Perhaps," Angela mumbled. No, too much pain connected with the shelter. "Rosa?"

"Yes?"

"You seem to know Susan well."

"I'm getting to know her."

"Does she seem stand-offish to you?" Angela regretted those words as soon as she spoke them. Maybe she was being too harsh.

"Stand-offish? Oh, I felt the same way when I first met her. It's just Susan. How do you say it? Reserved."

What was it about the look when Susan picked up the rose? "Reserved, yes, but there's a deep pain in her eyes."

———

Friday morning Angela received a text from Rosa.

> Not going to Susan's. Roberto had a bad night. Want to make sure he's okay.

Angela had no excuse now. She couldn't let the hostess down after she had prepared for them. She would have to go to Susan's house. Alone. But, in her mind, it wasn't Susan's house. It was still Cecilia's.

The house looked deceptively simple from the street, a neat bungalow two blocks from church. Blooming flowers bursting from window boxes gave it an English flair. Angela touched the doorbell and looked through the beveled glass panes of the heavy wooden door. A gray-and-white shaggy rug in the entryway seemed to brighten the staircase. That staircase. Memories flooded back of scraping off layers of shellac with Cecilia. Then their delight in uncovering a gem of beautiful red oak beneath.

Susan appeared, swinging the door open and blocking Angela's vision.

"Hello, come in, come in."

"Hi, Susan. Thank you."

"Rosa called me about her little boy Roberto not feeling well. I'm glad you could come, Angela. Right this way."

Angela's heart beat faster. Everything seemed new and old at the same time.

The white-painted kitchen cupboards with doors that reached all the way to the ceiling looked the same. But pale, monotone-colored canisters stood in place of Cecilia's brightly colored decor. The tiny sunroom, just wide enough for a kitchen table and chairs, still sported the white Cape Cod curtains. A glass-top table with a black wrought-iron frame replaced Cecilia's walnut oval table.

"I'm sorry, what did you say?" Embarrassed to ask Susan to repeat her words, Angela re-focused her attention.

"Coffee okay?" Susan poured coffee into an insulated carafe and the fragrance wafted over Angela.

"Mmm, smells like hazelnut, my favorite."

"Cream, sugar?"

"No, thank you. Black for me."

Susan hustled to remove a baking pan from the oven.

"Sticky rolls." Susan inverted the pan with a quick flip, but nothing came out. "Oh, it's living up to its name. I need—"

"A spatula?" Angela jumped up and reached for the wide silverware drawer, then stopped.

"Yes, that's the drawer. Make yourself at home."

Angela opened the familiar drawer. "Three hands needed for this operation," Angela said.

"Apparently so." Susan laughed.

Angela halted, realizing it was the first time she had heard Susan laugh. Susan didn't seem to notice as she rushed to the sink to soak the pan. Her smile faded but the heat of the steaming faucet transformed her face with a warm flush. Such a pretty young woman.

"I have a confession to make," Angela said.

Susan arched her eyebrows.

"You know, Pastor Christiansen and his wife, Cecilia, lived here. That is until she passed away."

"Yes, we bought the house from him. It seemed like the perfect home and he was so—" Susan hurried the rolls to the table. "—anxious to sell and move away after losing his wife. How very sad."

"Cecilia was my best friend."

"I'm so sorry."

"Thank you. The cancer came so quickly." Angela's eyes stung. "I spent so much time in this house, helping her renovate it. And, well, that's why it took me a while to accept your invitation."

"I wondered." Susan passed the rolls. "Tell me, what was Cecilia like?"

Angela shuffled a roll onto her plate, a smile curved her mouth. "Cecilia was my opposite. Although we had many interests in common. She was patient, I was impulsive. She was controlled, I could fly off the handle. By her example, she helped me mature." Angela's gaze met Susan's. "I always felt she brought out the best in me."

Susan's reticence dropped and she gave Angela a yearning look. "What better friend could anyone have? I understand how difficult coming here must be for you. I'm sorry."

"It's okay. I'm seeing the home differently." Angela looked up. "She's not here."

Susan straightened. "Excuse me?"

"I think I expected to see her in every nook and cranny. Cecilia's not here." Angela drew a sharp breath. She didn't know which came first—her words or an image God must have placed in her mind. As if He had pulled back a corner of a curtain just enough to give Angela a glimpse of His goodness. "She's in heaven." To be in heaven. A smile rose until she was beaming with such uncontrollable joy her heart seemed to take flight. Angela's eyes smarted. "Cecilia's in heaven. What a glorious thought!"

17

I t was Monday, Angela's day off, nothing but laundry and house cleaning on her schedule. She stared at a stack of mail Becca had brought in.

A common Manila envelope. But its contents weren't common. Crisp sheets emblazoned with "Certificate of Death." The lightheartedness of multicolored ink swirls through the paper belied the seriousness of something so final. Certificate of Death. What a name. Angela flung them on the kitchen counter and fled to her room.

"Mom?" Becca followed and knocked on her door. "What's wrong?"

Angela mopped her eyes and blew her nose. "Just need some time."

"Okay."

Getting the certificates was inevitable. But who knew a piece of paper would throw her back to the beginning of her grief? Shock. Pain. Anger.

Anger relived the event that shook her world. As if an

earthquake had split the ground they had built their lives upon. On one side, the life they had together. On the other side, Angela's present empty life. Her two lives divided by a chasm too deep to navigate. She could never get that first life back. That constant ache ... more than mourning for Todd.

Suddenly she realized she was also mourning for herself. The person she used to be. Todd's wife.

The clock chimed twelve. She found Becca in the kitchen tossing a salad.

"Sorry, Mom." She tilted her head toward a neat stack of mail with those glaring certificates on top.

"This isn't like me." Angela sat, head in her hands. "Why do I keep saying that? Exactly who am I? Crazy? That's how I feel."

"Stop it, Mom. You're not crazy. You'll get through this. We both will."

Angela crossed her arms. "A pep talk from my youngest child?"

"I'm not a child."

"No, a young woman."

"Now eat your lunch." Becca scolded and scooted a bowl in front of her.

"Don't push too far."

They both chuckled. It relieved the depression that had settled upon Angela. After lunch she gathered her mail, staring at the certificates. Who will need these certificates? She picked up the phone.

Her attorney's receptionist answered. "There is an opening at three-thirty this afternoon, or the next one would be in July."

"Today?" Angela said.

"Yes, a last-minute cancellation."

"I'll take it."

Three hours later, Angela walked through a lushly appointed reception area, down a hallway, while her attorney, Michelle Markham, made small talk. Angela drank in the surroundings. What would it be like to change her career? Work in an office, dress up every day? A vision of the flower shop's hurry and scurry, even getting grungy from the work, oddly comforted her. By the time they reached Michelle's office, Angela's thoughts had dissipated like the whiff of Michelle's heavenly perfume.

"I'm so sorry about Todd. How are you doing?" Michelle said.

Angela surprised herself by veering from her stock answer of 'fine.' "God is teaching me things about myself that I never understood before this happened."

"You've been through so much."

"Getting the death certificates this morning sent me into a tailspin ... re-living the trauma." Angela leaned back. "Sorry. You're my attorney, not a therapist."

"I can still sympathize."

"You're very kind."

Angela glanced at the tastefully decorated office and a clean desk holding only one folder. Michelle opened the folder.

"The probate, filed last month as you requested, has been recorded. It was simple with Todd's will, and you as his sole heir."

She handed Angela a seemingly endless checklist of items to attend to. Insurance. Deeds. Bank accounts. "Many will only need a copy of the death certificate. Some will require an original."

Angela nodded numbly.

"What about your home and business? I caution widows not to make any major decisions for at least one year if it's financially feasible."

"I plan to keep the business. It's my source of income. My home ..." Angela swallowed. "It's paid for, no mortgage, but it's a rather large house. I can't afford to maintain it. I plan to put it on the market."

"I'm sorry. That must be difficult. What about life insurance?"

"There's a policy from Todd's company." Angela named an amount. "Now that I have the death certificate, I'll meet with the Human Resources Department and sign off on the policy."

"Good."

Angela moved to the edge of her chair. "The most exciting thought occurred to me. I have three children. I could divide the insurance four ways. Todd's legacy. Think of it. My oldest daughter, finally on her feet after her struggle with cancer ... my son and youngest daughter just starting out ... what a difference it will make in their lives."

"Angela." Michelle's eyes grew large. She folded her hands in front of her. "Let's talk this through. Whose name is the beneficiary on the insurance policy?"

"Mine."

"And you agree Todd intended for you to have this money?"

She nodded.

"In too many cases, we see widows with grown children still thinking in terms of the family unit. Some feel guilty for not sharing everything with their children, while not recognizing the fact that their children still have their best earning years ahead of them. Years to build their own financial foundation." Michelle locked her gaze. "Some children take advantage of the situation or unknowingly give the wrong advice. And, sad to say, some widows end up penniless."

"That would never happen with my children."

"Perhaps not. But my job is to prepare you and help you establish the correct mindset. Think about the flight emergency instructions for every airline. 'First affix your own oxygen mask, then secure the masks on your children.' Same principle. Parents should take care they are fiscally stable first. And remember, your children aren't underaged dependents." Michelle's frown softened. "What does your retirement look like?"

"I have Todd's 401(k) account."

Michelle glanced at the statement Angela produced. "Retirement in fifteen to twenty years, I suppose?"

"Yes."

Michelle punched a calculator, then jotted notes on a legal pad for Angela to see. "Let's do the math. Would be nice if you can double the 401(k) amount. But, let's just say you increase by twenty percent. We'll do a worst-case scenario. Now let's add one-fourth of the insurance amount and amortize. If invested well, a minimum of five percent return should be doable. In fifteen years an annual income from interest would be—" She turned the calculator Angela's way.

"Below poverty level." Angela sank back. The leather chair squeaked in protest. "This changes everything. I was going to divide with the children and use some of my share to invest in the business, pay off loans, do some upgrades, and make it a viable business."

"Your business is how old?"

"Two years."

"Hmm, new, unproven. What if you pay off your loans and for some unforeseen reason your business folds?"

Angela crossed then uncrossed her legs. That struck a nerve.

"Well, I guess I would just find a job."

"And with your earning potential, how much would you be able to save toward retirement?"

"Not as much as Todd did."

"Let's look at investing all the insurance money and estimating the income you would receive. I'm not a financial advisor. I'll refer you to one, but I know the average rate of returns." Michelle's fingers flew across her calculator, and she penned several scenarios.

"Forgive me if I'm telling you what you may already know, but I don't want to leave out any point. If you continue to run your business and invest the money you receive from life insurance, you can draw dividends from that investment."

Angela blinked at the tidy sum.

"Dividends to supplement your income, gift your children, charity, or use for any emergency that may pop up. Or, once you're on your feet, leave dividends where they can grow your base. The best thing you can do for your children is to protect your assets and not become a burden to them in later years."

"Hmmm." Angela tried to absorb the details.

"Then, at retirement, you could draw from your 401(k) account and add that amount along with Social Security to your dividends." Michelle shuffled papers. "Remember, this is a business decision, not an emotional one. I know you'll do the right thing. Give it some thought. Ask a couple of trusted advisers, then make your decision."

As she left, Angela wondered who those advisers might be.

Maybe Wade, her accountant. Or Emerson. No, not Emerson. He was family. That could get messy. Todd, Greg, or Brock would have been her choice before. She had an inkling what they would say. Why was she having such a hard time letting go of what seemed like the perfect solution of dividing the money with her children? If not that, then what would be Todd's legacy?

18

It was Marge's turn to host the widow's meeting that evening. Angela walked the familiar pathway through Marge's garage to her back door, knocked three taps and entered.

"Come right in."

"Do you close your garage door at night?"

"When I think of it." Marge thumped a cutting board on top of the counter and grabbed a colander filled with veggies.

"Marjorie." Angela narrowed her eyes.

"Why should my friends have to use the front door?" A knock sounded. "That must be Caroline." Marge smirked and tilted her head toward the door.

Caroline tapped and walked in. The haunted look had disappeared. She seemed more like herself. "Mmm. Did you make your fabulous lasagna, Marge?"

"Just took it out of the oven."

Hugs and chatter followed and Angela and Caroline set the table and filled glasses.

"In this house, setting the table is the extend of my culinary contributions." Angela moved aside. "I'm going to sit and watch Julia Child perform."

"I don't have enough wine in the kitchen to be in her category." Uniform slices flew from a cucumber, cut with surgical precision. "And I have not learned to debone fowl." 'Fowl' came out with Julia's distinct accent.

Everyone laughed. For the first time in weeks, all three dived into their meal and thoroughly stuffed themselves.

"I don't think I'll ever eat again," Caroline said.

"You will," Marge said. "I'm sending leftovers with both of you."

Caroline groaned.

"Let's get comfortable." Marge led them from the kitchen.

"Easy to do." Angela followed. "It's like my second home. Todd and I spent a lot of time here."

"And Brock and I—before we moved," Caroline said, then brightened. "Marge, it's funny. The last time my kids visited, they mentioned your annual taffy pull for the neighborhood kids. So unheard of in this generation."

Angela smiled and nodded.

"Good times. Seems like yesterday. May sound strange to you, but I often feel Greg should come walking through that door any time now."

Angela caught her breath. "You too?"

Marge's fingers caressed the arm of Greg's recliner as she nodded.

"How many times have I imagined that Todd's in the next room? He just stepped out. He'll be back."

"Denial. I guess that's what they call it," Caroline said.

Angela scanned the living room of the three-bedroom ranch with its comfortable, lived-in look of disarray. She touched a quilt draped over the sofa.

"From the garage sale?"

"Yes. The fabric is old. Reminds me of going to my grand-parent's house."

Angela's fingers traced the star pattern. "Such tiny stitches, each so perfect. Lovely muted colors."

"Whenever my mother sees anything antique in my house, she reprimands me," Marge said. "She likes ultra-modern, nothing to remind her of the good old days."

Caroline frowned. "That's too bad. Brock never liked antiques, but I enjoy going back to the farm and seeing my mother's collections." Caroline stared at the floor. "Dad left everything as mother had it."

"How long has it been now?" Marge said.

"Six years," Caroline said. "You never get over losing your mother."

"No, I suppose not." Marge leaned back in Greg's recliner. "Other than adding the quilt, I haven't changed a thing. Greg liked his files and papers nearby. I didn't mind. I was never a neat-freak." She motioned to the stacks around the chair. "I wonder if they need any of these at the office. Guess I'll call Darren and let him look them over."

"Darren?" Angela said, "Oh, yes, Greg's engineer."

"Don't know what I would do without him." Marge fished out her workbook. "Anything new?"

Angela paused. "I tried to forget what happened this morning."

"What?" Marge said.

"Todd's death certificates arrived in the mail," Angela sighed. "That's not the worst of it. My behavior. My moods. Swinging from depression to anger and back again."

Marge nodded. "The smallest thing can set you off. I was searching the supply cabinet at the hospital for a notepad and the receptionist said, look, someone turned in a nice portfolio. She handed it to me with the words, 'lucky you.' Lucky me? I wanted to say keep the portfolio and give me back Greg." Marge straightened. "One has absolutely nothing to do with the other. But when you've lost the person who was your whole life ... silly, I know."

"No, it's not," Caroline said. "We can't stop our thoughts. Or emotions."

"Emotions. I was annoyed after the meeting with our attorney today." Angela winced. "Not 'our' attorney now—my attorney."

"What did he say?"

"She. Well, I had this great idea to invest in the business and pay off loans with part of the life insurance money to ease the pressure and then send some money the children's way." Angela sat up and filled them in on the attorney's advice.

Marge stared. "Greg and I have no children, so I don't face that problem. But you weren't thinking of dividing the insurance money with your children, were you?"

"I wanted to lighten their burden. Still do."

"Even after the attorney's advice?" Marge said.

"I wonder what Todd would have advised me to do?"

"I think we both know," Marge said crisply.

Caroline piped up, "Brock's death certificates came today, too."

"Haven't checked the mail for two days." Marge shook her head.

"Everything's tied up financially with Brock's estate, so there are no decisions to make yet. But I'm glad you shared the information. Your attorney's right. We need the correct mindset."

Angela steered them back to the workbook. "Well, I know why they call it a workbook. It's work to process your grief."

"I feel swallowed up in the tide," Caroline said. "So many conflicting thoughts."

Marge tapped her workbook. "I can see I would have continued to hide myself in my work if it weren't for these exercises."

"Agreed. 'Through the valley of the shadow of death.' I don't want to stay in that valley," Angela said. "But when will we make it through?"

"I wonder," Caroline said.

Late that evening, Angela sat with a cup of tea in her bedroom window seat. A gift bag from Susan held a devotional for widows. The short story ended with a reference from Psalm 18: "The Lord is my rock and my fortress and my deliverer, my God, my rock, in whom I take refuge." If she truly trusted the Lord to take care of her, couldn't she trust Him to take care of her children?

Suddenly she recalled Todd's words to the children years ago: "We'll give you a college education and the rest is up to you." He encouraged their independence. As their mother, she needed to follow through. She shook her head. Her prior reasoning fell like a row of dominoes.

19

The next day

Becca bounded into the flower shop with subs for lunch. "Here you go, Mom. I knew you and Rosa wouldn't stop for lunch."

"You're right." Angela quickly washed her hands. "Rosa, time for a break. Coffee? Forgot, you prefer tea."

"Yes, and thanks for bringing the hot water dispenser."

"Don't mention it."

"I'll have tea." Becca stepped up to the counter.

They ate lunch like a relay team, one eating while another attended to a customer or a phone call.

"I'm heading out with today's deliveries," Rosa said.

"Thanks, Rosa." Angela's phone chirped, a text from Michelle Markham with her recommendation for a financial advisor.

When the shop grew quiet, Angela called the number for an appointment.

"Might as well call HR for an appointment, too." Angela paced the floor holding her cell phone.

"Dad's work?"

"Yes."

"How do you do it?" Becca said.

"Take each day as it comes. The sooner I get this over with, the better." Angela turned back to her phone. "Human Resources, please."

After her call, Angela searched her dwindling garage sale stack. Trying to act casual, she pretended to occupy herself with draping a dresser scarf on a table and rearranging items on top as she said, "Tell me more about this young man I hear you talking to on the phone."

"Trevor? He hangs out with Molly's crowd. We don't really date, just sort of end up together."

"And Molly, she's becoming a closer friend?" Angela glanced at Becca's new cropped shirt, which barely touched the top of her jeans. When she lifted her arms, her bare midriff was in full view.

"I'm hoping she'll come to church with me."

"That would be nice."

"Don't you like her?"

"It's not that I don't like her. She's ... I don't know, she's so in love with her body."

"Mom! What a weird thing to say."

"I suppose."

"Well, now that you mention it, it's a fair assessment. I mean, the way she's put together."

"Becca, there's nothing wrong with looking the best you can. But when you add that much effort, it becomes clear you want others to notice. Especially men."

"Is there a message in this for me?"

"You've always been modest."

"Yeah, I remember how Dad felt on the subject." Becca's arms hugged her midsection. "I'd never want to disappoint him."

"I know."

Angela rubbed Becca's back and sent up a prayer for discernment.

Time to change the subject. "Becca, I'm thinking of ordering another line, accessories like kitchen towels, linens, soaps, to complement the antiques. I missed the gift expo, and I'll need your help."

Rosa returned and Angela pulled her into the discussion.

"Rosa, come and give me your input for a new line I'm ordering."

"Sure, happy to help where I can." But Rosa was side-tracked when a customer walked in.

"Maybe Angela can answer your question." Rosa guided a middle-aged woman to the counter.

"I noticed your wisteria vine blooming beside the front door. Such lovely lavender blossoms. Oh, my—I guess that's why your shop has the name and the lavender trim. I'm surprised to see it in this climate."

"Yes, it's a species adapted for Minnesota. It's been growing in my yard for years. I brought a slip of the vine to the shop two years ago, and now it's decided to bloom."

"Do you sell the slips? Because I sure would like one."

"I don't see why I couldn't start a few. I'll bring one in." Angela jotted the woman's phone number. Wisteria, long life. Angela had given the flower shop that name as a prayer for a long life to her business. May it be so. Her livelihood depended on it. No, she mustn't think that. She must trust God to take care of her.

An hour later, Angela called Becca to her office. Angela's tiny office wasn't much wider than the door to it and a small window that faced the shop. Her office was more like an oversized closet, but it served its purpose. "Check out these websites," Angela toggled to five different sites. "I want to appeal to everyone's taste and sense of color. Give me your vote."

"That's easy." Soon Becca added to Angela's list.

"Rosa? Come look at my laptop. What do you think?"

Rosa hesitantly pointed to one site. "I'm afraid mine would be Southwest colors of reds, oranges, yellows."

"Just what we needed—cayenne, banana pepper, lime. It's making me hungry." Angela keyed in her color selections and sent an order.

"Reminds me of taco Tuesday." Becca called from her art nook. "School lunches."

"You had tacos in Minnesota?" Rosa said.

"Of course."

"Mom, what about tea?"

"Sure. I had my coffee this morning. I'm ready for tea."

"I meant actually sell loose tea in the shop?"

Angela stared at Becca for a moment. "What a great idea."

Rosa joined them. "At the shelter, Miranda buys loose tea in bulk and combines flavors to make her special blend."

"Now that sounds like fun," Angela said.

"Let's try it." Becca smiled. "You can sell those empty tea bags to fill along with the loose tea."

"Okay, I'll check it out." Angela googled tea sources and jotted down some notes. "Just got a text. Bethany and Phillip are on their way."

"Hope it's before I leave. Finished only two signs today." Becca scrambled to complete her lettering. She was putting paint out of reach when the back door opened and Phillip shot in, running straight for Becca.

"Hi buddy, let me put these on the shelf." With a plaque in each hand, Becca reached upward.

"Let me see." Phillip jumped and grabbed for her arm. One by one, the plaques toppled to the floor.

"Phillip!" Becca yelled. She stomped her foot and stepped back from a smeared 'Life is Goo—' plaque. The other plaque landed upside-down, its semi-dry paint tattooing the tile floor.

"I'm sorry, Becca." Bethany flipped over a demolished sign.

"Well, there goes my afternoon's work." Becca rolled her eyes, hands on hips.

Bethany reached for paper towels. "Becca, he's two years old."

"I sorry." Phillip's lower lip trembled and his face scrunched.

"Hey, it's okay, Phillip." Becca hugged him and glanced at Bethany. "Guess I'm just not used to kids."

"Come over sometime. I'll indoctrinate you," Bethany said.

"I will. Don't know why I haven't spent more time with Phillip."

Becca cleaned the painting area and grabbed her backpack. "Time to head to work. 'Bye, gotta run." She waved and headed for the back door.

"Don't forget Emerson's birthday party tomorrow night, Becca," Bethany said.

"And don't forget the realtor is coming tonight," Angela said.

"I won't," Becca smirked. "And yes, Mom; I cleaned my room."

Phillip waved at Becca, then meandered toward Rosa, who was pushing the watering cart.

"You said the realtor's coming tonight?" Bethany said. "The Andersons?"

"Yes. Mary."

Bethany wandered to the middle of the room and stopped. "Wow!" She spun in a circle, arms outstretched. "What a difference. And look at this!" She touched a lamp. "Oooh, Retro. My favorite."

Walking to the back, she whispered to Angela, even though the shop was empty, "No tired-looking displays. Every inch of the shop is exciting now."

Bethany's hand flew to her mouth. "Sorry, Mom. That didn't come out right."

Angela laughed and drew her to the worktable. "Static displays lined up like the hardware store it used to be? You had it right."

"But I shouldn't have said it!"

"No worries. I have a new vision." Angela allowed her optimism to soar for the first time as she glimpsed items hanging from the ceiling, draped across walls, and flowing into an inviting array of upbeat home decor.

Rosa hugged Phillip, lifting him off his feet. He rewarded her with a round of giggles. Then Rosa handed Phillip a bucket. "Now, take this and help me."

Phillip began his job of picking up dead leaves while Rosa pinched and pruned. "I found one." Phillip ran to Rosa with a dried-up schefflera leaf in his bucket.

"Good," Rosa said. "Let's find more."

Bethany smiled. "Phillip has so much energy."

Angela waved a mug in Bethany's direction. Bethany nodded. Angela filled two cups and dipped a cinnamon spice tea bag into her green mug.

"Mom? That cup, isn't it—"

"Your dad's? Yes, I brought it back from the cabin." Angela ran her fingertips over the pine tree imprint. She had made peace with it. It had become precious. As memories threatened to overwhelm her, she cleared her throat. "Your energy coming back?"

"It's getting better. Thanks for not bugging me about it." Bethany pulled up a stool. "I almost have it down to a science. Eating a carb when I take my pill was a breakthrough."

"Learning curve, I guess." Angela sipped her tea then tackled the next order.

"No nausea for a week. We'll see if it continues." Bethany searched the ribbon spools until she found one to complement the flowers her mother had assembled. "It's hard not to look over your shoulder at where we were. We had quite a chunk saved for a down payment on a house."

"I'm so sorry, dear."

"But I mustn't forget what fighting cancer taught me."

"Taught you?" Angela's busy fingers froze.

"I remember buying a cute little print with a Bible verse because the color complemented my decor: 'I can do all things through Christ who strengthens me.'" A frown creased Bethany's forehead. "Then I faced cancer and learned to live that verse."

"I'm glad you shared that with me."

"Before cancer I had a Bible-verse-on-the-wall kind of faith."

"A Bible-verse-on-the-wall faith?" Angela inhaled sharply.

"That about sums it up. I thought I was a woman of faith. Then your illness. Then Todd."

Wisteria

Angela knew the long day would exhaust her, but when the realtor had offered an opening at seven p.m., she had grabbed it. Why put off listing her home? She turned onto Pleasant Street and one glimpse at her home answered that question.

The warm colors of the brick and cedar exterior showcased by the flowering spirea bushes, roses, and hanging baskets. Bianca wood chairs where she and Todd had sat in the evening filled the front porch. Everything said home.

Mary Anderson was a small woman and struggling to stay that way by the looks of buttons straining to escape her jacket. With military precision, she completed her walk-through and sat down on a stool in the kitchen.

"I'll just say up front, our biggest obstacle is the recent development on the south side." Mary tapped her pen on the counter.

"I didn't realize that."

"New builds saturated the market for the past two years with dozens of overpriced homes that didn't sell. The contractor bailed out. Now investors are scrambling to sell at whatever price they can get." She unbuttoned her jacket. "Your second obstacle. There's not a huge market for these older homes. You understand, I'm sure."

"I don't mean to sound as though I'm looking through rose-colored glasses, but I think it's stunning."

"You're the second owners? What is it, sixty years old?"

"Almost that old."

"We have to find a buyer interested in mid-century modern architecture."

"And look." Angela swept her hand in a wide arc. "Kitchen, dining room, living room, all together before an open concept was popular."

Mary's glance followed. "Fireplace in the center. The two-story wall of windows adds value. It's a beautiful home, and it will be a pleasure to show it." Mary's face lit up into a practiced smile that didn't quite reach her eyes. "There are very few homes for sale on lots this large with mature trees and beautifully developed landscaping." Mary whisked papers and a calculator from her briefcase. "My team put together comps of recent home sales in your neighborhood."

"Comps?"

"Yes, comparisons. Remember, tastes have changed. Try not to let sentimentality get involved with the sale."

How could she not get sentimental? While Mary filled out forms, Angela grabbed her laptop. Realizing she had not done her homework, she googled homes for sale in her zip code to confirm general home prices.

Mary passed the handwritten form in triplicate to Angela. "Here's a listing agreement ready for you at the selling price I would recommend."

Angela frowned. "Add ten thousand to that price and I will sign."

Mary paused, then said, "I have no problem with that. We can always go down, but we can't go up."

20

The next evening—Bethany and Emerson's apartment

Angela and Becca drove to Bethany's tiny two-bedroom apartment for Emerson's birthday.

Bethany greeted Angela and Becca with a brave smile. "I made a cake this morning. But, just as I promised, we're having takeout pizza."

Angela hugged Bethany. "As long as you don't overdo."

"Pizzz-aa!" yelled Phillip. He grabbed Angela.

"Hey, settle down, young man." Emerson corralled everyone into their small dining space. After they devoured the pizza, Bethany placed a beautifully frosted chocolate cake in front of her husband.

"Ahh, exactly what I wanted." He smiled at Bethany. "Best birthday present of all."

"I have a birthday!" Phillip said.

"Well, two months from now," Bethany said.

"How old will you be?" Becca said.

Phillip's head swiveled to his mother, who whispered, "Three."

"Tree!" Phillip giggled at their laughter.

Becca kissed his forehead. "You're quite a guy. Could I come over and play with you sometime?"

"Uh huh, swim?"

"While Mommy takes a nap?" Becca glanced at Bethany. "I think you're right. I need to spend more time with my nephew."

Bethany smiled.

Phillip stood in his booster seat to help blow out the candles. Emerson had to wrestle Phillip back into his seat before the cake was served.

"Presents!" Phillip squealed when Bethany mounded the gifts in front of Emerson.

"Okay, you can help me open the presents. Then it's off to bed," Emerson said.

Bethany leaned toward Emerson. "I'm not sure chocolate was the best idea before bedtime," she said.

A half-hour later, Emerson carried a chocolate-smudged Phillip down the hall to the bathroom.

Bethany trailed close behind. "Be back soon. I'll sponge off cake and we'll get him into pajamas."

Angela carried plates to the counter. "This is a small kitchen, isn't it?"

"Everything is small here," Becca said.

The dishwasher was humming by the time Emerson and Bethany joined them in the living room.

"Bethany tells me you listed with the Andersons," Emerson said.

"Yes, listed last night." Angela twisted her wedding ring. "And she'll give me a referral for a realtor to list the cabin."

Everyone turned and Becca gasped. "The cabin?"

Angela's hand covered Becca's. "We can't keep it. It needs a new roof, other repairs. Remember? Dad intended to take care of that this summer."

Becca's hand trembled as she pulled away.

On the drive home, Becca seemed to have recovered from the shock of hearing about the cabin—or was she putting on a brave face with her animated chatter? "And did you see Phillip's face when Emerson pulled out a Twins baseball cap? And Bethany put it on him and it fell completely over his ears!"

"Adorable."

Becca fell silent by the time Angela pulled into the garage. Nice try, Becca. Angela wasn't sure if the chatter was more for her benefit or her daughter's.

Angela sighed and headed down the hall to her bedroom. "'Night, Becca."

"What?" Becca stared blankly. "Oh, yeah, goodnight."

Angela picked up one book after another but pushed each one away. She moved to the window seat and pulled the reading light close. She was thankful no one could see her through the window. The canopy of mature trees offered concealment, a sheltering comfort. She pulled her journal out and started writing: "Fear not." A tear landed on her open page, dried and blistered one corner. Angela hugged the journal to her chest. "Dear God, the Bible says You put all our tears in a bottle." A bottle? "You'll need a fifty-gallon drum for my tears."

A knock broke her contemplation. "I saw your light under the door." Becca's eyes were red. "Mom, will it ever get any better?"

Angela motioned to Becca. "Come here." Piling cushions

against one end of the window seat. "They tell me it will." Angela put her arm around Becca and pulled her close. "Guess we'll find out together."

"What's going to be left of Dad when the house and cabin sell?"

"We have our memories, don't we?"

"Y-yes."

"We had the love of one of the greatest men on earth."

Her head nodded against her mother's shoulder. "I miss dad so much."

Angela held her and closed her eyes to more tears.

"You still have a father."

Becca stiffened. "But he's not here anymore."

"Your Heavenly Father is." Angela stroked Becca's hair, then leaned her cheek against the dark curls. "I'm afraid I didn't emphasize that enough to my three bees. We still have a Father looking over us, ready to comfort us and give us wisdom to live our lives."

"It's hard to pray. I get stuck." Becca sniffed.

"He hears you. He knows your thoughts, and He knows you're reaching out to Him." Angela told her about Bethany's experience of living the verses. "It's time to take those verses off the wall and into our hearts."

"Yeah, I guess that's where I've left them too, Mom."

"Shall I pray for us?"

"Sure."

"Dear Father, we honor and praise you for being the God of all comfort. Let our Bible verses on the wall sink deeply into our hearts. Not as a charm or a lucky rabbit's foot, but a testimony of our relationship with you."

Angela leaned back and closed her eyes. "We could make a

list of all the things we remember about Dad, all the things we are thankful for."

"A list?" Becca turned and frowned.

"Let me think." Angela persisted. "Remember that huge guest book they gave us at the funeral?"

"Ugh."

"I know. I stashed it away, never wanting to look at it again. But there was a section at the end with the heading of notes. I remember thinking, who would make notes?" Angela kissed Becca's hair where it parted on one side. "But wouldn't that be a perfect place to make our list? Someday we'll enjoy looking back at the names of the people who came to honor your father. Let's honor him in our own way."

Becca frowned but nodded. Inwardly, Angela groaned. This would take time to sink in.

21

A ngela continued to integrate her recent purchases alongside junk and vintage items. Plants and dried flower arrangements added color for a stunning effect. At least she thought so.

"My shop is full. First time in two years I've used all the space." Angela angled a display. Angles. Design is all about angles. "But no one sees it." She stopped at one of the large plate-glass windows and gestured at the highway. "I've put every enticing statement I can think of on our sign outside. Only our regular customers walk in."

She marched to the other side of the room and turned to face Rosa. "Look at the cars going by. How do I bring them in?"

Rosa shrugged, shoulders slumped.

Angela checked potted plants for moisture and continued her soliloquy. "On weekends people head north to their cabin. After all, Northgate is the gateway to the North. The town's slogan, right? That's what Todd and I used to do. Everyone who comes from the west goes by my shop to get to 35 and turn north. Could I cause a bottleneck at the gate?"

"A bottleneck?" Rosa frowned. "You want to stop traffic?"

"Whatever it takes."

Angela muttered and puttered. When she finally stopped long enough to gauge Rosa's reaction, Rosa was shakily fanning ribbon's loops, her face etched in eloquent distress. How little Angela knew of her.

"Rosa? Is everything okay?"

"Sure." But Rosa jumped when the phone rang.

After Rosa hung up, Angela touched her shoulder. "Rosa?"

Rosa stood still for a moment. "Today would have been our tenth anniversary, Carlos and mine."

Who was Carlos?

The bell at the front door sounded, oddly punctuating the pain in Rosa's face. But Rosa fought to adjust her expression. "I'll help them."

"No, stay here. I'll take care of them," Angela whispered. She recognized three teachers from Northgate's Elementary School and smiled.

"Very nice," One of them said as she studied the natural grass garland twining around a display of kitchen towels. They both stopped short at Angela's display of teas for sale. Each selected a different tea, then drifted out the front door with their small purchases. Angela sighed and turned to Rosa.

"Would you like to get together somewhere without interruptions? Maybe meet before work for coffee? Or tea?"

"That would be nice," she said, her voice unnaturally high with surprise.

"How about in the morning?"

"Sure. Roberto sleeps late. I could ask Arielle to come early."

"And I'd like to pay Arielle for the extra hour or two."

"I—"

127

"We'll call it a business meeting. The business of getting to know one another."

"Okay."

Thursday morning Angela headed to Old Main, the older section of Northgate, resplendent with tall, narrow brick buildings with ornate patterned false fronts. She swung behind a corner storefront, The Nordic Cup, dodging cars exiting a busy drive-through. A century ago, the building was a bustling mercantile.

Angela studied the well-preserved memorabilia displayed inside the coffee shop. Tiny drawers with glass fronts of faded gold-leaf scrolling decorated the shelves, and a huge bin formerly for penny candy now housed coffee beans.

The Nordic Cup hummed with business. Angela sank into a window seat, the same booth where she and Todd had always sat. Soon she spotted Rosa. A breeze swept her long hair into a dusky mass around her shoulders as she swung open the coffee shop door.

Angela met her at the counter. "So glad you could join me."

"Thanks for the invitation. My first time here." Rosa looked at the menu board. "What unusual names for coffee."

"See the soccer jersey on the wall?" Angela said. "Belongs to the owner of the shop, Bjorn Johnsen. He named the coffee shop's drinks after soccer plays."

An Oriental barista pitched the menu. "May I suggest Capocannoniere if you like a cappuccino, Powerplay with two shots of espresso; or for more of a punch, the Uff Da with three shots of espresso?"

Rosa studied the menu. "How about tea?"

"Yah, sure, ya betcha." She mocked the Norwegian slang and laughed along with them, her full dimples popping out. She pointed to a third menu board. "Lingonberry blend, green tea ... "

"I'll try the lingonberry," Rosa said.

"Hum, lingonberry?" Angela wondered about adding the flavor to her shop.

"Tea for you as well?"

"No thanks. It's morning. The Winger for me." Angela pointed to the mocha. "Now for pastries."

She hooked Rosa's arm and led her to a glass case. Soon, with hands full they walked to the corner window. Her favorite seat was still available.

"This spot okay?"

"Sure."

Angela slid into the booth. "Norwegian ancestry and Northgate fit together like lutefisk and lefse."

Rosa laughed. "I've sampled the traditional Norwegian foods. You can keep the lutefisk."

"I think you have to grow up with it, like Todd. He had a Norwegian mother and a Scottish father. His mother gave him a heritage—his father, his Celtic features." Angela ducked her head as she teared up.

"I'm praying for you," Rosa said softly. "I know you must miss him."

Angela nodded and stared at the frothy design in her cup. "Forgive me for these emotional ups and downs."

Rosa nodded. "Remember when I came to the shelter? Todd stepped up and found the Ellingsons, who needed a renter in their lower level. I'm very grateful. So kind of him."

"That was Todd's nature." Angela looked away.

"All the memories, all the adjustments you're making. Feels like a slippery slope, doesn't it?"

Angela caressed the wedding ring she still wore. "That's a perfect analogy for widowhood."

"Sometimes I think we live in two different worlds." Rosa laughed a high nervous twitter. "Or maybe I just feel like I'm living incognito. I've never talked about my husband, Carlos, have I?"

"No," Angela said. "And the women's shelter instructed us never to force a confidence."

"Thank you for not prying. I told Miranda the story before I entered the shelter. Would you like to hear about him?"

"Only if you would like to tell me."

"I would."

"I'm learning it helps to tell our story to others." Angela stopped a tear with her knuckle. "And, it's so hard to talk at the shop knowing interruptions could come at any time."

Rosa stared at the endless caravan of drive-through cars. "Carlos was very sweet when we first married." She ran her fingertips up and down the sides of her cup. "I met him through his sister. Such a sweet girl. She was our neighbor. Carlos came from Mexico, said he had a green card. He worked in a freight office in the old section of town. Often gone a week at a time making deliveries. We rented a nice home near my parents'. Roberto was born, and I couldn't have been happier. About the time our son started school, Carlos changed ... became agitated, sometimes violent. I finally understood his mood swings when he tried to tempt me to use drugs. He got angry when I refused. He talked about moving to Mexico, but I didn't want to go. So I made excuses."

Rosa glanced at customers chattering at nearby tables. She lowered her voice even more. "One day he disappeared. There was a sting operation. The freight company was a front for running drugs. He wasn't on the list of those captured, and we had no idea what happened to him." Rosa leveled her gaze at Angela.

Angela leaned forward as if those extra two inches could tune out the hiss of coffee machines and other conversations.

"I moved back to my parents' home. Then my father heard a rumor Carlos arrived in Mexico and died from gunshot wounds." Rosa squeezed her eyes shut. "What to believe? My father wanted me to disappear for a while. My mother insisted we stay. She wanted her only grandson close. I agreed with my father—protect Roberto, take no chances. My father had friends in Minneapolis, and they suggested we go live with them. We were afraid to get them involved. They told us about the shelter in Northgate. You must admit this is an out-of-the-way location."

"But Shepherd's Gate isn't a secured women's shelter," Angela said.

"I know. Before we left, I received a death certificate from Carlos' family in Mexico. That's why Miranda allowed me to join the shelter."

"Rosa, you're a widow, too." Angela reached across the table.

Rosa took her hand. "Almost a year. It's so hard to grasp."

"I'm so sorry. My heart goes out to you."

"Thanks." Rosa leaned back, stared at the ceiling then visibly relaxed. "I didn't want to talk about my past. But it's a relief to tell you."

"Here I am, wrapped up in my own world of grief, not even aware of how others around me are suffering." Angela's voice pleaded with Rosa to understand.

"Don't say that." Rosa lifted her soft brown eyes. "It's too new. You're still in shock. I know. I remember. I think God brought me here. I learned to trust in Jesus, to lean on him. I want to be a tower of strength like you, Angela."

"Is that how I appear?"

"Yes."

"If anyone had said that two years ago, I would have agreed." She shook her head. "I realize now I depended on my husband with God in the background smiling upon our marriage." Angela's gaze locked with Rosa. "Marriage can be an idol."

Rosa rested her forehead on her fingertips and nodded.

"I feel like a shallow Christian with a lot of Bible knowledge but little faith. I had to learn what the word 'testing' meant. My best friend, Cecilia ... I lost her to cancer. Then a bigger test came with Bethany's cancer. I didn't handle that well. Then I lost Todd."

This time Rosa reached out and gripped her hand.

"God promises never to forsake the widow." Angela smiled. "I can't explain what I'm feeling. A new peace, a solid determination to be honest with God. Might as well own up; He already knows my heart. Who am I to keep God at a distance?"

22

W hen Angela left the coffee shop and turned the corner of Old Main, her grief turned a corner, too. She resolved to let God's protection replace Todd's. She needed to turn to the only One who heals her hurt.

Working with Rosa assumed a new level of comfort and understanding that day. Sisters in faith, both widows.

Angela punched the buttons on her phone and smiled at Rosa. "What exciting news. Just got a text from Caroline. She got an offer on her house."

"How's the widow's group going?"

"In the beginning, a lot of tears. Now it seems there's more resolution, more comfort. I'm so thankful we decided to meet."

"The three of you ... must be very close."

"Getting closer." Angela scrubbed a tiny glass slipper with a toothbrush. Its ruby glow reminded her of the burgundy pattern in a hatbox, the perfect mate. "Rosa, would you like to join us? We'd love to have you, no matter where you are in the process."

"Thanks, but no. There was counseling at the shelter.

Miranda's a widow, and very sympathetic." Rosa stopped as a customer entered.

Angela recognized the owner of a local restaurant. "Hello, Maddie. How can I help you?"

Maddie had adorable blond hair chiseled short above a cute face with lips that smiled easily. "Shane here?"

"No, sorry. He left three weeks ago."

She stepped back, surprised. "Oh, I always paid him. Well, it's the end of the month. I'm here to pay my bill."

"I've got it right here." Rosa brought an invoice with a tally sheet attached.

"Two fifty? Oh, five weeks in June, right?"

Angela glanced at the entries. "Yes, that's right. Flowers for this week were picked up on Tuesday. That makes five orders."

"Still five percent off when I pay in cash?" Maddie unzipped a bank bag.

"Excuse me?"

"Shane said you okayed it." Maddie frowned. "That is your policy, isn't it? It sounded like a good deal when he approached me at the restaurant. It's really the only reason I ..." Her voice tapered off.

Angela did some quick mental figuring. Twelve-fifty wasn't that much. "Sure, we'll honor a discount. Let's see, I'll subtract the discount from the total and initial the corrected amount."

Maddie paid the bill and slipped the amended invoice in her cash pouch.

"Thank you," Angela said.

"Come and see us sometime." With a grin, Maddie strolled out the door.

Angela rang up the sale but removed all the checks and large bills from the cash register. "Rosa, do you know anything about Shane giving a discount for cash?"

"Hmm. I guess I never paid a lot of attention. But like she said, she always asked for Shane, usually came first thing in the morning before Shane left for deliveries."

Angela eyed the progress of orders for the day. "You can handle this, right?"

"Sure, not much going on today."

Angela slipped into her office. This was as good a time as any to make her deposit. She tore off her deposit ticket then flipped through the slips all the way back to the first of May to review cash deposits. Shane's precise printing stared back at her. The largest deposit of cash, the day after Mother's Day, seemed small. Mother's Day? "Money day," she and Todd had jokingly named it. She had worked twelve hours the Saturday before and let Shane handle the deposit on Tuesday since Bethany had an appointment that day. Except for Christmas and Valentine's Day, Mother's Day the next largest single day of income for the year. She scanned earlier months then compared them to the cash deposits made since Shane took over. Definitely much smaller.

Angela took her deposit tickets to the worktable. "Rosa, did you ever help with the deposits? Was that part of your training?"

Rosa frowned. "No. Never involved in the deposits."

"Okay. I'm just trying to catch up on my bookkeeping. Reacquaint myself with the cycles. Each season is different. That's a sweet arrangement. Who's it for?"

"A mom with a new baby girl. I remember Shane putting together one like this."

Angela drew squiggles on the deposit pad cover. "Rosa, tell me your impression of Shane."

"Such a nice young man." Rosa squinted at her work on a

135

brandy snifter with moss in the bottom and baby roses spilling over the top. "Fresh out of college, very smart."

Maybe Shane was smarter than either of them knew. "What did he talk about?"

"Family from Texas. Being from the Southwest, we had that in common. Shane's college debt seemed to hang over his head. He talked a lot about that." Rosa nestled a lacy bow inside the stemware. "How's this?"

"Perfect, Rosa." Angela smiled. "I'm pleased with your progress. Very creative."

"Thanks." Rosa beamed as if she'd just won a blue ribbon at the state fair. She added the arrangement to the van deliveries. "I won't be long."

When Rosa pulled away, Angela called her accountant. When she paused, Wade's voice grew terse. "Did you check your deposits daily with the sales totals?"

"In the beginning. Then he sort of took over, seemed to understand every aspect of the business. I thought Shane was a dream come true."

"You trusted him."

"I did. The deposits matched sales, but sales seemed low compared to last year. I just thought it a normal fluctuation with my dropping revenues." Angela's stomach growled. The scones at the coffee shop seemed a long time ago. "Unless he didn't ring up every sale and kept the cash. No, I mustn't say that. I don't know that for a fact."

"Angela, he could say he converted the cash to purchase coin and bills to stock the register, or any number of scenarios. Embezzlement charges require recorded proof."

"I wasn't thinking about charges. But if he is guilty, I just want a way to suggest he pay it back."

"It gets sticky. You're still charging him with a crime."

She had liked Shane. Yes, she had trusted him. Angela resisted the urge to bang her head against the wall.

She shifted gears as a mother and daughter walked in for their wedding planning appointment. Angela remembered the family from school activities. The new son-in-law-to-be was quite the basketball star. While they caught up on happenings around town, the trio sipped coffee in the shop's newly staged seating area. Angela traced the rough outline of pine trees on Todd's green mug. How she missed him. He would have made Shane's deceit easier to bear.

Eventually, the emotional day at the shop passed. En route home, a construction detour took Angela through streets of tidy but small homes. She slowed to study the area. Maybe a good place to move when her house sold. At one home, a couple who looked retirement age were busy moving a rack of lawn ornaments into a workshop and caught her eye. Angela pulled over for a closer look.

"Hi!" The ornament lady waved and sidestepped her backward progression with the metal rack on wheels.

"Leonard! For Pete's sake, stop. Maybe she wants to look at your stuff."

"Sorry. How 'do, ma'am?" He lifted a faded purple and gold Minnesota Vikings cap, brushed back his gray hair, and resettled the shapeless headgear. "With all the noise these things make, I didn't hear your car. You're sure welcome to look."

And look she did. Wind spinners of bright colors. Wooden whirligigs from birds to bears performed on a pole. Metal spirals danced in the wind.

"Your designs are so unique." Angela's spirits lifted. "Where do you sell them?"

"Just here in front of our house for now," the ornament lady said. "Too expensive to get a booth at the farmer's market."

A spark of an idea ignited in Angela's mind. Such a delightful couple. Could she suggest a solution to their display problem?

Becca was waiting inside the front door when Angela finally got home.

"I'm going out with Cole Richardson tonight. You've met him, Mom, remember?"

Good. Not Trevor. "Yes, but I know little about him."

"He's a Bible major, working for a year before he goes back to school. He doesn't want to be in debt when he graduates."

"Smart."

"He's nice. So far, our dates have been volunteering wherever he's needed." Becca stood in the hall, swiveling the toe of her boot on a corner of the tile. "But tonight we're going hiking."

"Why don't you invite him for dinner one Sunday? Let everyone get to know him."

"Okay. Oh, that's him." Becca came to attention and swung open the front door. "It's rare we both have a night off!" She turned with a glowing look on her face. Cole couldn't seem to take his eyes off Becca.

"Hello, Cole," Angela said.

"Hi, Mrs. McKinley."

"Where are you hiking?" Angela said.

"Bearpaw Path." Cole rushed to open the door for Becca and smiled. "No bears, but some great trails."

"Have fun." She waved as his pickup pulled away. Clean

138

silver sides ended in a tiny row of rust that made a filigree pattern from the wheel well to the back bumper.

Angela felt so inadequate. Todd could size up people, especially men. How she needed him.

"Todd, your baby girl needs your guidance," she whispered as she opened her front door.

Another night to get through.

Angela curled up in Todd's recliner, entertained the idea of waiting up for Becca, but finally headed for her bedroom. She tucked the sheet under her chin. Soon, blessed sleep took over.

"Hi, Angel," Todd said. He leaned over, planted a quick kiss, and vanished.

23

"Todd? Todd!" Angela bolted upright in bed.

Her eyes adjusted to the gray shadows of pre-dawn. "It was so real. It was so ..." She sobbed. "Real. He was right here. Right here with me."

Never had a dream affected her so.

She watched the sun come up. As she left home that morning, she couldn't stop thinking about the dream. Todd's voice. Todd's touch. With a heavy heart, she threw herself into her work at the shop.

"Ouch!" Angela banged her elbow against the handle of a cooler door she had forgotten to shut. She rubbed her elbow and closed her eyes.

"Angela, what's wrong?" Rosa said.

"Did you ever dream about Carlos?"

Rosa leaned her weight against the worktable. "Yes. Often."

"And in your dreams, he's still alive?"

"Every time."

Angela nodded and ducked into the bathroom. More tears.

An hour before closing, Angela made another trip to Olaf's

shop. Inspecting a distorted mirror with silver flaking off its back, she caught a reflection of her puffy, red-rimmed eyes.

Olaf glanced at her and backed up. "Avis, come here. You've got a customer."

Avis, Olaf's part-time helper, called over her shoulder in her cheery voice, "Olaf, you're behind on that refinishing."

"Quit trying to tell me what to do." Olaf's voice faded with distance.

Avis smiled her warm smile. "How can I help you, Angela?"

Angela gingerly balanced several items on the counter and pointed to a baker's rack behind her. "That should do it."

By the time Angela returned to the shop, a numbness replaced her tears.

An excited Rosa helped unload the van. "I can't wait to see what you'll do with this." She held up an industrial string holder covered in cobwebs.

Angela nodded. "Wait until you see what shows up tomorrow."

Rosa shook her head.

Angela watched from the back door until the sight of Rosa's rusty Cavalier faded. Suddenly the trip to Olaf's didn't seem like such a good idea. Spending money she didn't have for things she could have managed without. Why did she think shopping would ease the pain? Medicating, according to her grief study. Maybe elbow grease would be more therapeutic. Angela sorted and cleaned each item.

Rosa rushed in directly behind Angela the following morning. "Who is that in front of the shop? And what is he doing?" Rosa headed to the front door the next morning to find a curious display at one end of the parking lot.

Angela followed and inspected the whirligigs and spinners that sparkled and twirled in the wind. Since her shop was located close to a main highway the display should attract attention for Leonard's wares. "Leonard, you're here. It looks great."

"Already had three people stop by and two sales." Leonard Fredricks' smile lit up his round face. "I think you were right. This beats the back street I was on."

"That's what I hoped would happen," Angela said. "Leonard, I want you to meet Rosa."

"Nice to meet you, Leonard." Rosa singled out a spinner. "Look at the shapes. My son, Roberto, will love this. I'll take it. Just put it aside while I grab the money."

"Or, better yet." Angela paused to wind a trailing vine of wisteria to a post. "Come in for a cup of coffee. I'll show you around."

"Thanks, but I got my thermos." Leonard held up an ancient Coleman.

"I brought fresh blueberry muffins," Rosa called over her shoulder.

"Little lady, I believe there's a discount on your purchase." Leonard followed them into the shop.

"Wow," Leonard said as he passed through the front of the shop, "You're talented."

"Thanks, but I don't feel so talented with this." In the back of the shop, Angela touched a library table. "Trying to apply my limited knowledge of distressing wood."

When she lifted the table to move it to a better light, one leg slipped out and crashed to the floor.

"Here, let me help you." Leonard reached for the round tapered leg rolling in a semi-circle.

"How on earth did that happen?"

"The wood is stripped and the screws won't tighten down anymore." Leonard held up the leg and swiveled his finger over a hole with a split going halfway down the leg.

Angela's mouth fell open. "I wondered why the table was so wobbly."

"Just needs wood filler, glue, put in a vice overnight, and re-drill the hole. I can do that for you."

"Could you? I could use the help."

"I'm a tinkerer. It's what I do." Leonard rubbed his chin then glanced at the table leg he still held. "Best I remove the other legs and check them out as well."

Angela gladly handed over the table.

"No wonder it fell off. Two screws missing here from this bracket. I should have some that'll fit."

Leonard paused at a small table containing paint, brushes, and lettered signs in various stages of completion. "What's that you're working on?"

"My daughter is in charge of this project." Angela picked up a small placard displaying a painted word: Joy. "Wish we could make garden signs. This wood would never hold up outdoors."

"Where do you get the wood?" Leonard held up a thin piece of basswood.

"The hobby shop."

"Humph."

Leonard arrived the next morning, triumphantly carrying the library table.

"Now it's sturdy!" He jiggled the tabletop.

"It's like a new table," Angela said.

"Wait, there's more." Leonard returned carrying a bundle of pine boards, some with pointed staves attached.

"Will this work for outdoor signs?"

"Yes! Nice."

They both looked up when Becca breezed in the back door.

"Leonard, this is my daughter, Becca."

"Hi." Becca smiled and bent to touch the boards. "Did you make these?"

Leonard touched the brim of his cap. "Just some old scrap lumber."

"I think we have a new supplier," Angela said. Was it possible she had found help to repair her new purchases? And awesome boards to paint and sell? All this because she had offered a spot for someone to display their work?

24

The following Monday, Marge and Caroline met at Angela's house for their session. A hot day. The mosquitoes were hungry. No one even thought of going outside.

Marge glanced at Angela on the sofa and picked Todd's ample recliner. "Anyone interested in your house?"

"No." Angela twirled a lock of hair. "Maybe I should drop the price. Although I can't imagine why. No one has shown an interest."

Marge lifted her eyebrows at Angela. "I can't say I'm sorry. I can't imagine not having you next door."

Angela's eyes smarted. "I don't want to think about it either. Every change seems to have ripple effects."

Marge took a deep breath and nodded. She turned to Caroline. "How's your house sale coming, Caroline?"

"We are still negotiating. It's not a clean sale as I thought," Caroline said, "but I'm packing already. You are both invited to my house next Monday. That is, if you can handle the packing boxes."

"Won't bother me," Marge said.

Angela lowered her workbook to the coffee table. "Nor me."

"Think we'll find a garage sale?" Marge glanced at Angela then winked at Caroline. All three burst out laughing.

"Are the garage sale items selling well at the shop?" Caroline said.

"They fit in beautifully." Angela avoided their eyes. "The linens and glassware were just the touch I needed for the furniture from Olaf's. Our investment will pay off eventually."

"Our investment?" Marge laughed. "I only drove the getaway car."

"Marjorie." Caroline shook her head in a way that set her auburn locks dancing. "That was some heist."

"Seriously, your shop looks great," Marge said. "Come on, level with us. What else?"

"I hate to burden you with my problems." Angela paused, gauging their reactions to see if she should continue. "Okay, that's why we're meeting. Financially, I seem to have backed myself into a corner. Got carried away with new ideas and inventory."

"It isn't paying off for you?" Caroline said.

"Only a few of the big items have sold." Angela shrugged. "But let me tell you of something really sweet that happened last week."

Angela filled them in on Leonard's displays on Friday and Saturday. "Leonard is one of those talented individuals who is good at many things. He offered to help me repair some of my items that are a little too shabby. He also provided boards for yard signs and plaques for Becca to paint."

"That's exciting," said Caroline.

As always, the balloon payment tormented Angela. No

need to share that with anyone. Maybe the cabin would sell before December.

"Ever thought of being interviewed by the newspaper?" Marge said. "They're always looking for a story in a small town."

"That's an idea." Angela twirled a lock of hair around her finger and flipped it behind her ear. "My ads are so small I wonder if they are worth the expense. But a story with pictures may spark interest. Thanks for suggesting it."

"Might work," Caroline said. "More people walking into your shop just to check it out."

"There, we settled that," Marge said. "But your frown is still there. What else is bothering you?"

"Emotionally, I'm just not coping. I dreamed about Todd and cried for a whole day." Angela's voice broke. "We were one and now he's gone. My body feels ... like it's ... ripped in half."

"Exactly how it feels," Marge said. "With my sprinkling of Bible knowledge, that's one verse that rings true. Two become one. What does that leave when you're widowed? Am I half a person now?"

Angela bit her lip and Caroline pulled her close.

"Forgive me, I can't function tonight," Angela mumbled.

"Just sit back and relax." Marge picked up the remote.

With Marge in charge, by the end of their study, Angela felt more like herself.

"The fourth of July is Friday," Marge said. "Are you going to the cabin, Angela?"

"Not until late Saturday after I close shop. I've given Rosa the day off so she'll have a long weekend."

"That's too bad. Can't you leave on Friday? Caroline said. "Just stay closed all day Saturday?"

"Never a good idea for business. People expect you to be

open. I'll leave Saturday afternoon, drive back sometime Monday, and be here for our meeting. But the shop will be closed on Friday the fourth. Want to get together?"

"Sure, nothing on my calendar," Marge said.

"I'll be at the farm," Caroline said. "The kids and I are going to my dad's for a few days, even if we do get the cold shoulder from Aunt Jackie."

"Aunt Jackie is still Aunt Jackie, I take it?" Marge frowned at Caroline.

Caroline sighed. "She'll never change."

25

L eonard Fredericks hailed Angela from the flower shop's doorway the next morning. "Myrna wanted to come over and see the shop."

The ornament lady stepped around her husband. "Hi, Angela."

"Myrna, welcome!"

Fresh from the hairdresser with a hair helmet of steel-gray curls, Myrna extended her hand. "Hello, and this must be Rosa? I've heard so much about you. Did your son like the whirligig?"

"Yes, he loved it."

"Becca!" Myrna dropped Rosa's hand and hurried past her.

"You've met?" Angela said.

"Yesterday when she brought over that plaque." Myrna reached out.

Becca returned her hug. "Thanks again for those delicious chocolate chip cookies."

"We loved having you stop by. Come any time." Myrna

turned back to Angela. "With grandchildren scattered across the country, I miss having young people around."

Leonard bent over the worktable to admire Becca's work, a cursive 'Welcome' in brown on a turquoise board.

"I couldn't find the exact hardware you wanted," he said, "so I used brass pieces and hammered them to match."

Becca reached for the pieces as if they were pure gold and placed one on each corner of her board in progress. "Awesome!"

"What a difference. Never thought you could turn a piece of wood into something like that." Leonard smiled and turned to Angela. "I put new wheels on the tea cart. I'll bring it over tomorrow."

Myrna peeked at Becca's work. "Nice. I wanted to see what you are doing with all the boards Leonard chops up." Myrna's gaze shifted to the shop and she moseyed from one display to another. "And, my, what unusual home decor."

"Leonard's woodworking skills came to the rescue for several items, not to mention the signboards." Angela continued working on a fresh flower order. "Please feel free to look around."

Myrna nodded. "Years ago, I worked in a flower shop, waited on customers, swept up, and even put together bouquets. Everything has changed. It looks ... I don't know, trendy, I guess is the word. I'm still stuck in the lace and ribbon handicraft era." Myrna opened a nicked cupboard door with most of the paint peeled off. "Aren't you afraid a spider will jump out at you?"

Rosa laughed.

"I'm hoping they don't survive the fumigating from my disinfectant." Angela's eyes darted to the ceiling. "Of course, you never know."

Myrna jerked back from the cupboard, then laughed. "Well, thanks for the tour. Call me if you get behind and need help. I have a lot of time on my hands."

"Thank you, Myrna. If you're available during the holidays, I just might take you up on your offer."

Leonard held the door for her. "Be back in the morning." He reached up and jingled the bell. "With bells on."

Myrna looked back, rolled her eyes, and stepped through the door.

Angela turned to Becca. "So, you've visited the Fredericks?"

"Yes. Friday he told me where they lived, said to stop by anytime I had new designs to show him."

Rosa waved from the back door. "Making deliveries, Angela."

"Thanks, Rosa."

Becca turned to her mother. "I had a great idea I wanted to duplicate. So yesterday before work, I took my tablet to Mr. Frederick's. He helped me ... and here's how it's turning out." Becca pointed to her work in progress. She paused, her paint-brush in mid-air. "Kind of sad, really."

"What is?"

"Well, I could hear them arguing through their open front door when I arrived. Mrs. Fredericks was shouting at him." Becca shook her head and turned back to her painting. "I heard him say, 'for Pete's sake, Myrna,' and I heard her say, 'well, you know it's true, you pay no attention to me.' I didn't know what to do, so I knocked real loud as if I hadn't heard. I was desperate to finish the plaque. They said 'come in,' and I just walked in and smiled at them."

"Becca, they're a sweet old couple. All married people have their days."

Becca stared into space for a moment then resumed her painting. "I guess you're right."

That evening Angela couldn't calm her agitation. Myrna Fredericks persisted in Angela's thoughts. If she could bottle this despair and allow the Fredericks of the world to experience it, maybe couples would be gentler with each other. No one understands the finality of losing someone forever until it happens to them.

Angela darted to her bedroom, determined to take a walk despite the misty rain outside. She checked the back of her closet for something warm to wear and lifted a hanger. A whiff of Drakkar, Todd's favorite cologne, still lingered on his gray fleece jacket. Todd had put it around her shoulders on their last walk together. The memory hit her so hard she had to sit down. The jacket, on her side of the closet, had missed the purging. She hugged it as if it were a life preserver and closed her eyes.

First she wanted his things gone to avoid the pain. Now she clung to every item with his stamp on it. A torn sheet from a daily calendar where he had written, 'Angel, be home late, love you' was now too precious to part with. Silly, she told herself. But it was a connection to Todd and the days they had had together.

She forced herself up and donned his jacket. She would retrace the steps of their last walk. As she laced her walking shoes, the phone rang.

"Hi, Mom." Bethany's cheery voice came through the phone. "I'm bringing dinner over to your house tomorrow night so we can visit. Not sure what we'll have, but I'll think of something."

"There's hamburger in the fridge." Sudden elation over the thought of not eating alone overcame Angela. "Why don't you come early and use my kitchen?"

"Great idea. Phillip can play in the sandbox. He's been asking about that."

"The sandbox." Angela paused. "Todd built it when Phillip was still learning to walk."

"Yes, in the same spot where our old sandbox used to be."

Bethany had sounded happy, remembering. Would Angela find happiness in such memories someday?

The wet sidewalk stretched before her. Gray skies above, gray pathway ahead. Her steady cadence created a monotony that matched her mood.

26

The next day

Angela returned home from work to find Bethany setting the oven timer.

"Mom, you're home early."

"It wasn't busy this afternoon. Rosa will close shop."

Bethany hurried toward the scattered pieces of a wood puzzle. "Be careful, I haven't picked up yet."

"Don't bother until Phillip's finished playing."

Phillip sent his truck into a stack of blocks then turned troubled eyes to his grandmother as they tumbled across the floor. When Angela laughed, he giggled at his reprieve. His laughter filled the room.

Bethany poured Angela an iced tea.

"You're not overdoing?" Angela swallowed the cool liquid.

"No, Emerson will grill burgers, salad in the fridge, potatoes in the oven."

Together they retreated to the terrace. Phillip followed behind. It was a perfect July day.

"Becca's working?"

Angela nodded.

"I suppose she's working on the fourth?"

"Yes, low man on the totem pole. No holidays off," Angela said.

Phillip squealed and jumped in the sandbox.

"When are you and Emerson leaving for the cabin?"

"Friday morning. We'll get there when we get there. Wish you could ride with us."

"I'll drive up Saturday after work. We'll be together Sunday."

"Won't be the same without ..." The pain in Bethany's eyes matched her mother's.

Angela nodded. Fourth of July at the cabin without Todd. Another first to go through.

They sat in the shade, watching Phillip dumping sand.

"Busy young man." Angela smiled. "I'm glad you came over. I love watching him play."

"We alternate from the swimming pool to the playground and back to the apartment. Emerson said another year in the apartment and then we should be able to afford a house."

"You need more space." Angela sighed. "I need less space."

Emerson joined them and deftly lit the grill. "Anyone interested in your house yet?"

"No," Angela said. "My realtor called. I lowered my price to her original suggestion, but still no interest. It appears I have two choices." Angela tried not to let desperation creep into her voice. "Lower my price even more or wait until the bargain houses in the new development sell. Could be as long as a year."

"A year? Incredible." Bethany ran her fingers through her short hair.

"I'm not attracted to the new development. It's just a flat converted cornfield." Emerson closed the lid and scanned the shaded backyard. "The new homes are missing something with their proverbial decks up high, baking in the sun. Your terrace feels like being part of the backyard."

"I loved growing up here," Bethany said. "Something to remember when we look again for a house."

"Yes, a backyard that's already landscaped." Emerson smiled and glanced over their heads. "Hey, that vine is taking over."

Angela's wisteria vine had climbed over the top of the arbor and twined toward a clematis. The clematis, seemingly acquiescing the race of dominance, clustered low on the other side of the arbor.

"The wisteria is invasive, that's for sure. But the blooms are glorious." Angela sipped her tea. "Wisteria is symbolic of long life, immortality. They can live to be hundreds of years old. A wisteria in Japan is believed to be twelve hundred years old. Imagine."

"Oh, my. I had no idea of its history," Bethany said. "When you named the shop, I just liked the winsomeness of the word 'wisteria.'"

Angela's gaze swept over the projects she and Todd had completed over the years. The stepping-stone walkway weaving through the arbor, the rose garden in full sun, hedging the terrace. She sank deeper into the cushion on the lounge chair, enjoying her family.

"Daddy, look!" Phillip carried a small sand mold bucket to their little group.

"Hey buddy, let me see."

"There's more." Phillip pointed to a series of sand mounds resembling fallen cakes. Emerson followed him to inspect.

"He's so happy here," Bethany said.

"Bethany, it just occurred to me. Would you ever consider moving your family here with me for a few months and share expenses? There's plenty of room. I could cancel the listing until the market changes."

Bethany's mouth opened, but nothing came out for a moment. "I don't know what to say except, wow."

Angela leaned forward. "Shall we see what Emerson thinks?"

"About what?" Emerson called over his shoulder then he hurriedly flipped the burgers on a platter.

"If you like the idea of moving in with me for a few months," Angela said. "The three of you could have the two bedrooms in the lower level. Becca and I are upstairs."

Emerson closed the grill. "We could pay you rent?"

"Well, it just popped into my head. We all need to think it through. But maybe you could pay utilities and save your rent toward a down payment."

"Not pay rent? That would give our savings a real boost." His eyebrows lifted. "It's worth thinking about."

In the back of Angela's mind lurked the other alternative of paying her utilities with her charge card. The last thing she wanted to do.

Saturday morning—July 5th

Angela lifted a hamper into her car. It slipped, banged her knee, and landed on her foot. She grimaced and scrunched her toes until the pain stopped. Why did every effort balloon into a battle? She wrapped her arms around the hamper and manhandled it into the tiny backseat. In a full sweat, she headed to her room for a shower before work.

Why had her realtors chosen this weekend for an open house? Even showering was a task now. Angela scrubbed and polished everything in the bathroom so it would look its best. At least she would be out of town. That was a blessing, perhaps her only comfort as an extra-long day loomed ahead of her: first work, then driving to the cabin. She raced downstairs for breakfast.

"Where are you, Mom?" Benjamin walked down the stairs to the kitchen below. "I'll grab the cooler. Do you have it loaded with what I need to take for you?"

"Yes. Thanks." Angela watched his strong arms throw the full cooler over one shoulder. His muscles popped beneath his running shirt. She sighed. So easy, so simple. In no time they were back in the garage.

"What are you going to do with all this room? I guess if you ever bring your van home, you'll need all three stalls."

"Well, if Bethany and Emerson move in, they'll need a stall in the garage for their car."

"What?"

"I suppose I shouldn't have said anything yet. I offered to let them move in with me. They said they would let me know." Realizing Benjamin had been left out of the loop as far as family discussions were concerned, Angela hurried on. "My house isn't selling. They're stuck in a tiny apartment."

"Yeah, I guess so." Benjamin frowned and lifted a gigantic watermelon from the garage floor. "Whoa, how did you get this baby home?"

"Wasn't easy."

"Glad you did. Looks good. Same program every fourth of July, isn't it?"

"Yes." Angela paused. For now. When the lake home sold, everything would change.

She headed straight to the shop. As the quiet afternoon plodded on, she wondered about the wisdom of keeping her shop open. She walked into her small office and checked her cell phone. A text from her accountant, Wade Taylor. Angela frowned. Working on Saturday? Is he alone and bored, too? He offered to stop by the flower shop early on Tuesday morning for their follow-up appointment. Good. Prepping for that meeting should be simple. With hardly a smattering of customers, she closed the shop an hour early and hit the road for the cabin.

Stopped in traffic, Angela's mind wandered to the loneliness she felt watching cars full of families and couples. She dropped her head on the steering wheel. "Todd—" her voice broke. "Why did you leave me?"

27

Monday, July 7

After the weekend at the cabin with her family, Angela's thoughts continually circled back to her grandson. How quickly Phillip had accepted losing his grandfather. A grandfather represented by a few pictures on the wall. She could still hear his shriek of delight.

"Gampa!" Phillip's voice startled Angela's thoughts just like they had yesterday at the cabin when Phillip had seen a picture of himself with Gampa Todd on the mantelpiece. Angela wanted Phillip to remember Gampa as more than a photo. She hoped he would never forget he had had a Gampa who loved him.

The day slipped away. Getting farther behind with the housework she usually tackled on Mondays, she realized it would have to wait. She must be ready for Tuesday's meeting with her accountant. She willed herself to sit down at Todd's desk and make up for lost time. A new budget for Wisteria. Deep breath. She did a quick copy and paste from a previous spreadsheet. Simple enough. It took little time to project the sales she hoped would come her way.

Angela switched gears and met Marge in the driveway so they could ride together to their meeting at Caroline's. Marge wiggled into Angela's compact car, angled the vents, and leaned forward until it blew her hair away from her face.

"Ahhh, July."

Marge teemed with questions about Angela's weekend at the lake. "Why are photos popping out of this box in the backseat?"

"Oh, I forgot to take them inside," Angela said. "The realtor asked me to remove the family pictures."

"What?" Marge turned to get a better look. "It's the history of the lake home."

"Exactly. It means a lot to us but won't mean anything to potential buyers. It's our story of the lake home."

"I suppose you're right." Marge settled in her seat. "But it won't look the same."

"No, it won't." At least the few times she would be there before it sold. If it sold.

"You could have joined us," Angela said. "Or we could plan another trip to the lake—you, Caroline, and me. Just like old times. We could drive up—"

"No, thank you. I don't know when I would find the time. I took a weekend shift at the hospital for the extra money. After working at the hospital each day, I go to Greg's company and work until they close. It's just refreshing to hear you talk about it."

"Is everything okay?"

"Nothing I can't handle." Marge turned in her seat as a police car, sirens blaring, tore around them. "Glad I'm not driving through the city traffic every day." Marge snapped her mouth shut in a pursed frown.

Marge stared at the neat foyer. "Where are the packing boxes you said we'd have to dodge?"

"They're all upstairs." Caroline pointed to boxes lining the hall of the next floor. "As it turned out, there was plenty of packing to keep me busy on the upper level."

As usual, Caroline's dinner presentation was impeccable. When Angela offered her thanks, Caroline smiled. "You know me; all I need is a caterer or a deli."

"Sounds like a good plan." Marge lounged in a leather chair. "So, what's your opinion? I read women lose seventy-five percent of their friends when they become widows."

"Oh, no." Angela stiffened. "That can't be true. My friends would never ..." Angela's impulsive answer fizzled like air escaping a balloon. "Well, I've lost a few. The people Todd worked with who were friends. But he's no longer with the company, so I can see them dropping me as a friend. The people at church, I guess they haven't invited me to the get-togethers that consist mostly of couples. Maybe it's awkward for them." How awkward could it be? Todd and she would have included a widow. Or would they?

"Perhaps you're right. My steady friends are the ones I work out with at the gym," Caroline said. "I see little of the ladies from the church choir where I play—used to play."

Marge nodded. "I'm still a part of Greg's company, but he was the one who organized the get-togethers. He was outgoing, friendly, loved having people around. I just followed him."

"And I followed Brock. It seems our friends were his business associates." Caroline rolled her shoulders. "I don't want to continue any of those friendships."

"Well, I guess there's something to the theory. I'm going to stay positive and be thankful for the friends I have now." Angela opened her workbook. "I had time this weekend to reflect on the verses. Somehow, when you're up north surrounded by mammoth trees and a lake that goes on forever, you're more in awe of God. Aware of His question in Job, 'where were you when I laid the foundations of the earth?' And Deuteronomy, 'the secret things belong unto the Lord our God.'"

"The secret things?" Caroline interrupted. "What if the secret things have become your life and you find yourself living a lie? How do you cope with that?"

Angela's workbook slipped off her legs. She caught it close to the floor.

"Caroline?" Marge leaned forward.

"I have to ..." Caroline struggled for control. "I can't hold this inside any longer."

Angela tossed her workbook aside and grabbed Caroline's hand.

"The night before Brock left for the fishing trip, he couldn't find his favorite fishing hat. Such a minor thing. He became agitated. I tried to help him, but it provoked him more."

"That's the hat we found at the lake cabin?" Angela said.

"Yes." Tears poured down Caroline's face. "Then he exploded. He said, 'this isn't working anymore. I don't want to be with you.'"

Caroline struggled to go on. "There were clues of his involvement with someone else, but I ignored them. Well." A thin, brittle laugh escaped Caroline's lips. "It's obvious now, like the bill for a nine-thousand-dollar diamond necklace."

Angela gasped.

"Remember the Tiffany box at the cabin?"

Marge nodded. "And it's your bill to pay?"

"Already did. It's on Brock's credit card statement."

Caroline daubed at her face with a tissue. "It's odd how I put him on a pedestal. Excused everything he did. Even the growing verbal abuse. I look back and realize I walked on eggshells most of our married life. Dreading saying or doing something that would set him off."

What? Angela sat bolt upright. Caroline? The person who had it all together? The person most women envied with her looks, affluent lifestyle, position in the community? And Brock? Fun, loud, outgoing, but never appearing abusive.

"But the cruelest part was the funeral. Friends, businessmen, clergy, all praising him for being a man of integrity. Telling of his love and devotion to his wife and children." Caroline's voice broke.

Marge walked to the sofa and nudged Caroline to make room beside her. The three huddled close together.

"I played my part at the funeral. But now ... how can you mourn someone who caused you so much pain? Betrayal doesn't deserve mourning."

Angela waited, trying to reconcile this revelation with the man who had been their friend. Jovial, take-charge personality, always a big hug for Angela. But with Todd standing next to her, it never seemed inappropriate. The umbrella of a husband's love and protection. She missed that.

"He said he had planned to wait until after the fishing trip to tell me, but why wait? I could take the week to find a place to live, like one of the new condos."Caroline balled her hands into fists. "A condo, everyone's solution."

Eyes dry now, Caroline stared straight ahead. "If he had

waited, there would have been no final pain of rejection. I would have mourned the loss of my husband regardless of his personality defects."

Caroline leaned her head against the cushioned top of the sofa. "I'm not truly a widow."

"Of course you are!" Marge clenched her teeth. "Just because your husband thought of no one but himself, you're still his wife. You stood by him."

"You are just as much a widow as we are, Caroline," Angela said. "I don't know how you will sort this out, but ... " Angela stopped. Lost for words.

"And people say women are the weaker sex." Marge placed her arm around Caroline.

"We're here for you," Angela said.

Each with an arm around Caroline, Angela and Marge leaned their heads against Caroline's. No words, only shock.

28

Angela's accountant, Wade Carlson, was waiting in his car when Angela unlocked the front door on Tuesday morning. His tie did a jerky dance as he dashed to the door, but his sculpted hair remained in place.

"Morning, Angela."

"Morning. Lights are on over the worktable. We can sit there."

Wade peered through the shop's semi-darkness. "Quite a change since I was here last." Wade touched a roll-top desk displaying an ink well and quill then strolled behind the counter.

Angela followed. An accountant with the build of a full-back, aging well. "Coffee? It'll take just a minute to make."

"Sure, thanks."

By the time Wade had organized his printouts, Angela set a steaming mug and her new budget in front of him. "Here are my projections."

Wade sipped his coffee, pulled out his pen, and perused the first page line by line.

Wisteria

Angela gestured with a sweeping arc that included her display area. "I've added this new line of shabby/cottage mix."

Wade glanced around and creased his forehead until his eyebrows almost met. "What kind of investment?"

"On the next page." Angela pointed.

He marked his place and flipped the page. "You added personal funds?"

"Some." She thought of her near-empty savings account.

"Send me the amounts and dates. We'll post them as loans the business owes you." The lines on his forehead remained throughout his questions. He shuffled her papers until the edges were perfectly even then inserted them in her file. "Well, time will tell."

Wade pulled reports from his briefcase. "At least you're out of the red. Here's your profit-and-loss statement. A lot will depend on how well you do with the seasons coming up."

"Thanksgiving and Christmas." Angela crossed her arms.

"Those are the big ones. I noticed the checks to Shane stopped. You removed him after that fiasco?"

"Actually, he quit—before we had discovered anything."

"Even better. No unemployment insurance claims to challenge your premium rate."

"I know." She sighed. "All part of doing business."

He nodded. "You must have used last month's chart of accounts as your template because your quarterly expenses are missing from your projections." Wade pulled another item from his briefcase. He grimaced. "We rarely forget things like this. My assistant sends her apologies. She put the paperwork in your file instead of mailing it to you. Sorry. Here's your quarterly employee withholding statements for state and federal and your estimated income tax. Just include a check for each and pop it in the attached envelopes as you've always done."

Angela's stomach churned. How could she have forgotten? In the past, she had skipped her paycheck if funds were short. Leaned on Todd's salary.

As soon as Wade left, Angela gripped her hands, dropped her forehead to her knuckles, and inhaled deeply. Where would she get the money to cover quarterly taxes? Her salary, already cut to the bare minimum, would be needed for living expenses. Only one thing left to do. This would hurt.

"Todd." Angela stared across the empty room. "There'll be one more good-bye."

Rosa arrived and filled the hot water dispenser.

"Sorry Rosa, I got distracted and forgot to have your hot water ready."

"Not a problem."

Angela recovered and grabbed a broom. "Don't forget the *Gazette* is taking pictures of our shop this afternoon."

A customer wandered in and selected a whirligig. "Do you have a way to hang this in my garden?"

"I have just the thing." Angela stepped to a nearby display. "Here's a shepherd's staff, only double. One side for a hanging basket and one side for the whirligig."

"I'll take it!"

One of Angela's new customers, Harriet Jones, surveyed the cozy staged areas. She oozed style with her chic ankle pants, appliquéd shell, and sling-back flats. "What you've achieved is phenomenal." She touched a wall-mounted ladder-backed chair holding old magazines, mats, and a straw hat arranged on the rungs and seat.

"Thank you." Angela soaked up the compliment like a parched petunia finally receiving water.

"How creative." Harriet rubbed a tall headboard fastened atop a matching footboard with attached mirror and shelves.

"I could never coordinate everything quite the way you have." Harriet shook her head at a display going up the wall, items hanging from the ceiling. "We remodeled the kitchen, dining area, and added a three-seasons room, and I want this type of decor. Would you mind if I send over my interior designer? Would you point out this entire section to her?"

"I'd love to work with her, Harriet."

Angela had little time to think about that opportunity. A rush of customers occupied her time through the lunch hour.

After lunch, Emerson dropped in. "Bethany said you were making changes. Looks good." He tucked designer sunglasses into the pocket of his tailored shirt.

"Thanks. Glad you like it."

He picked up a metal spinner. "Hey, I used to have one of these." He twirled it and laughed like he had just reconnected with an old friend.

Angela smiled.

"Hi, Emerson," Rosa said.

"Rosa." Emerson nodded.

"Angela, I'm leaving now. Be back soon," Rosa called and carried the last plant out the back door.

Angela wiped her hands on her work apron. "Would you like coffee, a snack?"

"No, thanks, enough coffee today." Emerson smoothed his trust-me blue tie on his button-down dress shirt and pulled out a stool across from Angela. "Bethany and I have been talking about our family moving in with you."

Angela's stomach quivered. "Yes?"

"You're sure you could handle the noise, the inconvenience?"

"Actually, I would enjoy the company. It gets pretty quiet with Becca working evenings."

"It's anything but quiet with Phillip."

"Don't forget, he spent a lot of time with us when you traveled and Bethany was ill. But I want the two of you to be sure."

"And we want you to be sure it's right for you. We like the idea—but feel it wouldn't be right to pay only utilities and leave you with home insurance, taxes, maintenance. What if we pay utilities and a percentage of maintenance?"

Angela exhaled. "You would rescue me by paying utilities. How about utilities and the food you eat?"

Emerson shook his head. "All the food. You'll let us know if money gets tight?"

"I will."

"One caveat. Our lease is up in four-and-a-half weeks. Need to give a four-week notice. Would have to move fast."

"This is exciting. I'm ready when you are."

"We'll start this weekend. Maybe they'll rebate some rent."

"I'll help wherever I can."

A customer popped in, so Emerson waved and left.

Rosa returned just before Gwen Olstad arrived from the *Northgate Gazette*.

"Good afternoo-oon." Gwen's voice reached to the back room. "Wait. What do we have here?" She stooped and picked up an old tin sign. "Ueland Farm Equipment? That was my grandfather's company. I have to have it. How much is it?" She glanced at the price tag. "It doesn't matter. I want it," she said, holding it captive against her chest.

"It's in good shape, isn't it?" Angela said.

"Yes!" Gwen placed the sign on the sales counter and smacked both hands on top. "Can't believe I found this little gem. My grandfather left everything in the building when the business sold. The new owners changed the name and tossed anything marked Ueland."

"That often happens." Angela donned a clean apron. "Would you like coffee?"

"Thank you." Gwen plopped her camera bag behind the counter. "This okay?

"That's fine, and here's your coffee."

"No one paid attention to memorabilia then. I was young and couldn't have cared less." She dug into her other bag and pulled out her notepad and pen. "I'm so excited over the sign. How will I ever settle down to interview you?" She scooted onto a stool.

"And now." She took a deep breath, pen poised. "How long have you been in business?"

"Two years." Angela's eyes dropped to Gwen's bright red cupid's bow lips.

"And would you detail what your shop offers to the public?" Gwen slurped her coffee as if she thoroughly enjoyed the sound as much as the coffee.

Filling three pages of her notepad with Angela's answers, Gwen stopped only to snatch her sign when a customer meandered near the counter.

"You can place it here on the worktable." Angela patted a spot. "I'll wrap it for you."

"Don't wrap it yet, please." Gwen placed the sign on the worktable with her notepad on top. "I think I have all I need.

I'll submit it today. It'll publish the day after tomorrow." She added in a low voice, "They don't give us the space they used to. In times past, I could have given you a half page."

Gwen unpacked her camera. "Now, for the pictures."

Posing Angela and Rosa in front of a bright display, Gwen snapped her pics. Sweeping back to the worktable, she propped up her tin sign before a tiny American flag and aimed her camera. "I'll work this in somehow." She winked at Angela.

29

Angela faced her next good-bye. She spent Wednesday morning before work searching the car resale websites and lost no time listing her car online.

"Bumblebee." She sighed. "I have no other choice."

She washed and buffed the car. Her hands slowed. Todd had surprised her with this car three years ago on her birthday. Before the shop. Before Bethany's cancer. Before Todd's ...

This was her life ... split into "before" and "after."

The car queries were immediate. Late morning, a loose-jointed man in his thirties walked into the flower shop.

"That the car you got for sale?"

"It is." The only Mini Cooper in front of the shop, she wanted to add.

"Care if I take it for a spin?"

"I'll go with you. You may take it to the freeway and circle back around. That should give you ample opportunity to test it."

"Oh yeah, I suppose."

Angela turned to see Rosa following to the front door, watching them pull away.

He braked so hard when they returned that Angela folded at the waist, straining against the seatbelt.

"It's for my girlfriend. She needs a car, and she likes the looks of these." He unfolded his long legs and climbed out. "So how much would you actually take for the car? How about—"

"I gave you my price." Angela marched toward her shop.

"Yeah, but aren't you gonna come down any?" He followed.

"No." Angela surprised herself with her toughness.

"Well, that's kinda steep. I'll have to get back to you."

He was barely out the door when a bubbly young woman walked in and asked for a test drive.

They were soon back in the parking lot. "I love it, I love it!" The potential buyer hugged the steering wheel, her bouncy auburn curls tumbling forward in her face.

Angela smiled. Anything she offers even close to my bottom-line will seal the deal.

By afternoon the car was gone. The pretty girl with the auburn hair was all smiles. Angela drove to the license center, transferred the title, and deposited the check in her business account. One more good-bye.

When the Thursday edition of the *Gazette* arrived in everyone's mailbox, the shop hummed with people.

"Just had to come and check it out." A customer pointed to a copy of Wisteria's story that Angela had posted at the checkout counter. The customer plopped down her purchase of dried flowers arranged in an ornate basket.

Gwen had written a quarter-page story that included the

picture of Angela and Rosa. During a lull in the busy day, Angela poured water for tea for each of them.

"Here's the rest of the newspaper." Angela flipped through the pages. "Oh, my goodness, it's the Ueland equipment sign Gwen bought. She turned it into a half-page story."

"Let me see." Rosa peeked over her shoulder. "It's a history of the Ueland family."

"Ah, but look under the picture," Angela said. "At least she mentions purchasing it from Wisteria."

"That should help us."

"Let's hope so." Angela cut the story from the newspaper. Even as she spoke, she wondered if anything would turn the shop around. Would this effort fail as well?

An older woman known for her antique collection entered. She slowly gazed at each display.

Finally she walked to the counter and pulled a newspaper from her handbag. "Do you have any more of these?" She pointed to the story with the tin sign.

"No, I'm sorry," Angela said. "It's the only one we had."

"Well, thanks anyway."

She opened the front door to let three more people in.

"Not bad for a small town," said one shopper, looking down her nose at Angela's gaily painted green and red table with a black-and-white checkerboard top. But the woman's sauciness melted when her companion yelled, "mine!" and quickly snatched the table.

"Well, yes, I suppose it's okay if you're looking for a something quirky." The first shopper said.

The door closed at last and Rosa swept the floor.

"I think the newspaper article will be a success." Angela whispered a prayer to God to please let it be so. "As long as people come to see, the word will spread. Let's call it a day."

Not wanting to face an empty house, Angela drove straight to Bethany's apartment.

Bethany grabbed both of Angela's hands and pulled her inside. "I'm so glad you came over tonight."

"Gamma." Phillip giggled. "Glad you came."

"What a nice welcome," Angela said.

"I can't believe we're moving in with you."

"Move in?" Phillip latched onto Bethany's leg.

"I'll enjoy having all of you with me."

"Emerson has it all worked out. We're planning on six months, one year at the most. By that time, the market should allow you to get top dollar for your home, and we should be ready financially to purchase a house. At least that's what we're hoping will happen."

"Move in?" Phillip tugged insistently.

"Yes, we're going to live at Grandma's house for a while." Bethany pointed to the boxes against the wall. "That's why we're packing."

"Dylan, too?"

"No, Dylan will stay with his mom and dad."

"No, want Dylan."

"Who's Dylan?" Angela said.

"Phillip's playmate. They live in the next unit. Phillip and Dylan are together almost every day at the playground."

"Want Dylan!" Phillip whined and sobbed.

Bethany gave her mother a welcome-to-my-world look. Then a sly smile spread over her face. "Hmm, I wonder if Dylan has ever played in a sandbox."

Phillip's mouth closed and his eyes opened wide.

"Like your sandbox at Gamma's?"

"Yes!" Phillip squeezed her tighter.

"Maybe we could invite him over after we move." Bethany peeled his arms off her leg and walked him to a shelf of toys.

"How can I help you pack?" Angela looked at the open cupboard doors.

"Do you mean it? You're not too tired?"

"Of course not. It'll be fun. As long as you don't overdo."

Bethany smirked. "However do I manage each day, Mom?"

Angela rolled her eyes. "Accused of hovering again? A mother could have worse faults."

"True." Bethany laughed. "Emerson left for L.A. Won't be back until Friday night. Let me make a quick dinner. Then we'll tackle it."

Angela filled water glasses.

"We'll do a little each night. Furniture this weekend." Bethany looked up from her salad preparation. "Did you see the family text from Benjamin? Emerson recruited him, too."

"I hope Tatum comes along."

"Sounds like she will." Bethany whisked dishes to the table. "I'll clean the apartment the week after we empty it."

"You can box up your dishes, towels, and bedding and use mine," Angela said. "We'll find a place to store them."

Bethany turned to her mother with a peaceful look. "The dream is getting closer."

They bumped into each other in the tiny kitchen, laughed, and hugged from sheer delight.

"I hope the noise won't be too much for you," Bethany said.

"After long hours at the shop, my evenings are rather short," Angela said. "Besides, it's no fun coming home to an empty house."

Phillip's fork clattered to the floor. Angela jumped up to grab another. "Becca will go back to school soon. I'll have your family with me for several months, sell my house and look for a place to move next year. Surely that will make a difference in my financial situation."

Bethany squeezed her mother's hand.

Angela blinked, held her head high, and scanned the room. "So, what should we concentrate on tonight?"

They chatted, planned, and packed enough to load their vehicles.

Bethany opened her back door. "Good, you brought the van."

"Bumblebee." Phillip rushed out. "Where's bumblebee?"

"I'm sorry, Phillip. Bumblebee is gone."

"In the shop?" Bethany said.

"No, I sold it this morning."

Bethany gasped.

"I know." Angela leaned against the doorframe. "But I have three vehicles to insure and maintain. It was newer than Todd's Cherokee and worth more. I need the van for the business, so I'm driving it to work each day." Angela drooped.

"Sorry, Mom."

"I'll get through this." Angela headed out the door with a box.

The van filled quickly. Bethany's car held seasonal clothing still on hangers. Soon they were off to Angela's house.

When they got out of the car in Angela's driveway, Phillip squealed and tugged on Bethany's arm.

"Sandbox!" he shouted, pumping her arm until she almost drop a load of clothes.

"Careful, Phillip." She readjusted hangers. "As long as you stay in the sandbox while we're carrying boxes." Bethany walked him to the back door. "Lawn looks beautiful."

"I'm getting the hang of it," Angela said.

"Emerson will be glad to help."

"I need to learn to do it myself."

Angela made three more trips to her van and grabbed her mail while Bethany brought in the last box.

"Want some water?" Bethany called. "I'm going to take some to Phillip."

"Yes. Be right with you. Let me open my mail first."

She set aside a statement addressed to Becca. Strange. It looked like a credit card statement. Then, picking up an unmarked envelope addressed to her, she slit it open. Her first dividend check from her investment of Todd's life insurance. She clutched it, knowing she would put this into savings. There may be more unexpected expenses. Being blindsided was not a good feeling.

30

Just before lunch on Friday morning, Susan strode into Wisteria. "I'm here for another rose."

"Another baby at the shelter?" Angela turned to the refrigerated case and stopped. "A pink rose okay?"

"Perfect. A mother with a two-year-old son has a new baby daughter. Can't I pay you for this?"

"Please, let me contribute."

"Thank you. We'd love to have you come to our house for dinner on Sunday. You, your children, and your grandson? What do you say?"

"Oh, I'm afraid you don't know what you're asking. Benjamin and Tatum are coming on Saturday, will spend the night, and join us Sunday. So many of us."

"Good! We'll get to know them better," Susan said. A tiny smile played at the corners of her mouth. "I'd love it. I really would."

"Are you sure?"

"Yes, definitely." She caught Becca's eye. "Becca, I hope you can make it."

Becca rose from her painting table. "Thank you, Mrs. Bailey."

"Thanks. I'll check with the kids," Angela said.

Susan waved as she left the shop with her rose.

"Nice of her to invite us." Becca watched Rosa open every door, searching the coolers.

"Looking for something, Rosa?"

"Yes, the lavender vase bouquet," Rosa said.

"I see every color but lavender." Becca peeked over her shoulder.

"No, it's a vase covered with lavender stalks."

"Here it is." Angela shifted a bright birthday arrangement. "Pushed to the back."

"Wow. What is it?" Becca said.

"An herb-wrapped vase. This one's filled with English roses." Rosa proudly held up the creation. "Your mom's design. I'll put it on the table for reference."

"Why haven't I seen that before?"

"A recent idea," Angela said. "They're catching on. May become our signature piece."

"It looks like you just plucked it out of a garden." Becca watched Rosa. "I'd like to make one. Any more orders?"

"That's the only one today," Angela said. "But no reason we can't add another to the ready-mades. Rosa, would you like to teach Becca?"

"Only if you'll correct me when I'm wrong." Rosa glanced Angela's way.

"I promise." Angela continued working.

Rosa assembled tools and Becca leaned close. "Use a squatty six-inch vase." Rosa grabbed two clear vases and handed one to Becca. "Place a rubber band midway."

Rosa scooted a rubber band across the table to Becca, then

held up the lavender sprigs. "Trim these to six inches, the height of the vase. We're going to line up the lavender stalks vertically, completely covering the outside of the vase. See?" Rosa inserted the first lavender stalk behind the rubber band. "Don't worry, the rubber band is there just while we assemble it." Rosa's deft fingers worked quickly. "Finish with ribbon, tie one strand at the top, one at the bottom of the vase, remove rubber band."

"Or you could use twine," Becca said.

"Twine, I like that. Rustic." Angela retrieved the twine spool from the rack. "Try it."

Becca finished her vase and it tied with twine. "How's that?"

Angela tugged at the twine. "What do you think, Rosa?"

"I say dump the ribbon."

"Well said."

"Gotta run," Becca said. "A few errands before work."

"Thank you for helping at the shop." Angela stepped to the back door and spoke in a low voice. "It's none of my business. I'm just concerned. Was that a credit card statement you received?"

"Mom. Once I get paychecks rolling in ... " Becca looked at Angela, then quickly away. "I'll be caught up soon."

"Becca?" Angela said. "Do you have debt?"

"Yeah. Had to run up my credit card the last couple of months."

Angela noticed the cut and fit of Becca's new jeans.

"I know. Dad said to open it for emergency use only. But things have been pretty crazy lately." Becca sighed and hung her head. "No, that's no excuse. Every time I pulled out my card, I could hear dad's voice. It hurts. I won't let it happen again."

"Would you like an accountability partner?"

"No." Becca glanced away then back to her mother. "Yes. I guess I'd better face up to it or I'll never get back on track. I'll leave the bill on dad's desk so you can see the progress I'm making."

"You realize, financially, I can't help you now?"

"I would never ask you with all your shouldering."

Angela ignored her ringing cell phone till Becca was out the door.

Angela answered her phone and her heart fluttered in a happy dance. "Benjamin, of course you can come over tonight."

"Is Becca working?" Benjamin said.

Angela cradled the phone while she worked. "Yes, it'll be just the two of us. Unless Tatum is coming?"

"No, she's out of town."

When she hung up, a knot grew in Angela's stomach. Was something wrong? She and Benjamin usually talked once a week, but she had sensed nothing off-kilter with Benjamin.

"Benjamin's coming over to have dinner with me tonight."

"Quite a trip, isn't it?" Rosa said.

"Eighty miles one way. I guess he's staying over tonight. Not sure if Tatum will make it tomorrow to help Bethany and Emerson move. Forgot to ask." Angela's mind raced with logistics and menus. "Can you lock up tonight? Oh, I forgot. It's Friday."

"That's no problem. It's ... well, I mean, we haven't been busy."

"Go ahead and say it. Business is dead."

At 6:30 that evening, Benjamin breezed into the dining room just like old times. "Wow! Grilled salmon? It's good to be home." He hugged his mother.

"Good to have you home," Angela said. She hugged him, stood back, and traced her fingers along his firm chin. Just like Todd's chin. It was almost like Todd was with her. No. She mustn't even think that way. "Will you spend the night? Ready to help Bethany and Emerson move tomorrow?"

"Well, I'm going home tonight, pick up Tatum and come back in the morning."

"Oh. Such a drive for you."

"It's nothing, Mom. Just wanted to spend some time with you tonight," Benjamin said, his eyes bright as stars.

"Benjamin, that's—well, this is a treat." She passed the sautéed veggies and studied his face. "Okay, level with me."

The merriment in Benjamin's eyes increased. "Mom, can't you tell? I'm in love."

"In love?" she said, her words raspy. "Tatum?"

"Tatum."

Why didn't she feel completely at ease with this revelation? She remembered Tatum's involvement in her church and smiled. "And she's a Christian?"

"Yes."

"So, tell me about this wonderful woman?"

"What can I say? She's fun to be with, got a great sense of humor. We like the same things. When I'm away from her, I can't wait to see her again. You know, after she finished college, she found a great job in St. John, has gotten to know people, and has a church family that rallies around her.

"She needed that. She's not led the same kind of a life I have. As an only child, she didn't have a typical kid's life. Her mother went through one surgery after another. New treatments kept Tatum separated from her parents. I guess they shuttled her off to an aunt, a grandmother, back home with babysitters."

Angela stroked Benjamin's hand. So strong. It seemed like only yesterday this hand had brought her a frog one day, and a clutch of dandelions the next. "How long have you known Tatum?"

"Three months. But I knew from the beginning, she's the one."

"Why ... Benjamin, why the rush?"

Benjamin paused, his eyes darted to one side.

"Dad and I had this talk years ago. Remember the passage in the Bible where Paul said 'it's better to marry than to burn with passion?'"

"Yes, I remember the verse."

He flushed. "I've never been attracted to anyone like I am to Tatum. I'd walk through fire for her."

Then Benjamin's frame drooped. "I couldn't ... I didn't know who to talk to. It would have been easier if Dad were ..." His voice trailed off.

Then he frowned, his head snapped up, his eyes flashing. "I've been so angry about Dad. We lost him. Just like that!" He snapped his fingers.

"Benjamin, you seemed so strong. Why didn't you talk to me?"

"I tried to cope. Kept telling myself, be a man." He shook his head. "Easier said than done.

"But I had Tatum. Sympathetic, always listening whenever I needed to talk. I tried to be that person for her as well."

Angela closed her eyes as if to shut out her own neglect. Her son had to turn to a relative stranger because she wasn't there for him.

"One night she and her mom had an argument. She came to my apartment in tears. Told me about her childhood, her mother's chronic health issues, her absent father putting in sixty-hour work weeks. It was my turn to hold her and comfort her." He shook his head. "I'm not made of iron. Never been tempted like this. I want to get married right away. She seems to be for marriage but wants to wait a while. I'm hoping things will change once we're engaged."

Oh, why can't Todd be here? "Benjamin, don't rush things. Get to know each other. Become friends. You know I'll be praying, don't you?"

"Thanks, Mom. There's one more thing."

Angela glanced his way, waiting.

"She doesn't want to have kids. Says her childhood was rotten. What if she has her mother's genes? Passes them on to her children? But I told her it doesn't matter."

"You're okay with no children? Ever?"

"For Tatum? Sure. Who knows, she may change her mind."

"Benjamin, you can't go into a relationship thinking you'll change the other person."

"Well, then I'll change."

Angela sighed. Not the best solution. Is Benjamin mature enough for this big step? But when Benjamin set his jaw that way there was no use talking more about the subject. She forced her tone to be light. "I'm glad she's coming tomorrow. But we may overwhelm with our big family."

"For sure."

"Susan and Pastor Bailey invited all of us for dinner after church on Sunday. Will you and Tatum be able to join us?"

Benjamin looked down at his plate. "Maybe we'll stay. We'll see."

31

Angela left her shop early Saturday afternoon just in time to welcome the moving crew from Bethany and Emerson's apartment. In no time flat, they filled Angela's halls with boxes and furniture.

"Mom." Becca met her in the lower level. "I invited Cole to join us, but at the last minute he had to back out. Needed at home."

"Who's that?" Bethany pulled Phillip out of the mover's path.

"Cole Richardson," Becca said. "We've been dating about a month now."

"One of the Richardson kids?" Bethany smiled. "There was one in my class."

"Nine kids," Emerson growled. "I think there was one in everyone's class."

"I like big families. I wish—" Bethany hugged Phillip then followed the procession down the hall.

"Is this the spot to put our bed?" Emerson pointed to their king-sized bed already set up in Bethany's old room.

"No, the inside wall facing the window," Bethany said.

Emerson and Benjamin shot each other an exasperated glance that said, "women!" but shrugged and complied.

"Perfect." Bethany cheered them on and rushed to the cluttered hallway.

Emerson leaned an arm against a mattress up-ended in the hallway. "What shall we do with Bethany's old bed?"

"Let's see." Angela paused. "It goes upstairs into Becca's room. Becca's single bed will come down to Benjamin's old bedroom to give us two single beds in Phillip's new room."

Becca smiled at Bethany. "Hey, I finally get the queen-sized bed."

"Then tonight, everyone can sleep in their old rooms." Angela turned to Tatum. "I hope you don't mind sharing a room with Becca?"

"Should be fun." Tatum grinned at Becca.

"Hey, roomie." Becca high-fived her.

"What about the sofa?" Bethany frowned as they brought her cushy leather sofa to the lower level.

"We can't leave it in the garage. In wintertime the mice would find a snug little home," Benjamin said, resting his end of the sofa at the foot of the steps.

"I'll soon be going back to school," Becca said. "Let's squeeze it against the wall in my room. Plenty of room left for it."

Emerson moaned. "Back up the steps."

By evening, exhaustion hit everyone. Tatum received a full dose of a large-family experience as they retired to their rooms yelling goodnight to each other.

"Just like the Waltons. Remember the old re-runs?" Tatum laughed and headed to Becca's bedroom.

Sunday—The Baileys' house

Angela walked through the Bailey's front door effortlessly this time. Angela's family overflowed the living room and everyone relaxed in the warm welcome they received.

Tatum walked in the dining room just as Angela helped Susan carry food to the table.

"What darling figurines," Tatum said, gazing at the buffet.

"That's our family," Susan said, touching each one. "James, me, and the baby we named Stephen. Actually, we don't know if it was a boy or a girl. I had a miscarriage. Stephen would have been two years old."

Angela slipped an arm around Susan's waist. "I'm so sorry. I didn't know."

"Thank you." Susan's lip trembled.

Tatum made an about-face. "I'll see what happened to Benjamin."

Angela's gaze followed Tatum out of the room, wondering if she should go after her. Ask if she's okay? Or maybe just give her some space?

Returning home, Angela was working on clearing a path through boxes in the upper hall when her cell phone rang.

"Angela? Miranda Frandsen here. I'm wondering if you can help me at the shelter this afternoon. I have only one volunteer for our weekly Bible study, and he's leading the lesson."

Angela could hear Benjamin and Tatum in the lower level.

"I'm sorry, Benjamin and his girlfriend are here. Phillip is sleeping."

"Don't worry about it. Enjoy your family. I'll try a few others."

"Okay—" Headed to the steps leading to the living room, Angela almost dropped her phone. Someone was playing Todd's guitar.

"Oh, what's this?" Tatum touched sheet music on the nearby stand and strummed the guitar. Angela recognized the song Todd and she had sung at a couple's retreat.

Benjamin joined Tatum's singing. "Leaning, leaning, leaning on the everlasting arms."

Angela tripped on a step but caught herself.

"It may be old, but this is a new song for me." Tatum looked up smiling.

"Then I would say you did some great sight-reading," Angela said. "You have a lovely voice. The two of you harmonize well."

"Benjamin's singing pulled me along." Tatum ducked her head to reposition her fingers. Her blond hair swept across her face, almost touching the strings. She and Benjamin alternated singing the verses and choruses just like Todd and Angela had. Angela wanted to curl up in a ball and cry.

When the singing stopped, Angela composed herself. "Benjamin, Tatum, could I ask a favor?" Angela said. "I just talked to Miranda from Shepherd's Fold. They are looking for volunteers. Would the two of you like to sing that song this afternoon at their Bible study? Emerson and Bethany should be back before Phillip wakes up."

"What's Shepherd's Fold?" Tatum said.

"It's a temporary shelter for women who need help to get

back on their feet," Benjamin said. "It's an outreach of our church and churches in the Twin Cities."

"So what happens? What do they do?"

"A Bible study," Benjamin added. "Followed with snacks so the volunteers can get acquainted with the residents. I've volunteered over the years. Mrs. Frandsen invited me because she told me she likes to have godly young men as well as women reach out to the ladies. Be an example to them. Some of them have never attended a church."

"I see." Tatum straightened the guitar strap.

"I don't know." Benjamin's expression changed. He picked up the music, studied it. "Yes, come on Tatum. Let's do it."

32

The stucco building, once a Motel Six, had lain idle for years before it was converted to a women's shelter. Pink, red, and white impatiens spilled over the tops of two large pots on either side of the door. The building appeared anonymous until you got close to the door and could see the small vinyl letters spelling out "Shepherd's Fold." Angela wilted at the thought of her last visit. Todd was at her side.

The shelter's director, Miranda Frandsen, unlocked the doors. She opened the door wide and led them into the reception area. "Come in, come in. Angela, you brought Benjamin, and—"

"Hi, Mrs. Frandsen. This is Tatum." Benjamin shifted the guitar case and shook Miranda's hand.

"We sign in here." Benjamin motioned to the guest log and guided Tatum.

"Hi!" A little boy with uncombed blonde hair and runny nose flew to their side and wrapped his arms around Tatum's legs. His upturned face, split by an enormous smile, vied for her attention.

"Oh!" Tatum stiffened.

"So sorry, he don't normally do that." A young woman approached, carrying a newborn in her arms. "Austin, come here. You mustn't bother that lady." She pulled the little boy away by his collar.

Angela greeted the trio. "Is this the new baby Susan told me about?"

"Yes, she's Isabella. I call her Bella. Just came home on Friday."

Home. A woman's shelter? Angela's heart melted. The mother let go of Austin long enough to uncover a beautiful baby with a fringe of tawny hair on her forehead.

Angela turned to Tatum. "Look at those long lashes."

Tatum touched the edge of the blanket. A little hand fluttered against Tatum's hand.

"Ohhh." Tatum's face softened. "Look. What tiny fingers she has."

Angela marveled that a newborn was a mystery to Tatum. How much time had she spent around children?

"Hello, Mrs. McKinley." Cole Richardson, Becca's friend, slipped up behind her.

"Cole, how nice to see you."

Cole shook Angela's hand then extended his hand to her son. "Benjamin."

"Look who's here!" Benjamin clamped a hand on Cole's shoulder. "Haven't seen you since high school."

"Hey, remembered by an upperclassman!"

Benjamin smiled. "I don't think you've met Tatum."

Tatum stopped stroking little Bella's hand, smiled at the mother, then turned to Cole.

"Glad you're here." Cole shook her hand.

"Are you the leader tonight?" Angela said.

"Gonna try." Cole smiled and turned to Tatum and Benjamin. "Good, you brought a guitar. I'll show you where to set up."

He led them to the dining room. Folding chairs surrounded long tables for ten. "Would you like to lead them in group singing?"

Tatum smiled. "Sure. What song should I play?"

Cole pointed to tattered hymnals on tables. "I'll let you choose. As soon as you start strumming, you'll bring everyone together."

He was right. When Tatum slipped the strap over her shoulder, the children clamored around Tatum and Benjamin. After three songs, Angela realized she wasn't crying. It was the first time she had sung without tears since Todd's death.

Benjamin looked at the little group. "My mom and dad sang this song before he ... well, he's in heaven now." Turning, he hid his face and placed the music on the stand.

Even the children sat with eyes riveted to the young couple singing. Angela heard the third verse of the song as if for the first time.

"What have I to dread? What have I to fear?"

Angela squeezed her eyes shut. Todd standing next to her, his resonant bass harmonizing with her soprano flooded her. What have I to dread? She asked the question as a widow. What have I to fear?

Everything.

Cole opened his Bible to the book of Romans and summarized in a short message. He explained the message of the Gospel but kept it short, then bowed his head. "Dear God, I pray for the one who doesn't know you as their Savior that tonight would be the night they call upon you. I pray for those who have claimed the promise of salvation through Christ

Jesus. Strengthen them to face the days ahead. Guide our every decision. We place ourselves before you and claim your protection in our lives."

Seats creaked. Soft whimpers rose.

"In Jesus' name we pray, amen."

The chocolate-y smell of brownies pulled the children and their mothers to the kitchen area. Angela filled cups with milk, which disappeared as fast as she could fill them. She noticed Tatum following baby Bella's mother while Benjamin gave little Austin a piggy-back ride to a nearby table.

As the line dwindled, Angela grabbed a brownie and looked for a place to sit.

"My name's Lilly." A woman in her late twenties stepped forward. Her hair, dyed red and pulled into a tight ponytail that exposed her dark roots couldn't have been less becoming.

"Hi, I'm Angela." She motioned to a nearby table and Lilly followed.

"Yeah, I know. You're one of the women who lost her husband in that big smashup, aren't you?"

33

Angela's chest caved as from a blow, but she tried to keep her voice steady. "Yes. How did you know?"

"Everyone knows. It was on every news station."

"Of course." Angela took a deep breath.

"Well, don't worry. You're pretty, not that old. You won't be alone for long." Lilly shot her a sideways glance.

Angela clutched her neck.

"Lilly, what a terrible thing to say." An attractive forty-ish woman, with a trim figure, wearing a short-sleeved knit top, glared at Lilly from down the table.

"Huh?" Lilly smirked and leaned toward Angela as if they were close friends. "Shelly's always setting someone straight."

Angela thanked Shelly with her eyes. "Lilly, Shelly's right."

Lilly shrugged. "Guess so, but you'll find out it's no fun being alone."

Angela blinked. "There's nothing wrong with being a single woman and worse things than being alone."

"Tell me about it." Lilly slumped, her swinging foot thumping the table leg. "The last man I had beat me then took off with some ditz. I was working two part-time jobs, and I ended up with all the bills." Her eyes glinted. "Sure like to fix him."

"Sometimes it's best to forget the bad things that happened in our past." Angela looked away.

"Bet you never made any mistakes or did anything wrong."

A distant memory stirred Angela. Gossip that placed shame at her door, even though she was innocent. "I've made mistakes. As a teenager, I was headed in the wrong direction."

"What stopped you?"

"A godly grandmother who pointed me to the right path." She brushed brownie crumbs into a neat pile.

"No granny like that in my life." Lilly swiped Angela's stack of crumbs to the carpet and brushed her hands together in a tidy motion.

Angela gasped, but Lilly didn't notice. Shelly leaned back in her chair with a sigh.

"Are you a believer?" Angela turned toward Lilly.

"Trying. Just can't get into this Bible stuff. Who can understand it? And how do you stay awake long enough to get anywhere reading it?"

"Once you realize how much God loves you, you can't get enough of His Word." Angela realized the truth in her own statement and a calmness surrounded her. She wondered if Lilly would someday find comfort in God's word. "Can I show you?"

"Sure. Hey!" Lilly registered simultaneous surprise and anger as she watched Angela flip pages. "Do they let you mark up Bibles like that?"

"If it's your own Bible, and if it helps you to highlight passages, then there's nothing wrong with it."

Shelly scooted her chair closer across from Angela. "You marked some words in yellow and some in pink. Why's that?"

"Well, I'm a visual person. I underline verses I want to remember. Verses that illuminate a great truth, I highlight in yellow. On days I need more strength, I skim through my bible and read those." She turned a page. "If it speaks to my heart, I highlight it in pink."

"Like this part?" Lilly pointed to a verse in the book of Romans. Her fingers skimming down the page.

"Yes," Angela said.

"And then that's a truth 'cuz you highlighted it in yellow." Lilly found the verse Angela intended to read.

"That's right." Angela smiled. "It's written to believers: 'This is how God showed his love among us: He sent his one and only Son into the world that if we believe in Him we will have eternal life.'" Angela flipped to the book of Acts. "Believe in the Lord Jesus, and you will be saved.'"

Lilly fidgeted and Angela said, "Do you have a Bible?"

"They gave me a Bible. Maybe I'll mark it up." Her head swiveled back. "You got pretty hair. Is that Clairol? What shade?"

Angela slumped, feeling entirely ineffectual. "It's natural."

"Huh. Might've known. Well, you look good, you know, kinda put together." Lilly shifted her eyes and yelled across the room. "Hey, Jeanne, where's my sweatshirt I loaned you?"

Angela watched her dash away. "Did I say something wrong?"

"No," Shelly said. "Lilly's ... well, social skills aren't her greatest asset."

Angela tried not to stare at the scene Lilly created with the one called Jeanne. Angela turned her attention back to Shelly. "Have you been here long?"

Wisteria

"Only two weeks. I just returned to Northgate last year to take care of my Mom—" her voice broke. "Her cancer was so advanced. I lost her three months ago."

"I'm so sorry to hear that." Angela stretched out her hand to Shelly.

"Thanks." Shelly grasped her hand. "I had moved into her apartment, found a job in a service call center. But when I took so much time off work to drive her to doctors' appointments and chemo, they replaced me. By that time hospice was called in, and she begged me not to put her in a nursing home. So I took care of her. We survived on her Social Security and the odd jobs that came my way. After I lost Mom, I couldn't pay for the apartment."

"I'm so sorry."

"Thanks. She was my best friend." Shelly's lower lip trembled then she straightened. "Lost the apartment and put what furniture we had in storage. Lived in my car for a couple of weeks."

"Your car?"

"You can shower at a truck stop for ten dollars."

Angela darted a glance at Shelly. This lovely, intelligent woman? Could things get that bad, that quickly? "But isn't that dangerous? I mean, living in your car?"

"That's why I came here."

"I'm glad you did."

Shelly crossed her arms and studied her neatly trimmed fingernails. "I know what you're going through as a widow, in a way, because my husband deserted me, divorced me. After twenty years of marriage, he just up and left. Different, but same kind of loss."

Angela strained to analyze her statement. For certain the

pain was real for both of them. "It was a death, the death of your marriage."

"Exactly. Only, he's not dead. A month after our divorce, I walked into a convenience store and almost ran smack into him. It felt like someone had punched me in the gut. You can't imagine. I still tense up just thinking about it." Shelly closed her eyes.

"Would you like a hug?" Angela said.

Shelly nodded. Angela walked around the table and wrapped her arms around Shelly.

"I'll be fine." Shelly brushed back the curls that had fallen over her eyes. "Once I find a full-time job, save up some money, I'll be able to get an apartment. Until then, I appreciate having a roof over my head."

They caught sight of Miranda. Shelly carefully blotted the corners of her eyes with a tissue. "Thank God for that lady. She's a saint."

Miranda's body swayed from side to side as she ambled toward them. Her white blouse and gathered skirt fit snugly over her portly frame.

"What's this I'm overhearing?"

"I said you're a saint." A teary softness appeared in Shelly's eyes. "You seem to know what each of us needs most."

"Thank you. I hope that's always the case." Miranda smiled her beautiful smile and patted Shelly's hand.

A cry of pain split the air. Angela turned to see little Austin clutch his tummy.

"Here, take her!" Bella's mother thrust her sleeping bundle into Tatum's arms, grabbed Austin, and headed to the restroom.

"No, wait!" Tatum held Bella like a receiver not knowing which direction to run with the football.

34

Angela was thankful Marge hosted their meeting the next evening. Even a short time alone for Bethany and Emerson to settle into their new home would give them some breathing room.

On the surface, a calmness settled on the trio as they relaxed in Marge's living room.

"Angela, I guess your house is off the market," Marge said. "Quite the activity this weekend."

"Yes, a full house with Bethany, Emerson and Phillip moving in with Becca and me." Angela cocked her head. "But don't let that stop your trips across the backyard. They'll enjoy seeing you, too."

"Thanks." Marge glanced at Caroline. "Did your house sell?"

"We hit a snag with the potential buyer's loan request," Caroline said. "It may take some time. But, at least the house has my name on the mortgage. I won't have to pay to have it transferred."

"What do you mean?" Marge said.

"Maybe I shouldn't have said anything." Caroline closed her eyes and took a deep breath. "You see, Brock managed to transfer many of our assets into his name and to hide a few accounts. The attorney is still trying to find everything. I had hoped to keep this from the children, but they may find out anyway if it goes to court."

"Preparing for divorce and trying to keep assets from you?" Marge's hand slapped the arm of Greg's recliner. "The snake."

"This will be hard for them to bear. Especially Sydney. She idolized her father. Their personalities are so much alike." Caroline's eyes narrowed. "I don't think it will be nearly as hard for Joshua."

Why? Angela wondered, but Caroline didn't elaborate.

"Do they suspect?" Marge said.

Caroline shook her head. "No more than I did, I'm sure. I suppose I had better break it to them before we meet with the lawyer."

Angela squeezed Caroline's hand and got a return squeeze.

Caroline bit her lip, then relaxed. "Now, let me hear from you two."

"I have a prayer request. Please remember Shepherd's Fold." Angela told them of her visit the night before. "Some ladies there simply made wrong choices. You know, I feel like I'm about two mistakes away from being there myself."

Caroline turned to face Angela. "Oh no, we would never let that happen to you."

"Thanks." Angela's heart twisted. "But I understand more and more how it happens. I wish I could be more help."

"How do women end up there?" Caroline said.

"Physical or emotional trauma, some learning disabilities, not good with critical thinking, and some, just one terrible circumstance after another." Angela recited the mental list she'd formed when she couldn't sleep the night before.

"And one woman in particular, while caring for an aging parent, simply ran out of funds. She needs to get back on her feet again. A sharp, intelligent woman. She's just staying at the shelter until she finds a job."

"I'm glad you volunteered. Glad you have that special talent," Marge said.

"Sometimes all it takes is a listening ear." Angela opened her workbook. "How did it go last week?"

"I confess, I barely made it through," Marge said. "But what I read was thought-provoking."

"I'm still stuck on 'who am I?' The question forces me to recognize I need to redefine myself. I'm no longer Brock's wife." Caroline sniffed. "How do you gain solid footing after your world crashes around you?"

"I can't say," Angela said softly. "I know I'm a widow. And guess what I did? One night I pulled out our concordance and looked up the word 'widow,' then read each verse under that heading." She swallowed the lump in her throat. "We're a big deal to God. The verses tell how God protects the widow. The Lord watches over the widow. The widow is never alone."

35

Angela opened her shop Tuesday morning with coffee on her mind. The aroma of Sumatra roasted beans filled her senses as she strolled to the worktable. Until she turned around. Halting in mid-step to the cooler that held her flower inventory, she gasped. How could this have happened?

All the fresh flowers drooped. Brown-edged chrysanthemums. Shriveled roses. Gladioluses prematurely budded. She opened the door and recoiled from the stench of damp, decaying plants. Heat hit her face. She jiggled a few buckets of flowers. They flopped haplessly, devoid of water. "It all evaporated? How?"

"What happened?" Rosa entered with one foot poised to leave.

"No refrigeration in this case on the hottest weekend of the summer. Leave the back door open. I'll get the fans going."

The phone rang. "Let it go to voice mail." Angela directed. "This is more important."

For thirty frantic minutes, they emptied buckets, snipped

stalks, tossed foliage, and sprayed air freshener throughout the shop.

"Who should I call? There must be a label. Oh, here it is." Angela circled the faulty case and found a weathered sticker with what she hoped was still current information. She picked up her cell phone.

Rosa pointed at the Tuesday orders. "We needed three dozen gladioluses from Friday's shipment for today's orders."

"Delivery truck's left St. Paul, so no chance to add to our order." Angela's hands covered her face for a moment. She tried not to assign a dollar figure to the loss.

"Sorry," Rosa said as she slipped the salvageable flowers into the one working cooler.

Angela shook her head. "All part of doing business." What was the loss? Hundreds of dollars?

Rosa spread out the shop's order slips. Angela took stock then made a quick trip to her supplier. After lunch, while they crowded the fresh supply of flowers into the working case, a service truck drove up. A middle-aged man with straggly, shoulder-length hair sauntered through the back door.

"Hi." He grinned as if the tag on his shirt was all the introduction needed. "Which one is it? Oh, yeah, I can see from here."

He popped off the refrigeration unit cover and stared. After fifteen minutes, his grin returned. "Need a new compressor. No fixing her. I'll call around, try to find you a good deal. But we're looking at four, maybe five hundred bucks minimum for the unit and labor."

"Isn't there a warranty?"

"Not on a unit this old."

Angela gritted her teeth. Anger would solve nothing. Angela thanked him and opened the back door, watching his truck back away with a roar. She slammed the door. "Get a haircut!"

Angela retreated to the break table. She needed strong coffee. After one sip, the shop bell rang. A young woman in a red dress complemented by a voluminous scarf strode to the counter.

She slung her ironed-straight hair back and extended her hand. "Hello, I'm Jenny Myers. Are you Angela?"

"Yes, I am," Angela said, connecting with a firm handshake.

"I'm Harriet Jones's interior designer. She asked me to drop by." Jenny turned and scanned the shop. "And I can see why."

"So nice to meet you." Interior designer? Harriet had followed through? Angela tried to appear calm, but her heart was pounding. She led Jenny to her largest display. "Let me show you what caught Harriet's eye."

Jenny nodded, pulled out a tape measure and notebook and went to work.

"Just call me if I can help." Angela took a deep breath, thankful that the scent of lavender fields met her nostrils.

"No problem," Jenny's singsong voice called back.

Angela drifted back to work. The clip-clop of Jenny's heels signaled she was still surveying the displays. Less than twenty minutes later, Jenny hurried to the counter.

"Here are the items we're purchasing," Jenny said.

Angela tried not to let her mouth drop open when she read the list. "Great!"

"I want the two fluted jardinières, but could you switch the dried grasses to incorporate these colors?" Jenny held up an arrangement.

"Yes, certainly." Angela made notes.

"Awesome. Now, if you would give me a total, we can put it on my charge. I don't mind telling you," Jenny said, "you've saved me a lot of grunt work tracking down the accessories we needed for that remodel. I have in mind the rest of the furniture that will give Harriet the look she's after."

"More than happy to do it," Angela said.

Rosa and Angela easily lifted a modified dresser into Jenny's van.

"Sorry, I'm not much help." Jenny grinned and pointed to her four-inch heels. "An appointment later this afternoon."

"We don't mind," Angela said. "Looks like we'll need my van, too. Will someone be there to help unload?"

"Yes, definitely. You know, there are two more designers in our downtown office. Do you have business cards I can pass around?"

Angela raced inside and grabbed a stack. She tried to keep her hands from shaking as she handed them over. "Just call me when you are looking for something specific and I'll post it online for you."

"Thanks. Here's my card for future reference." She flipped a card out of her bag and waited while they loaded the flower shop van.

Jenny's building on the northwest side of Minneapolis had a garage. Angela followed close behind and watched Jenny commandeer two men to unpack the goods. Word spread quickly, and Jenny's coworkers gathered with oohs and aahs for their favorite pieces.

Angela headed back to the shop with a stream of ideas buzzing through her head. But nothing could overpower the elation dancing in the back of her mind. Jenny had dropped twenty-five hundred dollars, just like that!

"Quite a hole to fill." Rosa stared at empty displays. "What are we going to do now?"

"I already have a plan. We'll start with the ivory and brass pieces in the back room." Angela grinned. "Remember, this is a good problem."

Between customers, they sailed through reorganizing displays and restocking the shop before closing time. A good day. Until a text from Benjamin stopped her cold.

36

Angela retreated to the privacy of the van, her hand shaking as she called Benjamin.

"Mom, our time at the shelter was an eye-opener for Tatum."

Angela exhaled in relief and tried not to read too much into Benjamin's excited voice as she answered him. "In what way?"

"She's had limited exposure to children, but I think she fell in love with the baby. You should have seen her face when Bella was shoved into her arms. She said later the feel of the helpless, warm body, so trusting, made her want to hold on to her and not let her go. She had no idea a baby could make her feel that way."

"Bella, the sweet baby."

"I don't know if she'll change her mind about having kids, but she said she wanted to become more involved with the work at the shelter. I mean, like drive over from St. John to volunteer. Maybe once a month."

"Miranda will appreciate that."

"She really has a heart for helping people."

"She must. She sounds like a wonderful Christian."

Angela sat motionless in the van after they hung up. Maybe Tatum was more mature than she had appeared. Oh, that Tatum would make a good wife for Benjamin someday. Angela pulled tissues from her purse. Why couldn't Todd be here? Why couldn't she fly into his arms and sob out this complicated task of being a mom to adult children? How to avoid stepping on delicate male egos? Todd would have known.

A few minutes later, Angela arrived home to the pleasant aroma of simmering marinara sauce.

Emerson opened the back door with one hand, tugging at a struggling Phillip with the other hand. "Phillip, it's time to come inside and wash your hands before dinner."

"No. Want sandbox." Phillip plopped in the doorway. His high-pitched cry filled the room.

Angela turned to Bethany. "How was your day?"

"Laundry, cleaning, getting settled." Bethany raised her voice. "It was great."

"Hands. Now. Because I said so!" Emerson swung Phillip over one shoulder and proceeded down the hall.

With everyone finally at the table, Emerson dove in, piling pasta onto his plate until Bethany elbow him.

Emerson stopped. Tongs in hand. "You pray at every meal?"

Bethany took his hand. "Would you like to lead us in prayer?"

Emerson shot her a quizzical look but joined hands with everyone and mumbled a quick prayer.

"Good day at the shop, Mom?" Emerson said.

"Good day shop, Gamma?" Phillip lifted a spaghetti-sauce face.

"Chew and swallow your food before you speak," Bethany said.

"Thank you for asking, dear." Angela patted Phillip's cheek with a napkin. "Well, it started out with the setback of a broken compressor—but ended with a huge sale."

She elaborated on both. So good to have someone to listen, to sympathize, to rejoice.

Angela slept soundly that night.

"Good morning, I'm Paul, here to replace the compressor."

Angela did a double-take. A professional stood in place of yesterday's wise-guy. She led him to the case and watched him remove his well-cared-for tools.

An hour later, he neatly coiled an extension cord without a crease or twist. "That's a used compressor I installed, but it has a year's warranty. Call us if you experience any trouble."

"Thank you, I will." Ashamed of her anger the day before, Angela marveled at the way God had provided for her needs. Funds already sitting in her bank account would pay the bill. Even with her lack of trust, He still had blessed her.

She exhaled slowly. "Rosa, I'll make deliveries. I feel like venturing out."

"Okay. Orders are ready." Rosa helped her load the van.

Same route, same people, same stops as before Todd's death. She received no dreaded looks of pity on the familiar faces. The world had moved on. Angela wasn't sure if that comforted her, but at least it wasn't as torturous as she had imagined.

About to pull out of a business complex, she paused as someone waved at her. It took a moment to recognize Lilly with freshly bleached blonde hair. At least the dark roots were gone.

Angela hit the button to open the window on the passenger side.

"Hi, Lilly, headed somewhere? Can I give you a lift?"

"Job interview." Lilly opened the door and tried for the seat three times before she could hop in with her tight skirt and high heels. "Getting tired of cleaning jobs."

"What kind of job interview?"

"A sales associate at Walmart."

Angela stifled her reaction. "No problem. It's on my way. Did you bring another pair of shoes for your walk home?"

"No, I'll take 'em off and go barefoot if my feet hurt."

Angela dropped Lilly at Walmart and thought of the shelter residents, their uphill struggle, and their need for something as simple as job hunting skills. Someone should volunteer.

Her mind slipped into neutral until she noticed an oncoming car. A police car. It was Officer Brown, the police officer who brought the news of Todd's death. Their eyes met. He nodded.

Angela blinked back the tears as best as she could. She wasn't sure how she found her way back to the shop.

Busyness could remedy her disorientation. She picked up an order slip.

"All they specified was a tall narrow bouquet," Angela mumbled as she measured and clipped flowers for height and filled a vase with a conical styrofoam form. Despite the vague order, a pattern emerged. Lavender carnations offsetting pale green spider mums that spiraled up and around a mass of orange and yellow Gerber daisies. She stood back, surveying the effect.

Rosa interrupted her train of thought. "Phone's for you."

Angela was still staring at her arrangement when she answered the phone.

"Hi, Angela. It's Gwen from the *Gazette*. You have such a flair for decorating, and I need your help. Can you look over my house?" Gwen never minced words. "Maybe one evening? Or, during the day, if that fits your schedule better?"

"Decorating? But, I'm not a decorator."

"You know how to blend antiques. Just try it, okay? Make suggestions. If you take one look at my house and can't do anything with it, I understand. I can't do anything with it, either." She laughed. "I'll pay you a consultant's fee just for an evaluation. How's that?"

"Sounds intriguing." Angela looked up. Her flower shop was empty except for Rosa. "Okay, but only pay me if you like the results."

Angela shook her head and smiled. An appointment next Tuesday evening. To do something she knew how to do only intuitively.

"What's so funny?" Rosa said.

"It seems I'm a decorator now. That was Gwen. She needs help arranging her antiques and finding a spot for the sign she bought from us."

"Well, if anyone can do it, you can," Rosa said.

"That remains to be seen."

37

Marge and Caroline got an unexpected bonus the following Monday when the widows met for dinner at Angela's. Phillip, the great little entertainer, treated dinner as a party. His mouth dropped open when Angela set a three-layered coconut cake in the middle of the table.

Then his face fell. "Gamma? Where's the candles? Like Daddy's cake?"

"That's only for birthday cakes, dear."

Phillip's brow creased. "Oh." But he forgot about candles after his first bite.

After dinner, Emerson stood and nodded to Marge and Caroline. "Enjoyed having dinner with you, ladies. But we have some serious movie-watching to do." He saluted with a DVD case. "An old classic, but Phillip's favorite."

"A frozen swirl and his peanut," Phillip said.

Bethany giggled and took his hand.

"What's funny, Mom?"

"It's about a squirrel and his acorn."

"That's what I said."

Wisteria

Three widows held back laughter until the bedroom door closed behind Phillip.

"You have a charming grandson," Caroline said.

"He sure is," Marge said. "Reminds me of Bethany with his blond hair."

Everyone drifted toward the living room.

"You and Todd always shared your children with us. Greg's business was our baby." Marge sighed. "It's been fun watching them grow up. Now your children have children."

"I heard you dropped off a box of goldfish crackers for Phillip."

"I like to see his face light up." Marge tilted her head. "Caroline, what about your house?"

"Negotiations with the buyer are going nowhere. But I plan to move on schedule."

"Do you know where you're moving?" Angela said.

Caroline shook her head. "I have this dream of building a house that suits only me. Doesn't that sound selfish?"

"No," Marge said. "We need dreams. Now more than ever. You've raised your family. The next house should meet your needs."

"Not sure where to stay short term. I've been spending a lot of time at the farm with dad." Caroline opened her workbook. "Marge, how about your week?"

"Nothing new," Marge said. "I still go from work at the hospital to work at Greg's company. Other than the two of you and my other next-door neighbor, I don't visit anyone much. But I don't feel isolated." Marge lifted one shoulder. "It's as if the best part of me is gone. I enjoyed working. I left our social life with Greg. He was so involved with people, making friends wherever he went. I didn't bother. I guess I wasn't interested."

"You'll always have a friend in me." Angela leaned toward Marge.

"And me," Caroline said.

"You two are like family. The sisters I never had." Marge's emotional armor seemed to chink with that declaration.

"That ties in with our assignment," Angela said. "How did you answer the questions about relationships?"

"The relationship with my children," Caroline said, "that's something I have to work on constantly."

"Ditto." Angela swiped at her furrowed forehead.

Tuesday evening, Angela stood in Gwen Olstad's living room, awash with the typical I-don't-have-a-clue decorating style. A sofa guarded by two lamp tables sat flush against the wall, facing two matching chairs flush against the opposite wall. A plethora of antiques flanked the remaining walls and adorned the fireplace mantel. Adrenaline surged through Angela. She couldn't wait to rip into that room.

"You have some beautiful pieces." Angela touched a pie safe in mint condition and walked around the circumference of the room. "My first suggestion would be..."

Gwen leaned forward. "Yes?"

"If you place a chair on each side of the fireplace to frame and draw attention to it, and move the sofa here, facing the fireplace ..." Angela stepped back. "That would open the room and create a flowing traffic pattern."

"Listen to you. I thought you said you weren't a decorator."

"Oh, I pick up things from books and magazines."

"Then let's do it!"

"Okay. But first, do you have more antiques you'd like to incorporate?"

"Do I!" Gwen hustled toward the dining room. "Let me show you the whole house because I want to change the entire main level, not just one room."

Angela stopped Gwen in the kitchen. "What about your oak cabinets? Would you ever consider painting them?"

"What did you have in mind?"

"Something dark, like a charcoal gray." Angela pointed to the space above the cabinets. "That would showcase your teapot collection above the cabinets. Draw the eye up, enlarge the room."

"Uff da!" Gwen reverted to the Norwegian exclamation for bafflement. "But I like the idea."

"We could stagger the height of the teapots, sitting one on top of that spice box, one on top of the bread box, and a few teapots nestled in front."

"I'm making a list. Now, there's three bedrooms upstairs."

"Lead the way."

Returning to the living room a few minutes later with an armful of accent pieces, Angela stood back. "What about your drapes? Are you attached to them?"

"Well, no. They need updating."

"Can you see how the light-colored drapes draw your eyes to the windows rather than to your antiques? You could eliminate the drapes and still have the blinds when you need privacy."

"You're right. I've noticed that effect in new homes. I should try it."

"Think about it. Shall we tackle the living room now?"

Gwen nodded. Soon they had stacked different sizes of small wooden chests beside the fireplace and topped them with family treasures. A stained glass panel became a room divider. The pie safe became a bookcase with a frayed-edge quilt draped over the top and doors left open.

On one of their trips upstairs, Angela touched a roll of cloth at the foot of a bed. "What's this?"

"I intended to transform it into a throw." Gwen grimaced and unrolled a beautiful piece of tapestry. "But never had time."

"We could display it on the wall."

"The wall? Great idea!"

In the dining room, Angela transformed the wall above a sideboard with the tapestry. Then she headed back to the living room.

She stood the Ueland Equipment sign in the middle of the mantel and flanked it with pewter candlesticks on one side, an old scale on the other. "What do you think?"

"Angela!" Gwen stepped back, clasped her hands in front of her. "My sign. It's the first thing they'll see when they enter the room. Exactly what I wanted."

Angela smiled. "I think we've accomplished a lot in one evening."

Gwen handed her a check.

"Gwen, this is too much."

"It's the going rate. I checked. Can't tell you how happy I am with what you've done tonight. When word gets out," Gwen tilted her head, "and I have contacts. This could open a whole new career for you."

38

F ootsteps echoed as Angela and Marge entered Caroline's skeleton of a house a week later. Most of the furniture remained, but the homey items were packed away. Boxes lined the walls all the way to the living room.

"Sorry. You know me. I enjoy being organized." Caroline lifted her hands. "I waited until our meeting to share more bad news."

Baxter scurried around each of them, wondering why no one paid attention to him.

"The house didn't sell. The buyers pulled their bid."

"Oh, no." Angela rubbed Baxter's ears and he settled down.

"Well, it is a lot of money." Caroline perked up. "As I mentioned last week, I'm moving, regardless. An empty house shows better, I'm told. Say, let's eat. I'm hungry."

The trio settled in the dining room to the luscious deli fare Caroline provided.

"Where are you moving?" Angela said. "Have you decided?"

"For now I'm moving in with Dad and Aunt Jackie."

"Good idea," Marge said. "Let's see, is that farther? No, you're closer to Northgate."

"That's the problem as the kids see it." Caroline sipped her bottled mineral water. "Well, a problem for Sydney. Joshua already lives close to dad's farm. Only Sydney feels I'm deserting her by leaving the Twin Cities."

"Will you miss it?" Angela circled her arm to encompass the grandeur of the great room and sighed.

"An ostentatious house? Brock enjoyed the house and the cities, not me." Caroline wiped a speck from the spotless table with her napkin. "When I finish packing, most items will go into storage. I'll leave the furniture the decorator ordered to stage the downstairs. For showings and open houses everything should be neat, sparse, and clean."

Marge laughed. "They won't find a speck of dust."

"What?"

"You seem obsessed with your housecleaning. Wish I were the same."

"OCD Brock called it." Caroline grimaced. "No, you don't, Marge. It's a terrible way to live."

"Terrible?" Angela said. "Why do you say that?"

"I can't even go to bed at night if there's one dirty dish in the sink."

"If you could bottle and sell that trait, I'd place my order." Marge surveyed the perfect shine on the hardwood floors.

"I would trade places if I could." A pucker of worry appeared between Caroline's eyes.

"We love you just the way you are." Angela's hand settled on Caroline's arm.

"Thanks. I'm glad I have one friend." Caroline smirked at Marge then laughed good-naturedly.

"Sorry, didn't mean to tease you. Can we help you move?" Marge said.

"Thank you, but no. You both work full time. Just your moral support is a tremendous help." They finished clearing the table, and Caroline led them into the living room. "Tell me what's going on in your lives."

"I'm thinking of a project for the women's shelter and looking for volunteers," Angela said.

"What's up?" Marge said.

Angela related the encounter with Lilly's inappropriate interview attire.

"They watch too much TV," Marge said. "The real world's a shock."

"I'm sure she thought she looked nice." Angela shook her head. "But maybe we could help. Be an example to them. Help them identify their job skills, write a résumé, prepare for interviews."

"Whoa," Marge said. "That's quite an undertaking."

"I know, but they would improve their chances of finding employment with more guidance," Angela said. "How about it, Marge?"

"Sorry, I'm spread thin right now," Marge said. "What about the shelter? Isn't that part of their program?"

"They depend on volunteers for much of the instruction of this type. The director focuses on Bible study, drug rehab, admin ... she can only do so much."

"After the move, I could use a distraction." Caroline leaned toward Angela. "I'll be able to give you a date by next week."

"Thanks, you're an answer to prayer." Angela opened her workbook. "Do you realize that we'll finish our twelve weeks of sessions in another four weeks?"

"I hate to see it end." Caroline clutched her workbook.

"It doesn't have to," Marge said. "We could just get together when everyone's available. Maybe once a month?"

"That's true," Angela said.

"Let's do that," Caroline said. "Let me say this week's lesson spoke to my heart. And some days" —Caroline put her face in her hands for a moment— "some days I forget about the past year when we were building the house, the time when Brock became a stranger. I remember our life together, before. Bumpy, but together as a family. I miss our life as a family." Caroline rubbed her left third finger, devoid of her wedding band. "I flip-flop back and forth. I loathe him. I love him. It's odd. It was sweet in the beginning."

"How could it be odd to concentrate on the earlier days of your marriage? Remember the good. Somehow deal with the betrayal and put it behind you." Angela looked at her own left hand with the diamond Todd had given her and wondered if she would ever remove her ring. "Easy for me to say. I've not been in your shoes. Do you think talking with a counselor would help? A good Christian counselor?"

"No." Caroline's firm chin rose. "I'm not depressed—I'm sad. I prefer to work it out alone."

"You be the judge. The medical world offers a lot of support," Marge said.

"I keep wondering if we could have saved our marriage, given more time." Caroline's voice deepened. "Doesn't matter. I need to let go."

Marge folded her hands in her lap. "Our grief recovery sessions have helped me take the journey, as they call it. Otherwise, I'm sure I would have been stuck without a window of hope."

"Window of hope," Caroline echoed. "Yes, after working through the grief as we have, I can see that."

Angela opened her workbook. "Look at their statement, 'Who am I to question God?' God chose to take Todd home. It still hurts. What can I say? But, somehow, the pain isn't as raw."

Caroline cleared her throat. "Another thing I've been obsessing about all week. Why? The why of it all."

"I'm a realist." Marge tapped the cover of her workbook. "I liked their answer. In fact, I found it profound." Marge leaned closer. "Even if we knew why, they would still be gone."

39

Mid-August

It just took one cool Minnesota August night to turn many of the sumac leaves brilliant red—heralding autumn's arrival. Autumn. Angela's favorite time of the year. Just its name lifted her spirits as she opened the flower shop with Becca in tow.

"Becca, your work this summer—from yard signs to these delicate pieces—what a boost to the shop." Angela cradled a pale pink plaque trimmed in a string of pearls.

"Thanks for letting me experiment." Becca's small paint brush dotted a line of white trim on a black background. "It's relaxing. Look what I'm painting."

"Christmas!"

"Yes. I hope to finish Christmas plaques before I go back to school."

Angela glanced over Becca's shoulder. "A three-dimensional snow man. How did you do that?"

"A little trick of the trade." Becca grinned.

"Let me see." Rosa joined them, then shook her head. "Totally not ready to even think about snow."

"Glad you're planning ahead." Angela's smile dissolved. Christmas. Without Todd.

On the pretense of helping Rosa clear off a dresser she had sold, Angela rushed to the front to hide her tears.

"Wait, I'm taking the dresser and everything on it." The customer held up her hand. "I have to snap a picture." She laughed and pulled out her phone. "I'll never remember the way you arranged it."

Finally, the bigger items were selling.

That evening after dinner, Bethany shooed everyone into the living room while she stayed in the kitchen, filling glasses with ice. "We have a birthday party to plan." Her voice rose to reach them in the next room. "Sunday is Phillip's birthday."

"My birthday? Daddy, my birthday!"

"Who should we invite?" Emerson shifted his laptop.

"Dylan!"

Emerson grimaced. "Well, maybe celebrate with him one day during the week."

"I called Uncle Benjamin today and left a message for him and Tatum to come," Bethany said.

"Okay. And Gamma."

Everyone laughed.

"I wouldn't miss it for the world." Angela lifted Phillip onto her lap.

Bethany's cell phone rang. "Mom, can you grab it?" she called from the kitchen.

"Hi, Benjamin. You're on speaker phone with Mom, Bethany, Emerson and Phillip."

Benjamin's voice came over the line. "Hey, everyone. Got the invite to Phillip's birthday party. We'll be there."

"Wonderful," Angela said.

"And, Mom, would you believe Tatum's birthday is Friday?" Benjamin said. "Maybe we can celebrate both at once. Do you think Phillip will mind?"

Angela turned to Phillip. "Shall we celebrate two birthdays at once?"

A cheer from Phillip split the air.

Angela smiled. "I suppose you heard the response?"

"Yeah, we'll be there. Things are going good, Mom. Real good."

Angela glowed from Benjamin's last remark. She took him off speaker and lingered over his call for a couple more minutes.

"Benjamin's bringing a cheesecake for Tatum so Phillip won't have to share his cake." Angela announced.

"Good idea. She's a little old to be blowing out three candles." Bethany placed the last glass on the coffee table. "I wonder how old she is?"

Sunday morning after church, Angela's home swelled with family. The meal was a success with Emerson and Benjamin working the grill. Cole Richardson, Becca's friend, joined them, so Phillip gained one more fan to entertain.

"Glad you're here, Benjamin," Emerson said. "Wanna help me at the cabin next weekend? September. Time to winterize the boat ..."

"Maybe get in some fishing?"

Emerson smiled.

Angela looked away. No buyer for the cabin. Insurance, taxes due. Would the roof hold up one more year?

After the meal, Benjamin lifted Phillip and placed a balloon on his booster seat. "There's a present inside. All you have to do is sit down hard and pop the balloon."

Phillip plopped squarely on the balloon then bounced up and down. "It won't pop!"

He leaned to his left as far as possible and looked at the balloon. He didn't notice his mother on the other side, fumbling for the pink ribbon pin she wore, and pricking the balloon. Bang! No one was more surprised than Phillip.

"Look what fell out." Bethany retrieved a tiny envelope.

"What is it?" Phillip held up a plastic card.

"Looks like a credit card." Cole smiled at Phillip.

Phillip's face fell.

Benjamin laughed. "No, it's a gift card. Phillip, you can buy toys with this card."

"Mommy, look. I buy toys!"

"I see," Bethany said. "Won't that be fun?"

Benjamin moved behind Tatum's chair. "And a balloon for Tatum." Ignoring her you-must-be-kidding look, he motioned for her to get up.

"Pop it, pop it!" Phillip clapped.

Tatum shot Benjamin a withering look but sat on her balloon. Phillip covered his ears but squealed with delight at the big bang.

Tatum stood. "It looks like a long ribbon and ..." She pulled the white ribbon until something shiny clinked against her chair. She gathered it to her and gasped. Tears welled in her eyes. She covered her mouth and almost fell into her seat.

Phillip turned sad eyes to her. "No card for toys?"

Benjamin took her hand in both of his, the ribbon and its dangling engagement ring entwined in their fingers. He dropped to one knee by her chair and gazed at Tatum through misty eyes. "I love you, Tatum. Will you marry me?"

Tatum leaned forward and planted a quick kiss. "The answer is yes."

The dining room erupted with shouts, screams, and hugs.

"What a surprise. What a wonderful surprise," Bethany said.

Angela kissed Tatum's cheek. "My new daughter."

Glancing at Cole, she wondered how he would take being in the middle of a family drama.

Cole stood behind Becca, wide-eyed. He recovered and shook Benjamin's hand. "Congratulations."

"Not even a clue," Becca said.

Emerson gripped Benjamin's shoulder. "You sure put one over on us."

Phillip tugged Angela's arm and whispered, "Did she like her present?"

"Yes, oh, yes, very much."

Phillip broke into a big smile. "Good."

40

Late September

Angela returned from her morning delivery of two arrangements and tried not to cringe at the low count. How much gas and time had she burned? Enough to make essentially no profit after expenses. But sales should pick up soon.

It was a perfect day to play hooky—rather, scout for shabby chic. Attending a popular flea market and antique show today should yield enough items to take her home accessories business through Christmas.

Angela filled her insulated mug for the road trip. "You'll be okay at the shop alone today, Rosa?"

"Sure." Rosa scanned the scant five orders spread on the worktable. "But how will you tackle the antiques by yourself?"

"I roped Caroline into going with me."

"Good. Bring back lots of treasures."

"I'll try."

Did it make sense to pull money saved toward her balloon

payment? Spend money to make money? What else could she do? December would boost her bank account. Or the sale of the cabin. Something would pan out. Surely.

When Caroline came through the back door Angela ran to give her a hug. "I've missed you since our weekly meetings stopped."

"Getting together once a month is not enough." Caroline returned her hug.

"Agreed."

"Can't believe I've waited so long to visit your shop. I want a grand tour when we return." Caroline's eyes darted about the room before she and Angela slipped out the door to the van.

"Be happy to show you around."

"I have my eye on a couple of pots of those glorious russet mums." Caroline pointed to plants in the front of the building when the van circled around. "That's one thing Aunt Jackie and I have in common, a love for flowers."

"Do you enjoy living on the farm?" Angela headed south for the hundred-and-fifty-mile trip.

"Yes. Hard at first. But now I'm settled, baby grand and all." Caroline grimaced as she picked up her travel mug in the roomy center console.

"Uh, oh. Do I sense a bone of contention?"

"You might say that." Caroline peeked at Angela and smiled. "It scrunches the living room furniture together. Dad doesn't seem to mind."

"Aunt Jackie?"

"She's not saying much."

"Setting boundaries, right?"

"Right. I'm getting better." Caroline sipped coffee. "It's time we planned a trip to Shepherd's Fold."

Angela set the cruise control and relaxed. "What new skills could we teach the residents?"

"I was a server during my college years," Caroline said. "I think there are courses offered now. Food safety? I could check."

"Would you? That's ideal. I was thinking of helping them draft a résumé. Marge said she might come after work at the hospital. She's wants to offer a short course on surfing the web for job openings."

"I'll make notes." Caroline pulled a tiny notebook from her bag. "We have a long trip ahead. Might as well plan."

They made good time until they neared their destination and turned off the interstate.

"What's this?" Angela slowed.

"A round-about." Caroline said. "They're nice once you get used to them."

The round-about made Angela feel like one of the Shriner's synchronized motorcycle riders in a fourth of July parade. She zipped and threaded her way and finally made her turn. Traffic slowed, and a town appeared.

"Wow!" Caroline said. "Never expected this."

"The Internet says this is the fifth largest show in the country."

The town no longer resembled a town, but an endless flea market. Tents and booths stretched along every street and in front of people's houses. A young man waved Angela into the yard of a private home to park her van, his fees proudly posted. She quickly complied.

"Feels strange dragging a garden cart," Angela said as the two of them lifted it from the van. "But it's big and has wheels."

"Oh, you're not out of place." Caroline laughed and

nodded to people who pushed past with shopping carts, wheel-barrows, and children's wagons, with and without children.

"Now remember, I'm here to guard your purchases while you shop." Caroline dodged a bicycle and manned her post behind the garden cart. "If I see anything that interests me, I'll let you know."

"This is perfect. So glad you came."

An hour later, they pulled her bulging cart to the van.

"This is fun." Caroline shook her head. "A new experience for me."

"Me too. Do you need help lifting that?"

"Why do you think I work out?" Caroline's bench-pressed biceps flexed as her arms circled a wooden barrel.

"I'm impressed." Angela carefully nested breakables in the van.

"Bucking hay bales for Dad last summer probably fine-tuned my routine."

"You?"

"The crew didn't show up one day, so I volunteered." Caroline smiled wryly. "It shocked Aunt Jackie. I think that was my motivation."

"You never cease to amaze me."

"Being a widow changes a person. I'm doing things I never dreamed of doing a year ago. Where there's a will, there's a way."

"I've coined a new phrase," Angela said. "Where there's a widow, there's a way."

They eyed one another then burst out laughing.

"How true," Caroline said.

"Let's choose a different area." Angela checked the van's location and noted the street sign.

"Glad you have a good sense of direction." Caroline

followed her trek up the hill.

"There's Olaf. Do you remember him? Antique shop in Northgate?"

"The junk shop? Yes, I remember him."

"Olaf, I didn't expect to see you here," Angela said.

"And why not, I'd like to know?"

"It surprised me. So far from home." Angela smiled as she glanced at Caroline standing back with a puzzled expression.

"Olaf, I've never seen this lamppost in your shop."

"Just got it in. Make me an offer."

Angela lowballed it and was surprised when he took the offer.

"Just one catch," Angela said.

"Oh, yeah?"

"My van floor is full of breakables." Angela walked past the lamppost. "Can you truck it back for me? I can pick it up at your shop later."

"Humph. I suppose. Maybe I'll have an empty truck," Olaf cackled then stuck out his protruding jaw as Angela counted bills into his hand. He gave her a receipt and taped a "sold" sign on the lamppost.

Caroline glanced back as they walked away. "Always an interesting chap."

Angela shook her head. "Some people are hard to understand."

"True."

Circling past the booths, they finally arrived back at the van and unloaded their wares.

"Hi, Angela!"

Angela twisted her neck in the direction of the greeting. "Why, Trudy? Trudy Bauer? I'm surprised to see you." The unpleasant memory of the conversation in the shop with Trudy

soon after Todd's death flooded back to Angela. Trudy's asser-
tion that she would soon talk to Todd every day. Well, of all the
phases of mourning she had been through, at least that had
never happened.

"So this is where you get the stock for your high-end shop?"
Trudy called. She wagged her finger at Angela and hurried to
catch up with Arnie, who waved and kept walking.

Angela frowned and whispered to Caroline, "And there's a
law against that?"

Caroline jabbed Angela. "You'll get wrinkles from that
crease between your eyebrows."

"I must be getting tired to let Trudy get under my skin,"
Angela said. "It's long past lunchtime. Maybe the food line
won't be so long now."

"Guess where I'm headed?" Caroline crossed the street and
slapped her money on the counter.

"Mmm, I can't resist deep-fried cheese curds." Angela
ignored grease stains dotting the paper tray and popped one in
her mouth.

The smell of sloppy joes led them to the fire station. All the
garage doors were open, fire trucks and emergency vehicles
lined the street to allow use of the entire station floor.

"Look at the sign. 'All proceeds go to purchase equipment
for our volunteer firefighters.'" Caroline glanced at the crowd.
"Dad has been a volunteer for years."

"He has?" Angela surveyed the sawhorses-and-plywood
sheet tables with a few people clustered around.

"Yes, in the rural areas there are no fire stations such as
Northgate has. It's all volunteers. Let's donate to their
fundraiser."

"Gladly." Angela appreciated the short lines in the middle
of the afternoon.

"So nice to sit down." She plopped into a folding chair and lifted her feet, doing tiny circles in the air.

"Haven't been shoved so much since I spent a day in Tokyo." Caroline rubbed her arms. Her smile showed her enjoyment. She picked up her sloppy joe and laughed when half the filling fell back on her plate. "Good thing they provide a plastic fork."

"I've found so many items for the shop. Good prices. Profitable day."

"And it's good for me to get away and give Aunt Jackie some space," Caroline said.

"I'm glad you recognize that. It's a change for her as well."

"She has managed Dad's household for the last five years. I'm trying to ease in and make myself useful. I'm sure we'll find some common ground."

Angela nodded. "She's a widow too, isn't she?" Angela said.

"Yes. Husband killed in Vietnam. They were only together about six months, I'm told. They married soon after high school. As far as I know, she has had no one else in her life all these years."

A siren drowned out Caroline's last words. Men behind the counters peeled off aprons. Shouting at each other, they grabbed gear from lockers and suited up amid an ordered chaos then swarmed to the nearby trucks.

"What happened?" A bystander shouted.

"Car on the interstate hit a bridge abutment head-on."

"Bet they're all goners."

Their words stomped on Angela's heart like the boots hitting the steps of the emergency vehicles.

Caroline's hand shook as it closed over Angela's.

"Just when you think you've got control," Angela whispered.

41

The next day

"Mom, your phone's chirping." Bethany pointed with a breakfast bowl to the far side of the counter.

"Angie?"

"Grandma? How nice to hear from you." But Angela could not detect the usual cheerful tone in her grandmother's voice. "Is something wrong?"

"It's Raymond," she said. "We lost him Tuesday night."

"I'm so sorry."

"Thank you, dear. He's been suffering, but he's with the Lord now."

With the Lord. Just like Todd.

"I wish I had known him better. How are you doing?"

"I'm sad. I miss him. I'm also relieved. Does that sound terrible? No more pain for Raymond. We had two years to prepare. Two years to say good-bye."

"That's so sweet." Angela eked out the words.

"You know, he didn't want to be a burden to me. He even helped me plan the funeral."

"When is it?"

"Tomorrow. Friday. I know you're busy, but I wanted to let you know."

"I'll be there." Angela ached to see her grandmother again. She didn't know how she could possibly arrange to get there, but she'd find a way.

"Are you sure? You have a flower shop to run. I'll understand if it doesn't work out."

"I want to be with you. I miss you."

"I miss you too, Angie girl. If you can come, I'd love for you to stay with me."

"Thank you." Angela closed her eyes.

Bethany hugged her mother. "Grandma Em?"

Angela nodded. "Yes. Grandpa Raymond passed away, and the funeral is tomorrow. Oh dear, Friday. When the shop is open late."

"Mom, if you want to go, I'll help at the shop. I'll ask Dylan's mother to watch Phillip. I know the ropes, remember? Before cancer?"

"And even when you were ill. I remember the holidays when you pitched in."

"I needed to feel useful."

Angela smiled and shook her head.

"I don't know." Angela caught Phillip as he raced from his bedroom toward her.

"Gamma." He hugged, let go, and headed to his booster seat for breakfast.

"It's Thursday. If I book a flight and leave tonight, spend Friday, Saturday there, come back Sunday ..." Angela put her head in her hands. "The loaded van from yesterday's trip. How much can I get unloaded today?"

"Rosa and I will work on it," Bethany said.

"Maybe I was too hasty to promise—Todd always said I was impulsive."

The trip could set her back several hundred. The niggling fear of the balloon loan due at the bank in December surfaced again.

The four-hour flight from Minneapolis to Atlanta and the long drive northwest to Aunt Rita's house were not nearly as exhausting as the brief night. Aunt Rita was accustomed to staying up late. She chatted until midnight, seemingly oblivious to Angela's weariness, and recounted everything that had happened in Beaumont Springs for the past six months. Finally Angela seized upon a lull, excused herself, and fell into bed.

The next morning Angela's sister, Lorrie, drove Angela and Rita down the last hill into Abbeyville, her grandmother's hometown. A steeple and bell tower came into view, and special memories of the place where Lorrie and Angela had spent their summers stirred in Angela's heart.

Aunt Rita, in the back seat, leaned forward. "Wow, haven't been to this church in years. Metal siding instead of chipping clapboards. Spanking new doors. When did that happen?"

Lorrie maneuvered her car into the freshly painted lines of a new asphalt parking lot. "And who paid for it all?" Lorrie's gaze took in the scene.

The heavy scent of roses and mums met Angela as they were ushered to the pew reserved for the family. She scooted beside Lorrie.

Angela twisted in all directions. Where was Grandma
Emmeline? How was she holding up at the age of ninety-three?
Angela looked past three generations of Raymond's family
squeezed into two pews.

Finally her grandmother appeared on the arm of
Raymond's eldest son. Her age lines more creased than ever,
but a gentleness and peace about her gave her face a special
beauty.

Angela's eyes smarted. She squeezed them shut to block
the tears, but they still slid past her lids. Tears for Todd,
rather than Grandpa Raymond. Tears for herself, rather than
her grandmother. Angela fought her feelings by focusing on
her surroundings. The church's interior seemed frozen in
time. It looked identical to how Angela remembered it as a
child when she and Lorrie spent time with their
grandmother.

The pianist swayed and pounded the keyboard. Angela
leaned close to Lorrie and whispered, "Mrs. Fox?"

Lorrie nodded. "You got it."

Aunt Rita glanced their way.

The hymns were sweet, the Gospel message was clear, and
the Bible verses made her heart yearn for heaven. The tears
disappeared and the service wrapped her in peace.

Angela rode with Lorrie and Aunt Rita to the burial.

"Why did I wear this thing?" Lorrie pulled a scarf from her
neck. It fell across the front seat in a puddle of flowery pastels
that didn't quite match the crisp lines of the black pin-striped
suit she wore.

"It's almost October. Who would believe such humidity at
this time of year? Let's crank this baby up." Lorrie flipped
switches until the car's air conditioning blasted full force.

"Amen to that." The words seemed to be the extent of Aunt

Rita's religiosity. "I'm so used to being cold in the diner air conditioning that I can't take the heat when I come outside."

Angela smiled. "If I could only soak up the heat to take back to Minnesota."

At the shaded gravesite, Angela hugged her grandmother long and hard, silently sharing her pain. Holding her close couldn't fill the emptiness of losing one's husband, but it said, "I understand." This sisterhood of widows was a club no one wanted to join.

Reluctantly, Angela let go. There would be time later for more hugs and certainly tears. But in the welcoming privacy of Grandma's home. Angela turned and paid her condolences to Raymond's family, leaving Aunt Rita deep in conversation with one of Raymond's daughters.

Lorrie nudged Angela. "It's too hot. Let's go." Without waiting for Angela to respond, Lorrie headed toward the car.

Angela caught up and glimpsed tear streaks on Lorrie's face where her makeup had run. "Lorrie, you're crying." When was the last time she had seen Lorrie cry? She couldn't remember. "You must've been close to Raymond."

"No, not at all." Lorrie waved her off and blew her nose. "I'll try to stop by Grandma's tomorrow."

What was she not saying? Had something upset her? "Are you okay?"

"Yeah, sure. I'll start the car."

When Aunt Rita finally rejoined them, they headed back to the church.

Aunt Rita switched to the front seat beside Lorrie. "Now, got your luggage, Angie? You're sure the Kellers are taking you and Grandma Em home?"

Grandma Em? Why would her own daughter always call her mother Grandma Em? Somehow, Angela could never add

'Em' to Grandma's name. A simple Grandma seemed more respectful.

"Yes," Angela said. "And they have a van to carry any plants or flowers she decides to keep."

"Good, because we won't have time to come back for hours if they don't. I've got to get changed and show up for the dinner crowd. Good night for tips. We'd better run. It's a half-hour to Beaumont Springs." Aunt Rita slammed the car door.

Angela stood in the middle of her grandmother's living room, holding a peace lily. "Where shall I put the plant?"

She scanned the room. A towel draped across the top of a recliner signaled what must have been Raymond's favorite chair—and his use of hair oil. Angela smiled. Her grandmother, always prudent.

Grandma lifted an aging rhododendron from the lamp table. "This needs to go to the sun porch. Let's put the lily here."

Each plant found a new home. "How about a quick nap for you?" Angela drew her grandmother to her bedroom and lowered the shade.

"It's almost three o'clock. I never sleep in the daytime." But she sat on the edge of the bed. "Maybe I'll just put my feet up." Angela untied her shoes. "Goodness! You'll spoil me."

"I wish I could." She kissed Grandma's forehead and watched her lie back, shoulders relaxed.

Just as Angela remembered, the refrigerator was always stocked with sweet tea. She poured a glass and wandered to the front porch. Angela tested the old swing. It still creaked. Just like when she was a child, swinging in it with Lorrie. A climbing rose on one side and vines on the other offered seclusion but left enough open space for the late afternoon breeze. Angela turned and settled in a tiny tucked-away daybed, intending to close her eyes for only a moment.

A shrill ring jolted her awake.

As Angela pushed the screen open, her grandmother held out the phone. "It's for you."

"Thank you." Everything blurred as Angela left the bright sunshine and her eyes adjusted to the dim hall light inside. She seated herself and picked up the telephone.

"Angie. Hey, Angie-baby!"

42

"Remember when I used to call you that, Angie?"

"Who is this?"

"It's Harrison Connor! Your old high school sweetheart."

Angela stumbled onto the bench next to the telephone. Her stomach lurched.

"Missed you at the high school reunion last month."

"Harrison, I just lost my husband."

"Oh, yeah, that's what the gang said. Hey Angie, I'm all kinds of sorry about that. Man, that's rough."

Did he expect her to respond?

"Say, heard you were here for a funeral. I thought maybe you and I could get together. You know, have a couple of drinks, talk 'bout old times."

Or old sins? Angela shook her head. "I'm sorry, it's just not possible."

"Well, I thought, I mean, you're here and I'm here. Might s'well get t'gether."

Did he slur his last words?

"No, thank you. I'd like to spend as much time as possible with my grandmother before I go back."

"Well, if you change your mind—"

"Sorry, Harrison. I won't."

Angela braced her back against the wall. Acid rose in her mouth, along with unwanted memories.

Harrison Connor from high school. Good-looking, popular, rich. She hadn't even been on his radar. Not until the summer after her senior year. Her Aunt Rita had encouraged her to take a job at the diner where she worked. The job and tips brought a windfall of spending money, and she spent every penny on herself. Clothes, makeup, and a new self-confidence morphed her into a different person—pursued by Harrison. She ran with a crowd whose sole ambition was to have fun. Guys flirted with her. Girls envied her. The new-found attention intoxicated her.

Before college started in the fall, Harrison took her to an unchaperoned party at a remote cabin. He kept saying, "tonight's the night." What did he mean? Did he plan to propose? Her heart fluttered. Marriage? At her young age? The thought took her breath away.

With no adults present, the party continued late. The drinking didn't shock her because their outings revolved around drinking. What shocked her was Harrison's behavior. His swagger. His lopsided grin. Then he grabbed her arm.

"Bedroom's open!"

Was he serious? She froze in fear. He clutched her around the waist. She twisted and pushed against him. Thrown off-balance, he tripped over a carton of empty bottles. She broke free. Everyone laughed and surrounded Harrison, helping him, falling against him.

Angela raced through a side door. Dodging cars parked in the yard, she reached the highway. A blessed road sign halted her. "Abbeyville, three miles." Her grandmother's house. She could make it. She ran on the berm, staying in shadows. Bushes and briars tore her clothes. One of her slippers came off and stuck in mud. She jerked it free and tugged on the dirty slipper. Three miles seemed like thirty miles. Finally she staggered, out of breath, up the front porch and pounded on the door. When her grandmother unlocked it, Angela fell into her arms. Then she sobbed out the entire story.

Not the story told in Beaumont Springs.

"Angie?" Her grandmother snapped her out of her reverie when she stepped into the hall. "Is it too early for supper? Why, what's wrong? You're crying?"

"That was Harrison Connor on the phone."

"Who? You don't mean that boy from high school—"

"Yes, the one that spread all the gossip."

"Well, of all the nerve. He's got you all upset. You're okay now. Go wash up and let's eat. You'll feel better."

Her grandmother ushered Angela into the bathroom and picked up an ice cream pail full of water. "Let me get this out of your way. When I take a shower, I always catch the cold water and save it to water my flowers. You'd be surprised how long it takes for the hot water to kick in." She lifted the pail higher. "A gallon every time. Gotta save on that water bill whenever I can."

"I ... guess so." Poverty and penny-pinching had disappeared from her life after Angela's marriage, shrugged off as a thing of the past. She never dreamed of worry about electric, heat, or water bills. Now that could change depending on her business.

Angela felt better after splashing water on her face and lathering her hands with her grandmother's homemade soap.

She sat down to a table laden with all the typical foods

provided for grieving families by a loving church. Her grand-mother blessed their meal.

"Angie, did you take a nap, too?"

"Didn't mean to. But yes, I fell asleep."

"You're probably worn out after your trip." Her grand-mother paused. "Do you want to talk about that monster who called you earlier?"

Angela laughed at the imagery. "Maybe I'm overreacting. He was just being the typical Harrison. But I feel so—"

"So what?"

"Ashamed. Dirty. Guilty. The way I behaved after high school ... I brought it on myself."

"Children do stupid things sometimes. You have children. You know how they act."

"Yes, they made their mistakes." And still may. Angela's thoughts flittered to her two unmarried children. "But who wouldn't believe Harrison's version of what happened?"

"Enough people heard your story. There were enough inci-dents, and his taking advantage of other girls, to validate your version." Her grandmother relaxed in her chair. "Remember what the Apostle Paul said about himself? 'I am the chief of all sinners,' and at another place he talked about forgetting what is past and pressing on. Angie, what happened, happened. All we can do is confess and ask Jesus to forgive any wrongdoing on our part."

Angela shook her head. "My mistakes, that incident ... the self-loathing that came from that night ... lingered with me for years. I blamed myself for the humiliation I endured from the town's gossip. I was so gullible." She straightened her shoulders. "It's hard to forget."

"Remember, every time you relive the past, you make it the present."

"God is so good to me. Why do I choose to wallow in the past?"

"Turn it over to Him." A well-worn hand closed over Angela's. "Look how David struggled in the Psalms. Sometimes we misunderstand what grace is all about."

Angela's other hand touched her heart. "Grace."

"Everything happens for a reason, Angie. Did you ever think if that incident hadn't happened, you may never have wanted to get away? Or gone to a Christian college?"

"Met Todd?" Angela smiled. "Have a wonderful family?"

"A turning point in your life, and you chose the right path."

43

Angela awoke to the sweet song of wrens. She lingered in bed, enjoying the concert. Her grandmother's sheer curtain billowed and fell in the breeze, marking time with the wren's song. She closed her eyes.

Memories of college life swept over her. The Bible study she and her roommate joined. The questions she raised. Know the Lord personally? Know guidance and peace when struggling with the questions of life? Know where they would spend eternity? The assurance of those precepts backed by Bible verses drew her to a campus group. A group showing the alternative to the drinking lifestyle of the young people she had known.

Then she met Todd. He led the group, set an example, and blazed a trail for others to follow. Angela's sophomore year they dated.

And he became the center of her universe.

Angela rolled out of bed. Her hand smoothed and tucked the sheets, as she reveled in her grandmother's embroidered pillowcases trimmed with hand-crocheted lace.

Wisteria

Angela paused at the kitchen door to listen to her grandmother softly humming "Blessed Assurance."

"Good morning, Angie. Have a cup of coffee. I'll have our breakfast ready in a jiffy."

"Can I help?"

"Now don't spoil my fun. How often do I get to wait on my granddaughter?" She cracked eggs into a bowl and saved the shells. Grandma called eggshells black gold. Good for garden compost.

Her grandmother stretched to open cupboard doors, pulling her thin housedress askew and showing a neatly placed patch under her arm. The door slammed shut, but not before revealing bare cupboard shelves.

"Grandma, are you doing okay? Financially, that is?"

"Oh, Land o'Goshen, yes," she said. "The Lord takes good care of me."

"But, I mean, do you have enough food to eat and clothes to wear?" Angela rushed the words in one breath.

"You mean because of the way I live and the fact my dresses aren't the newest import from Paris?" Grandma chuckled until the bib on her apron moved up and down. "Child, when you've done without for most of your life, it's the only way you know how to live. No need to be wasteful."

Still not convinced, Angela stared at the worn vinyl floor and wondered if she should press the issue.

Grandma peeked in the refrigerator. "Angie, would you mind running down to the cellar and fetching a jar of strawberry preserves? I don't like to bring the canning upstairs until the weather gets cooler. You'll find the preserves in the same place as always, on your left, top shelf."

"Sure, I'll get it."

The dankness of the basement was oppressive. Still, it was

249

cool. She and Lorrie had played with dolls there to escape the summer heat. The ceiling was so low Angela instinctively ducked even though it was almost a foot above her head. At the far end of the basement was a small, dark room her grand-mother called the root cellar. The familiar clicking sound of a chain being drawn from the ceiling fixture flooded the room with light. No wonder the cabinets were scanty. Row after row of canned fruits and vegetables. And there on the top shelf, jellies and preserves. Fully stocked. Her eyes swept the room. What had seemed only a chore in her childhood now became an astonishing wonder. She stretched for the strawberry preserves and watched the patterned glass jar reflect the light. The ruby chunks and tiny black seeds swirled together in an exquisite pattern.

"Angie? Did you find it?" Grandma's voice drifted from the top of the steps.

"Yes, Grandma." Angela hustled up the stairs.

"Sorry I took so long. Couldn't help staring at your canning. What a beautiful sight."

"Guess I never thought of it that way, but you're right. When it's all finished for the winter, it's a sight to behold."

"I can't believe you're still able to keep up."

"People from church prepare the garden to plant and help me with the picking and putting up." She tilted her head at Angela. "They say they want to learn from a pro. I guess there are a few tricks you need to learn.You have to accommodate for the poor soil we have, add compost to have a good garden. Guard against the insects constantly. The raised beds that Raymond installed made such a difference." She hustled baked oatmeal with raisins to the table.

"Let me help you," Angela said, adding a platter of eggs and sausage to the full breakfast.

Grandma took Angela's hand and bowed her head. "Dear heavenly Father, we praise You for Your bounty and goodness to us. We would be lost without You. Bless my girl, watch over her, and show her the plan You have for the rest of her life. Give her strength to go on without her husband. May You be glorified in all we do. In Jesus' name we ask, amen."

"Thanks, Grandma." Angela picked up her fork. "I love your prayers."

"I pray for you every day, Angie-girl."

Her grandmother poured glasses of orange juice and passed biscuits. "You know, I will miss Raymond so much." Grandma pulled out an embroidered cotton handkerchief and wiped rheumy eyes. "You just went through that. You're so young, and it was so sudden. We haven't talked about Todd yet, have we?"

"No, we haven't."

"Want to tell me a little more about what happened?"

"I do. It seems every time we widows share our stories, we heal a little more."

Grandma patted Angela's hand. Angela briefly described the accident but dwelled on the adjustments and her get-togethers with two other widows. With her Grandmother's sympathetic listening ear Angela felt as though she carried a lighter burden.

They lapsed into silence. Sausage grease congealed on the platter, but neither of them seemed inclined to deal with the dishes or leftover food.

Grandma shifted her weight. "Raymond lost his wife five years before we married. He had that nice pension from the chemical company, invested well over the years, so he told me. I wouldn't know about those things. Raymond did a good job of putting everything in a trust to take care of me and leave plenty to his children as an inheritance, which is the way it should be.

I found out he's the one who maintained the church building. He left a small trust for the church, too. He wanted to build me a fancy house, but I convinced him I liked living here. So after we married, he moved in with me."

Grandma chuckled. "Rita and Lorrie thought he was penniless. I let them think what they wanted. I'm only telling you because you seem worried about me. Your Aunt Rita and Lorrie know nothing about my affairs. They seem downright ashamed of me, but that's okay. I don't run in the same circles they do." She laughed that cute laugh of hers, "hu-Huum," the last syllable rising to soprano.

"You saw them pat me on the arm yesterday and say, 'you look real nice, Grandma Em,' as if surprised that I owned a nice dress." Grandma's fingers smoothed the pin-tucked trim on her worn short sleeves. "I always dress nice when I go to church. I always honor the Lord. If they would only come to church, and I pray every day they will, they'd see for themselves.

"Well, I don't mean to speak ill of them. Your grandfather died when Rita and your dad were teenagers. Times were hard. Then I married Paul, my second husband, after they had moved out on their own. He only lived three years after we married. This is his house. He had no children and left it to me, bless his heart. He died exactly one year after your mother. If I hadn't been so busy nursing him, I would've taken you and Lorrie in. But Rita seemed to have a purpose when you two went to live with her. Your dad, Cary, liked the arrangement. I guess they thought I was too old for the responsibility. At least I had you and Lorrie every summer. Lots of wonderful memories."

"Yes, there are." And some of them were still visible in the kitchen. Like the aged Donald Duck cookie jar always filled with treats. The red and white canisters her grandmother carefully cleaned when she and Lorrie got sloppy making cookies.

"I never expected to marry a third time, but Raymond was such a sweet man. He became a good friend."

"He's the only great-grandfather my children ever knew."

Angela thought of the trips Todd and she had made with their children. More good memories. Without a word, Angela and her grandmother both rose and cleared the table.

"What a breakfast," Angela said. "Let me do the cleanup."

"Let's wash up together."

"Just like we used to do." They laughed like two schoolgirls.

"I'll wash, you dry," Grandma said.

After they finished the clean-up, Angela studied the familiar backyard through the kitchen window. "Grandma, there's a magnolia tree down in the backyard."

"Yes. Malcolm, next door, asked me if it was okay to let it fall in my yard and lay there until he has time to chop it up and cart it off."

"But the leaves are green. Why did he cut it down?"

"In the way. He plans to build a shed back there."

"Wow. Do you know what I have to pay for magnolia leaves?"

"What on earth do you do with magnolia leaves?"

"I use them for fillers in arrangements, and the dried leaves make beautiful wreaths. Do you think he would let me have some leaves?"

"I don't see why not. They're trying to get rid of the tree." Her grandmother hung her apron on the same hook where it had always hung.

"Great. This is like gathering a harvest. Do you have extra trash bags?"

"I do. Let me call Malcolm and let them know what you're doing."

"Oh, Grandma, I hate to run out on you. I'm here to help you."

"Nonsense. Can I help?"

"Oh, I'll just pack a few branches for fresh arrangements then snip off leaves and stack them for wreath making."

"Bring a branch on the back porch, and I'll get to work snipping leaves. You'll need the pruning shears."

"It'll be like old times, you and me working together again."

"I hope the neighbors don't see me, having fun the day after Raymond's funeral."

44

Angela had just returned from shipping the box of fresh magnolia branches to her shop when the screen door slammed. At the squeak of sneakers on the hardwood floor, Angela stepped into the hallway.

"Lorrie." Angela hugged her. "Glad you're here."

Lorrie exhaled shakily. "Me, too."

"Something to eat?" Grandmother called. "We had lunch, but I can get out leftovers. Or coffee?"

"No, I'm fine," Lorrie said. "Well, maybe coffee."

"Will we be more comfortable in the living room with our coffee?" Grandmother said as she filled their cups.

Lorrie planted her elbows on the kitchen table. Strong afternoon sunlight accented her face, blotchy and without a sign of makeup today. "No, what I've got to say, well, I'd rather it be eyeball to eyeball."

"What on earth—" Grandmother said.

"It's about the funeral. The service. I mean the preaching."

Lorrie nervously traced the outline of a red rooster on the

plastic placemat. "I know you took us to church, Grandma Em," Lorrie said. "I told everyone I was a Christian when I wasn't."

Grandma nodded.

"I never confessed my sins, afraid I'd have to stop having fun." She scooted back in her chair. "Ran with the wrong crowd, as you well know." She tilted her head toward her grandmother. "Odd. Some of them are dead now. Car wrecks, drug overdose, alcohol abuse. The ones who survived moved away. They got out of town, out of Beaumont Springs."

Lorrie glanced at Angela then looked away. "After Todd's accident, something happened that I can't explain. Life doesn't go on forever."

Angela flinched.

"I applied for a job with that new company in Fairmont. Customer service. They seemed to think my years as a waitress equipped me for handling people. They were right. I enjoy what I'm doing."

Angela squeezed her arm. "I'm so glad, Lorrie."

"I like my customers, but the people I work with ... would you believe most of them are Christians?" Lorrie glanced at Angela. "I've had a hard time fitting in, felt like an atheist around a bunch of holy rollers, as we used to call them. Their quaint little 'bless you' to everyone, 'I'll be praying for you' conversations, Bible verses on their desk, all rubbed me the wrong way. Until Raymond's funeral."

A smile on Lorrie's face replaced the scowl. The hard lines faded. "The message made me see myself as a phony. I wanted you both to know that late last night I followed Pastor's prayer and confessed my sins. I'm trusting Jesus with every part of my life. All the hard parts I didn't want to admit were there and those parts that didn't work no matter how hard I tried."

Grandma grasped both Lorrie's hands while Angela jumped up and hugged Lorrie's shoulders from behind.

"Dear Father," Grandma bowed her head. "Thank you that Lorrie found her way home. Guard her against Satan's attacks that every new believer encounters. Lead her to a church, a body of believers. Give her help from the Word. In the name of our Savior, amen."

"Grandma Em, I already have the answer to the last part of your prayer." Lorrie sat back. "I've found my church right here in Abbeyville."

"You don't say." Grandmother smiled. "You couldn't make me happier."

"This is too much." Angela dabbed her eyes with her napkin.

"Well, Abbeyville is closer to where I work than where I live now." Lorrie walked to the sink and dumped her coffee. "I'm thinking of moving here, finding an apartment."

"Why not live here?" Grandmother said.

"In your house?"

"Sure. I've got a spare room."

"I don't know."

"Well, give it some thought. I could take care of you."

"I should take care of you, just like you took care of us." Lorrie said. "Maybe this is my chance to do that."

Grandmother smiled at Lorrie. "Angie and I are having a Bible study from the Psalms this afternoon. Can you join us?"

"Sure," Lorrie said.

"Let's go to the living room." Grandma Em shooed Angela and Lorrie ahead of her.

Before sitting, Angela stopped beneath her parents' wedding picture.

Grandmother stopped behind her. "Cary and Esther. You

both look like her. I wasn't a Christian when your dad and your Aunt Rita were born. Named them after movie stars from my day, Cary Grant and Rita Hayworth." Grandma hobbled to her platform rocker, shaking her head as she walked. "Only visited church when the mood struck."

"How did you become a Christian? I don't think you told us."

"It was your mamma, that saint of a young woman. Pulled me into the church in Abbeyville. Your father, Cary, too. That's where I met Paul, my second husband. He was a deacon there. Later told me he had been praying for me since I lost your grandfather. They had one of those tent revivals just like Billy Graham used to do. Cary and I both dedicated our life to Christ. That's what the preachers called it back then. Still feel my heart swelling at the memory of your mother's solo that night, 'Just as I am.'"

"If only she had lived." Lorrie's wistful expression mirrored Angela's.

"We don't know the whys of life. But we know the source of all knowledge." Grandma reached for her Bible. "You'll find a couple more Bibles in that bottom drawer."

"Wait, let me get my notepad." Angela hurried to her room and back, sitting with her favorite purple pen poised.

"Well, isn't that cute," Grandma said. "One of those gel pens, right?"

"Yes, how did you know?"

"Oh, I keep up with the young ones." Her grandmother opened a drawer and pulled out a pink roller ball pen. "I save it for church."

"You're precious." Angela swung one leg under her to get comfortable.

Wisteria

Defying the heat of the day with drawn shades, oscillating fans, and icy drinks, the three pored over Psalm 103 in the cozy living room.

Lorrie left them in the late afternoon.

"Seems all we do is eat." Grandmother laughed as she and Angela headed to the kitchen to pull out leftovers for dinner.

A few minutes later, Aunt Rita breezed into the hall. "Hello, anybody home? Oh, here you are."

"Hello, dear," Grandma said. "Join us for some supper?"

"Don't mind if I do. Can't stay long, though."

Rita arrived dressed for something other than a family dinner. Bright red dominated her color scheme, from her Capris to her sequined T-shirt. She shrugged her designer shoulder bag until it hit the floor like a sack of flour.

Grandma stepped around it, pulled out her chair, and bowed her head with a blessing.

"Would you look at this food? Now there's a casserole for you." Rita dipped a large spoon into chicken and broccoli covered with toasted almonds. "Those gals at church cook better than any restaurant in town."

"They did an amazing job, didn't they?" Angela passed scalloped potatoes to her grandmother.

"I remember when I was in Minnesota for Todd's funeral some lady brought over a casserole." Aunt Rita snickered. "Called it a hot dish. Did you ever hear of such a thing? I wanted to ask if there was anything in it or did she just heat up a dish?"

Angela laughed. "Oh, that's what they call casseroles in

Minnesota. I've been there so long, I've gotten used to their term. I think it's kind of cute."

"Well, it sounded strange to me." Rita mounded a second scoop on her plate.

After they polished off the meal, Angela sliced a pecan pie, her favorite, one of the few things she and Aunt Rita had in common.

"Angie, by any chance did you get a call from an old flame?" Rita's eyes twinkled.

"What are you talking about?"

"Why, Harrison's back in town. Harrison Connor. Walked in the diner day before yesterday."

"Did you mention to Harrison I was coming to the funeral?"

"Well, of course I told him. And I said you might need cheering up."

Angela clenched her jaw. "Aunt Rita, I don't need cheering up, especially from Harrison."

"Now, Angie, don't go gettin' on your high horse. He's quite a guy. I saw nothing wrong with your just chatting with him. You never know—"

"But I do know." Angela said with uncharacteristic intensity. "With his lifestyle, I could never be friends with Harrison."

"Rita." Grandma shook her head.

"Okay, okay." Rita added more whipped cream to her pie. "I guess I'll never understand you. And you said Benji's engaged? When's the date?"

"Yes. Benjamin is engaged. They're talking about a June wedding."

"Nice, a June wedding. So, you two have any plans for tonight?"

Grandma Em refilled their cups as she answered. "Yes. I wish you could join us, Rita. Malcolm and Ella next door invited Angie and me over. We always have a good time making popcorn and playing games."

Angela picked at her pie. "Such good neighbors."

Rita pushed her plate away so fast the fork rattled. Angela caught the eye roll.

"Oh, look at the time. Sorry to eat and run. Meeting the girls."

Angela followed her to the front door. "I'm going to church with Grandma in the morning. Would you like to join us?"

"No, my only day to sleep in. Should I pick you up early in the afternoon and we swing by my place before Lorri takes you to the airport?"

"Sure, Aunt Rita."

"I've found a box of stuff you and Lorrie might like to go through. I invited her over, too."

"What do you mean? What kind of stuff?"

"Oh, things your dad left. Memories, I guess."

"Okay." What could be in the box? Angela watched her aunt gather her bag gingerly, careful of her manicured nails.

Grandma had whisked leftover food into containers. "Take some food home with you."

"No." Aunt Rita frowned and held up her hands. "I won't be home for hours."

Angela followed Aunt Rita to the door and held out her arms. "I love you."

Rita forced a deep chuckle. "Love you, too, honey." She gave Angela a one-arm hug and hustled to her car.

Angela retraced her steps back to the kitchen. "I never know quite what to say to Aunt Rita."

Her grandmother rested her sudsy arms on the old iron sink

and stared out the window. Angela's eyes traced her wrinkles. In the evening light she looked her ninety-three years. "Is Rita really my daughter?"

45

The next afternoon

Angela surveyed the exterior of Aunt Rita's house. Not much had changed on the outside. The single driveway ended at the slanted carport. Stones and rocks still stood in for landscaping.

"Aunt Rita, just look at those beautiful geodes, broken open and sparkling in the sun. I remember Lorrie and me dragging them home. Do you remember that?"

Rita glanced where Angela pointed. "I gave up pulling weeds and just give the rock garden a good spray now and then with herbicides. I'm thinking about having someone dig it up and seed it, make it part of the lawn."

The rocks Angela and Lorrie collected? Angela's heart tugged as she followed her aunt into the kitchen.

"When Lorrie gets here, I'll pop a pizza in the oven. You still drink diet Coke?"

"No, thanks. I'll grab water."

"It's cooler in the living room." She motioned with a glass in her hand where a window air conditioner blocked most of the light.

"Oh, what a relief." A blast of cool air met Angela as she sat on a tight-looped davenport that must have been fifty years old.

"Yes, don't know what I'd do without it. I'd never get to sleep at night." She poured diet Coke over ice. "Don't know how Grandma Em can live without an air conditioner."

"I asked her that, too. She said she's used to it."

"That's the difference between us."

"Well, I guess your circulation changes when you get older. She wore a sweater last night when we went next door."

"A sweater? Yes, I've seen her do that. How was game night?" Rita snickered.

"It was fun." Angela smiled. "We had a plan before we left. You know how Grandma always liked to play Scrabble? I told her we'd play as a team. She did really well. We won."

Rita adjusted the three bracelets on her left arm. "Oh, yeah?"

Even with the noisy air conditioner, they both heard the back screen door slam as Lorrie walked into the kitchen.

Angela jumped up and hugged her sister. "I'm so glad we get to spend more time together."

"Me too, Angie." Lorrie returned the hug then flopped in the nearest chair.

Aunt Rita lifted her glass and laughed. "Get your own, girl. You know where it's at."

"I think I will," Lorrie said. As she stood, she humphed at Angela. "See what I still have to put up with?"

Angela remembered Lorrie and Aunt Rita sparring with each other and changed the subject. "So what's this about a box?"

Aunt Rita cleared the coffee table then reached for a box by the wall. "I cleaned out Cary's apartment years ago." Rita firmly set her glass on her coaster and stood up. "Your dad had this box in his closet. It's been in my attic all these years. I guess I forgot about it. Maybe I wanted to forget about it. It's stuff a person packs away when they lose someone. Pictures of him and your mom, some baby pictures. Why don't you two sort it out and take what you want?"

Lorrie's chin trembled. "I remember Mom." She glanced at Angela. "You were too young."

"I know." Angela swallowed and leaned forward. "And I was nine years old when we lost dad."

Lorrie removed the cardboard top and stared at the framed photo on top. "Look," she said. "They must have taken this when they were dating."

Angela smiled. "They were so young. That chin, the full lips. Doesn't Bethany remind you of our dad?"

"Yeah, I think you're right," Lorrie said.

"And our mom, the tilt of the head. Becca has her build. I can't wait to show these to the kids."

They uncovered an eight-by-ten hand-colored portrait of Lorrie. Lorrie turned it over and pointed to her name and date on the back.

"Wow. I would have been three years old," Lorrie said. "Sorry, I don't see one of you. Things got crazy, I hear, after you were born."

Angela and Lorrie unwrapped a copy of their parents' wedding picture, identical to the framed copy at grandmother's house. A layer of newspapers lay below. Wrapped in the center was something heavy.

"A Bible." Angela touched it with awe.

"You take it Angie. Grandma Em said I need one of those new study Bibles."

"A study Bible?" Rita said.

"Yes." Lorrie ducked her head then looked Rita in the eye. "Aunt Rita, I've become a Christian."

Rita's mouth fell open.

"I know God has forgiven me for what I have done in the past."

Rita scrambled out of her chair and headed for the kitchen. "Ready for that pizza yet?"

"Not yet." Lorrie looked at Angela. "Maybe later after the big meal at Grandma Em's settles."

"Humph." Rita returned with another diet Coke and curled up in her chair.

Angela couldn't help but cry as she held her mother's Bible. "Lorrie, she's waiting for us in heaven," Angela whispered.

"Oh, for Pete's sake." Rita flipped her hand, bracelets clacking together.

"She died from a disease, didn't she?" Lorrie said.

Rita swirled ice in her glass. "A kidney disease. The Staleys all died young."

They had emptied the box and separated the baby pictures. Most were photos of Lorrie, only three of Angela. Little baby eyes stared back. Her eyes. She sat on the floor with everything spread around her trying to re-construct a childhood she was too young to remember. Had she seen these pictures before Todd's death, she would have been delighted. Todd's death and the reality of great loss changed the way she viewed a loss of any sort. How long would the sober side of life dominate her thoughts?

Angela and Lorrie separated their baby pictures, then ran to the photo center to make copies of the snapshots of their mom and dad.

"We might as well head back to Aunt Rita's," Lorrie said. "We have two hours before I need to take you to the airport."

"Let's do. I think she was expecting us back." Angela said as they drove back to Aunt Rita's. "Wasn't Grandma delighted to have us both in church this morning?"

"I'd forgotten how much I enjoy Grandma Em's company," Lorrie said. "Lately I've stayed away from her too much. Just got together on Christmas and holidays."

"Why did you do that?"

"Guilt."

Angela nodded.

"You know that look she gives you?" Lorrie pulled past the geodes as far as she could into the driveway and stopped behind Aunt Rita's car. "Combination of sad and disappointed?"

"I remember. Got my share of those."

"Really? You were everyone's favorite, the perfect child. Well, except for that time after you graduated from high school."

Angela frowned and pushed through Rita's flimsy back door.

"Aunt Rita?" Lorrie sat with her back to the window, same chair she always took. "What do you think about me moving in with Grandma Em?"

"Well, what won't you do next?" Rita looked over her glasses at Lorrie. "What if she gets sick? Would you still stay with her?"

Lorrie swallowed. "I hadn't thought that far ahead. But if I can keep her out of the nursing home, I'd be willing to try."

Ginny Graham

"Good," Rita said, "I'm no nurse. It was hard enough raising two little girls."

"Have we told you how very thankful we are that you gave us a home?" Angela said.

"Only about a ka-gillion times." Aunt Rita brushed off the sentiment like flicking a fly from the pizza she was popping into the oven. "Well, we made it, didn't we? Cary was good about taking care of the financial end. We were poor but had plenty to eat. Your dad loved you. Just couldn't get over losing Esther."

Her dad. Angela recalled the man who seemed a stranger. So few were his visits to them. "I guess." Angela forced the words out but couldn't stop the frown.

"Whatta you mean, you guess?"

"I don't know. I lost my husband. I'm still trying to stay involved in my children's lives. I don't want them to lose a mother as well."

"It's different for men. 'Specially as young as Cary. What's a man know about little girls?"

Angela smoldered inside. They were his little girls. They needed love. Why did Aunt Rita always defend him?

Aunt Rita plopped napkins on the table. "Well, Lorrie, it's a free place to live."

"Aunt Rita! I would pay Grandma Em."

"She could probably use your help with the bills. Can't imagine how she makes it. But she never complains."

Angela looked out the window to hide a half-smile. The geodes in the backyard sparkled, smiling back at Angela.

46

Northgate—the following Tuesday

A ngela arrived early at the flower shop determined to prep and stage as many items as possible from her antiques and collectibles she had purchased the week before. Her excitement from the flea market "finds" had cooled. Had that been just a week ago?

She fought to organize her thoughts. "Rosa, if you'll put together wreaths with the magnolia leaves, I'll refill the displays."

"Wreaths?"

"I brought magnolia leaves from my grandmother's yard." Angela opened the carton she had shipped second-day air. "I'll take some home to dry in the sun this week."

Angela bent back the carton flaps and halted. "What's this?"

She found a white envelope taped inside one flap with her name written in her grandmother's familiar script. "Excuse me, coffee break time. I just have to read this." When did Grandma have time to open and reseal the box?

Angela slit open the letter as she walked to the break table. She smiled. How she missed her grandmother already. The envelope contained a hastily scrawled note, "I know travel is expensive. It was so good to see you. Remember how much I love you, Angie." Ten one-hundred-dollar bills were tucked inside the note.

Angela covered her mouth to stop a sob.

"Bad news?"

Angela recovered and shook her head. "No. Just a sweeter-than-life grandma." Did her grandmother know what a chance she had taken putting cash in a shipping box? No matter. Her heart was in the right place.

Rosa touched the leaves. "They're nicer than leaves from our supplier. What did you have in mind?"

"A thick border of magnolia leaves, stuck into the foam, ends pointed out around the perimeter." Angela marshaled her thoughts and placed a few leaves around a wreath form. "Add moss to cover the styrofoam, fillers, and hydrangea blooms. I think we have a good supply of them."

"I'll get the glue gun," Rosa said.

Rosa turned out wreaths with such intensity that, when customers walked in, they seemed more interested in watching Rosa work than in placing their order. Several walked out with a magnolia wreath among their purchases. Rosa stacked and stored the finished wreaths in record time, but she hardly spoke a word.

"What do you think?" Angela called from the back room and held up a child's toy wagon. "Add succulents to it, a tiny bridge, make it a fairy garden?"

"Sure, nice," Rosa said.

Angela couldn't understand Rosa's reticence. "Was it hard for you last week with me gone?"

She clipped her words. "No." Rosa said too hastily. "Everything ran smoothly. Great working with Bethany."

"Rosa, you seem edgy."

She shook her head. "Roberto, at school."

"What do you mean?"

"They tease him. He's different. Hispanic." Rosa completed a new order. "In Arizona we weren't minorities."

"Don't several boys in his class go to our church?"

"Yes, Jaxson for one." Rosa stopped and scrunched her face. "He's the ringleader."

"Oh, dear. Have you talked to his teacher?"

Rosa shook her head and kept her attention on a transparent silk bow she coaxing around a vase.

Angela spun Rosa around. "You need to talk to his teacher."

The phone interrupted Angela. Rosa leaped to answer it.

Frustrated but unsure how to help Rosa, Angela added the little wagon, still empty, to a display. She could fill it later. Rosa would talk when she was ready. In the meantime, Angela needed to move pots indoors before winter. A brisk wind hurried her efforts.

"Can I help you with that?" Lilly hurried along the sidewalk, a light jacket flapping around her hips. "At least I can open the door for you."

"Hi, Lilly. Thank you." Angela pulled the pot against her chest, thankful that her apron could catch the grit and grime.

Lilly walked in front of her, gazing at the displays. "Never been in here before. Wow."

"Then let me give you a tour." Angela noticed her frown.

"Naw, what would I do with it if I found something I liked?

271

Especially antiques." Lilly squinted at a kerosene lamp. "Anything else I can help you with? Ain't doing much."

"Thank you, no. Can't think of anything."

With a wave of her hand, Lilly retraced her steps to the front door.

"Oh, wait," Angela said. "Something I need to pick up. Would you like to ride along with me?"

"Sure."

"It's a lamppost. If I had someone sitting in the van to steady it, the globes wouldn't have to be removed. It's just across town at Olaf's."

"Olaf's?" Lilly flung the words over her shoulder. "You couldn't drag me to Olaf's with a log chain."

47

"What was that all about?" Angela said. "I don't know." Rosa's puzzled look met Angela's. "Lilly's a peculiar one."

"That she is."

A retired woman in a jogging suit whom Angela recognized as a former clerk in the Save-Mor walked in, her eyes searching.

"May I help you?" Angela said.

Playful blue eyes met hers. "I was over at Gwen's house," she said. "How do you do it?"

"Do what?"

"The decorating. Could you repeat that look at my house?"

"To be honest," Angela said, "I don't know. At Gwen's house, everything fell into place."

"Well, would you be willing to try?"

"Of course." Angela made an appointment with her for Thursday evening.

While Rosa sat with a bride-to-be planning her flowers, Angela wandered to her office to update her calendar.

"Hi!"

Angela jumped, sending vendor orders to the floor. Her insurance agent, Kent Hargrove, filled the doorway of her office.

"Kent, I didn't hear you come in."

"Sorry. Didn't mean to startle you." He beamed at her. "Mind if I sit down?" He wiggled into the cramped space. "Saw you sitting back here all alone."

"I was thinking of calling you."

Kent sat up straight. "You were?"

Angela gestured to her shop. "Have you seen the new line, my new inventory? I'm wondering if my insurance coverage should reflect the change."

"Absolutely." Kent created a ceremony of removing his jacket and draping it over his chair. "If you'll give me an inventory list with prices, my camera's in the car. I'll make a few notes and update your policy."

"I'll copy the inventory list I just gave my accountant."

Kent snapped photos while Angela juggled the phone and walk-in customers.

"Won't take long." Kent held up his notes.

"Don't forget your jacket."

Before long, the shop filled with people. For one glorious hour, shoppers overwhelmed them. When the hubbub abated, Angela reached for an empty vase to start a phone order. She froze like a statue at the scent of Drakkar.

"Excuse me?"

Angela took a deep breath and tried to smile at a contrite young man at the counter.

"How may I help you?" she said.

"Do you have flowers that say, 'I was a jerk'?"

"I've heard of that dilemma, and we have just the solution."

His eyes lit up when Angela brought out a small vase of apricot roses.

As suddenly as they came, everyone disappeared, leaving Angela with her thoughts and the memory of Drakkar cologne. She retreated to the restroom and leaned her head against the closed door. "How long, Lord?" she whispered. "How long will memories stab me?" A tear was her only answer.

"The water's hot," Rosa called.

Cloistered in her office, Angela gratefully sipped tea and checked emails. A cozy office, hot tea, and soft music put her in a world of her own. She closed her eyes.

"Afternoon, Angela."

Had she missed the bell again? She looked up. Kent was back. He dropped his jacket on the back of the side chair and adjusted the cuffs on his long-sleeved shirt. "Ah, that feels better."

He opened his briefcase with a flourish. "Here you go."

Angela glanced at her watch. "That was fast. It's only been two hours."

"No appointments this afternoon, and it's important that you have adequate coverage." Kent pointed to the paperwork and explained the basis for the additional charges.

"Yes, I agree," Angela said. "Everything looks in order."

"Here's a pen."

"Thank you." She quickly signed each line flagged with a sticky note arrow.

Angela accepted the copy Kent held out to her, set it aside, and picked up her schedule. "Again, thank you, Kent."

"My pleasure." Kent lowered his voice. "Angela, I just wanted to say I'm really sorry about your loss, losing Todd. My wife's been gone two years now."

"I remember, Kent. I'm so sorry. It's hard, isn't it?"

"Well, yes, it was. She was the only gal I ever dated." He sat up straight, sucked in his slightly bulging middle. "You see, I want to meet others now. But I don't really know how to go about it. How do you start over at my age?"

Angela shrugged and managed a tight smile.

"Angela, if you ever need someone to talk to, or maybe run out to dinner with, would you call me?"

"I have my children, my church, the shop. My life is rather full."

"I know, I know. But before they start calling you, I want you to know how I feel."

"They?"

"Angela," he attempted a coy look with one eyebrow raised. "You know you're a beautiful woman. Don't worry, you'll have men calling you."

Every muscle in Angela's body stiffened. "Kent. I just lost Todd. It seems like yesterday to me. How can you even suggest such a thing?"

"Sorry, didn't mean to upset you. You know I'd never do anything like that." Kent stuffed his briefcase. Apologizing profusely, he grabbed his jacket and left.

Angela dumped her cold cup of tea and refilled her cup. The hot water dispenser wasn't the only thing steaming.

"There you are," Rosa said.

"Do I have a sign on my back?" Turning, Angela picked up an order and began assembling it. She gritted her teeth and recounted Kent's visit.

When she finished, Rosa's eyes flashed. "Patan, qué insensible."

"What?"

"Sorry. The rat, insensitive."

"I feel so ... I don't know how to describe it ... violated."

Angela stabbed a firm stalk into the wet Styrofoam mixture. "I'm a married woman." Another stalk. "Well, okay, I was a married woman until a short time ago." She slammed her hands to worktable. "I don't want to think about other men yet."

Angela trimmed a spray of alstroemeria and exhaled. "If a widow had said that to me a year ago, I'm not sure I would have understood."

"I know of widows who start dating a few months after losing their husbands."

"Me too. I thought nothing of it."

"Everyone's different. You and Todd were so happy."

"Can't imagine a life with someone else. Maybe that will change someday. I don't know. But right now I'm still trying to accept my new life. I don't need any ... complications."

"I hear you."

"I almost came unglued with Kent. And now I feel guilty. I should have handled it differently. With gentleness. He's a widower."

Rosa assembled sweetheart roses in a bouquet and shrugged. "Maybe it's a wake-up call. Someday you'll laugh over this." She smiled. "But he's right, you know. You might as well prepare yourself."

Angela studied Rosa. "Oh, Rosa, is that what you faced? I'm so sorry. Of course, you've had to deal with things like this."

"Hey, it's life. You sort of expect these encounters."

Suddenly Angela saw Rosa in a new light. The determined, spunky way she carried herself. A woman living alone, like Angela. It was obvious Rosa had developed the street smarts to handle herself.

Rosa shrugged. "You learn to behave differently around men."

Still disturbed, Angela left work early. Exercise. That's what she needed. She hit the sidewalk for a run. Her arms pumped, her feet ate up the ground, and her knees barely felt a jar. She stopped when she reached a park bench on the trail a mile from home. Todd called it their halfway point. She removed Todd's jacket and tied the sleeves around her waist. Drakar. Again? Twice in one day? The scent was getting fainter on the jacket but still there. It was past time to throw it in the laundry. Was she ready to let go of one more connection to Todd? She shook her head, knowing she didn't want to weather another wave of grief. Not after today's experience at the flower shop.

Her ringing cell phone jerked her back to the present. "Benjamin, perfect timing," Angela said. "I'm out for a run."

"Hi Mom, just getting home from work. Tatum's visiting her parents in California. She wanted me to go with her, but I don't have that much vacation. Think I'll just take the Red Eye Friday night and spend the weekend with them."

"I'm glad you'll be getting to know them." Angela tried to picture what Tatum's parents would be like based on the scant comments Tatum had made. "I can't help but wonder about her dad. Do they have a good relationship? I'm sorry. Maybe I shouldn't ask."

"It's okay. I'm still getting to know her." Benjamin paused. "From what she's said, it sounds like Tatum's dad didn't interact with her a lot, working too many hours, as I mentioned before, too busy building a company to build a relationship with his daughter, or his wife."

"So they're her role models for marriage?"

"That about sums it up."

"I'm seeing a new side of Tatum," Angela said. "My heart goes out to her."

"Tatum agreed with me to start pre-marital counseling. She actually suggested Pastor Bailey. He made quite an impression on her. She thinks he's a squared-away guy. He's willing to meet with us once a week in Dresden, where his mother lives. It's halfway between St. John and Northgate. He counsels from a book defining the Christian marriage."

Benjamin mentioned an author Angela recognized. "I'm so glad you're building a foundation for a godly marriage." Angela thought back to Tatum's busy father. "It's so sad Tatum couldn't have had a dad like your dad. He wasn't perfect, but he treated his daughters like gold, didn't he?"

"Yep. And he expected others to treat them like gold. Narrowed the list of guys they dated. I can only hope to have his wisdom someday. Well, if we should have children."

"I'll keep praying."

Angela re-tied the jacket sleeves and another whiff of Drakar reminded her of Todd. If only he were here to counsel Benjamin and Tatum. Had Benjamin gleaned enough wisdom from his dad over the years to carry him into the next phase of his life? To set-up a home that honors Christ? She would trust God that he had.

48

Thursday evening, Angela called on her new client. Not only the woman's husband but also their next-door neighbors eagerly escorted her through the front door. "Is it okay if we watch?" the neighbors said. "Be happy to move furniture or whatever you need."

"That might work well."

As the evening progressed, Angela found she could fly through the rooms. Point. Command. The furniture moved.

"Hey, I like this," Angela said as the men collapsed after moving a piano to three different spots. "I have a crew to allow me to view every option of furniture placement."

At 10 p.m., exhausted, she walked in the door of her home. Phillip came running up the steps toward her.

"Daddy yelled at Mommy."

Angela's stomach tightened. What had she walked into? She expected bumps in the road with blending two families, but ... there was no turning back now. She put her arm around Phillip and proceeded down the stairs. "Phillip, what are you doing up so late?"

"I dunno." Phillip shrugged.

A bedroom door opened. Bethany walked down the hall into the kitchen, her posture stiff. "Hi, Mom. There's a plate of leftovers if you'd like to warm them."

"You shouldn't have, but thank you. I will."

"No trouble. Here's your water, Phillip. Come with me. Bedtime."

Phillip toddled to his room as Angela carried her dinner to the table. She glimpsed Emerson in the living room, TV remote in hand but a blank screen before him.

"Hi Emerson," Angela called across the room. "How was your day?"

Emerson frowned. "Strange day. Had the staff meeting yesterday, just like normal. Today my manager's office is empty. Cleared out."

"Your manager left?"

"He had no choice."

"Oh."

"Yeah. Oh. Guess things exploded after I left last night. I'm just hoping none of the debris lands on me. Lots of gossip but few facts."

"I'm glad you told me, Emerson. I'll be praying."

"Sure, thanks." With a lopsided grin, Emerson looked up. "Who knows, maybe they'll offer me the position."

Returning, Bethany darted a glance his way.

"Hey, I'm sorry. I didn't mean to take out my frustrations on you," Emerson said in a voice soft and low. "Come here, sit down. You've been on your feet all day."

Bethany allowed him to pull her next to him and plopped on the sofa.

49

Monday, October 6th

As previously planned, Angela met Caroline at the front door of Shepherd's Fold.

"Caroline, you look great."

"I don't know why I'm so nervous." She twisted her hands. "Do I look ready to waitress?"

"You do, most appropriate." Angela lifted her briefcase. "I brought my laptop."

Miranda Frandsen unlocked the door. "Come in. How lovely to see you both."

"Hello, Miranda," Angela said. "This is Caroline Chadwick."

"Thank you for coming," Miranda said. "I am so excited, and so are my girls."

"Marge is working but passed along these notes for the residents."

"Oh yes, she's the web guru you were telling me about?"

"Well, no, she's just had experience searching for employees. She sent detailed information about web lookups for job openings."

"That will help. I wish we had more laptops for the ladies to use. However, many are using the library for that purpose. It's helping them to get out more, learn something new." Miranda tapped the sheaf of papers Marge sent. "Be sure to thank Marge for me."

"Will do. We'll see her tonight."

Caroline read aloud the Bible verse murals plastered on the lobby wall. "'I am the good shepherd.' 'I came that they might have life and have it abundantly,' 'I am the gate; whoever enters through me will be saved.'" Caroline pivoted back to Miranda. "You've covered the walls. That must inspire everyone."

"I hope so. Our Savior, He's our comforter and our guide." Miranda smiled and halted.

"Before we go any further I'd like to share our expectations for our volunteers. You've heard this before Angela, but it may be new to Caroline." Miranda paused. "Many well-meaning volunteers from the community breeze in to instruct and offer a myriad of advice and suggestions to our residents. Sometimes, not understanding why no enthusiastic response met them, they soon stopped coming. You see, the residents need to trust their instructors first. To know someone is sincerely interested in them. Most of all, our residents need to learn to hope again. Hope. To believe their future can be bright. Along with you, I want the best for our residents."

"Thank you for sharing that with us," Caroline said and Angela nodded her agreement.

"Now, I'll take you to the dining hall, ladies. Sorry I can't stay. But if you need me, my office is right across the hall."

Angela fell into step beside Miranda.

"Elise is here," Miranda said as she opened her office door. "Remember her? Austin and Bella's mom?"

"I didn't know her name, but I remember her." How could Angela forget the young mother who introduced Tatum to a newborn baby?

Miranda lowered her voice. "Elise's husband did an about-face, and they're back together as a family. He encourages her to volunteer with us. She's in charge of the nursery this afternoon."

A loud wail from beyond the half-door to the nursery stopped them. Angela peeked in. "Hello, Elise. Is that Bella?"

Elise looked up from diapering an angry, squirming three-month-old. "Hi! Yes, it's time to eat, and Bella has no patience."

Bella, the loudest voice of all.

The sound of a piano met them before they reached the dining hall.

"Scott Joplin?" Caroline said. "Someone's playing ragtime."

Lilly looked up, and the notes to a jerky rendition of "The Entertainer" crashed.

"Lilly, I didn't know you played the piano." Angela rushed toward her.

Lilly stood up and frowned. "Used to. Mom taught me chords. I play mostly by ear." She crossed her arms, gestured at the stack of hymnals on top of the old upright piano. "Can't seem to get the hang of playing hymns, though."

"I'm sure you could pick it up quickly," Caroline said to Lilly as Lilly retreated hastily into the kitchen.

Angela pulled a table to the front. "Hello, ladies."

Several residents milled around the dining hall, a study in wariness mixed with curiosity. Angela took a deep breath, plugged in her computer, and set her case aside.

"Would you like coffee?" Lilly called.

Angela placed her water bottle on the table and noticed Lilly sizing up Caroline from head to toe. "Yes, please. How about you, Caroline?"

"Yes, thank you. Can I help you carry them?" Caroline said.

"Sure." Lilly frowned.

"Hi, my name's Caroline."

"Hi. Lilly." Lilly turned and hit the handle on a large coffee pot. "Black okay? I know that's what Angela drinks."

"Yes." Caroline reached for both cups, but Lilly was faster and snatched a cup for Angela.

"Got it," Lilly said. She passed Caroline and marched to Angela's table in the front of the room.

"Thank you, Lilly." Angela took a sip and counted seven women finding places in the front two rows. "One more coming, is that right?"

"We're just waiting for Peyton," Lilly said with authority.

A young woman rushed into the room carrying a notebook.

"You must be Peyton." Angela smiled.

The young woman with dark circles under her eyes nodded. "Hi."

"Okay if I open with a word of prayer?" Angela waited until heads bowed or nodded. She kept the prayer short.

Caroline, wearing a white shirt and black slacks, stood. "How many of you have worked in a coffee shop or a restaurant?"

Two women raised their hands.

Lilly rolled her eyes and met Angela's glance.

"So have I." Caroline raised her hand in a comradely manner. "Let's go over a few points." Caroline spoke of importance of sanitation, then demonstrated a simple table setting. No matter how dressed-down Caroline tried to be, she looked like a supermodel as she walked back and forth carrying a loaded tray giving hints and instructions.

Angela slipped into the kitchen to assemble snacks. She noticed the resident's intent faces following Caroline's twenty-minute talk.

When Caroline finished speaking, Angela called from the kitchen. "Let's take a break."

While Peyton and Lilly haggled over what hummus was, Angela's gaze scanned the women who gathered. Would Angela be able to lift these women's sights above the immediate? Would they learn to believe in themselves again?

Caroline volunteered to clean up the kitchen while Angela made her way to the front.

"Time's up. Bring your food along if you're not finished." Angela waited while the group reassembled.

"Now, what type of job interests you?"

"CEO," Lilly said and grinned at the person sitting next to her.

"There's nothing wrong with that, Lilly." Angela clamped her lips together to hide a smile. "If you have experience in management, the educational credentials required, the skill to run a company, and get along well with people, I encourage you in that pursuit."

Lilly scowled at Angela.

"Anyone else?"

A young woman who introduced herself as Jasmine raised her hand. "I'd like to—" she swallowed. "Be a nurse. Someday."

Angela smiled. "My daughter wants the same thing. She's working as a medical aide this summer. Minnesota offers a short course to qualify you as a personal care assistant. Have you applied for your PCA training?"

She nodded. "That's where they said I needed to start. Miranda helped me apply."

"That's excellent, Jasmine."

A young girl with a purple swath of hair hanging limply over one eye sat up straight. "I want to do hair."

"Do you enjoy working with other people's hair?"

"Sure, a fun thing to do. Cut and color hair all day."

"Maybe you could ask for a few volunteers and practice?" Angela said. "Just remember, most hairdressers don't have paid benefits."

Blank stares met Angela. "Many hairdressers have no employer but are under contract to the shop where they work," Angela explained. "In other words, they are their own small business. No benefits like vacation, paid time off, or contributions for retirement."

"No vacation?" The wannabe hairdresser gasped.

"Depends on the working arrangement you make with that shop. If a shop contracts you for your services, then you are a sub-contractor. They don't pay you for time off. So think about your future, even retirement at your young age. Ask questions. Find out if you are an employee of the shop and what benefits the shop offers. Or, are you under contract to the shop."

A neighbor elbowed the purple-hair-swath-lady, and everyone laughed.

"My occupation presents the same shortcomings," Angela said. "As a small-business owner, you're the one responsible for setting aside money for your time off and for your retirement." Angela flinched and hoped no one noticed.

Peyton raised her hand. "I want to finish college and get a degree in marketing."

"Did Miranda show you the applications, Peyton?"

"We're working on it. Just been here a week."

"I'll be interested in hearing how it's going." Angela paused and smiled at Peyton.

"Let's talk about your interview." Angela touched on the importance of making a good first impression. The value of eagerness and self-confidence.

"What if you don't feel confident?" blurted out Lilly.

"Fake it 'til you make it, as my kids say." A couple of smiles but otherwise stolid looks met Angela. That went over well.

Angela inhaled and plunged forward. "Dress the right way for the job you pick. If the job is for plant assembly work, you'll need sturdy clothing and sturdy shoes." Angela motioned to her clothing. "I'm wearing my shop uniform, lavender polo and khakis. Nothing that will get caught in a conveyor belt, right? Caroline modeled waitress clothing. If you're working in an office, business casual. Slacks and shirt, no jeans or T-shirts. Choose sensible heights on shoes because you may do a lot of walking. Have you taken advantage of the clothing donated to the shelter?"

Angela paused as five people raised their hands. This was harder than she thought it would be. Had she been clear? Easy to understand? Had she given too much detail? She felt so inadequate.

"Good. Who has a résumé?" Only one raised her hand. "You'll a yellow pad, pen, and a sample résumé on the table in front of each of you." Angela moved quickly through the room. "You'll see my instructions on top of the résumé." Angela held up a single sheet. "You have permission to use the Shepherd's Fold address and phone number while you are here."

Angela paused. "Don't let gaps in your work history discourage you. You'll have interests, skills, and experience that you may not think will help you, but let's list everything."

Miranda joined Angela and Caroline as they walked

behind the women, offering help. Their eagerness raised Angela's spirits. Maybe her efforts today would have an effect after all.

After a long afternoon, Caroline and Angela packed up.

"I'm going back tomorrow," Caroline said. "Miranda offered her computer to help them type their résumés."

"Fantastic. It's too bad Marge couldn't come."

"At least she agreed to meet us for a bite to eat. I'm afraid she's working too hard."

After their hellos, Angela and Caroline gushed about their experiences at the shelter.

"Gracious." Marge's amused expression brightened her face. "I'll check it out just to see why you two are so excited."

Angela's brows knit. "Well, excited, tempered with a feeling of insecurity that I don't have the training to meet their needs."

"Remember," Caroline said, "we did the best we could. The fact that they took part in the process says a lot."

"Of course, you're right."

"You gave them your time." Marge added. "They must know you didn't have to do that."

They touched on random topics to bring each other up to date. A lone man openly stared at the three of them as he passed and exited the restaurant.

Angela shifted her position and met Caroline's glance. "Any strange encounters with men for the two of you?"

Without naming the person or his position, Angela related her insurance agent's clumsy moves.

"Oh yeah," Caroline drawled, "There's nothing like being

called pretty lady by your butcher as he hands you a package of pork chops."

Angela laughed to hear Caroline mimic the guy who flirted with her.

Marge shook her head. "A Harley guy tried to pick me up. Not sure how he thought I would climb on the back of his motorcycle. Wouldn't I make a fine Harley babe?"

Laughing with friends and realizing she wasn't alone made Angela's experience with Kent seem trivial. It receded into the background as it should.

50

"Saturday. Week's almost finished, Rosa," Angela said. "Tomorrow we rest."

"I'm looking forward to it." Rosa hummed as she pinched back plants and picked up leaves.

"Nice to see you so happy. Anything happen?"

"I did what you suggested, talked with Roberto's teacher." Rosa watered a droopy African violet. "You'll never believe what she said. Seems his teacher minored in Spanish and was about to introduce the language to the classroom. Yesterday she spoke to Roberto in Spanish then asked him to translate to the class. She announced he would help her teach Spanish words each week to the class. Said she depended on him for the correct pronunciation."

"Was he an instant hero?"

"Something like that."

Angela hugged Rosa quickly as the phone rang.

"Angela." Rosa held up the phone. "For you."

Angela shifted the phone to make notes as the request became clear. "Let's schedule that for one evening next week."

Angela finished her conversation and turned to Rosa. "Remember the lady I helped with her decorating? That was a referral. Her next-door neighbor wants their house staged because they're moving."

"How exciting! Things are picking up."

A delivery man sat boxes inside the front door. She held the door open just long enough for him to let another Arctic blast of air into the room.

Rosa caught a ribbon, pulled back a balloon that had taken flight, and shivered. "Won't be long."

"Winter's coming," Angela said as she toted boxes through the shop. Rosa went after the last box, and Angela hurried to remove the large bills and checks from the cash register. "Time for a bank run." She slipped into her office chair and sorted the cash on the desk before her. "We need more ones, two rolls of quarters," Angela mumbled as she flipped open the cash box.

"Angela? Is that you?" A young woman strode through the shop. "Just wanted to tell you the good news." She skirted around Rosa and halted in front of Angela's desk.

"Peyton?" Angela stopped counting bills and scooped the stacks into her cash box.

"You remembered my name!" Peyton glanced at the box just before it closed. "Oh, sorry. I shouldn't be back here."

"Not a problem." Angela rose and pointed Peyton to the worktable. "The deposit can wait. What good news?"

"School. I was late, but they let me jump into some classes and I'm commuting from the shelter. Now I've found a part-time job in the school's cafeteria, and I'll share housing with two other girls. I'm so excited."

"Wonderful. Calls for a celebration if you don't mind watching me work. Coffee? Tea?"

"I'm trying to enjoy tea. Don't want caffeine added to my list of addictions."

"This is my favorite. A custom herbal blend that's become a big seller at Wisteria." Angela pointed to an open bag of colorful tea and filled a cup with hot water. "Which school?"

"U of M."

"But we have several Christian colleges—"

"No openings until January. Just couldn't wait."

"But what about the program Miranda outlined for you?"

"I don't think I need it. Rehab helped."

Angela stacked ribbon spools in their slots and cleared off the worktable. "Will you find a church nearby?"

"I'll try. Depends on whether someone will pick me up. Miranda contacted a friend in Minneapolis."

"Peyton?" Angela waited for her to make eye contact. "I'm praying you find a church family."

"Thanks." Peyton gulped her tea. "Better run. Still some packing to do. Susan's driving me to my new apartment right after church tomorrow. Thanks for encouraging me. I couldn't leave without saying good-bye."

Angela hugged her and watched her dash out the door into the crisp air. "We might as well lock up, Rosa. It's almost five."

Rosa agreed and finished her round with the dust mop.

———

Angela arrived home surprised to find the dining room dimly lit by candlelight. She waited for a joyful announcement, but instead detected a strain in the air as Emerson closed a quick table blessing.

"A guy with a master's degree got the job," Emerson announced.

"I'm sorry."

"I'll probably have to train him." Emerson viciously forked a T-Bone and held it up. "That's why we're celebrating with steak tonight. Trying to keep a positive attitude."

Bethany patted his arm. "You're still the best."

Phillip stabbed a stalk of broccoli and waved it high. "The best, Daddy."

"Thanks, pard." Emerson laughed. "I shouldn't have gotten my hopes up. Too young. Haven't proven myself yet."

"Someday. It'll happen." Bethany smiled.

Emerson nodded but didn't look convinced.

"It'll happen!" Phillip repeated exuberantly.

Angela smiled at Bethany with that private smile only mothers understand. "Thank you for that little blessing I call a grandson."

At that moment, Angela's cell rang. "Hi Marge, are you coming over?"

"Sorry, not tonight. Too much going on. Did you get my email?" Marge said. "Another website for job openings?"

"I did, thank you. Monday afternoon I plan to hold another class at the shelter. I can't believe the response I'm getting. Still, I'm disappointed that one opted out of the program and started school at the U."

"Sounds like she's motivated. She'll be fine."

"I suppose. But she's going to the University, not the environment we wanted for someone just out of rehab. So many temptations."

"Hey, I went to the U, and I turned out okay." Marge snickered.

"Yes, you turned out just fine," Angela said.

"Caroline told me she's giving piano lessons at the shelter," Marge said.

"Awesome! I didn't know that."

"Angela, you always get so excited when we talk about the shelter."

"That's because these women have a way of grabbing your heart."

51

Friday, November 28th

Another month slipped by, but Angela hardly noticed. She lay in bed and tried to remember snuggling with Todd. Nothing warm and cozy about a single body in a king-sized bed. She stretched and opened her eyes. A glow outside competed with the darkness. Every Minnesotan knew what that meant. 'Scattering of light' was the official term. Like a child at Christmas, she pulled on her robe and ran to the window seat. Snow-glow! It transformed bushes into sparkling mounds. Frosted trees became the stuff of a fairyland and the sky was so luminescent that she didn't need to turn on any outdoor lights to enjoy the beauty.

She took her time getting ready for work, waiting for the snowplows to do their job.

She had just flipped light switches in the shop when the telephone rang.

"Angela, this is Trudy. You remember the fundraiser is tomorrow night, right?"

Angela's heart somersaulted then dove to her knees.

"No one thought of table decorations." Trudy paused. "I'm so new at this."

"Always my responsibility the past two years," Angela said. "I can't believe I forgot," Angela said.

"Well, you can't remember everything."

"Let me see what I can come up with. I'll call you back."

"Are you sure? Because we could try something different this year."

Angela reassured Trudy and hung up the phone. She hastily surveyed her flowers, with an eye on economy. She had enough chrysanthemums in the case to put a bud vase on each table. No, that would look tacky. The centerpiece and decorations for the stage were her contribution each year. Her name as a florist was on the line. She picked up the phone, determined to find a solution.

Soon she had Trudy on the phone again. "Will a potted plant on each table be okay? Mostly potted azaleas and kalanchoes in pinks. I hope it doesn't clash with your colors."

"Pink is our color!" Trudy said. "Pink and silver."

Angela hung up the phone with ideas and anxiety churning in her head. She snagged Rosa as soon as she came in for her late shift.

"Rosa, I forgot about the fundraiser for the shelter." Angela ran a jerky hand through her hair. "It's tomorrow night."

"Uff da!" Rosa said.

Even in her agitated state, Angela had to smile at Rosa's adoption of the Norwegian vernacular. "No worries, Brogger's has an overstock of potted plants that I will gladly take off their hands. We can put a plant on each table and auction them off at the end."

"Great solution. No vases, no flowers to arrange."

"The only wrinkle is I have to drive to North Minneapolis to pick them up this afternoon. Will you be okay?"

"We'll make it work."

The next morning Angela warmed the van for fifteen minutes before loading the plants. She blanket-wrapped tall ferns and added pink balloons to decorate the stage where the auction would take place.

"I don't think we've ever stuffed this many balloons in the van." Rosa laughed.

Angela smiled at the bubble-gum colored clouds floating in the back of the van.

Arriving at the local Lion's Club, Angela recognized several volunteers working with Miranda. Everyone helped Angela unload the van. Soon silver tablecloths with silver sprinkles down the middle came to life with pink blooming plants.

"Beautiful flowers," Miranda said. "How are you doing today?"

Angela's eyes smarted.

Miranda hugged her. "Just remember, you're also on my prayer list—" Miranda cut her words short with a deep breath.

Angela stepped back. "What's wrong?"

Miranda paused then chuckled. "For a seventy-seven-year-old woman, nothing. Nothing at all. Be sure to join us tonight."

Angela paced her bedroom floor. What about the gala? She had been so focused on the centerpieces that she'd forgotten what the evening actually entailed. It was more than a fundraising auction—it was also a banquet and gala. She and Todd had attended every year. Her dress, purchased last year at a clearance sale, waited in a clothes bag. But how could she go now? Without Todd? She argued with herself for fifteen minutes then pulled the emerald dress from the closet and flung it across the bed. Bits of glitter caught rays from the setting sun. Their sparkle gave her courage. She could envision Todd looking at her with his slow smile. "Angel, you'll look beautiful," he would have said. With fresh resolve, Angela decided, she would go. She would go with Todd.

A quote from one of the many books for widows she had read came to mind. "Are you hanging on to your fifty percent of a marriage contract, which is null and void?" Although those words still shocked her, she said aloud, "Yes, I am. It's a comfort to pretend. I will go to the banquet with Todd just as I've done every year." Thank goodness Bethany and her family were visiting Emerson's parents in Wisconsin for the weekend. No one could hear Angela's musings.

After she showered, she continued her conversation, forgetting her resolution never to talk to Todd. She dried and scrunched her hair, remembering how Todd had made every outing a special event. She arranged most of her hair on top of her head, letting the balance cascade over her right shoulder. Taking her time with her makeup, she could almost hear Todd's sweet comments. "There's my angel face."

Angela slipped into her dress, searched for just the right jewelry, and passed Todd's ties still hanging in the armoire. Ties forgotten during last summer's purge of Todd's clothing hung like glistening flags.

The rest of his things could go, but not his ties. She grabbed one with just a touch of emerald, placed it on the side of the bed, and gently smoothed the silky surface.

"Now you'll match me." She breathed a sigh.

Angela continued her illusion as she drove, parked her car, and found her way to the banquet room. She wasn't alone. Todd was with her. The delicious click of her high heels reminded her of their outings in the past. She opened the door and removed her coat. Heads turned her way. Lifted eyebrows and surprised expressions bordered on shock. Suddenly she realized how she must look to others.

"Angela, wow, you look great." Trudy Bauer reached her side and tilted her birdlike head.

"Thank you," Angela said and drew a sharp breath. How would she ever get through this evening? She shouldn't have come. It was too soon to attend a gala affair dressed to the nines. Almost like celebrating.

"We have one extra chair at our table," Trudy said. "Would you like to sit with us? Just like last year?" She guided Angela to a table below the stage.

Ironic. Trudy, who spoke to her dead father every day. Exactly as Angela had done with Todd today. Angela realized it was time to put aside her animosity for Trudy and be thankful for the friendship Trudy offered. We all have our quirks. Trudy had shown a good heart by donating her time for the gala.

Trudy's husband, Arnie, stood. "Hi, Angela. Join us?"

He pointed to the two extra chairs next to him.

Trudy took over. "Let's see, that chair is for Arnie's mom. We'll put you next to her and beside our new neighbors, Jeremy and Monica." Trudy bubbled and spoke to a couple already seated. "This is Angela. She owns the flower shop. You know, Wisteria Floral?"

"No, I'm sorry, I don't," Monica said and turned to Angela. "We're so new we don't know anyone except Trudy and Arnie and a few people from Jeremy's work."

"Nice to meet you." Angela nodded their way and quickly slipped into the chair. "Thank you for letting me join you."

"Hello!" A man touched the back of the empty chair between Angela and Arnie. He was so close the whiff of his breath mint was nauseating. "Is this seat taken?"

Angela froze. Could the evening get any worse?

Arnie lifted his hand. "Yes, Kent, I'm afraid it is. Sorry. My mother asked us to save her a seat. She should be here any minute."

Angela's insurance agent, Kent Hargrove, hovered over the empty chair, so Angela turned to the new neighbor. "Monica, how long have you lived in Northgate?"

"Three weeks. Jeremy's CEO at Holcomb's."

Angela swallowed hard to keep bile from rising in her throat.

"Oh, wow!" Trudy said. "What a coincidence that you should be seated at the same table. Jeremy took over Todd's old job."

Hot tears stung Angela's eyes, but she managed a smile.

"Oh, you're Todd's wife?" Jeremy said. "I've heard plenty of good things about him. Happy to step into a position with a well-trained staff, thanks to him, I'm sure."

"Thank you." Angela's words squeezed through her throat.

"Let me introduce myself," Kent said, striking up a conversation with Jeremy. Kent stepped behind Angela to shake his hand but returned to the same spot beside Angela until Arnie's mother claimed her chair.

"Oh, let me help you." Kent pulled out the chair, tried to assist, but almost tripped the little old lady as she maneuvered herself and her large bag into her spot. Kent gave up and stood behind Arnie's chair.

Angela noticed Arnie fighting a smile.

Several people who had worked with Todd stopped and said a few words to Angela.

"Angela, so nice to see you," said the wife of Todd's former CFO. "You must come over for dinner sometime. How are your children?"

Dinner? Previous years they had been together continually. With Todd gone, she had dropped off their radar. But that was only natural. Their friendship no longer held her interest. Angela answered and asked appropriate questions as more people crowded forward. Everyone seemed to fairly gush when they spoke to Jeremy and Monica.

"Ladies and gentlemen." The emcee's microphoned voice filled the room.

All but one person quieted down.

"—Drop-dead gorgeous."

Angela's head swiveled. Kent was staring directly at her. Red in his neck worked its way up to his face like a candy thermometer in hot syrup. He retreated hastily to another table.

Three hours later, Angela faced reality when she entered her dark house. Todd was gone. Why pretend he was still here? She picked up his tie from the foot of the bed and held it to her cheek. The cool satin brought a sob. Time to let go. The tie slithered to the floor as she fell to her knees. "Dear Lord, I have no one. It's just me now. I'm all alone."

"You have Me," the Lord seemed to say to her heart.

Angela spent a long time on her knees that night. She recognized her preoccupation with Todd for what it was—an impediment to healthy healing. But more than that, an insult to God. A lack of trust. How had this happened? How had she crawled backward into this web of despair?

"Dear Lord, he's not coming back," Angela prayed. "Todd is not in the next room. I'm not the mature Christian I thought I was. I have a long, long way to go; but I'm depending on You to see me through." Trust. "I trust you to guide me and teach me on this new path." But what next?

52

On Monday morning, Angela drove back to the hall to pick up the ferns. The wind almost ripped the van door out of her hands. How would she get her ferns back to the shop in one piece? She surveyed the hall remembering her initial elation when she walked in Saturday night. What a train wreck that had been. She couldn't wait to grab her ferns and leave.

Miranda seemed to be everywhere supervising the cleanup. When their paths crossed, she put a soft hand on Angela's arm. "Where's that lovely smile?"

"Miranda, how nice to see you."

Miranda leveled her gaze at Angela. "Do you have to rush off to work?"

"Shop's closed on Mondays." Angela relaxed and smiled.

"We're almost finished here. Can you stop by the shelter for a visit?"

"Love to," Angela said. "Let me run these back to the shop so the plants don't freeze. I'll be over, say, ten o'clock?"

As she headed down the hall at the shelter, a whiff of something cinnamon-y met Angela's nostrils. Someone must have just taken rolls out of the oven. She reached Miranda's door, but Lilly called to her before Angela could open it. A different Lilly, her expression soft.

"Take these to Miss Miranda, okay?" She held out a plate covered with a towel.

"Thank you, I will."

"Come in." Miranda lifted the towel and inhaled deeply. She chuckled and lifted a tea cozy off a ceramic pot. "It's all about staying warm when you live in the North. Would you like tea?"

"Perfect," Angela said and settled at the other end of the sofa.

They nibbled on rolls as Miranda shared recent happenings at the shelter. Miranda decisively sat her cup on the table. "Remember, I'm here for all women—not just women in the shelter," she said.

Angela tried to smile, but her face crumpled. Miranda shifted toward the center of the sofa and put both arms around Angela. It felt so good to be held, to feel Miranda's hand lightly rubbing her back.

"I thought I was healing and helping other widows to heal, but look what I've done."

"What have you done?"

"Saturday night. The way I dressed."

"I thought you looked lovely. Something more must be bothering you."

Angela took the tissues offered. "My frame of mind. That whole day. I was with Todd. I dressed ... I laid out his tie, pretending he would put it on and go with me."

"Why do you suppose you did that?"

Angela rubbed her forehead. "I think a part of me thinks he will come back. He'll need," her voice broke, "his ties. As long as his ties are hanging there, he's not gone." Tears slipped down her face.

"It's easier during the week. I'm at work. There's no time to think about Todd. I'm in denial, aren't I? Back to the denial stage."

"Denial takes away the sharpness of the pain."

Angela continued as though talking to herself. "I'm ashamed to admit I pretended Todd was still with me."

"Do you know where Todd is?"

"Yes, praise God, he's in heaven." Angela leaned back and closed her eyes.

"Based on the testimony he gave right here at this shelter, I believe he is, too." Miranda sighed. It sounded like a sigh of longing.

"And I have heaven to look forward to, meeting Jesus face-to-face, reunited with loved ones." Angela straightened. "Before I went to bed Saturday night, I felt the Lord speaking to my heart. He made it clear He is taking care of me, wants me to lean on Him. That was Saturday. This is Monday. I'm finding it so hard to put into practice. I trust the Lord. I know He listens to me, but it was so easy to tell Todd. There are so many things going on ... I just want Todd."

Miranda patted her hand. "I remember when Roscoe passed away. It was forty-seven-and-a-half years ago."

Forty-seven-and-a-half years. Angela studied the other woman. Would she continue to count by the half-year? "So, you were younger than me?"

"Yes. Two children still at home." Miranda picked up her Bible. "Jesus wants to comfort us. I'll send a few verses home for you to study." Her hand trembled as she thumbed through pages.

Miranda eased her Bible into her lap. "I recently read a message for widows that stated as Christians we are called to be widows. Now, let that soak in. We did not ask for it, would never have chosen it. But widowhood is a calling from God. He has work for us to do. The suffering shapes us. Gives us compassion for others we never possessed before. What else is he calling you to do, Angela?"

"I'm not sure. To make a success of the flower shop? That's my priority now because it's my livelihood."

"That's a notable calling. To work where He has placed you to work. That's important. Just listen to Him, pay attention to His leading. Is it the business that has you tied up in knots?"

"Not totally." She gently placed the empty teacup on the table. "Although financially I'm concerned about meeting my payments and staying afloat. But my relationship with God, the relationship with my children, and filling this empty hole in my heart that Todd has left ..."

"Your burdens are too heavy. Let's give it to the One who bears our burdens." Miranda placed her hand over Angela's and bowed her head.

Later that evening, the widows gathered at Marge's house. No more workbooks, no videos, just conversation.

"I have a confession to make," Angela said. "Lately, I've been living as if Todd is still here, talking to him, pretending he is walking beside me. Saturday night I completely went over the edge."

Angela recounted her attendance at the gala. "I don't know what possessed me. I wanted him back so much. I wanted that feeling of going out again with Todd. I made a total fool of myself."

"I can relate," Marge said. "I can see it happening to a widow. Isn't this part of the mental coping we do? Errors in judgment, social mishaps?"

Angela shrugged. "How long?"

"No one can answer that," Caroline said.

Marge headed for the kitchen. "As long as it takes."

"Can you forgive me?" Angela said.

"Forgive you for what?" Marge returned with the hot chocolate pot.

"For pretending to be someone I'm not. For pretending I have it all together."

"We're not here to judge, remember? You're safe," Caroline said.

Marge refilled their cups. "It's our learning curve."

"I'm determined to reinvent myself. And who I am. I'm not Todd's wife anymore. Even my role as a mother is being redefined. The kids treat me differently. Before there were two of us. A team. One balancing the other. Now there's just that one vulnerable person in their lives. At least that's how I sometimes feel."

"Vulnerable," Caroline stared at her clasped hands. "I don't like the feeling."

"And, from my personal experience, I don't believe there's any such thing as stages of grief. There's no way it's as orderly as that," Marge said. "It's merely a convenient list of emotions we can expect to experience."

Caroline nodded.

"I agree." Angela crossed her arms. "It's nice to know we're not alone in our feelings. I wanted to come clean with you. I've been saying reach out to God while I reached out to Todd. God is so patient with me." Angela swirled her cup of hot cocoa with marshmallows melting on top. The cup's warmness reminded her of Miranda's words warming her heart. "I spent an hour this morning with Miranda Frandsen. What a comfort to talk to her. Shall I share what she said?"

"Of course," Caroline said.

Marge nodded.

"We studied verses in First Corinthians. The married woman cares about the things of the world, how she may please her husband. But the unmarried woman cares for the things that belong to the Lord, how she may please the Lord." Angela clasped her cup tighter. "I want to focus on being the woman who pleases the Lord."

53

What a blessing for Angela to be in church the following Sunday with her children. Benjamin beamed at everyone as he guided Tatum through the crowd. Angela stopped to chat with friends then edged her way to the back door. Rosa and Roberto reached the door just ahead of Angela.

"Roberto, mañana?" A young voice called.

"Mañana." Roberto waved and joined his mother.

"Wasn't that—" Angela said.

"Yes, Jaxon," Rosa said. "Seems they have a lot in common. They're best friends now."

"I have a feeling the Lord is going to bless all of Roberto's tomorrows." Angela exchanged a smile with Rosa before parting at the front door.

Angela and her crew headed home and Phillip's non-stop chatter entertained them as Emerson's SUV crept through partially snow-plowed streets.

Emerson hoisted Phillip over his shoulder and bounced

him all the way to the dining room. He nodded to the couple relaxing on the sofa. "You beat us home."

"We didn't have a little one to collect," Benjamin said.

Tatum caught Phillip's hand. "May I sit next to you?"

"Okay."

"We're going to the women's shelter this afternoon," Tatum said. "Anyone want to come along?"

"Oh, yes, let's do." Bethany turned to Emerson. "Phillip's nap should be over by three."

Emerson shook his head. "I need to plan a campaign for a new customer. This afternoon is the only time I have available. You and Phillip could go."

Bethany sighed.

"Can we borrow Dad's guitar again, Mom?" Benjamin said.

"Yes, I forgot to bring mine along," Tatum said.

"Of course," Angela said. "It's good that someone's using it."

Tatum wiggled in her seat and Benjamin gave her a knowing look.

Lunch was a quick affair. But, before anyone left the table, Tatum clutched Benjamin's hand.

"We can't wait any longer." Tatum's eyes sparkled. "Tell them, Benjamin."

"Okay, you two," Emerson said. "You've been ready to explode all morning."

Tatum hunched her shoulders to her ears.

"Happy news, sad news." Benjamin glanced at Tatum who frowned. "Well, for Mom maybe."

Tatum scrunched her eyebrows and leaned against Benjamin. "The company I work for is opening an office in San Diego and they've offered a promotion if I move there. I can't think of living away from Benjamin until we're married next June."

"I think San Diego will be a great place to live," Benjamin said. "I've started a job search and it looks promising."

Angela tensed as her mind went in several directions. "When are you moving?"

"First of the year," Tatum said.

"So we've set a date for the wedding." Benjamin squeezed Tatum's hand.

"Christmas Eve," Tatum said.

"A wedding on Christmas Eve?" Bethany said. "What could be more perfect?"

Angela exhaled slowly. "Wonderful."

"Next month? A wedding that fast?" Emerson's voice rose.

"We'll have a small wedding with just the family present. Then a large reception in San Diego in June as we planned," Tatum said.

"Where's the wedding?" Bethany said.

"Right here in our home church," Benjamin said. "We talked to Pastor Bailey during our counseling sessions. He has us on his schedule for an eleven a.m. wedding. We waited to tell everyone face to face."

"You have such a stately old church. I think it's the perfect background for a wedding," Tatum said. "Mom and dad will join us. Our relatives and friends in California will attend the reception in June."

"Nice." Angela's voice rose. "Tell me more."

Benjamin bowed to Tatum. "Take it away."

"Oh, it will be so simple." Tatum clasped both hands. "Only immediate family. A suit for Benjamin, no tux. Simple dress for me. I'll just carry, I don't know, maybe some long-stemmed white roses and fling them over one arm. Nothing elaborate. That will come in June."

"What about food? A wedding breakfast or lunch?" Angela twisted her wedding ring, realizing she would be expected to host the event. Her heart sank. Her hectic December schedule. The bank note, a ticking time bomb. Joy, exhaustion, and fear battled for first place in her mind.

"Oh, I hadn't thought about that." Tatum tapped her chin with one finger. "A wedding breakfast sounds nice."

"Mornings don't agree with you." Benjamin gave her a side-long glance.

"You're right. And, there'll be so much to do the morning of the wedding. I suppose a luncheon would be best."

"Traditional Christmas fare would be a snap to prepare." Angela's mind turned to a turkey roasting while they were off attending the wedding, salads waiting, crock pots bubbling.

"Well," Tatum said, "let's give it some thought."

When wedding talk faded, Angela glanced at Benjamin, then Emerson. "Remember when we removed dad's clothes from the closet last summer? We missed his ties. They were hanging on the door inside our armoire. Perhaps the two of you could choose any you like, and I'll give the rest away. Well, okay, I'm keeping one tie that I bought him when pink was an in-color for men."

"Sure, Mom. I'll let Benjamin go first," Emerson said. "Pink's back in, you know."

"Too bad." Angela laughed.

Tatum touched Benjamin's arm. "You could wear one on our wedding day."

Benjamin smiled in a way that reminded her of Todd. "Wearing something that belonged to dad."

Relief gushed from Angela's heart. "I guess that's what prompted me to think of it. I was hoping you'd feel that way."

54

Concentrating on housecleaning proved to be a difficult task Monday morning.

Angela stopped dusting their family portrait and stared out the window. "California."

"What's that, Mom?" Bethany said.

"I'm thinking about Benjamin and Tatum moving to San Diego." Angela wiped the lamp table thoroughly as if she could wipe away the happenings of the last few months. Todd gone. Benjamin moving to what seemed another world. "I hoped our family would always live close."

"Lots of families have children spread across the country."

"I guess. I broke away from my family."

Bethany rubbed her forehead. "Mom, let's take a break."

While Phillip waged a noisy war with action figures in his room, mother and daughter huddled over coffee.

"Things will work out." Bethany flicked a short strand of hair. "Nothing's ever as it seems on the surface."

"Is something bothering you?"

"I'm concerned about Emerson. Spiritually. I've prayed about it, but ..."

Angela's left hand touched Bethany's while the glitter of their two wedding rings winked at them.

"I'll just say this. He goes to church, says all the right things, but he's not living them."

"Have you talked to him about it?"

"Just skirted around the edges. Didn't go well."

Angela nodded.

"We seemed to have drifted. The cancer, the strain of his job." Bethany tightened her jaw and sniffed. "Maybe he drifted from the Lord as well."

"That can happen ... to any of us." Angela looked away.

"Everything was about me. My cancer. No time for us as a couple."

"You have a built-in babysitter now. Why don't you get re-acquainted? Go out, just the two of you?"

"Maybe that would help." Bethany jumped as Phillip exploded into the dining room, his makeshift cape flowing behind.

"You're a wise woman. You'll work this out."

Bethany nodded. "Thanks for listening."

"I'll pray," Angela said.

"That's what I needed to hear."

Angela started a load of laundry and checked her notes for her last class at the shelter.

"Oh, the time." Angela hesitated.

"Mom," Bethany said, "I'll finish your laundry. I'm caught up."

Angela closed her briefcase. "Thanks. I wouldn't be in such a rush except I asked Miranda if she would give me a half hour."

"She reminds me of Grandma Em."

"They are a lot alike." Angela swept Phillip's toys from her path. "I've got to run. Don't forget your sword, Phillip."

The strains of *Leaning on the Everlasting Arms* met Angela at the front door of Shepherd's Fold. Her throat tightened, but no tears escaped as she walked to the dining hall. She was indeed thankful for those Everlasting Arms. She sank into the nearest chair and closed her eyes until the song ended.

"Lilly," Angela said, "you're playing beautifully. I hear you've been taking lessons from Caroline?"

"Yeah, when she can make it. Said she doesn't like to travel in the ice and snow. But I'm practicing just like she told me to do."

"I love that song you played."

"Yeah, me too. It's the one that boy and girl did last summer. Your son and his girlfriend?"

"Yes, Benjamin and Tatum." Angela felt her heart tug at the mention of his name. He would be so far away. How often would she see him? Would Tatum follow in her father's footsteps and put her work before family? No. Surely not. She seemed to love people too much, loved to serve in her praise team at church.

"They're nice. Came to our Bible studies a couple of times and always sang again."

And that too would end, but Angela would let Benjamin and Tatum break the news. She quickly prepped the room for coaching with the residents.

"My practice hour'll be over soon."

"Take your time. I'm meeting with a couple of gals who are

still looking for a job, but first I have an appointment with Miranda."

"I go to work at seven tonight." Lilly smiled. "At Walmart."

"How's it going?"

"So far, so good."

Angela hurried down the hall. Something about Miranda's cozy office helped Angela unwind.

"I heard Lilly playing hymns. Nice touch on the keys. Who would've dreamed?"

Miranda sipped her tea. "Thanks to you and Caroline, a noticeable change has come over Lilly. She's quieter. She's spending time in her Bible. Last night during our study time, I sat next to her and noticed many underlined passages. She whispered, 'Angela said it was okay' and applied her high-lighter."

Angela smiled and inhaled her tea's spicy fragrance. "I can't believe it. Praise God. Makes all the work worthwhile."

"That's why I love where the Lord placed me. No place I'd rather be," Miranda said.

"It's your calling. That's plain to see."

"He puts us where we're needed."

"Sorry I won't be able to teach classes on Monday after-noons again until after the first of the year. We're ramping up for Christmas at the shop. I'll be working every Monday to keep up."

"I understand. I appreciate the time you've volunteered. Now, let's talk about you and your Bible study. Did you journal?"

"It was awesome. Things came to mind. I wrote 'Dear Heavenly Father' each day and turned it into a prayer journal."

Miranda smiled and reached for Angela's hands. "Let's thank Him."

Wisteria

Too soon their time was over. Back in the dining hall, Angela surveyed her group.

"Only three of us left," Alexis said.

"Don't know if I'll ever find a job." Hillary huffed with a dejected look on her face.

"I don't see why not," Angela said. "Thank you for being so prompt today. One of the most important traits of an employee is showing up for work on time every day. Now tell me about your job hunt."

Angela worked with each one. She was packing up an hour later when Lilly came running in from the hall.

"Angela." Lilly panted. "Glad I caught you."

"What's wrong?"

"It's Olaf. He's in the hospital. Will you take me?"

"Slow down," Angela said. "Catch your breath. Who are you talking about?"

"Olaf. Olaf Hansen."

"Olaf? The antique shop Olaf? But, I don't understand—"

"We've got to hurry. Will you take me?"

55

Angela broke every speed limit she dared. "Lilly, why would the hospital call you?"

"Can't we go any faster?"

"We'll be there soon."

Lilly grimaced.

"But I don't understand. A month ago you wouldn't go near Olaf's shop."

Lilly sat ramrod straight, her protruding jaw set in stone. At the hospital, Lilly raced ahead of Angela to the emergency room.

Angela caught up with her just in time to hear the receptionist ask Lilly, "Are you next of kin?"

"Yes. Lilly Hansen."

Angela frowned. Why hadn't Lilly mentioned this before? Like when she refused to go with her to pick up a lamp post at Olaf's?

"I'll wait here, Lilly," Angela said, motioning to a chair.

"No, I want you with me."

The receptionist smiled at Angela. "Are you related as well?"

Angela shook her head.

The receptionist's sympathetic gaze shifted back to Lilly. "I'm sorry ..."

"Where is he?"

"Please wait here. It won't be long. I have paperwork for you to fill out."

Lilly scribbled so fast that Angela wondered if she skipped pages altogether. The receptionist's phone rang. She jotted something and handed Lilly a slip of paper. Lilly's hand shook as she read it.

Still not making eye contact with Angela, she dropped the paper in Angela's lap. "Here's the room number. I'm going up with the gurney."

Angela hesitated. Would Lilly return for her? Probably not. She waited fifteen minutes then navigated the maze of halls until she found Olaf's room. She stopped short at the door. With their backs to the door, Lilly and a nurse huddled in deep conversation. Rhythmic beeps pierced the otherwise quiet room. Angela shrank to the side of the door to give them privacy. She couldn't help overhearing.

A crisp voice rose over the beeping. "The MRI shows a thrombotic stroke." The voice could just as easily have been delivering an anatomy lecture. "Therapy may decrease the aphasia."

"The what?" Lilly's voice was high and pinched.

"Speech. Problems with his speech."

Angela slipped away and wandered the halls, her eyes straight ahead, but sounds were not so easy to block. Murmured family conversations. Moaning coming from one room. TV blaring in another. Monitors beeping. Antiseptic smells. They overwhelmed her. How many families were facing a new normal that only time could redefine? She circled the hallway until she thought it was safe to venture into Olaf's room.

With a wet washcloth in hand, Lilly motioned Angela into the room. Olaf looked pale and small, hooked by tubes and cables to blinking machines. His eyes were closed.

"Pops always liked a washcloth on his head when he didn't feel good." Lilly gently rubbed the cloth in place. Olaf breathed a sigh of relief.

Angela gulped. Pops?

The next day

"Rosa, I'll make the deliveries today. Remember Olaf? He's in the hospital. I think I'll stop by his room."

"Oh?"

The hospital was her last stop, and Olaf's her last delivery.

Lilly rose when Angela walked in. "Flowers. You brought flowers." Lilly set the bouquet on a nightstand.

"How is he doing?" Angela whispered.

"About the same. They said he has a good chance of recovering." When Angela nodded, Lilly continued. "Do you know the lady that works at the shop? Avis? They said she saved his life. It happened at the shop. She came this morning and told me all about it."

In a low voice, Lilly recapped the story. Incoherent sounds from Olaf drew Lilly to his side. She rubbed his arm. "It's okay, Pops. I'm right here."

His eyes closed, and Lilly stepped back. "Mom always called him Pops."

"I didn't know," Angela said.

"I guess that's the way I wanted it. At least when I first came back to Northgate and to the shelter." Pain filled Lilly's eyes.

Angela wrapped Lilly in a hug.

Lilly crumpled against Angela. "I want to be a daughter to him now."

"I'm glad to hear you say that," Angela said.

"Not much I can do here, they said. I have to go to work again tonight. Can't lose my job." Lilly stepped closer and pulled her father's gown up over his shoulder. "Pops would understand."

"I'm sure he would."

"Need to talk to you. Need to talk to someone." Lilly glanced toward the bed. "But not here."

"After I close shop tonight, do you have time for coffee before you leave for work? Say, five-thirty?"

"Sure."

"I'll pick you up here?"

"Okay."

A nurse appeared, checked Olaf's pulse, and entered chart notes.

"Sorry, I must be going." Angela moved toward the door, casting one last look at Olaf. "Is Avis running the shop?"

"Just doing her regular shift, four hours in the afternoon. Closed the rest of the day, she told me."

Olaf opened his eyes and called out incoherently. His eyes closed again.

Lilly cocked her head. "He does that a lot."

Rosa looked up when Angela returned. "Did you see Olaf?"

"Yes. He had a stroke."

"That's so sad," Rosa said. "No family to be with him."

Angela caught herself just in time. Better let Lilly share what she wanted to share.

"Well, Rosa, it's time we thought about gearing up for the Christmas rush," Angela said. "I asked Myrna Fredericks to come in for half-days beginning tomorrow. I'm hoping she'll be a big help."

"Nice." Rosa smiled. "I like her."

As Angela worked, she wondered what Olaf's recovery would mean to Lilly. There was certainly a lot of history there that Angela wasn't privy to. History and bitter feelings that somehow adversity was smoothing out. Angela attached sprigs of bittersweet to a pine wreath. Smiling, she remembered when she and Todd had found wild bittersweet on one of their hikes. It surprised her that she could smile. Bittersweet. So like memories. Sometimes bitter. Sometimes sweet. Sometimes both.

56

Angela followed Lilly's hunched shoulders to a quiet corner at the Nordic Cup.

"I forgot to ask if caffeine keeps you awake." Angela sipped her mocha. "But I guess it doesn't matter if you're on your way to work."

Lilly nodded. "They're moving Pops to a nursing home soon to start therapy." Lilly slurped the foam on her latte. "He seemed a little stronger this afternoon. They're working with his speech already."

"I'd like to visit him."

"He'd like that." Another slurp. "Guess you're wondering about all this."

Angela crossed her arms and leaned back. "It's none of my business. I'm just concerned about you. Don't feel obligated to tell me anything."

"I don't." Lilly brushed hair out of her eyes. "He's my dad. I told Miranda about him when I first came to the shelter. I told her I hated him.

"Well, you know Miranda: 'honor your father' and all that.

It was a tough pill to swallow. He used to say 'you're just like your mother'—until I wanted to be just like my mother. Mom was twenty years younger than him. She always called him an old miser. He never would give her any money. When I was eleven, she ran off with another man." Lilly shifted in her chair. "When I was sixteen, I ran off. A lot has happened."

Angela leaned forward, twisting a strand of hair.

"Did I tell you I'm a believer now?" Lilly rolled the bottom of the cup in a circle, sloshing the latte dangerously close to the edge. "I thought you just confessed your sins, trusted Jesus, and He changed you. Not that easy."

"No, we're not robots, are we?" Angela said. "We still have free choice. Still have to overcome our old nature."

"Miranda told me to read my Bible." Lilly's face relaxed. "I know so little, but I know I'm a child of God. It's a whole new world. I want to do the right thing. When I heard about Pops, I got real scared. Not sure he understands, but at least I told him I was sorry."

"God allowed you to tell him."

"Does God work like that?"

"I believe He does."

"Well, when I saw him in that hospital bed, he seemed so helpless. The old Pops sorta faded away. I just wanted to take care of him."

"God gives us that love, Lilly. Love we never had before."

"You sound like Miranda." Lilly hooked her cup handle and swung the empty cup back and forth with one finger. "I'll never be like her."

"What do you mean?"

"Always has the right Bible verse on the tip of her tongue."

"Don't expect it to happen overnight. Those things come from reading and memorizing His Word."

Lilly propped her elbows on the table. "Don't think I'll ever get there."

"A year ago, did you think you would be where you are today?"

"No. No way." Lilly laughed.

"We learn at a different pace. We're all different, but God has a plan for each of us."

At noon the next day, a banging at the back door brought Angela to the rear of the shop. Opening the door, she came eye-to-eye with Myrna glaring at the door handle. Leonard Fredericks' wife, the ornament lady-now-floral-shop-employee, stood outside frowning at the door handle.

"There's a trick to this door handle. Let me show you." Angela scooted through the doorway and closed the door behind them. "Lift the handle like this and twist to the left."

"Let me try." Myrna lifted, tugged, and groaned. The door opened. "That's easy enough."

"Back door. Another repair on my landlord's to-do list," Angela said.

Myrna stomped snow from her boots. "Afternoon, Rosa."

"Welcome," Rosa said. "Happy you're here."

"I know I'm early, but I've been looking forward to working here so much."

"Good," Angela said. "Christmas rush will soon be upon us and we can use your help. I know we agreed on four hours a day, but would you be able to work all day tomorrow? We open shop at ten."

"Sure."

"Just for one day." Angela pointed to containers of bulk tea and a stack of small bags. "I'm having an open house with a contest to let customers vote for the tea blend that will be called "Wisteria Tea."

"Interesting." Myrna leaned forward to sniff. "But what if you don't want to make a pot of tea?"

"Easy. Here are empty tea bags to fill and slip into your cup. Now, the cinnamon spicy one is labeled Wisteria A. This one with the beautiful colors is labeled Wisteria B. I'll mix it precisely and have small bags of each for sale. We'll set up a table for the tea and Christmas cookies." Angela scanned the back room. "So much to do. Your help will be appreciated, Myrna."

"More than glad to do it," Myrna said.

Myrna had many questions, but an extra pair of hands eased the workload. The day sped by.

An exhausted Angela looked at the clock four hours later. "I think it's close enough to five to close the shop."

She headed to the front to lock the door, but someone opened it.

"Hi, hope we're not too late?" A flushed face appeared below an odd-shaped felt hat.

"Peyton. How nice to see you." Angela opened the door wide. "No, you're not too late."

Peyton motioned to two girls who entered, then quickly ducked behind a display to examine a metal board of magnets. "Friends from college. No classes tomorrow, then we're spending the weekend in Northgate with their relatives."

"Come in. Can I help you find anything?" Angela blinked as one girl's hoodie slipped to reveal a mass of unkept hair. Somehow she didn't fit Angela's image of a college student, even in these days of ripped jeans and ratty T-shirts.

"Actually, could I use your restroom?" Peyton said.

"Sure. Do you know where it is?"

"I do. Saw it last time I was here."

Peyton hurried to the back, and Angela got a jumpstart on shutting down for the evening.

"Nice working with you, Myrna." Rosa slipped into her jacket and picked up the scarf Myrna dropped.

"I'm just thrilled to be here." Myrna looped her scarf around her neck.

"Thank you—" A voice from the front door halted Angela.

Then another voice. "Forgot my money. I'll come back another day."

"Bye, thank you." A high-pitched voice called from outside.

"I guess Peyton left, too. I'll check." Angela noticed the restroom door ajar. "Yep, light's out. I'll lock the front door." On the way back, she emptied her cash register. It was too late to make a deposit today; the bank would close before she could get there. The cash box clunked as it slipped into its drawer of the desk. She grabbed her bag from the office and flipped off the lights.

57

The next morning

Angela rolled out of bed, wishing she could replace her shop uniform today with the new T-shirt Becca had given her. It so summarized her life: "Work, Eat, Sleep, Repeat." She dressed and met Emerson in the kitchen.

"You're up early," Emerson said in a low voice.

"Lots to do ... decorating for Christmas." Angela popped an English muffin in the toaster and reached for the skillet.

"Still time for eggs?"

"Of course. You know I never go without breakfast. How's work?"

"Work? Oh, you were in bed before I got home last night. No promotion for me at present, but the reorganization in my territory is just as good as a promotion. The new boss wants all the west coasts, including my territory. That's where he's from. Kids live there. Suits me just fine. I'll have the Midwest now. Be home most nights."

"Great news. I'm so happy for you."

"Thanks." He flipped through the mail. "A very early Christmas card for you."

"Oh." Angela halted. "Tom Christiansen. Cecilia's husband."

"Pastor Christiansen? Didn't he become a missionary?"

"Short term. Returning in May, he says." May 15th. The one-year anniversary of Todd's death. Angela rubbed her forehead. "Wants me to go with him to the gravesites for Cecilia and Todd."

"That'll be painful."

"Yes."

"Hang in there. Gotta roll." Emerson grabbed his mug in one hand and briefcase in the other. "Coffee's fresh."

"Have a good day." Angela watched him head to the garage. "I'll leave your coffee for Bethany. Too strong," she muttered and made her breakfast sandwich to go. She glanced at the Christmas card again. Tom Christiansen. How was he handling the loss of Cecilia? Does it get easier after three years?

The shop door opened freely. Did she forget to lock the deadbolt last night? She shook her head and tried to bury the feeling she'd never left the shop.

Angela put a pot of water on the hot plate and checked her decorated table in the middle of the shop. Myrna had numbered the tea servers and put slips in front of each for the voting of their favorite tea. The slips would double as names to be drawn for prizes at the end of the day.

The tea could wait until her customers appeared. She needed coffee. Soon the smell of Guatemala dark roast filled the back room. Ah, it's the little luxuries.

Two hours later, Angela greeted Rosa and Myrna. "Did you notice if I locked up last night?"

"No, too busy pulling my stocking cap over my ears." Rosa stomped snow from her boots.

"Hmm. It was unlocked," Angela said.

"And nobody bothered a thing." Myrna glanced at the clean shop. "That's a small town for you."

"Rosa, would you pull deliveries first?" Angela headed for her office. "Then we'll set up for the contest to choose a Wisteria favorite tea."

"Sure. Looks like quite a load to deliver today." Rosa opened the cooler door.

Angela muffled a scream.

The cash box with checks littering the floor lay at her feet. "Empty! How could this have happened?"

Myrna cowered in the doorway.

"I'll call 911." Rosa marched to the phone.

It was just the impetus Angela needed to get moving. "Do you know how much money—this shouldn't have happened. Too busy to make a deposit this week," Angela muttered. The money set aside for the balloon payment to the bank just shrank.

"They'll be here in ten minutes." Rosa gazed around the shop. "They said not to touch anything."

"I only see the cash missing." Angela reached for the checks, then froze, left them on the floor, and inched out of her office. "Can't even set up the register." She glanced at the cash register drawer. "Loose coin is still in the till."

"Well, if that don't beat all." Myrna peeked in. "Guess the change was too much trouble to gather."

Angela pulled out her checkbook. "Rosa, here's a check. Run to the bank and pick up ones, fives, and tens so we can make change today."

"On my way." Still bundled up, Rosa took the check and strode out the back door.

"What about the cops?" Myrna stood frozen at Angela's elbow.

"Myrna ... I'm sure they'll be most thorough. And we'll help the police in any way possible." Angela squinted at the displays in the shop a person could hide behind. Her heart raced.

Myrna lifted clasped hands against her chest. "Never been involved in anything like this."

"It's okay. The officers are on their way."

"I know, just this funny feeling."

Angela gripped Myrna's shoulder. "I'll make a sign for customers to announce a delay in opening. Myrna, can you tape it on the door?"

Today. Of all days. Her open house, the tea tasting and voting contest, people arriving soon.

"Sure." Myrna paced to the front and applied the sign. "There's a squad car!" Myrna called, taking long strides back to the worktable.

Angela's heart sank. Great advertising. They parked in front of the shop.

Then she chided herself for being irritated. Those men and women laid their lives on the line every day to protect her.

"Hello. I'm Deputy Makayla Johnson." A young officer followed Angela to her office. "Any cameras inside? Any knowledge of other businesses in the area with outdoor cameras?"

Angela shook her head. Officer Johnson continued firing questions to reconstruct the previous day. After she interviewed Rosa and Myrna, the officer came back to Angela's office.

"Do you make a deposit every day?"

"I will from now on." Angela sighed. "It's been three days."

They compared the cash register reports to the deposit slip and arrived at an estimated amount of cash missing.

When the officer paused to study her notes, Angela stood. "Okay if I work while we talk?"

"Not a problem," she said, following Angela to her table set aside for tea sampling. "Do you leave the cash register drawer open at night?"

"Yes, when we bought the machine, the rep advised us to leave the coin in an open drawer," Angela said and pulled a box of sample cups from under the table. "They said the loss of loose change is cheaper than repairing a drawer that's been crow-bared open."

Makayla smiled. "That's been our experience."

"Why would they leave the checkbook and the checks?" Angela pointed back to her office.

"Who's going to cash the checks? Your checkbook presents a whole new problem for them. Probably just after the quick cash."

Angela's shoulders slumped.

"Let's get back to your customers. This young woman you spoke of, your last customer, a student at the U?"

When she zeroed in on Peyton's visit, Angela frowned. "Yes."

"Two friends from school with her?"

"Yes, that's how she introduced them."

"When they left, how many people did you see leave through the front door?" Officer Johnson's glance swept the room, including Rosa and Myrna in the question.

Myrna stopped winding ribbon. "I wasn't paying attention."

"I glanced up and only saw two people," Rosa said.

"Was one of them Peyton?"

"I—I think so. I guess I don't know."

"How about you, Mrs. McKinley?"

Angela arranged voting slips on the table and set a gift-wrapped box in the middle with a hole to receive them. "I didn't have a clear view of the door. I heard three responses. Someone outside said "Bye, thank you.' I just assumed it was Peyton."

"So she could've remained inside?"

"I checked the bathroom before I left, and the light was out." Angela chewed on her lower lip. "No, not Peyton. I'd never believe it of her after her hard work to rehabilitate."

"Excuse me? Rehabilitate?"

"Yes, drug rehab. I met her at the women's shelter."

"Did she know the location of the cashbox?"

"No." Angela grabbed a stack of Christmas napkins from a box under the table. "Wait. One day Peyton walked into my office to tell me about school. I scooped cash from the desk, placed it in the cashbox, and slid the box into the bottom drawer. Yes, I guess she knew. But how could this have happened? I must have left the door unlocked. Would she have come back later and tried the back door? It makes no sense."

"Unless she never left. Maybe hid behind a display or in the restroom?"

Myrna's hands flew to her neck. She stared in horror at the restroom as if it still hid a thief.

"Could you look and see if anything was disturbed?"

Angela raced to the restroom. Pulling a curtain aside, she exposed a small closet with shelving halfway down for supplies. The bottom half was big enough for a person to squeeze into hiding. A plunger, bowl brush, and cleaners clustered on one side rather than spread across the space as Angela always kept them. The tiny space glared at her.

"Obvious, isn't it?" Angela's hands clenched into fists.

"So she hid there while we locked up?" Rosa said.

"Then took the money and waltzed out the back door," Myrna said.

Officer Johnson continued to take notes. "That's a possibility."

58

December 2

Christmas rush. Sink or swim. Angela welcomed it with open arms. This month would determine the shop's survival. An amber glow of twinkling lights transformed the shop displays into a fairyland of gifts. Animated red, green, and silver decorations blended with poinsettias of varied colors. Her spirits lifted.

Even the bell over the door seemed to chime a holiday tone as three shoppers shuffled in as soon as Angela unlocked the door.

"I see exactly what I need." A young woman wearing a puffy down jacket gathered three wall plaques Becca had designed. "My mother, my mother-in-law, myself." She giggled.

"Any more of the snowman?" asked another.

"Yes, let me get them." Angela turned to a bin behind the worktable.

"Oh, can I come and see?" she said.

Angela cringed, thinking of the disarray. "Well, just be careful where you step. Don't trip."

They trooped back and flipped through stacks as if they were at a Macy's sale table. Ten minutes later, they walked back to the counter carrying their purchases.

"Got it! I didn't see this one anywhere in the store." One held up a plaque with a silhouette of a star and manger, 'Behold Our King.'

"And your tea contest?" Another spoke up. "Which won?"

"Number two, the herbal blend." Angela pointed to the bags with a cello window and bright colors peeking out. "It seems to be a hit. Would you like to try a bag?" She smiled recalling how hard the three of them had worked to keep hot tea on hand for her delighted customers. How exhilarating it had been to see her shop overflowing with their eagerness.

"Should we?" one asked.

Each stacked a bag of tea on top of their purchases. Angela never thought she'd be grateful to have sore fingers and achy wrists from assembling so many bags of tea. But now she overflowed with gratitude—for aches, a full store, and happy customers.

The puffy down jacket lady hugged Angela. "Merry Christmas."

Out the door they sailed.

"I love my customers, especially this time of year. Excitement in the air, the countdown to Christmas, no place I'd rather be." Angela turned to Rosa and smiled. "Did I tell you I'm meeting Caroline and Marge tonight for dinner? Kind of an early Christmas party for the three of us before the holidays take over."

"What a great idea." Rosa smiled and answered the phone. "It's for you. It's Lilly."

"Just wanted you to know they moved Pops to the nursing home." Lilly sounded happy.

"Oh." Angela groaned inside. The shop was busy. Tonight was dinner out with Marge and Caroline. She had put aside thoughts of visiting Olaf. "I'm sorry I haven't been back to see him."

"That's okay. He's doing much better. He liked those flowers you brought. They didn't quite make it with the move, but I'll buy him more. Maybe one rose. I can pay for it. I'm working now, you know."

"I won't have time to visit, but I can drop it off tonight. How about after five?"

"Sure. I'll still be there."

Angela resisted the urge to bring a bouquet to Olaf. The goal of the shelter was to help women become independent and Lilly could only afford one rose. Angela respected her request.

That night she clutched the wrapped rose against her as the wind tried to snatch it away. It was a short drive to Northgate Care Center. The blonde brick building was ablaze with lights. The rehab section consisted of a corner where two hallways met. She soon found Olaf's room and Lilly.

"How much?"

Angela named the price and watched Lilly proudly count out the bills.

"That lawyer Pops knows came to see him today. Mr. Brecken was real nice. Said they would get things worked out, whatever that means. They wanted me to move into Pop's house to look after things, but I told him loud and clear." Lilly's voice grew strangely thin. "Never!"

"It shouldn't be this hard to get together when we live next door," Marge said, pushing her car door open for Angela.

"We're burning the candle at both ends," Angela said.

"That would explain it."

"Thanks for driving." Angela squinted at the slushy ruts defined in the headlights. "Looks like the storm will hold off."

"Don't count on it."

They met at Patrick's Place, a restaurant halfway between Caroline's new home and Northgate. The restaurant glowed with holiday lights.

Angela and Marge gratefully left the frigid air at the door for the building's warmth. Caroline waved from a booth in the corner. Her hair was shorter and fluffed around her face. She looked much younger. Her black coat tucked snugly around her shoulders made a perfect backdrop for her auburn hair.

"Is it too early to say Merry Christmas?" Caroline said. Gold gift bags with sparkly tissue sticking out the tops marked Angela's and Marge's places.

"No, never too early. Merry Christmas." Angela added red and green bags to the table and pulled her coat closer. "I think I'll keep my coat with me, too."

"Really? My sweater's warm." Marge fished two boxes from her bag.

With so much catching up to do, they somehow managed to order food.

"Let's open our presents," Angela said. "My first of the year."

"Let's!" Caroline laughed.

Chocolates from Marge, a journal with a matching pen from Caroline, and a necklace from Angela lay sprawled on the table.

"Chocolate is always perfect," Angela said. Caroline agreed.

"Oh, I love it." Caroline held up the necklace. Her fingers touched the word 'Faith' on a hammered copper plate hanging from a simple silver chain. "I think I'll wear it." She unhooked the clasp and slipped it around her neck.

"Me too." Marge laughed as her fingers fumbled with the clasp.

"Let me help you." Caroline lifted the chain around Marge's neck.

"Whoa! Your hands are cold as ice."

"Sorry." Caroline rubbed her hands together and tried again.

Angela sat back and twisted a lock of her hair. "Caroline, are you playing your piano?"

"A little." Caroline stared at her ringless hands, her long artistic fingers idly tapped the tabletop. She turned toward the window, now splattered with clumps of snow. "My heart's not in it."

"I can understand."

"I feel guilty because the piano takes up all that space. I try to play a few minutes each day. Something from memory. I haven't unpacked my music."

"I think I mentioned that Benjamin and Tatum are getting married on Christmas Eve?"

"Yes, how lovely." Caroline's lips curved in a smile, but her eyes were sad.

"Tatum asked me to arrange for a pianist. I wonder if you would do us the honor and consider playing for the wedding."

"I don't see how I can." Caroline's fingers grasped her necklace.

The following Sunday

During their impromptu lunch after Sunday services, Bethany squeezed next to Tatum. "Here's our thoughts for the wedding luncheon menu. Does a traditional Christmas dinner sound okay?"

"Christmas dinner?" Tatum picked pepperoni from her slice of pizza.

"Yes," Angela joined them. "The turkey could be ready soon after we return home. I have a great recipe for mashed potatoes with sour cream. Keeps hot wonderfully in a crock pot."

"Hmm, no." Tatum tapped the list. "Mother is lactose intolerant. No sour cream. But plan whatever you like. You could have that as a side and have something like buttered asparagus for mother. I'll be too excited to eat. But I must tell you, I really like the idea of a finger food luncheon the best."

"Finger food?" Bethany looked at Angela as if for help.

Tatum brightened. "How about salmon or spinach and goat cheese canapés? Or, better yet, fig and chèvre canapés? To die for! Oh, and maybe artichoke bruschetta? Do you make a white Mornay sauce?"

"No." Angela noticed Benjamin fade to the living room with Emerson. "I suppose I could learn."

"It's easy. I could—no, I guess I'll be rather busy, won't I?" Tatum glanced at their menu. "Red grape Waldorf salad? Interesting. What's that?"

"An apple salad," Bethany said.

"Oh," Tatum said.

Wisteria

Angela sensed Tatum's reluctance. Her menu and her carefully timed plans for the reception flew out the window. Canapés had to be made at the last minute. She reminded herself to breathe, even though the air seemed sucked out of the room.

59

Wednesday morning

Angela arrived at work an hour earlier than usual. Rosa was right behind.

"You're early." Angela's eyebrows lifted.

"I dropped Roberto off at school, wanted to make sure—" She stumbled over her snow boots and caught herself.

"Rosa, don't you feel well?"

"I'm fine." Rosa dipped her head. Her long hair fell forward, but not fast enough to hide her red, puffy eyes. "Not much sleep last night."

"Here, sit down. The water's hot." Angela scooped loose tea into an empty tea bag.

"But there's so much to do."

"Then I'll work, and you collect yourself."

"There's no collecting." With a sigh Rosa dropped in a chair and buried her face in her hands.

"I might as well tell you what happened." Rosa sat up suddenly. "I need to talk to someone." Her eyes met Angela's.

344

"At 3:00 a.m., someone knocked at my door. My landlord had made a trip to urgent care two nights before, so I thought they needed help but were afraid to startle me with the doorbell. Without thinking, I opened the door. And there stood Carlos."

"Carlos?" Angela dropped a bucket of holly on the table. "Your husband? He's alive?"

"Quite a shock."

Angela plopped onto the nearest stool and clamped hands over her mouth. "Oh, dear."

"He hugged me, kissed me, and told me how he had longed to take me in his arms again. Before I could recover, he rushed past me and barged into Roberto's bedroom. Carlos picked him up and said, 'it's Papi!' Roberto could hardly open his eyes. He said 'Papi?' then closed his eyes and went back to sleep. I coaxed Carlos out of his room and closed the door. Carlos pulled me down beside him on the sofa and said he wanted to explain everything. His explanation was sketchy. He talked in circles. He had mentioned his father to me before. Carlos always had undertones of respect in how he talked about his father. I never knew what to make of Carlos' offhand remarks about his father. Laughing about the way his family grew marijuana in the mountains, it sounded to me like the way they grow corn in Minnesota. Last night he finally confessed that he had always worked for his father, learning the business since he was a child. It was his father who had suggested he move to Arizona and set up a front for their business. He was all for Carlos marrying me and pretending to live a quiet, normal life."

Rosa lifted her chin, eyes set. "I stopped him and asked about the death certificate I received."

Angela leaned forward.

"When we were married, Carlos would leave for a week at

a time to go on the road ... supposedly to make deliveries. After the sting operation I found out from his sister it involved drug dealing for his father. He knew he couldn't risk going back to Arizona after having escaped. Carlos said he was hoping the authorities would find out about the death certificate and quit looking for him. Can you imagine? He was willing to just drop his life with Roberto and me and begin another life in Mexico."

Angela shook her head.

"Then Carlos took my hand and said he was finished working for his father. He had seen too many men die. His own brother died a month ago in Mexico at the hands of another gang. Carlos said he had turned his back on that life. While he was saying this, he wouldn't look me in the eye. I knew there was more that he wasn't telling me. Then Carlos became animated and told me about a friend in California who operated a tire center and wanted Carlos as his partner. He said that's why he came, to take Roberto and me with him. Right away."

Rosa crossed her arms. "His story had too many holes in it. So, I told him no. He said, 'Don't tell me no. Your my wife. You'll go where I say.'"

I was frightened. I said go ahead to California without us and find a place for us to live first. His eyes became hard. I don't think he expected me to refuse him.

As Rosa's words picked up steam, so did the size of her hand gestures—until her sweater sleeve slipped toward her elbow.

"Rosa?" Angela hesitantly reached toward a black and blue mark on her arm. "Did he hurt you?"

Rosa covered the bruise with her sleeve. "It happened when he held my arm tight and wouldn't let go, that's all."

"That's all? Rosa!"

"I know. Carlos hasn't changed. He learned that the only way to deal with life was aggression. Otherwise you got walked on ... taken advantage of. That's how he's wired. That's how he survived. I don't believe for a moment he would cut ties with his father, even if he wanted to."

Rosa rubbed her forehead. "It was getting light outside. I could hear my landlords upstairs. Carlos berated me. Demanded I go with him. Grabbed my arm. Dragged me. Practically carried me. I kicked. Knocked over a floor lamp, shattered the lightbulb. I struggled. We ran into the coffee table. He hit his knee and grabbed it. That's when I jerked loose from his grip."

Rosa glanced at Angela. "Mr. Ellingson called from upstairs, 'Are you okay, Rosa?' Fear flashed across Carlos' face. Then his voice hardened. "I'll go without you." He shoved me to the floor and stormed out the door."

Rosa straightened. "I can't believe I stood up to him."

Angela squeezed Rosa's hand. "You had divine protection."

"I know." Rosa exhaled shakily. "The Lord protected me last night."

"I'm so thankful."

"Angela—" Tears carved a path through Rosa's make-up, pulling black mascara in their wake. "I lost a husband. Then to find out he's alive and have to push him away?"

"A nightmare. I can't imagine what you're going through." Angela shook her head.

"If there's a connection with his father's gang, he may have headed to Phoenix, to his sister's. I called my parents. It shocked them."

"Rosa, we should call—"

"No!" Her eyes widened. "No police. You don't understand. It's complicated."

Angela frowned. "It's against my better judgement. I mean, what if he's still in town? Let's think this through. Who could advise you? What about Miranda?"

"Yes, I'll try Miranda."

While Rosa spoke to Miranda, Angela turned on lights and unlocked the front door, allowing Rosa some privacy in her conversation. Angela also called Myrna for "reinforcements." Relieved to have Myrna on her way, Angela returned to the worktable and began working at lightning speed as a customer wandered into the shop. Angela smiled and bundled up an order with one ear listening for Rosa in the back room. Three more people perused the aisles and exclaimed over the displays.

After the customers left, Rosa, now looking more fresh-faced, approached Angela. "I have to leave to pick up Roberto. Miranda is letting us move into the shelter until she finds a safe house."

Rosa jumped at the sound of her cell phone and wandered the length of the back room. When she approached Angela, the color had drained from her face.

Angela ducked behind the cooler, pulling Rosa with her, out of sight of any customers who might enter. "Rosa!" The words were a hoarse whisper. "Did something else happen?"

"I told you about my father's friends, Roan and Meilie in Minneapolis? That sweet couple from back home? I don't even know their last name. But somehow Carlos remembered and found them. Yesterday he shouldered his way into their house and threatened Meilie, trying to find me ... when she pulled my address, he shoved her hard against the wall, snatched her purse, her money, her credit cards."

"Oh, no."

Rosa blinked. "I need to go."

Angela nodded as her eyes filled with tears. Rosa quickly

hugged her before rushing out the back door. Angela stared at the door and prayed for Rosa's safety.

While Angela helped customers, Myrna walked in, hung up her coat, and brightly greeted the ladies waiting at the counter. Angela flashed her a strained smile of gratitude.

An hour later, business in the shop slowed. Angela removed her apron. "Myrna, I'm making deliveries. I'll be back soon."

Angela mechanically dodged slush on the sidewalks while juggling her flower creations, her thoughts rarely straying from Rosa. Soon she was back in her van, heading toward the shop, still wondering how Rosa would escape Carlos.

Frenzied honking and noisy flapping snapped Angela out of her rolling thoughts. She hit the brakes as a new-looking car in the opposite lane braked to avoid hitting a gaggle of Canadian geese in the road. The driver slammed to a stop amid squawks and fluttering wings while one goose scraped across his hood of his car. That Buick ... Kent Hargrove. Angela couldn't suppress a smirk as she proceeded slowly. At least he has insurance, she thought, then sobered instantly when the air filled with the sickening sound of crumpling metal.

In her rear-view mirror, she could see a vehicle had plowed into the back of Kent's car. She had a glimpse of Kent, his face red. He seemed to be delivering an angry lecture to—was that Cole, Becca's friend? Surely not. By now, she was too far away to tell. The car behind Angela honked. She couldn't keep driving this slow; traffic was getting heavy.

When Angela returned to Wisteria, Myrna was busy helping a customer choose a centerpiece. Angela fished out her vibrating cell phone and read a text from Becca.

Cole. In a fender bender.

349

Myrna looked up from closing the cash drawer. "Something wrong?"

"Yes. That really was Cole in that fender bender I just saw."

She quickly texted Becca.

Angela's heart sank. Cole probably had no collision insurance on his old clunker. This would seriously dent his college fund. "What a day. So many things happening at once."

By late afternoon, Angela had to face the fact that Rosa may be gone for a while. "Myrna, would you be able to work all day while Rosa's away?"

"I don't see why not. Kinda fun, getting out of the house," Myrna said. "Where's Rosa? She okay?"

"Personal business," Angela said.

"Hmm." Myrna swept around her feet.

Angela moved to one side. "Thanks. I'm feeling knee-deep in ribbon ends and clutter."

"Sweeping's what I do best." Myrna vigorously scooped the litter into a dustpan.

Angela bent over a large box and separated fragrant spruce tops. "The front porch pots are selling fast."

"Everything's selling fast." Myrna rapped the dustpan on the edge of the trash can.

Angela breathed a thankful prayer. But she added a postscript: that God would place her on steadier ground. The aftershocks of this latest development with Rosa would take time to settle.

60

W orking on Mondays during December was a given. But Angela was actually looking forward to the long day. Becca had come home unexpectedly because of emergency repairs at her school, so her extra set of hands at the shop would lighten Angela's load.

The phone buzzed as Angela stuffed lunch in a bag.

"Sorry to call so early," Miranda's raspy voice came on the line.

"Do you have a cold?"

"I do. Many with colds at the shelter. I always shake them off. I'll be fine."

"Everything okay?" Angela said.

"No, I have terrible news. Rosa received a phone call from her dad last night. Apparently Carlos, her husband, made it to Phoenix, but—" Miranda did a poor job of muffling her cough. "In an auto accident, apparently fleeing from the police, and died en route to the hospital."

"Oh, no." Angela sat down hard on a kitchen barstool. Thankful Rosa and Roberto had not been involved. "I can't believe it. He's gone? How can anyone be a widow twice?"

"It's tragic."

"Poor Rosa. How is she?"

"She's shaken as you can imagine. But things are happening fast. No time for her to give way."

"Is there anything I can do?"

"That's the reason I'm calling. Her dad purchased their plane tickets, but Rosa and Roberto need a ride to the airport. Their flight leaves at noon."

"I'll take them."

"And Angela, I'm so sorry to hear about the robbery at your shop last month. The police questioned all of us at the shelter. One resident heard they arrested Peyton and her friends this past weekend."

"What will happen to her?"

"It doesn't look good. Probably a jail sentence, rehab again."

"I feel so sorry for Peyton."

"Sorry you had to suffer the loss in your business."

"My insurance paid most of it. They covered it after my deductible."

"Praise the Lord. And—keep praying."

"I will." Angela closed the call and motioned to Bethany and Becca.

"Girls." Angela rubbed the back of her neck.

"Oooo." Becca scooted around the corner. "Haven't heard that ominous tone in a long time."

Bethany scowled at Becca and shook her head. "What is it, Mom?"

"I only have a moment to spare, but I need to tell you about

Rosa," Angela said. "Without going into a lot of detail, her husband, Carlos, has died."

"She had a husband?" Becca joined her.

"I'll let Rosa tell you the details when she returns." Angela shook her head. "She and Roberto leave this morning to fly to Phoenix for his funeral."

"We know so little about Rosa," Bethany said.

"Apparently she was in danger. She's safe now."

"But the shop. Your busiest time of the year," Becca said.

Angela shook her head. "I know."

Becca touched her mother's arm. "I'm headed to the shop, Mom."

"Me, too." Bethany grabbed a loaf of bread. "I'll make sandwiches and take Phillip along. We'll get as much done as possible."

"Thanks." Angela's lip trembled. "You don't know how much I appreciate that."

Angela rushed to the address Miranda had given her. Rosa and Roberto stood in the entryway with packed bags.

"I'm so sorry, Rosa." Angela reached out and hugged her.

Rosa's face was thin and drawn as she nodded and stepped through the door. "Thank you for driving us."

"Hello, Roberto," Angela said.

"Hi." Roberto grinned and slipped on his backpack as if ready for a new adventure.

Angela squeezed Rosa's hand.

Buckled in the back seat, Roberto made his voice as loud as he could. "I'm going to Phoenix to see mis abuelos."

"His grandparents," Rosa said.

"Do you remember your grandparents?" Angela said.

"Oh yes, when we lived in Phoenix," Roberto said. "And I remember Papi."

Angela's eyes smarted. He must not know. Was Rosa waiting until they were with her parents to tell him?

Rosa glanced at Angela and shook her head. "I'm so sorry to leave you alone at the flower shop at this time of year."

"Don't worry. Becca's home from school early for Christmas break and Bethany volunteered to help. We'll be fine." Angela slowed for a snow-drifted section of highway.

"I dreamed about Papi," Roberto said. "I dreamed he came to my bedroom one night and held me."

"That's a nice dream, Roberto." Angela white-knuckled the steering wheel for no reason related to the road conditions.

The congested airport drop-off area left little time for words before the glass doors closed on Rosa and Roberto.

Angela would put in the extra hours. She would make it. Rosa would soon be free to come back and make a fresh start, now knowing the truth about her past. In the meantime, Angela would weather December's business with her daughters' help. December. A wedding to look forward to. Angela's mind shifted to a planning mode and her heart lifted.

———

Later that evening, Angela's phone rang.

"Hi, sis."

"Lorrie," Angela said. "So nice to hear from you."

"So, Benjamin is getting married on Christmas Eve?"

"Yes. Isn't it exciting?"

"It is. Grandma Em asked me to tell you she's sorry she

doesn't feel up to coming." Lorri hesitated. "But I would like to come. Do you have room for me at your house?"

"Oh yes, Lorrie! Can you get away?"

"I have vacation time coming, and I'd like to see everyone again."

"And we'd love to see you."

"It's been a long time."

"It has. Remember, it's Minnesota. Bring warm clothing. Layers of warm clothing."

61

The next day, again, Bethany and Phillip joined Becca and Angela at Wisteria. She would work longer hours and try not to wonder if everything would get finished. Myrna proved good with the customers and meticulous with orders, but Angela's mind reverted to Rosa throughout the day.

"Look Gamma." Phillip unpacked his books and placed them on the break table. "Mommy says this is my job." He hugged his mom's old copy of *Curious George*.

Angela and Bethany exchanged smiles.

"I brought my Spiderman sleeping bag."

"Did I hear you are three years old, Phillip?" Myrna said.

"Yep." Phillip swung his legs back and forth in the break room chair, both elbows on the table, chin on his hands.

A captivated Myrna continued. "My grandsons are five and seven years old."

"They live with you?"

"No, they live in Pennsylvania. But I'll see them at Christmastime. We leave Friday morning."

Angela tensed. "That's right. You told me you could only work through Thursday this week." Not Friday. Our busiest day.

"Um hum," Myrna said.

"I'm having Christmas too, Gamma." Phillip piped up in his high voice.

Angela sorted orders by date, trying not to think how Rosa always handled the responsibility.

"Gamma?"

Angela smiled.

"Phillip, remember we each have our job to do." Bethany touched one finger to her lips.

Phillip frowned and unpacked more books.

"Angela, look at this Christmas cactus, mashed on one side." Myrna held up the pot. "Looks like somebody dropped something on it. What should I do with it?"

"It's trash." Angela motioned to the trashcan.

"Oh, no," Myrna said. "Can I take it home and nurse it back to health?"

"It's yours," Angela said.

Myrna wrapped the pot and set it next to her purse. "I've finished watering plants. What now?"

Angela paused. "I don't know. Let me think."

The phone rang. "There, my next assignment," Myrna said.

Myrna put the caller on hold. "It's the bank, wondering why the open house flowers haven't arrived?"

"They're ready in the case," Angela said. "Wait. Were we supposed to deliver?"

The tag said deliver.

Angela lifted the enormous arrangement from the case, her hands shaking. "Tell them it's on its way."

"I can drive the van," Bethany said. "Let me take them. Come on, Phillip. We're going for a ride."

Becca leaned forward and whispered, "Mom, I'll find things to keep Myrna busy. I know what needs to be done." She tipped her head toward Myrna polishing the glass in the front door.

"I'd appreciate that so much. I'm terribly distracted today." Angela breathed a sigh of relief. "Myrna, would you like to help Becca? I've loaded her down with things to finish."

"I'd love to, Angela."

Bethany was wiggling Phillip's boots over his socks when her buzzing phone stopped her. "A text from Tatum." Handing her phone to Becca, she said, "Asking if we can be bridesmaids. Said she wants both of us."

"Oh, that's sweet of her."

"And she would like us to wear red. Do you have anything in red?"

"Red sweater, but it's pretty tacky." Becca brightened. "Time to go shopping."

"At least you look good in red."

"Oh! The flowers for the wedding. How could I forget?" Angela said. "I'd better add that to my order for next week."

"What's this?" Myrna said. "Whose wedding?"

"My son, Benjamin, is getting married on Christmas Eve," Angela said.

"How nice. And you're decorating the church?"

"Only a small wedding for the immediate family."

"I see." Myrna twisted wire together and handed a bow to Becca. "How's this?"

"Perfect size for my arrangement," Becca said. "Aunt Lorrie will be here, too. Arriving late Saturday night."

Angela tried to recount her ever-growing to-do list. Every

item made her chest constrict more. Prepare a room for Lorrie. Plan the wedding reception. Stay ahead of business at the shop. Angela ducked into the restroom just for a moment to get control. She leaned against the door, closed her eyes, and reminded herself to breathe.

62

Saturday, December 20

Angela had put in long, steady days the past week. Business boomed. Her feet had been numb each evening, but she made it.

Rosa had texted every day. Then early Saturday evening, she called Angela at home. "I found a church just like our church in Minnesota. Angela, he preached the Word straight from the Bible at Carlos's funeral." There was joy in her voice. "My family heard the Gospel."

"I'm so glad, Rosa." Angela sank into her favorite chair and put up her feet.

"This is difficult for me to say," Rosa said. "My mamá isn't doing well. She needs me. Roberto is happy here. I'm home, and I'm happy. Angela, I've decided to stay."

"Rosa." Angela's feet hit the floor. Her action startled her family who were each busy in their own corner of the living room. The looks of concern on their faces reminded Angela that Rosa now safely enjoyed a family as well.

Angela struggled to keep her voice level. "Rosa, I love you and I want you to be happy."

"Thank you. Love you, too," she said. "Makes the decision more difficult."

"Don't feel bad about staying." Angela swallowed hard. "This completes the circle, don't you see? You came to the shelter. You've mastered new skills and proved you can not only survive but also provide a home for you and your son."

"You're so right." Rosa paused. "Angela, we took our clothes, but my car, the household items in our apartment—they're not much, but I want to donate them to women at the shelter."

"That will be appreciated."

"I'll try to be an example to other women just like so many of you have been for me."

"I couldn't ask for more."

Angela hung up the phone and stared at the Christmas tree in the middle of the living room, but its bright lights and reflecting ornaments blurred.

"Rosa's staying?" Bethany said.

"Yes." Angela managed a crooked smile.

"Wow. Hard to run the shop without her."

"But she's with her family."

"We'll miss her and Roberto." Bethany settled Phillip on her lap.

Angela closed her eyes.

"What time's Aunt Lorrie coming?" Emerson said.

Angela clutched the arms of her chair, glanced at the clock, then relaxed. "She changed to a later flight. Arrives at eight. I should leave in an hour."

"I'll drive you," Emerson said.

"I'd appreciate that."

"I go too?" Phillip said.

"Who's staying home with mommy?" Bethany squeezed him until he giggled.

Snow fell in lazy flakes during the drive to Minneapolis.

"Thank goodness she's flying into MSP instead of the main terminal," Emerson said. "And glad I'm not fighting my way through it each week anymore."

"You're home most nights. That means so much to Bethany and Phillip." Angela checked her messages as they rushed into the airport. "Lorrie's text says to meet her at baggage pick up number two. What did we do before cell phones?"

She followed Emerson down the escalator. "There she is!"

Lorrie trotted to them as quickly as she could drag her luggage.

"So good to see you!" Lorrie hugged Angela tight. "Emerson, last time I was here, it was for your and Bethany's wedding."

"Hi, Lorrie." Emerson squeezed her shoulder and took her luggage.

"Was it that long ago?" Angela said.

"Wait here." Emerson looked at Lorrie's imitation leather jacket and furrowed his forehead. "I'll get the car. It's not far."

Lorrie shivered as she climbed in the back seat.

"I have another heavy coat. It'll fit you perfectly," Angela said.

"Thanks."

"How do you enjoy living in Abbeyville?" Angela said.

"I'd rather be there than anywhere else." Lorrie said.

"Even your own home with some hunk of a guy?" Emerson smiled into the rear view mirror.

"Fat chance of that in Abbeyville." Lorrie's laugh rang out.

Soon they were pulled into Angela's driveway.

"Still an awesome house," Lorrie said as she entered Angela's home.

Angela guided her to the living room. "We moved Phillip in with his parents so you can have his room while you're here."

Lorrie looked around. "Where's your room?"

"Upstairs, remember?" Angela said. "Get settled then come to my room for a nice long chat."

"Like the old days." Lorrie grinned.

In the kitchen, Angela warmed a heating pad and felt her energy return as she mounted the steps and entered her room.

A knock on the door and Lorrie entered wearing sweats. "I don't think my feet will ever be warm again."

"Yes, they will." Angela flipped the comforter on one side of the bed. "Hop in. It's warmer. We'll have a slumber party."

Lorrie climbed in, screeched, and jerked her feet back. "What's that?"

Angela uncovered a bumpy rectangle. "A homemade heating pad."

Lorrie rested her feet on its top. "Don't tell me you made it?"

"No, the youth group at church. Their fundraiser, flannel filled with shelled corn. I just took it out of the microwave."

"Aren't you afraid you'll have popcorn?" The two giggled with abandon, erasing years between them.

"I needed you, Lorrie. I'm so glad you're here."

"Me too."

"It's a busy household. While I'm at work—and how I hate to leave you alone during the day—I want you to come to my

363

room for peace and quiet when the household gets rambunctious."

"It's okay. I understand you have to work."

"Here's mother's Bible. There's a chair or the window seat. Make yourself comfortable whenever you come in." Angela turned the Bible's pages. "It's well-used but there's not a single mark in this Bible, other than her name and the family history in the center."

"Grandma Em told me they used to believe it a desecration to underline or make notes in the Bible."

"So it was out of respect?"

"Yes, I think so." Lorrie reached out and touched the satin-smooth page. "It's almost like Mom is here with us."

"I know. Such a comfort. So glad Aunt Rita kept it for us."

"Guess what? Aunt Rita came to church last Sunday evening with Grandma and me."

"An answer to prayer."

"Yes. It's a start."

"Grandma tells me you've joined the church choir."

"Singing in choir makes me feel closer to God." Lorrie smiled and looked up as if she could see straight through the ceiling, past the starry sky, into heaven. "It's a whole new world. I can't believe it. I can't believe my Heavenly Father was there all along waiting for me to take the first step."

———

Sunday, December 21

The church's beauty washed over Angela with all the best that Christmas had to offer. A 12-foot decorated pine tree domi- nated the area behind the pulpit. It wrapped Angela in a warm blanket of joy. She smiled at Lorrie, tucked beside her in the pew. Pastor Bailey's Christmas sermon extended from the birth of Christ to His sacrifice on the cross and His resurrection.

When the service was over, Lorrie scooted to the aisle, turning to let Angela go ahead of her. Too late Angela saw Kent stepping backwards in the aisle to allow a couple out while in deep conversation with another man. He backed smack into Lorrie.

"Oh!" He wheeled around with surprising agility, grabbing Lorrie's shoulders with both hands to steady her. "I beg your pardon. Wasn't watching where I was going. Are you okay?"

The corner of Angela's mouth crinkled in a smirk. She expected Lorrie to react the same, but Lorrie's face flushed, and she batted her eyelashes.

"I—I'm okay," she stuttered.

Lorrie never stuttered in her life. Not Angela's older sister.

"My name's Kent Hargrove. I don't believe I've seen you before?"

"Kent, let me introduce my sister, Lorrie."

"Your sister?" Kent's eyes dipped to Lorrie's ringless left hand and back to her face. "Yes, you look a lot alike. Will you be staying long?"

"Only a week."

"Please excuse us, Kent." Angela touched Lorrie's arm to guide her up the aisle.

"Very nice to meet you," Kent said.

Little boys clamored around Angela, halting her progress out of the sanctuary. One tugged on her arm. "Where's Roberto?"

"I'm sorry." Angela recognized Jaxon, the former tormentor. "He and his mother are in Arizona now. Did you know his grandparents live there?"

Jaxon's forehead wrinkled. His mouth drooped.

"I'll tell him you asked about him when I talk to his mother."

"Okay!" the group shouted and left en masse.

Angela had to face the truth: Rosa and Roberto were not coming back. The words replayed in Angela's head, but she pasted a smile on her face, opened the door, and took Lorrie's arm. "It's so nice to have you. Glad you'll be here for the wedding," Angela said.

"I'm so happy to—ohhh!" The wind took Lorrie's breath as she maneuvered across the parking lot. She slammed the car door after her and laughed when Angela took the driver's seat. "This long quilted coat you loaned me?" Lorrie turned to Angela. "Felt like wearing a mattress when I zipped it up this morning. But boy, am I glad to have it!"

"You look very Minnesotan."

"Do you ever get used to it?"

"Yes, you shiver through a couple of winters, change your mindset, then you're home free." Angela left the church's congested traffic and headed to the business section. "On your right is the shop."

"Wisteria!" Lorrie leaned forward when Angela slowed down. "Look at that sign. You always loved the color lavender. From what I can see, it looks just the way I imagined."

"We'll drive over one day this week, and I'll show you around." Angela looked at the sign she forgot to take down about a sale that ended a week ago, thought about the back room piled high with unpacked boxes to break down, supplies to organize, and felt tired. Really tired.

63

Monday morning at Angela's house—December 22

Angela patted the assembled tableware for the wedding reception. "I think we've organized, planned, and prepared as much as possible."

"I agree." Bethany washed jelly off Phillip's face and hands and watched him speed to his toy corner. "It'll be a great reception."

"I still think you should have told Tatum what we're up against at the flower shop," Becca said.

"No. It's her wedding. She should enjoy it," Angela said. "A caterer will prepare the bulk of the menu. That's a load off my mind."

"I'll drive to Minnetonka tomorrow to pick up your order," Bethany said.

"Thanks. What would I do without my girls? Still going to the shop with me, Becca?"

"Yes, Mom."

"I'll take care of the local shopping," Bethany said. "Should get the baking finished today."

"We'll tackle what's left to do tonight together." Becca beamed.

"You're forgetting one thing." Lorrie walked up behind them.

Angela caught her breath. Her mind whirled. What had she forgotten?

"Big sister's here now. You can count on me when you're in a pinch."

Angela slowly exhaled and hugged Lorrie.

Soon the house was immaculate, items checked off lists. Bethany and Lorrie formed a great working team in the kitchen. Angela and Becca set off to the flower shop.

"At this rate, we should have tomorrow's deliveries ready to go first thing in the morning," Becca said as she pressed soil around a maidenhair fern.

"Tomorrow will be a hectic day. All orders picked up or delivered since we're closed Wednesday and Thursday. I'll miss out on the last-minute Christmas Eve shoppers, but it can't be helped." Angela smiled at Becca. "We did it. I paid off balloon payment at the bank this morning."

"Thanks for the check, Mom," Becca said. "You shouldn't have, but I can use it for those college expenses."

Angela felt one burden roll off her shoulders. She let the contentment seep through her.

"Calls for a celebration," Becca said.

"Isn't a wedding enough of a celebration?"

Becca laughed, then sobered. "That's odd. Someone's knocking at the front door."

"Happens all the time." Angela walked through the darkened room and unlocked the door. "Sorry, normally closed today, but may I help you?"

"Yes, I'm a resident from the woman's shelter." Her head drooped before she continued. "Susan Bailey, the pastor's wife, told me to see you. I saw your van out back and thought I'd take a chance." The huddled figure clutched her coat tighter, shivering. "Susan said you were looking for a new employee?"

"Yes. I will be. That is, I am. Come in." Angela stepped aside and stared at the woman's perfectly tapered blonde hair.

"I see you're working. Please go ahead. I don't want to interrupt what you're doing. We can talk while you work." She followed Angela through the quiet shop to their worktable with the fluorescent lights glowing overhead.

"My name's Angela. This is my daughter, Becca."

"I'm Sally. Sally Griswold. Nice to meet you both." She stepped back and studied Becca's arrangement. "What lovely colors. I just moved ... well, ended up in Northgate. I'm looking for a job, and I have experience in floral."

Angela almost dropped the bucket she was returning to the case. "You do? Tell me about your experience."

Sally unzipped her coat and let it fall on a nearby stool. A thirty-ish Barbie doll emerged: long neck, thin arms and pencil body apparent through a snug sweater.

"Well, I lived in Bloomington."

"Minnesota?" Angela said.

"No, Illinois." Her eyebrows lifted as she scanned the room. "Seven years in floral design. A rather upscale shop. I'm sure I could be an asset to you."

369

"We're small," Angela said. "I can only pay the going rate." Angela name a wage per hour.

Sally blinked, but Angela continued.

"When can you be available?"

"Why, any time. What were you thinking?"

"Tomorrow."

Becca flipped on a few lights and watered plants.

Sally lowered her voice and leaned toward Angela. "I'll be perfectly honest with you. I'm recovering from a devastating relationship. He kept the Beamer. I drove an old rust bucket to Minnesota because ... well, my family lived here when I was a child. Happy memories." She shook her head. "Couldn't find a job. Ran out of gas and money. A woman at the motel was nice enough to tell me about Shepherd's Fold."

Sally met Angela's gaze. "The answer is yes, I can start tomorrow. And the wages are just fine."

"We're almost caught up with orders," Angela said. "But tomorrow there will be more to download and our walk-in customers to handle."

Sally nodded. "What a life you lead. Your own flower shop, always a dream of mine."

"Something I always wanted, too." Angela glanced her way.

Angela walked her to the front. "I'll see you tomorrow morning at nine, Sally."

Becca pushed her watering cart closer. "Mom, why are you frowning?"

"She couldn't be a more opposite to Rosa." Angela removed the key and watched the red taillights disappear. "Think she'll show up tomorrow?"

64

True to her word, Sally arrived at nine the next morning and seemed eager to dive into work. Angela watched her choose flowers, including a half-dozen long-stemmed roses.

"Wait," Angela said. "That's a sixty-dollar arrangement. That allows for only two roses, depending on the cost of the other flowers."

Sally checked the amount on the order slip. "Sorry, I forgot to check your prices. I'll be more careful. Our lowest-priced arrangement was one-fifty."

Angela blinked, then stared at Sally's triangular arrangement with lovely sweeping points. "Nice!"

"Awesome," Becca said. "I know just the ribbon for those colors."

"Uh, no. Bows are passé," Sally said. "Well, except for the funeral bouquets."

"Oh." Becca studied Sally's arrangement. "So how can I make mine look more like yours?"

"You've got a great start. But, there are too many flowers. You've lost your lines. May I?" Sally removed one-third of the flowers. "Pick out the blooms you want to showcase and give them some room. Sometimes less is more."

"Wow, what a difference."

Angela noted the improvement. "You're adding style to our shop. We can learn from you."

Customers spilled into the shop, orders disappeared, and the crew worked even faster.

"Before I forget, we'll need the white roses for the wedding tomorrow. I set them aside. Yes, here they are," Angela said.

"A wedding? On Christmas Eve?" Sally said. "How romantic. Tell me about the flowers they ordered."

"My son is getting married," Angela said. "His fiancé wants to carry long-stem white roses over her arm. I'll have an arrangement for the altar, one for the reception table at my house, and I guess that's it. A small wedding, only immediate family."

"I've always loved doing weddings. Are you using tulle?" Sally said.

"Never thought of it. There's a bolt behind the tissue paper."

"That's always a nice touch for the bride's flowers." Sally reached for the tulle and caressed the soft fabric. "Protects her arm. Even after you de-thorn the roses, there's still a roughness that could catch on delicate clothing. Just a thought."

"Good idea." Angela glanced her way. Must be quite a story behind Sally's experience.

"Would you like me to assemble the altar arrangement?" A soft expression around Sally's eyes slowly spread and curved her lips. "Oh, it's your son. You probably want to do them yourself."

"Not necessarily." Angela melted when she glimpsed the

next arrangement Sally was creating. "Please, go ahead. I'll do the bride's roses."

A gust of cold air reminded Angela to ask her landlord to build a double entryway for the back door when she signed a new lease.

"Hi, everyone." Bethany closed the door. "Had lunch? I brought a few snacky items for you."

"I'm famished," Becca said.

Sally peered around her arrangement.

"Bethany, I want you to meet Sally," Angela said.

"Mom told me an angel dropped out of the sky yesterday." Bethany nodded Sally's way.

Soon everyone was talking at once. Only Phillip said nothing. He just stared at Sally's manicured red nails until the front door opened and a mother walked in with her four sons.

"Phillip, whoa, stay behind the counter, remember?" Bethany caught Phillip as he started to follow a little boy. "Time we started for the cities."

"Bethany, thanks for picking up the food," Angela said.

"You're doing okay?" Bethany said.

"Yes." Angela looked around the room. "We're cruising."

"Come on, bud, finish your cheese and we'll take the apple with us." Bethany cleared the break table and stuffed her squirming son back into his snowsuit.

"Coffee or tea, Sally?" Angela said.

Sally wandered to the break room picked up a bag of Wisteria Tea. "Oh, what's this?"

"Our special mix of tea."

Sally smiled. "That's what I'll have."

Customers swarmed in for pickup orders. The shop hummed.

"Lorrie!" Angela watched her sister walk in the front door with Kent Hargrove close behind.

"Kent called and asked me to lunch." Lorrie tilted her head at Kent.

"Don't want to take her away from you in the evenings." Kent smiled at Lorrie. "Just thought we'd have lunch then stop in the flower shop and say hi."

Angela closed her gaping mouth. Kent courting her sister? Of course, Lorrie had no idea of his past interest in Angela.

Kent halted at a display of toy tractors. "Would you look at this? Replica of an old IH 240. Reminds me of growing up on the farm."

"Oooh," Lorrie gushed.

Angela turned away to hide a grin. Lorrie wouldn't know an International Harvester 240 from a tricycle. Between helping customers, Angela watched, incredulous, as Lorrie and Kent made their way around the room.

Kent took Lorrie's arm and guided her toward the display case. "We can't leave without flowers for you, Lorrie." He pointed to an arrangement with Angela's trademark of dried lavender stalks around the vase. "How about this one?"

"Pink roses. Perfect," Lorrie said.

"Aunt Lorrie, let me help." Becca seated the arrangement in a box, cushioning the bottom with paper and protecting it with more paper over the top.

Lorrie ducked into the back room and hugged Angela. "Gotta go."

"Sorry I don't have more time to spend with you," Angela said.

"Trust me, it's okay." Lorrie beamed and caught up with Kent. She accepted the arm he extended to escort her out the door.

"Was that your sister?" Sally said.

"Yes. Sorry I didn't introduce you."

"I can see you're related. Same build, beautiful blonde hair. Do you have other siblings?"

Angela shook her head. "No, just the two of us." The phone interrupted, and she answered the call. Listening, she moaned.

"What's her room number?" Angela scribbled a note. "Can she have visitors? Thank you for letting me know."

"What happened?" Becca pushed a miniature Norway pine to the staging area.

"Miranda was hospitalized last night." Angela brushed a tear aside. "Pneumonia."

"Oh no," Becca said. "At her age ..."

"The shop is quiet for the moment. Let's pray, shall we?" Angela and Becca bowed their heads where they were standing. When she looked up Sally was busy inserting fillers for the background of a fresh arrangement.

"I'll make her a special bouquet," Angela said. "I know her favorite flowers."

"Extra orders for the hospital here. Wanna take 'em?" Becca said.

"Angela," Miranda's voice was a whisper. The oxygen tube dented her face. An IV ran into her left hand.

Angela kissed her forehead then unwrapped the bouquet.

"Daisies." Miranda's voice grew stronger. "In the middle of winter."

65

Christmas Eve

Before dawn, Angela crept from her bed and knelt at the window seat. She studied the frostwork in the corners of the glass, far more intricate than any lace a wedding veil could boast. She remembered her own wedding day and bowed her head. What would Todd have said to Benjamin today? What more than she had already said to him? What more than Pastor Bailey had said? Her heart was full. "Bless them, dear Lord," she prayed. "May You be glorified in their lives."

A soft tap on her door ended Angela's prayer. She ushered in Lorrie carrying two cups of coffee.

Angela took a cup and motioned to the chair. "Thank you. You're up early."

"Always." Lorrie balanced her cup and picked up a devotional. "I started reading this yesterday. Why didn't they have devotionals when we were young? Maybe they did, and I wasn't paying attention."

"We seldom went to church, remember? Only in the summer at Grandma's."

Lorrie nodded. "Grandma Em. Feels like sitting at the feet of a saint. She found a study for new believers, a book for each of us. I'm sure she knows most of it by heart, but she gets so excited as though she's hearing it for the first time."

"A Christian never tires of hearing the Gospel again." Angela drained her cup, wrapped her arms around her legs, and placed her chin on her knees, drinking in this moment with Lorrie before the day's activities claimed her. "I'm finished with that devotional. Why don't you take it home with you?"

"Thanks, I will."

Becca and Bethany's voices floated up the stairs. Lorrie stood. "Finished? I'll take our cups with me."

Angela dressed and rushed downstairs to finish the food prep for the reception.

Lorrie stood in the dining room next to Bethany. "How much time do we have before leaving for the wedding?"

Bethany checked her watch. "Exactly three hours. Plenty of time to set up for the reception."

Lorrie glanced at the sheet in Bethany's hand. "You have a diagram of the table?"

"Showing the location of each dish." Bethany pointed to plates temporarily serving as stand-ins for each platter.

"Your planning goes way beyond me," Lorrie said. "But how can I help?"

"Glad you asked!" Becca handed a box to Lorrie and balanced another against the table. "Plates set at the beginning of the buffet line. Silverware and napkins stacked at the other end."

"Now, where's the spot for the bouquet?" Angela brought a

Ginny Graham

long low arrangement of white roses, white snapdragons, red berries, and sprays of fragrant spruce to the table.

"The paper strip in the middle of the table marks its spot," Bethany said.

While the ladies prepared the table, Angela could hear Emerson's and Benjamin's repartee. Emerson played his part of the best man well, telling stories of disastrous weddings and honeymoons until laughter prevailed over Benjamin's wedding jitters. Soon Benjamin sounded an alarm to hurry everyone to dress. Angela showered and changed into a taupe wool suit with matching silk blouse. She tucked her mother's Bible under her arm. It would feel like taking her mother to the wedding.

Lorrie, Phillip, and Emerson followed Benjamin and Angela into the church.

"Don't worry, we're right behind you." Emerson smiled when Benjamin turned. "We've got your back."

Benjamin grinned. "As long as there's not a target on it."

"What can I say? You'll be a married man soon."

"Okay, you two." Angela scolded.

"Nice tie," Angela whispered as Benjamin hung up his overcoat.

"Thanks, Mom."

Tears in Benjamin's eyes caught Angela by surprise.

"Your father would have been so happy for you and Tatum."

"If only Dad could have been here." Benjamin blinked and rubbed the end of the tie between his thumb and forefinger.

Angela straightened the knot on his tie. Her fingers

378

lingered over the smooth satin. Todd's son. Benjamin beginning a new family.

Benjamin spotted Tatum's parents waiting in the foyer. "Mr. and Mrs. Edwards, soon-to-be Mom and Dad. I want you to meet my mother, Angela." Going down the line, he named each one.

"How do you do?" An older version of Tatum stepped forward and nodded to each family member in turn. Mrs. Edwards was small, slightly bent, but there was nothing frail about her voice or the presence she exuded. "Angela, Emerson, Lorrie, my pleasure. Please call me Olivia. This is Jim."

Tatum's father nodded curtly.

"Ohhh," Olivia tensed but shook the small hand extended to her. "You must be, uh ... "

"Phillip," he said, "Only I have to be quiet."

Everyone laughed at his candor.

"We enjoy your daughter so much," Angela said. "She's lovely."

"Why, thank you," Olivia said. "We're growing very fond of Benjamin and looking forward to getting to know him better."

"Yes," Jim Edwards piped up, crossing in front of Olivia to stand by Benjamin's side. "You'll be moving to San Diego and I plan to show you around our firm." Jim put a hand on Benjamin's shoulder. "Maybe we can talk you into joining us."

Benjamin smiled in lieu of an answer. Angela's heart skipped a beat. Her thoughts lingered on Tatum's mention of the long hours her dad worked. No time for family.

The sound of Pachelbel's *Canon in D Major* on the piano drew everyone's attention to the front of the church. Angela smiled. Caroline's fingers flew effortlessly over the arpeggios that created a beautiful counterpoint to the melody. Her flawless execution created a work of art at the keyboard. Caroline was back.

Pastor Bailey tapped Benjamin's shoulder. "Are you ready?"

When Pastor Bailey took his place, everyone's focus shifted to the sanctuary. Olivia's face was a study of surprise and enjoyment as she gasped. "What an exquisite spray of flowers on the altar," she whispered to Angela as they parted.

Angela exhaled. Sally was truly a gift. How comforting that God had prepared a helper for her. Not just one helper, but also Bethany, Becca, Lorrie to see her through.

Benjamin escorted Olivia down the aisle and returned for Angela. She folded her hand over his arm and squeezed it. Angela blinked back tears when Benjamin patted her fingers.

Benjamin took his place beside Emerson. Becca, then Bethany proceeded down the aisle with measured steps. Both wore a red top with a red lace band around the hips above long black skirts, carrying nosegays of Lilly-of-the-valley and baby white roses.

"Hi, Mommy!" Phillip whispered loudly as she passed.

Bethany stared straight ahead, but her smile deepened. The music rose in volume, signaling everyone to stand and face the back of the church. Angela waited to turn. She wanted to imprint on her mind forever the joy lighting Benjamin's face watching his bride.

Tatum's white velvet top fitted her snugly above an organdy skirt. Billows of white floated around her feet as she walked toward them on her father's arm. In the crook of her left arm, long-stemmed white roses nodded and danced nestled among ferns and white tulle. Narrow satin ribbon toppled over the bouquet with lover's knots tied around sprigs of baby's breath at their ends.

"Do you, Benjamin, take Tatum to love, honor, and cherish, until death do you part?" Pastor Bailey said.

"I do." Benjamin's firm voice repeated his vows to Tatum.

Angela's attention wavered, haunted by memories. What about after death? Do you stop loving, honoring, and cherishing them?

Hardly.

66

Christmas Day

Angela awoke with dread that something was terribly wrong. It took her several minutes to clear the sleep flog from her mind and register that dread. Oh, yes. Christmas without Todd. The desire to stay in bed overwhelmed her. She rolled on her side with life's if-onlys flitting through her thoughts.

Sounds of people stirring tugged at her heart. She could either share a happy day with her family, or she could give in to sorrow.

A sense of urgency usurped her depression. Why miss a single minute? Throwing her robe around her, she combed her hair, brushed her teeth, and flew down the stairs. Down where the gifts, her family, and the fragments of her life awaited her.

Phillip squealed when he saw his dream come true with a red bow tied to its handlebars. Angela eased into Todd's recliner and pulled an afghan close. She was so disarmed by

Phillip's squeals of delight with each gift that her tears and joy couldn't be separated.

Emerson coached Phillip on his new balance bike. A bike with no pedals, just kid power to scoot him down the hall and back.

"Merry Christmas." Lorrie perched on the chair beside her. "Your eyes are red."

"I'm a mess, aren't I?" Angela said.

"No." Lorrie shifted her weight and eased herself back into the chair. "I can't imagine what you're going through."

Angela reached out, and Lorrie gripped her hand. "So glad you're here."

"I wish Benjamin and Tatum could have stayed for this morning," Becca said.

Bethany arched her eyebrows. "Seriously, Becca?"

"Oh." Becca's face flushed. They both laughed.

Phillip parroted the last comment he had heard at the reception. "She had to get off her feet because her toes were pinched, 'member?"

Snickers blossomed into full-blown laughter. Phillip's frown deepened.

"Phillip, want to hand out the presents?" said Emerson.

"Okay."

Emerson whispered in his ear.

"For Gamma." Phillip dumped a box in Angela's lap and sailed back to the Christmas tree. Angela held it close, wanting to savor the moment of watching her family—the most important gift of all.

Phillip couldn't resist tearing into a present labeled for him. He wrinkled his nose when he pulled out a scarf.

"Is that yours or is it mommy's?" Emerson said. "Let's try it on mommy." Emerson wrapped Phillip's scarf around Bethany's neck.

Phillip laughed. "It's too little!"

Emerson tugged the stocking hat on one side of Bethany's head while Phillip's peals of laughter filled the room.

Angela watched the byplay and smiled. The way it should be. With Bethany the center of her little family, and Gramma fading into the background. Somehow it was easier to fade when Todd was beside her. Becca pulled a chair closer to Lorrie and they launched into an animated discussion of the popular Christmas movie they had seen. All the family noise around her and she felt lonely. She shook herself. Buck up. Life isn't about you.

Phillip resumed his job and bounced across the room. "For Aunt Lorrie."

"What's this?" Lorrie removed tissue from a gift bag and pulled out a silky scarf in muted shades of green and orange. "I love it." She draped it around her neck and flipped out her long, blonde hair.

"Great colors," Emerson said.

"Gamma, open it!" Phillip yanked wrappings from the box Angela held. She laughed and helped him.

"The guest book?" Angela paused. Todd's funeral. Someone had slipped a picture in the cover opening. Todd, one hand on the top of the screen door, elbow bent, holding open the door at the cabin. His tall, lanky form. His handsome grin. His red-and-black plaid shirt. "My favorite picture."

"Gamma, don't crwy," Phillip said. "I wrote something."

"Remember when we talked about making notes last summer?" Becca opened the book to the middle and pointed.

"Oh, my." Snapshots on one side of the page, an envelope

taped to the other. Angela pulled a sheet from an envelope and read. "'I remember Dad, by Bethany.'"

Bethany sat cross-legged on the floor in front of her. "We each wrote a letter to you of our favorite memories with our favorite photo of dad. Benjamin dropped his off so we could complete the book."

Angela turned the page to a picture of Benjamin in his scout uniform with Todd pinning a badge to a little puffed-out chest.

"Look, Mom," Becca said. "Dad helping me blow out candles. He loved teasing me about wearing a chocolate cake."

"Oh, look," Lorrie peered over Angela's shoulder at the Danish-style table. "It's the same dining room table."

On the next page, Phillip's envelope appeared with 'Grampa' written in a large, shaky print.

"Now this is a true legacy for Todd. A legacy of the love of his family." Angela touched a picture of Phillip sitting on grandpa's lap driving the lawn tractor. "I've never seen—"

"I had forgotten we took this one," Bethany said. "Found it when I was scrolling through photos."

"It must've been—"

"Yes." Bethany leaned closer. "First of May. The last picture of dad."

Angela and Lorrie found themselves alone in the kitchen after the noonday meal.

"Kent's picking me up at seven for dinner tonight. I came to visit you, but he's so lonely. Has no one in Minnesota."

"I'm glad you two met." Angela trimmed the turkey carcass. "You're free to bring him here."

"I'll mention it to him." Lorrie washed her hands and opened freezer bags. "I've met no one like Kent. Well, you know the choices we have in Beaumont Springs."

Angela raised her eyebrows. "I do."

The murmur of voices in the living room and the hum of the dishwasher blended together as Angela and Lorrie enjoyed their world of sisterhood.

"He tells me he's a Christian and was quite involved in a church when they lived in Iowa."

Angela helped Lorrie stack sliced turkey in the fridge. "I know little about him. I heard he bought the agency from a college friend. He and his wife moved here a few years ago. They settled on the east side of town. His wife, already being treated for cancer, died a year later." Angela reflected she should have been kinder to Kent. The death of a spouse, the same grief she was processing.

"Must've been hard for him," Lorrie said.

"I'm sure it was. He became friends with Pastor Bailey and joined our church a year ago. Kent and Wade, my accountant, golfed with our pastor. Todd talked about joining them ..."

"He mentioned golfing with the Pastor, but I don't remember hearing about Wade."

"Wade's rather quiet."

The two sisters spent the afternoon visiting until the darkness of evening reminded them that some in their family may actually be hungry.

Angela stacked cups and plates. "Do you think everyone's ready for hot cider?"

"Nice."

Angela placed a tray on the coffee table. Lorrie followed with sandwiches.

"Oh!" Becca headed upstairs. "Just got a text. Cole's here."

Angela could hear excited greetings as Becca brought her guest to the living room.

"Merry Christmas, Cole," Angela said. "You're just in time."

"Merry Christmas to you," he said.

Becca turned to Lorrie. "Cole, this is my Aunt Lorrie."

"Nice to meet you, Mrs.—?"

"Miss. But you can call me Lorrie."

Everyone helped themselves and drifted into little clusters, except Phillip. With red cheeks and a lilting voice, he danced from one group to the next.

Lorrie fidgeted then finally stood. "I think I'll see if I have something that matches my new scarf," she whispered to Angela and headed down the hall.

Angela ran up the steps and rummaged through her closet. Grabbing a sweater and two blouses, she rushed to Lorrie's room.

"Knock, knock."

Lorrie opened the door. "What do you have there?"

"Just in case you didn't bring the right color, try one of these."

"Just like old times." They giggled and Lorrie found a blouse she liked.

"Would you like for me to arrange your hair?"

"Oh, would you?" Lorrie said.

Angela moved a chair in front of a full-length mirror. She swept the sides back and perched her fingers on the top of Lorrie's head. "Now, what do you think?"

"Yes! Do it."

"Let me find a curling iron."

"I have one." Lorrie stood. "Next to my roses." She touched

the lavender sprigs on the vase and handed the curling iron to Angela.

Angela curled and pulled and fussed until they were both satisfied with the results.

Bethany knocked. "Kent's here."

Lorrie gasped.

"Good. Time for a grand entrance," Angela said to Lorrie.

Kent reached the bottom of the stairs and stopped dead in his tracks when Lorrie entered the room.

His eyes took in the clothes, the hair, her glowing smile. "Wow, you look great."

"Thank you," Lorrie said. "Merry Christmas."

She held out her hand and Kent took it in both of his.

"Merry Christmas, Lorrie."

She looked flustered but pulled Kent around the room. Kent spoke to each one—until he got to Cole.

"Kent, this is Becca's friend, Cole," Lorrie said.

The color drained from Kent's face.

"We've met," Cole said, "Merry Christmas, Mr. Hargrove." He reached out his hand and Kent pumped it awkwardly.

67

Friday, December 26

Angela had gotten through her first Christmas without Todd. Her lips trembled as she picked up the guest book with all the children's photos and memories of their dad in it. Guest book. More like a Going Home Book. That's what she would call it. She flipped to the middle, slipped each hand-written sheet out of its envelope, and read each note again.

Becca's right. There aren't enough tissues.

Angela closed her eyes and leaned against her pillow. The memories still pained her. But they were a sweet pain now.

By the time she finished reading a chapter in her mother's Bible, she could hear water running downstairs. She joined Becca for breakfast and backed up when Becca sneezed.

"God bless you," Angela said. "Catching a cold?"

"Yes, Bethany's had it, Phillip's had it, and now me."

Angela ran her fingers across Becca's shoulders as she slipped onto a stool beside her. "Was it late when Cole left last night?"

"No. Cole and I both work this morning."

"I guess Lorrie was out late last night. She's usually up by now." Angela loaded her plate into the dishwasher. "Are you ready for the mess we left on Tuesday?"

"We trashed the place, didn't we?"

"Mm hmm. Riding with me?"

"Sure. I'll grab my backpack."

Angela opened the shop's back door to a war zone. "It's worse than I remembered."

Becca laughed. "Looks like our dorm room."

"I hope you're kidding."

"Come see sometime, when I'm not expecting you." Becca nudged Angela's shoulder.

Angela froze.

"What is it, Mom?"

Angela snapped to attention, her nostrils flaring. "Nothing. I thought I smelled something."

"Good. I thought for a minute somebody robbed the place again." Becca grabbed the key ring and laughed. "They would've broken their necks trying to get out the back door."

Angela headed for her office, anxious to deposit Tuesday's revenues.

"I can't believe I forgot to take the cash home. You would think I had learned my lesson."

"It's been a hectic time, to say the least."

Angela breathed a sigh of relief at the total and slipped her deposit into a bank bag. An added blessing. Seed money for ramping up to Valentine's day. She and Becca swept, stacked, and hauled empty boxes to the dumpster.

At one o'clock, Bethany arrived. "I brought lunch. Leftovers."

"Perfect," Angela said. "But should you be out again? Becca said you had a cold?"

"I'm fine. Just totally stopped up. Can't smell a thing."

Phillip unzipped his coat and dropped it on the back of his chair as if it were time for work.

"How's my favorite helper?" Angela smiled at Phillip. "We're just cleaning up the shop. No deliveries."

"I'll keep you company. Phillip and I needed to get out," Bethany said. "Hey, mom, the baker's rack by the front door, the one you painted orange, gold, and green—I think it would look cute in your kitchen. We could use an extra shelf."

Angela crossed her arms and nodded. "Amazing how the color combinations come back in vogue. You're right. It would fit in the recessed area that leads to the dining room."

Bethany unpacked lunch on the break table. "Where's Sally?"

"She mentioned she had committed to work in child care at the shelter. Said she would report back tomorrow."

"What's Aunt Lorrie doing?" Becca snatched a sugar cookie.

Bethany carried a small plate to Phillip. "Sleeping in, then spending the day with Kent."

"It's going to be hard for her to go home." Angela closed the display case and stared at the back wall. "Where did this brown spot on the wall come from?"

Becca squinted at the spot, roughly the size of a silver dollar. "Don't know. It's not paint."

Angela shook her head. "If these old walls could talk ..." As if in reply, the fluorescent light above the back door flickered. *Great.* Something else to add to the maintenance list.

Becca grabbed a tissue and blew her nose. "We're out of waxed wrappers."

"I opened a new carton," Angela said. "Was about to put it on the rack."

"I can do it." Becca ran to the far corner of the back room. She pulled full sheets and added a small stack to the worktable.

The front doorbell dinged. Becca rushed to the counter and waited while an elderly woman shuffled toward her. "Hello, Mrs. Dexter. Bet I know what you want."

"Yes, I'm here for a pink carnation. Christmas is over. Time to treat myself."

Angela smiled. Even Becca was familiar with the story of her corsage of pink carnations her husband had given her for their high school dance.

"Maybe I should make my deposit before the bank closes," Angela mumbled to Bethany. She slipped the bank bag into her generous apron pocket behind her cellphone.

Becca wrapped a carnation with a fern frond and handed it to Mrs. Dexter. "There you are. Happy New Year."

Mrs. Dexter peered around the room. "I noticed an odd smell when I walked in. Something burning?"

"What?" Angela wheeled around and sniffed. "I thought the same thing earlier. But no, nothing's burning."

Mrs. Dexter shrugged and picked up her flower. She was halfway toward the front door when two pops like a rifle shot sounded. Before Angela could react, something behind the discolored spot on the wall exploded. Flames shot from the electrical outlet above the brown spot. Grayish-white smoke rose to the ceiling, rolling toward the front of the shop.

"Out!" Angela shouted. "Everyone out! Where's Phillip?" Bethany picked up Phillip, looking for his jacket. "No! Just go." Angela pushed them out the back door.

The room filled with smoke. Angela ran to the front of the shop, looking for Becca. Feeling in her apron pocket, she clutched her cell phone; but it slipped back inside as she ran into Becca crossing the middle of the shop.

"Where's ... fire extinguisher?" Becca coughed. Her hands flailed at the smoke as she headed in the opposite direction.

"No. Out!" Angela gulped more smoke as she spun Becca around and shoved her toward the front door. Angela tried to pull her collar over her mouth, but it slipped as she half-dragged Becca along. That must be the front door. Angela reached out. They both went down.

"Mrs. Dexter!"

"Mmm, fell," came the muffled response.

Angela threw her body against the front door and kicked Mrs. Dexter's bag into the opening. Whoosh. Fresh air.

"Try to get up!" Angela commanded Mrs. Dexter. But she didn't move. "Becca, grab her underneath one arm. I'll get the other."

Cold, clean air continued to rush in. In response, the fire roared with triumph at the gust of oxygen.

"Father, help!" With a strength she didn't know she possessed, Angela helped Becca drag Mrs. Dexter partially through the door. The brace of cold air seemed to revive Mrs. Dexter. "Can you stand?" Angela tried to haul Mrs. Dexter to her feet.

Smoke and heat blasted through the open door. "Mrs. Dexter, you have to move!" Angela kicked the bag out of the way. She pulled Mrs Dexter from the door.

Angela dropped to the sidewalk. Where was her cell phone?

A siren drowned her thoughts. Numb and exhausted,

Angela seemed glued to the sidewalk. Soon a man rushed up beside her.

"Anyone still in the building?" He looked around as he checked Mrs. Dexter.

"I'm okay," Mrs. Dexter mumbled. "Where's my carnation?"

Angela shook her head. "No. Bethany, Phillip ... pushed out ... back door."

"Their ages?"

Angela tried to respond, but a fit of coughing stopped her.

"Twenty-six and a three-year-old," Becca said.

Angela jerked upright, disoriented. "Mrs. Dexter?"

Angela followed his nod toward a blanketed figure on a stretcher being loaded into a rescue vehicle. How had they arrived so quickly? Had she passed out? Time seemed suspended. Mrs. Dexter clutched a bag to her chest with crumpled tissue paper sticking out the top.

Someone threw a blanket over Angela's shoulders and pulled her toward a patrol car parked a block away in the middle of the street, blocking traffic. Angela cried when she looked into Officer Jammal Brown's face.

"You're going to be okay," he murmured. He helped her into the patrol car parked a safe distance from the shop. "I heard the call, was in the area."

Brown shoved a water bottle in Angela's hand. "Swallow," he commanded. "Another ambulance will be here soon to check you out."

Angela's nose and throat burned. She tried to swallow. It hurt too much. Everything hurt too much. "The fire?"

"Ma'am, the firefighters just arrived." Black smoke billowed, obscuring the shop's front windows. Angry flames roared through the smoke and reached greedy arms to engulf the front of the shop. Heat withered the lacework of wisteria vines at the entrance.

A huge pillar of flame shot up from the back. Flames lapped the roof. Fire trucks crowded the space in front of the patrol car and ambulance.

"Bethany! Phillip!" Emerson's voice penetrated the patrol car window.

"Sir." Officer Brown touched his shoulder. "Who are you looking for?"

"My wife! My son!" Emerson's jaw was set rigid as granite.

Angela closed her eyes and prayed they were safe.

Someone in the ambulance beside the patrol car noticed him, stood up, and ripped a mask from her face. Bethany.

Emerson cleared the distance to her in three leaps. "Thank God! If I had lost you—"

Shouting drowned out all other conversations. Paramedics urged Angela and Becca out of the patrol car. "We're taking you and everyone who was in the building to the emergency room. Can you walk?"

More sirens blared. She stumbled past the back of the fire truck obscuring her view of her shop. Walked behind the water lines from fire trucks. Then her shop came into view again. Water streaming from a fire hose looked like a tiny string amid black clouds. Angela's eyes seemed glued to the building. This couldn't be happening. Not after all her hard work, the note paid, her security in sight.

68

The next afternoon

Wisteria. That symbol of long life hadn't held true for her business. Angela stood in front of a bizarre scene. Falling wet snow pockmarked the piles of debris. Through the skeleton of wall frames, her blackened van and Bethany's SUV completed the desolate scene. The gray ash, lying deep beneath a silence pure and smooth, like burned out craters healed with snow.

Angela lifted the yellow fire line tape that outlined the empty space that once was her shop. She had to come. She had to witness the desolation first hand. The death of her dream. Everything she had built, believed in, and bore the burdens for, lay in ashes at her feet. All that remained of what little security she'd had was dust. Was her future as bleak as that devastated plot of ground?

The mechanical whir of a car window sounded behind her. "Mom, it's not safe. You shouldn't go any farther," Emerson called.

"I know." Angela picked her way to the edge of a pile of rubble. Emerson wouldn't understand why she had to physically touch and witness the scene to say good-bye.

"Mom?" Emerson climbed out of the car.

"Just give me a moment."

She kicked something half-buried under ash. A spiral of smoke rose as the ashes fell away. A wire frame. The baker's rack. The one Bethany wanted to take home.

"Why, Lord?" She clenched her fists. "I'm not angry. I just want to know why. *Okay, I am angry.* Who wouldn't be? You brought my shop back to life. And now it's dead, too."

Wind tore Angela's hood away. Snow pelted her forehead. Icy pellets like tiny BBs assaulted her neck. She backtracked and slipped into the warm car.

Emerson patted his camera. "I took pictures for your insurance agent. Ready?"

Angela looked straight ahead, resisting the urge for one more look. She and Emerson drove home in silence.

Lorrie met her at the door with arms open wide. "Are you okay?"

"It's all gone." She fell into Lorrie's arms.

"I'm so sorry." Lorrie tightened her grip.

Angela patted Lorrie's back and backed up, bumping into Lorrie's luggage in the hall. "Wish you could stay longer."

"Me, too."

"I'm tempted to follow you." Angela took Lorrie's arm and started down the steps.

"Why don't you?"

"Paperwork, insurance claims. Too much happening." In the kitchen now, Angela reached for a cup. Even Todd's green mug with the pine trees was gone. Lost in the fire. "Maybe later."

Lorrie joined her for coffee. "Angie, I hope you don't mind, but Kent is taking me to the airport tonight."

"Mind? Not at all," Angela said. "You two really hit it off, didn't you?"

"Yes. I like Kent." A serious look replaced her smile. "But I want to talk about you. When are you going to rebuild?"

"Rebuild?" Angela coughed and rubbed her throat.

"The shop."

"Must I think about that now?"

"Why not?"

"Lorrie, I lost my shop yes-ter-day," Angela said.

"So?"

"Besides, I don't know if I will rebuild. How can I?"

"Where's the spunk? My little sister always had spunk."

"Start over again?" Angela slumped. "Just the thought is overwhelming."

"But you can do it. Just think of it this way. You start clean. Put it together from the ground up. I know that appeals to you."

"Humph." Angela stole a glance at Lorrie. "Maybe."

Lorrie wore her determined look. "Think of the things you didn't like about the old shop. They're gone."

"That much is true."

"You can do it. I know you can." Lorrie rested her hands on Angela's shoulders and shook them with sisterly kindness. "A sister can say these things."

"You're good for me, Lorrie."

It was harder than she thought to say good-bye to Lorrie. Kent schlepped her luggage while the two sisters hugged, held back tears, and could hardly let go of each other's hands long enough for Lorrie to get in the car. Lorrie waved until the car disappeared from sight.

Angela called her grandmother before the tears could have

their way. "Just wanted to let you know Lorrie's on her way home."

"My dear," Grandmother's soft voice quavered over the phone. "Lorrie told me what happened. I'm so sorry. I've been praying for you."

"Thanks, Grandma."

"Is everyone okay?"

"Everyone's fine. It's just such a shock."

"It would be." Her grandmother sighed deeply. "What a week. And Benjamin has a new wife?"

"It was a lovely wedding." Grateful for the change of subject, Angela curled onto the window seat of her bedroom and described the day. "Happy bride and handsome groom. Lorrie was so much help. She fit right in. And Grandma, she's growing spiritually, isn't she?"

"Yes. It shows, doesn't it?"

"It does." Angela caressed her mother's Bible. "We had some sister time together."

"I'm so glad. My girls."

When Angela started coughing, her grandmother finished the call.

Angela headed downstairs. Phillip with sniffles had gone to bed early. Becca was at a movie with Cole. Thankfully, Angela didn't have to think about making dinner. Emerson had insisted on doing it himself. Hamburgers with all the garnishes. And his best effort at mac-and-cheese. Although it came out in one large lump when he spooned it into a serving bowl.

"Well, I can't go wrong with coleslaw from the deli," Emerson said, and blessed the food.

"Before another day goes by ..." Emerson paused, "I want to apologize to my wife and to her mother, who've had to live with me." With elbows bent, fingertips splayed at his temples,

Emerson turned to Bethany. "I've placed too much time and importance on getting ahead in business. Do you think it's too late to change? I could have lost you. My wife. My reason for living. My son." He stood and Bethany flew into his arms.

Angela delighted in the loving look they shared. When they sat back down, Bethany gripped Emerson's hand. "Praise God."

"And we've got great news," Emerson said. He glanced at Angela. "We've talked it over and we want to purchase this house."

"What?"

"It's perfect for us," Emerson said. "With my bonus, we've saved enough to cover the down payment."

"Mom, the best part of all is you can still live here with us," Bethany said. "You have your room upstairs and we have ours downstairs with ..." Bethany glanced at Emerson. "Well, someday we'll have more children."

"I don't know what to say." Angela's eyes filled with tears.

"Mom? Don't you like the idea?"

Angela nodded. A sweet pain shot through her. Our home. It's going to be our children's home. What could be more perfect?

"We don't want to force you into anything you don't want to do," Emerson said.

Angela stood. "The answer is yes—and I want a hug."

"Oh, Mom," Bethany said. "I'm so happy."

"Me, too."

"I can't think of another house that even meets the advantages I've found in this house." Emerson pointed out the things he especially liked.

"To think Phillip will grow up where I grew up," Bethany's eyes sparkled. "Same school, same park to play in."

Wisteria

Later, after helping clean the kitchen, Angela glanced at the dining room table and stopped. The arrangement from the wedding reception still graced the table, its blooms hanging on. Her last flowers from the shop. She tugged at one white rosebud, carried it upstairs, and cuddled the rose in her palm.

Its outer leaves were turning brown. She pulled a brown petal and let it flutter in her lap. Then the second. Then the third. She dropped the spent petals in the wastebasket and stared at the beautiful rose left. It was perfect. Not a trace of a scar from having lost outer petals. A new beginning for the rose. Could that happen to her? She laid it against her cheek and inhaled the fragrance. If she put it in water overnight, it would be open tomorrow. In full bloom.

69

December 28

Before services on Sunday morning, the church coffee shop was lively.

"Angela?" Sally Griswold, her employee of one day, minced toward Angela in high-heeled boots. "I can't believe it. Your shop. How utterly dreadful. Are you okay?"

"I'm fine, thank you." Angela kept her coffee close and dropped out of the crowd.

"You will rebuild, won't you? Wow, booming business."

"Remember, Sally, that was the day before Christmas Eve. Everyone was picking up Christmas orders. It was our busiest day of the year."

"True." Sally let her bag fall from her sloping shoulder as they each found a chair. "How soon before you're up and running again?"

"It will take time to put a new Wisteria together." Her thoughts took the direction of rebuilding without a hitch this time.

"If you still want me, I'll be there as an employee."

"Want you? Of course I do. You're one talented lady."

"Thanks."

"But it may be a month or two."

"Don't worry. I'll find some odd jobs to fill in. I'd better get in line for coffee."

Angela scooted her chair to make room for others and allowed her coffee to cool. She had no choice because almost everyone who walked by had something to say. The lukewarm liquid felt good as she swallowed.

"Angela?" Wade Taylor shook his head. "Sorry to hear about your shop. I'll get paperwork in order and let you know —" Someone jostled Wade as he searched in vain for seating. "We'll talk later."

She nodded, finished her coffee, and slipped away to her usual spot in the auditorium. Sally's beautiful creation, the arrangement for the wedding, graced the altar.

Residents from Shepherd's Fold filled the back section with Susan in their midst instead of Miranda. Susan caught her eye, waved, and walked over.

"Thanks for your text." Angela scooted to make room. "But there was nothing anyone could do."

"Your flower shop." Susan exhaled, shaking her head. "How are you holding up?"

"Just thankful everyone's okay."

"Yes, very thankful."

"Any news about Miranda?"

"She's still in the hospital," Susan said.

"I'd like to see her. Things have been so ..."

"She understands. She has her daisies from last week and talks more about them than any of the other flowers she received."

"I can't get away until tomorrow," Angela said. "But I'll see her then."

"Even better. I'm sure there will be lots of visitors today," Susan said. "May tire her out."

Angela laid a hand on Susan's arm, "Speaking of tired, is this too demanding for you? Additional work at the shelter? You look rather pale."

Susan's face flushed. "No, I'll be fine. Several people have volunteered to fill in the gaps."

People crowded in and Susan returned to her seat. Pastor Bailey's sermon, 'If the salt has lost its savor,' pushed through Angela's weariness and reached her heart.

There was no time for reflection. Angela had committed to picking up Phillip while Bethany and Emerson helped set up the cafeteria for the catered lunch. Angela rounded a corner to see Phillip blast out of Junior Church. "Da-deeeeeee!" He latched onto both legs of Wade Taylor.

"Hey, watch out!" Wade tottered from the impact. Trying to avoid Phillip, Wade lost his balance and crashed into the opposite wall. With a frown, he flung his hair back in place and reddened as he saw Angela approach. "A lot of little monsters running around loose." He laughed and awkwardly straightened.

"Phillip, that's not Daddy." Angela took Phillip's hand. "Say you're sorry to Mr. Taylor."

"Sorry, Mr. Taylor," Phillip mumbled.

"You're fine, Phillip." Angela tried not to coddle him. He was in the wrong, but her hand was gentle on his shoulder. "Please excuse him. His father is wearing a dark suit this morning, so he flew straight to the pinstriped legs."

Wade bent one knee and leaned until he was eye level with Phillip. "Hey, that's okay, young man." He straightened and grinned sheepishly at Angela. "I'm not used to kids. Forgive me for reacting the way I did."

"Don't give it another thought," Angela said.

"So, this is your grandson? Aren't you a fine-looking fellow?"

Phillip peered at Wade while leaning closer to his grandmother.

Smells of the catered lunch wafted their way as Wade followed them down the hall. "Are you staying for lunch?"

"Yes. Bethany and Emerson are on the work committee, so I came after Phillip for them." She switched her bag to the other shoulder and gripped Phillip's hand.

"Again," Wade leaned toward Angela. "So sorry about your shop. Will you rebuild?"

"The idea appeals to me."

"Makes sense." Wade nodded. "Say, why don't we get together and chat? Would you like to go out for dinner tomorrow night?"

Angela stiffened. Where did that come from?

"No, no thank you." Angela paused. "Wade, you're one of the nicest men I know. But, frankly, I'd like to see you and Melanie get back together."

Wade stepped back as a cluster of teenagers ran past them. His eyes shifted.

"Where is she now?"

"Minneapolis, I hear."

"Why not call her?" Angela said over her shoulder as they reached the fellowship hall. Was she being tactless? Perhaps. She didn't know their story. Oh, dear. Why had she stuck her nose into someone else's business? She turned and guided Phillip to the booster seat Becca had waiting. Suddenly fatigue overwhelmed her.

"Becca, do you feel up to driving home when you've finished your meal?"

"Sure, I feel fine."

"I need to rest."

They cut their visiting with others short and headed for the car.

"Mom, I'll have you home in no time. Would you like to take the back seat and lie down?"

"No. Feels good to sit up. I'm just wiped out." Angela gripped the armrest as the jeep fishtailed sideways. "Becca!"

Becca swung the steering wheel into the skid. "Sorry, Mom. I'll slow down. The salting is still doing its work."

"Road salt."

"What's that?"

"The sermon title."

"Oh yeah, road salt. Catchy."

"Until you compare it to your life." Angela opened the Bible on her lap. "It spoke to me, Becca. I can't explain it. Let me read it again. 'You are the salt of the earth. But if salt has lost its taste, how shall its saltiness be restored? It is no longer good for anything, but to be thrown out, and trampled under people's feet.' Or tires. Like road salt. I don't want to be road salt."

"Mom, you're the salt of the earth." Becca spoke in a soft voice as their car wallowed its way homeward.

Home again, Angela closed the door to her room. She fell on her knees beside the open rose. Her own life was more than half spent. What remained? She bowed her head. There were no words. She waited. And listened.

70

S moke burned Angela's eyes, nostrils, and throat as she fought her way to Todd. It hurt to yell. Could he not hear her? Why did he continue through another doorway, down another hall? She called again. Where were they? Not at the shop, not in their home. Just endless rooms.

"Mom!" Becca's voice cut through the chaos.

"W—what?" The bedroom light glared in Angela's eyes.

"You were calling for Dad. A dream."

"Ooooh," Angela moaned and wondered why her throat wasn't scratchy. "A fire." She rolled on her back and lay staring at the ceiling. "I thought I was doing so well. Over it. Ready to move on."

"Just a nightmare, Mom."

Angela felt surprisingly rested the next morning even after her nighttime ordeal. She needed to make her bank deposit.

Searching the laundry room for the clothing she had worn the day of the fire, she retrieved her bank bag.

It still smelled of smoke.

"Thank you, Father." She whispered her gratitude that she had safely tucked the bag into the pocket of her apron. It would have been difficult to recreate sales totals accurately without the register slips. She reached for the phone then stopped. Instead, she emailed the info and the deposit amount to Wade and asked for a current balance sheet.

As she hit send for the email, her cell rang.

"Angela! Wait till you hear the good news." Lilly gushed. "Pops is getting better. The doctor said they would release him in three weeks at the rate he's going."

"I'm so glad to hear that," Angela said.

"I was reading the paper last night and Pops noticed the last page, this big section about new condos for sale. Took a while to understand, but I finally got it out of him. He wants the two of us to move into a condo. He knows I don't want to go back to that old house where I grew up." Lilly paused. "I can take care of him."

"Lilly, I'm proud of you. It's the right thing to do."

"Yeah," Lilly's voice was soft. "Everything's different. Everything's changed. Thanks for your ... prayers."

Despite the chaos in her life, Angela's heart soared when she hung up from Lilly's call. Almost a storybook ending. No, a beginning.

After lunch, Angela hurried to the hospital. Miranda had been moved to a pleasant private room.

"Hope you're not too tired for a visitor?" Angela said.

"Not at all." Miranda punched buttons to raise the head of her bed. Except for her oxygen canula, Miranda looked like her old self. "My daughter Nancy just left to run some errands."

"Sorry I missed her."

"Have a seat." Miranda motioned to the chair by her bed. "Nancy wants to head back to Albuquerque tomorrow to miss the New Year's Eve airport traffic on Wednesday."

"Yes, New Year's Eve."

"I can imagine the thoughts going through your mind." The lift of Miranda's eyebrows held a shared sympathy anticipating what Angela would say.

"First one without Todd."

Miranda nodded. "And I'm sorry for the new trial you're going through. Susan told me about the fire."

"I'm undone. Thought I had mapped out my life, and now I'm facing a world turned upside down. Again."

"I can imagine." Miranda smoothed the sheet across her midsection. "Why do you think it happened?"

"They suspect old wiring."

"No. This trial. Why do you think this trial happened?"

Angela slumped in the vinyl padded chair. "No idea."

"God always has something in mind. We just have to pray and wait for Him to reveal it. What are you thinking of doing?"

Angela glanced out the window. "I'm thinking of rebuilding the shop. I'll still have my clientele; I could possibly branch out into interior design. Or, I could do an about-face, go back to school, get a master's degree in counseling, social work."

"Do any of those options excite you?"

"Excite me?"

"Yes, where is your passion?" Miranda's eyes sparkled.

"Passion for work is the farthest thing from my mind.

Maybe it's just the past week. The business crazy-busy. Benjamin's wedding. And then the fire."

"That would cloud everything—"

A fit of coughing halted Miranda's words. Angela rushed ice water to her and watched her slowly drink it through a straw.

"Ah, that's better." Miranda rested a moment before resuming her train of thought. "We'll pray for guidance. My life at the shelter ... the Lord made it clear He chose me. It was His plan, and I've tried to follow. I've never regretted it."

"You've helped so many people."

"Only a vessel. God works in our lives as we submit to His will."

"What a joy it must have been to serve Him for so many years."

"It was. I'm pleased with the way it worked out. But doing the work He puts in front of you, making that a ministry to Him, that's what's important."

"I can see that. Pray for me."

"I am."

"Thank you." Angela leaned in close. "Now, tell me about your health condition? That is, if you're up to it."

"I'm not surprised at what they found," Miranda said. "My heart. The tests show hypertrophic cardiomyopathy. Now that's a mouthful." She shook her head. "Haven't taken care of myself as I should. Carrying extra weight and getting all the diseases that go with it: heart problems, diabetes, high blood pressure. All that contributed to complicating the pneumonia."

Angela took her hand.

Miranda's smiled faded. "Self-control. One of the fruits of the Spirit. Why didn't I apply it? I should have known better. Always so much to do. It was easier to grab a donut, sandwich, cookie, the foods that fatten you up." Miranda smacked her thigh. "It's a wake-up call. But I can't continue in my condition. I'll have to give up my work."

"At the shelter?" Angela said. "You *are* the shelter. I can't imagine it without you."

"Nonsense. The Lord will raise up another."

71

Two days later

Anxious to plow through the insurance paperwork, Angela enlisted Emerson's help. "I don't know how to thank you for taking time off work this morning," Angela said. Emerson turned into a strip mall. The tower sign, third plate down, prominently displayed the name Kent Hargrove Insurance.

"I'm more than happy to," Emerson said. "You shouldn't have to pass through this alone, not when you have Bethany and me."

Kent must have been watching for them. He opened the door and steered them to his office. Angela's folder sat on his desk with partially completed forms on top.

"Shouldn't be any problems." Kent settled in his chair. "You insured the contents of the building for—" Kent ran a finger down the far right column and named a figure they had agreed on. "That amount will vary depending on the inventory left at the time of the fire."

"I brought a list of inventory." Angela opened her briefcase. "As detailed as I can remember. You have the pictures you took when we updated the policy?"

"I do."

"This is from the accountant." Angela handed over a copy of an email. "Wade said to call him for other reports you may need."

"Oh, Wade's your accountant? Good."

Emerson reached inside his jacket. "Here are the pictures after the fire."

"Thank you." Kent took the pictures, shaking his head. "Tragic. They linked it to the old wiring?"

Angela's shoulders tensed. "Yes."

"Now, a few questions, a few forms to fill out, and your signature is all we need."

With forms completed and papers signed, they rose to leave.

"By the way." Kent stood. "I enjoyed getting to know your sister, Lorrie."

"She felt the same way," Angela said.

Kent smiled. "Quite a gal. Yep. Quite a gal. We're staying in touch."

They shook hands. Angela thanked him and numbly walked out of the building with Emerson.

"I'm glad you were with me, Emerson." Angela buckled her seat belt. "I'm still traumatized by the fire."

"The least I could do." Emerson gave her a sideways look as he backed out. "How are you set, if I may ask, financially?"

"The insurance money, added to income for December, should be enough to set up shop again."

"So that's the plan?"

"Seems my best option."

"I suppose so." Emerson headed home.

"I called Mary Anderson about rentals. She mentioned a few possibilities. You know small towns. There's never a lack of empty storefronts."

"Unfortunately, that seems to be the case."

"She'll call back with appointment times, hopefully for Thursday after we get past New Year's Day." Get past. That seemed to be her *modus operandi*.

"Let me know when you narrow it down. I'll be happy to give you a second opinion, if that would help."

"Always," Angela said. "Todd picked out the last one. I thought the building was too large. He convinced me it was perfect for expansion. It was."

"The next will be great, too. Just wait." Emerson turned onto their street. "Bethany said she'd have lunch ready. I might make this a habit."

Angela's phone rang when they had finished lunch. "It's Lilly," she whispered, covering the phone and walking away from the dining table.

"I just heard about your shop," Lilly said. "Sorry, Angela."

"Thank you, Lilly."

"Say! Can't wait to tell you the good news. We've got a fantastic idea for you. Pops wants to know if you'd like to take over his shop?"

"Well," Angela said, "I'm not sure that would be in my line."

"Sure it is. You'd be good at it."

"Actually, I'm thinking of rebuilding Wisteria."

"Oh. Sure you don't want to think about it?"

"No, thank you. I'm optimistic about pursuing this." Angela tried to stifle her laughter as she hung up.

Bethany cocked her head. "Mom, what's so funny?"

"Should I go into the antique business?" Angela filled Bethany and Emerson in on the call and the invitation to purchase Olaf's shop.

"With a little effort," Emerson said, "your personality could morph into Olaf's."

"Thanks a lot." Angela stuck out her chin.

Emerson laughed. "Well, nothing like keeping your options open." He stood and stretched. "I'll be home early so we can celebrate New Year's Eve. Are you sure you don't want to go out with us, Mom?"

"No, Phillip and I have plans."

After Emerson left, Angela talked Bethany into taking a nap with Phillip while she took Bethany's shift in the nursery at Shepherd's Fold.

Susan met her at the door. "Angela, I'm surprised to see you."

"Bethany's cough is lingering. Just in case she's still contagious, I told her I'd fill in."

"We love our volunteers." Susan's hand shook as she locked the door after her.

"Susan? You're even more pale today."

Susan surprised Angela with a smile. "It's okay."

Angela frowned and opened the door to the nursery. She stocked the tiny fridge with juice boxes. Mothers brought their children. New children. New residents.

She bent to greet a boy about Phillip's size. "Hi, I'm Angela."

"Ang-La," the boy said.

"No." A little girl towered over him. "She said Angel."

"Angel?" One mother leaned over the half-door.

"It's Angela." She smiled and extended her hand.

"Nice to meet you, Angela, and thanks for watching Kia." A young woman with a gaunt figure shook Angela's hand.

Kia lifted a firm chin. "I like Angel better."

"Me, too," chimed in a third child. "Angel." He seemed to enjoy the way it rolled off his tongue.

Angela's throat tightened, but no sharp pain followed. Coming from the lips of those little ones, Todd's special name for her warmed her heart. She herded them toward an opened picture book on a small table to draw them into the Bible story she had prepared.

Susan returned. "Did you hear the good news? They'll release Miranda from the hospital tomorrow. She's moving to Northgate Care."

"Good." Angela lifted a one-year-old to her lap. "I'll stop by after she gets settled."

72

January 2

M ary Anderson not only sold residential but also dabbled in commercial real estate in Northgate. More than happy to help Angela, she dug up two possibilities for a new shop.

"What do you think, Angela?" Mary touched the white picket fence attached to the wall of a former dress shop. "I can see this renovated into a floral business, can't you?"

"Possibly."

"Let's head back to the office." Mary shivered and locked the door behind her.

Next door, stately columns caught Angela's eye. "What about this building?" She could see a spacious interior. Touches of brass inside the dark interior reflected the brightness of the day. "It's right next to the coffee shop."

"The old bank building?" Mary glanced at the building and fished for her car keys.

"Yes." Angela slid into Mary's car.

"Mrs. Paulson owns it." Mary maneuvered into Main Street traffic. "The last time I talked to her, she wasn't interested in selling or leasing the building."

"Mrs. Paulson who lives three blocks from me?"

"Yes, it belonged to her father. They built a new bank, but the family kept the old building. Are you acquainted with her?"

Angela craned her neck for another look. "I've helped her clean up flower beds in her yard. She always waves when I pass."

"You might call her. You're not a realtor. She may be more receptive to you."

Back in Mary's office, Angela watched her make a pot of coffee. Coffee from a can.

"I think the dress shop would be the quickest renovation for you."

"I agree, but it's so small. No room for the antiques and home decor that seemed to go over so well." Angela unzipped her jacket but left it on.

"That's true. And the first place I showed you today?"

"No, too far off the beaten path and next to an empty warehouse."

"If you're in no hurry, I'll put the word out to our team. I'll see what we can dig up."

"Thanks. I don't want to rush into anything."

Angela drove straight home and called Mrs. Paulson. She sounded delighted to have a visitor and asked Angela to come right over.

Mrs. Paulson's driveway had several cracks, but the brick-and-stucco Tudor-style home was in perfect shape. Angela let her eyes wander over the one-hundred-year-old mansion. Built on the edge of town long before the addition of Angela's subdivision, the Tudor mansion had progressively become engulfed in the middle of residential expansion.

Angela rang the bell and could hear Mrs. Paulson's shuffling steps. "Coming," she called.

So much for insulation a hundred years ago. Angela could clearly hear a bolt turn, a chain slide, and there stood Mrs. Paulson holding onto a walker.

"Hello, Angela. Come in." She skillfully backed up her trusty walker.

"Thank you." Angela closed the door behind her. An ornate staircase led the eyes to a brass chandelier hanging from the upper story. It ended a few feet above a table containing a massive vase of dried flowers, their colors a perfect complement to the floor's round Persian rug. "How are you doing, Mrs. Paulson?"

"I can't complain. Still getting around. My brain still functions well enough to play bridge." Her smug smile testified to her passion for the game. "Come this way. I made coffee. If you'll carry the tray to the den, we'll be perfectly cozy there."

Angela tried to keep her eyes straight ahead, but her head swiveled in every direction as she gawked at the interior. It was the first time she had been inside the home. They had always sat on the front or back porch having lemonade. French doors to her left gave a glimpse of a living room lost in a time capsule. Mrs. Paulson looked back while Angela twisted her head toward the French doors on the right, guarding a dark library.

"Perhaps you'd like to take a tour after we have our coffee. You've never been through the house?"

"No, I haven't. It's breathtaking." Angela grabbed the swinging door to the kitchen.

"Thank you for holding the door. I have to back through when I'm alone. Not the most graceful trick, I can assure you."

Mrs. Paulson chuckled. "Now just add the coffee pot, and the tray's ready."

"Oh, what a lovely tray."

Mrs. Paulson led the way to a small den to the left of the kitchen.

"You're right. This is a cozy room," Angela said. A fireplace with a carved black walnut mantel, emerald green tile above and below, shot merry flames from converted gas logs.

"Just set the tray right here in front of the sofa. Forgive me for not being the proper hostess. I'll let you serve, if you don't mind. I'm a bit clumsy." She parked the walker, straightened up, and chose the plush old Morris chair closest to the fireplace. "Just black coffee, please, and a couple of cookies on the side. You can set it here." Mrs. Paulson motioned to an ornate table next to her chair. "I practically live in this room. My bedroom's directly behind me."

Angela glimpsed a dark room with shades drawn, casting shadows on a canopy bed with luxurious tapestry hangings on each side.

"I keep most of the house closed off in winter. Just open it up once a month for my bridge club. It's quite an ordeal and requires the help of many people." Mrs. Paulson flexed arthritic fingers. "They are so nice to humor an older woman. When I was your age, I belonged to three bridge groups, don't you know?" She delicately sipped coffee.

"I suppose the way I've lived my life sounds rather frivolous. I tried to get involved in humanitarian efforts, volunteered for every drive and bake sale that Northgate held. Even tried to help at Shepherd's Fold when it was in its infancy. Just wasn't for me. I hope God will forgive me for just sending money its way instead of my time."

Angela had heard bits and pieces about a foundation the

Paulsons had established for Shepherd's Fold. Wondering if she dare comment on her generosity, Mrs. Paulson's next comment saved her from answering.

"But, enough about me. I'm so sorry you lost your husband last spring. You're so young to be a widow."

Angela touched on the happenings in the last seven months. She lingered most on the Miranda's wise teaching that had helped grow Angela's faith.

"Ah, yes," Mrs. Paulson said. "Miranda's a true mentor to many women."

Angela refilled their cups and pondered how to approach Mrs. Paulson about her bank building. Should she just dive in? Breathing a prayer, Angela related her plans to rebuild her flower shop. Then she mentioned passing the bank building and recognizing the value of transforming it into a shop.

"My." Mrs. Paulson set her cup on its saucer and gave it a slight turn. "What an interesting idea."

Angela sat on the edge of her seat. "The uniqueness of the bank building would draw people inside. Just as converting the mercantile into a coffee shop has made the Nordic Cup a popular gathering place. I love to see buildings with such history re-purposed."

"You know, that building is one of seven banks my father owed in the state of Minnesota. I planned to be a career woman and began my first job there. That's where I met John. It's the old story. Fall in love and thoughts of a career go out the window. What a wonderful life we had together. But I always insisted we keep that bank building even after we sold all the others. Just closed it up when they built a new one. Sentimental, I guess."

Angela's heart warmed to Mrs Paulson. What an unusual

life she had lived. "The ties we hang onto, sentiment becomes a part of our soul."

The mantel clock ticked as they both stared into space. Mrs. Paulson turned to Angela. "What about employees? Do you have someone to help you?"

"Yes, one loyal employee who needs a job badly. Sally Griswold. She's living at the women's shelter until she gets on her feet."

"Did you say Griswold? I haven't heard that name in years."

"Yes, her family lived here years ago she told me, then moved to the Chicago area when she was still a child."

"Why, I wonder if they could be my husband's relatives? His mother was a Griswold. In fact, it was his Griswold cousin who encouraged him to move to Minnesota." Mrs Paulson displayed a V-shape wrinkle between her brows. "I heard the next generation, his cousin's grandchildren, moved to Chicago. There was a divorce. Children split up. I lost touch with them after my husband died."

73

I t was after five and already dark when Angela completed a quick tour and closed the door on the dignified home. Mrs. Paulson was dubious at first about turning the bank into a floral shop, but seemed to warm up to the idea as they talked. With sparkling eyes, she gave Angela permission to try, along with the name of her lawyer who was the custodian of her affairs. Angela started her car and stared at the home lit by landscape flood lights. Mrs. Paulson lived alone in three rooms of a mansion of many rooms. A huge house to maintain and a fortune to manage. There was something to be said for the uncomplicated life Angela now lived.

A pang of sadness hit Angela when she reached home. The soon-to-be Bethany's and Emerson's home. Everything about her future was in limbo.

After dinner, Angela sat on the sofa next to Becca. "I'm

looking into the possibility of leasing the old bank building downtown."

Becca smacked the cushion. "Mom, are you kidding?"

"Quite serious."

"Next to the coffee shop?" Bethany called from the kitchen.

"That's the one."

"For a flower shop?" Bethany joined them in the living room. "It would take a magician to pull that off."

Angela smiled. "Emerson, are you free one day next week to go along and give me your opinion?"

"When?"

"As soon as I can set up an appointment with the custodian."

"Just let me know which day. I'll check my calendar," Emerson said.

"I'd love to explore that old cave." Becca wiggled under a throw. "Well, it always looked like a cave from the outside. But, I'll be back in college as of Sunday. I miss all the fun," Becca said.

"I promise to leave plenty of fun for spring break," Angela said.

Becca wrinkled her nose.

"A text from Benjamin and Tatum." Angela punched her phone. "Lunch on Sunday?"

"Cool," Becca said. "And then he'll be moving."

"We'll enjoy them while we can."

Angela tried not to think of the Sunday dinners ahead without her son and his new wife. She must trust the Lord to watch over Benjamin and Tatum. Focus on making their last week together as happy as she could.

"I'm still trying to picture that bank building as a flower

shop, Mom." Bethany tilted her head against the cushions and stared at the vaulted ceiling.

Angela's mind wandered to possibilities in marble teller cages with brass trim. Home furnishings could meander around, fill up the former office area. Some fun lighting and lamps could mix well with the space. She propped up her feet and stared at the fireplace, mesmerized by the flames.

"Mom?" Bethany said. "You're a million miles away."

"Sorry, what did you say?"

"Just wondering if painting this teak paneling a creme color would take away from the mid-century modern look?"

Oh, dear. Angela's mouth twitched and she tried not to overreact. "Yes, I'm afraid it would. The woods, generally teak, red oak, and rosewood, were a major theme in the craftsmanship for mid-century modern homes. Of course, you can veer from the traditional look if you like. It'll be your house."

"I suppose." Bethany's eyes studied the rich, glowing woodwork.

"I'd like to keep it the way it is," Emerson said. "How many people own a piece of history?"

"Just thinking of brightening up the interior." Bethany jumped up at the ding of the oven timer.

Their discussion continued through dinner, but Angela was distracted.

"I think I'll visit Miranda tonight." Angela stood. "She just moved to the nursing home. She may be lonely."

Becca looked up from the dishwasher she was loading. "Mmm. Sure Mom."

Angela stopped by Olaf's room, but he had so many visitors, she only stopped in to say hello. Lilly pointed the way to Miranda's room then hurried back to be with Olaf.

"You're leaving?" Angela couldn't believe what Miranda was saying. "I'm losing you, too?"

Miranda smiled ruefully. "Sorry. My daughter, Nancy, lives in Albuquerque. Only natural I go stay with her. Nancy's retiring soon."

"Of course. You're right." Angela smiled and felt ashamed of her reaction. "A warmer climate, too."

"How are you doing?"

"Still feeling at loose ends. Shop's gone. House is sold," Angela said. "Listen to me. I'm dumping on your shoulders."

"I can take it."

"Well, I looked at several buildings for a flower shop. I'm impressed with the old bank building."

"The bank building?"

"Guess maybe it's the challenge of pulling it together that draws me."

"He gives each of us special talents. Sometimes we just need to spread our wings."

"We'll see."

"Hand me my Bible, please." Miranda's face glowed as she flipped a few pages, pointed, and held it out to Angela. "You read it."

Angela cradled the Bible in both hands. "'Bless the Lord, O my soul, and forget not all his benefits, who forgives all your iniquity, who heals all your diseases, who redeems your life from the pit, who crowns you with steadfast love and mercy, who satisfies you with good so that your youth is renewed like the eagle's.'"

"Do you feel it?" Miranda sighed. "That little gust of wind under your wings? Lifting you?"

Did she? Did something stir her heart from those words? Would her future differ from what she imagined?

Miranda settled back. "Not long after I lost Roscoe, I read about the freedom for a widow. Well, the last thing I wanted was freedom. I just wanted Roscoe back. But, as the Lord led me along, it became clear I could never have devoted time to ministry at the shelter and taken care of Roscoe, too. The Lord knew best."

Angela closed Miranda's Bible. "I remember running errands, keeping an eye on the time, thinking I must be home in time to make dinner for Todd. Then realizing there's no one to make dinner for. I had the freedom to shop as long as I wanted. I felt guilty for even thinking such thoughts."

Miranda nodded. "A bittersweet dichotomy. I know. Becoming a widow was not what I would have chosen. But the Lord led me to a ministry at the shelter. And now He has other plans for me." Miranda smiled. "I heard you were at the shelter on Monday. Thanks for volunteering."

"No need to thank me." Angela pulled a strand of hair and wound it around her finger. "The work is very rewarding."

"Why don't you take my place at the shelter?"

"Miranda. That's impossible. What about Susan?"

"Susan's not feeling the greatest, a little poorly lately."

"Poorly?"

"It'll pass," Miranda said.

Was that a little curl of a smile around Miranda's mouth? Maybe it was just Angela's imagination.

"So, what will you do?" Miranda said.

"A flower shop is my best option. Flowers. Right now, that's all I know."

"Flowers?" Miranda said. "Maybe God is saying the women at the shelter are His flowers."

74

The next day, Angela received a group text from Marge and Caroline and shot back an answer.

> Coffee shop on Saturday morning? Unheard of for me! I'll be there.

Enjoying new freedom like a little girl skipping school, Angela parked her car in front of the bank building next to the coffee shop. Could this be her new shop? A new sign would fit over the old one. Wisteria. Should it be Wisteria Floral? Or Wisteria Interiors? Or a combination of the two? She climbed the steps, shaded her eyes, and studied the interior. The marble counters topped with a fencing of brass bars enclosing the teller's cages gave an appearance the bank had never closed. A movement on the reflected glass caught her eye. Angela wheeled around.

A young woman stood staring at her. "Aren't—aren't you Angela?"

"Yes, I am."

"You probably don't remember me."

"I remember you. Kia's mother? The nursery at the shelter?"

"Yes." Her face brightened. "You're all she talks about now. And the Bible story of Jesus calling the little children around Him. She tells the story to the other children. Makes them sit on the floor around her. I think she pretends she is you."

"You have a sweet little girl."

"Thanks. Well, I better run. I just made a delivery across the street."

"Wait. What's your name?"

She edged along the sidewalk, her hand lifted to push open the door of Nordic Cup. "Sierra."

Works at the coffee shop. Nice. Whatever direction her life took, Angela vowed to find time to volunteer at the shelter. Following Sierra into the coffee shop, the sounds and smells enveloped Angela. Caroline waved from a padded chair, and Marge breezed in the door to join Angela in line.

"What are you having?" Angela stepped back to join Marge as the couple in front of them moved to the pickup area.

"Same as always. Scissor Kick, extra shot of espresso." Marge nodded to the barista.

"Hi, Sierra. I'll have the same." Angela darted a glance at Marge. "Might as well be daring today."

"Coming right up." Sierra smiled brightly and turned to the myriad of equipment.

With lattes in hand, they made their way to Caroline.

"So sorry about your shop," Caroline said.

"Thanks. Appreciated your call after the fire." Angela sank into a plush chair.

"Will our lives never settle down?" Caroline said.

"Mine's getting more complicated." Marge turned toward Angela. "But nothing like yours."

"I'll be fine. I'm tracking down a very promising building. The old bank building next door."

"What?" Marge tucked her chin and frowned.

"You always were one for the impossible." Caroline laughed and picked up a dollop of whipped cream and sprinkles with her coffee stirrer.

Angela joined in her laughter. "Impossible may be the word."

"Next to the coffee shop might be a plus," Marge said.

Angela nodded. "Snuggled in the old section of town. Main Street. It's not on the main highway, so I wouldn't have the visibility I had before. I hope my old clientele remains loyal." Angela absently tucked her hair behind her ear. "Now, I want to hear about you two. Have a nice Christmas?"

Caroline's index finger circled the top of her cup. "Joshua joined us at the farm. Sidney and Dalton went to his folks in Ohio. First time they've done that. But then, things between Sydney and me have not improved."

"Sorry, Caroline," Angela said.

"Well, the four of us had a great Christmas," Caroline said.

Angela smiled. "Thanks again for playing at Benjamin's and Tatum's wedding. Marge, I wish you could have been there."

"Me too. Christmas Eve dinner turned into luncheon this year. You know we always took turns on Christmas Eve, my sister-in-law Pam and I. So that's where I went. With Greg's family."

"You weren't alone on Christmas Day, were you?" Angela said.

"No. In fact, Pam invited me for Christmas day. But I already had plans." Marge shifted her weight. "I joined Darren Jackson and his family. He invited me because he said he always feels like the odd man out in his family, being single. Well, I know how that feels now, so I agreed."

"Darren? The engineer?" Angela leaned forward. "How was it?"

"How was what?" Marge said. "Oh, you mean dinner at the Jacksons'? It was okay. Big family, lots of noise. Darren and I finally went to my house for some peace and quiet."

Angela and Caroline exchanged a look.

"How's your dad, Caroline?" Marge said.

"Dad's great, still active, always working," Caroline said. "Why don't you come out to the farm for dinner? Tuesdays are a rather long night. Both Dad and Aunt Jackie go bowling at seven. We could have an early dinner with them and then have the house to ourselves."

"Sorry, this coming Tuesday night won't work for me," Marge said. "Having dinner with Darren."

Marge laughed. "Why are you staring? Oh, a plump, gray-haired, unattractive middle-aged woman like me?" She shrugged. "Darren's an old bachelor. I doubt if he thinks of me as a date."

"You're certainly not unattractive, Marge," Angela said. "And you're fun to be with. I don't know why he wouldn't want a date with you."

"Me either. You're a lovely person," Caroline said.

"We're not at the dating stage, strictly business. Some things still don't add up. Darren's helping me investigate. That's all."

Angela looked up when she heard a familiar voice place an order and say to his companion, "Would you like anything else? No? Then I'll have what she's having."

"Angela?" Marge followed her gaze. "Isn't that Wade Carlson, your accountant?"

"Yes, and his wife, Melanie."

"I heard they were ..." Caroline said. "Oh, I must have been mistaken."

Angela watched the couple's progression. Wade found a table nearby. Angela tried not to stare, but she might as well have been part of the paneling. He had eyes only for Melanie.

75

"Angela? I don't believe we've officially met. Nordstrom's the name, Dale Nordstrom."

On Monday afternoon, when Angela and Emerson met at the bank building, an older gentleman came forward.

Angela shook his hand. "Thank you for opening the building. This is my son-in-law, Emerson Dahl."

"Pleasure to meet you, young man. Turned up the heat this morning," he said, rubbing his hands together. "We normally keep it just above freezing to protect the water pipes."

"Are the plumbing and wiring in good working order?" Emerson asked.

"Let me show you. The electrical box is right this way."

A florescent bulb flickered above Angela's head. Instinctively, she ducked, a chill coursing up her spine. "Go ahead, Emerson. I'll look around this area."

Row upon row of dropped fixtures hung from the ceiling. More than half were dark. A high ceiling. That's impressive. Makes the room look spacious. A metal cabinet clinked shut. Muffled footsteps approached.

"Well, this building is about thirty years behind your last building," Emerson said.

Angela nodded. "What about the counters?"

Nordstrom glanced at the dusty marble. "I've got a man that can clean it out for us. I'm sure there's a market for recycled marble countertops if you don't want them. See anything you want to keep?"

"I'm not sure." Angela motioned to the floor. Black and white hexagon-shaped tiles created an old-fashioned geometric pattern on the floor. "Removing the counters would leave bare spots in the floor, right?"

"Yes, never be able to replace the tiles. Too bad you can't just use it as it is."

"Well, it's overkill for counter space, but I like marble for a backdrop."

"You'd save us a lot of money if you leased it as is." His voice echoed to the plate-glass windows.

"It has possibilities." Angela warmed to the thought of preserving the history and integrating flowers and home furnishings.

Banking meets decor.

"Let me take some measurements."

***

Instead of driving home, Angela drove to the care center to see Miranda. A woman, flipping up the hood on her jacket, almost ran into her at the door. When the woman lifted her head, it was her pastor's wife, Susan. Susan with a white face.

"Susan?"

"Angela, I know how I must look." A nervous giggle escaped Susan's lips. "I thought I could make it home. Just came from the restroom." She clutched her stomach. "Didn't make it."

"Wait a minute. You were sick to your stomach and you're smiling?" Angela pulled her from the traffic in the doorway. "You're not ..."

"Yes. I'm pregnant," Susan whispered. "It feels so good to tell someone. Only please don't share it yet. It's only been three months. James and I are waiting ..."

"Of course. I won't say a word. I'm so happy for you."

With her eyes twinkling, Susan slipped out the door.

Does Miranda know? She must. Angela remembered Miranda's comment that Susan was feeling poorly. Let Susan keep her beautiful secret a little longer.

Angela chatted with Miranda in her room and absent-mindedly pinched a spent bloom on a vase of daisies. "I'm headed to the shelter at three," Angela said. "My heart goes out to the new women I've met. So much potential. They need someone to believe in them. To affirm them."

Angela smiled. "Observing the couples at Christmas reminded me of how Todd affirmed me without saying a word. I can see how I must transfer that confidence of Todd's affirmation to me as his wife to God's affirmation of me as His child. Once I learn, maybe I can pass it along to the women at the shelter."

"The Lord has given you a heart for them."

"Once I rebuild the business, I'll make time for them."

"Even after the ordeal with Peyton?"

"The theft at the shop?" Angela inhaled sharply. "Yes. I hated to press charges, but my insurance agent assured me it was for the best. She needs to face the consequences of her actions." Angela rolled the spent blossom in her hand and tossed it in the trash can by Miranda's bed. "Why did she do it?

She was clean. Spent all that time in rehab. She had her life ahead of her."

"The crutch, the reliance on drugs or alcohol, becomes their answer to coping with life. It becomes their god. Take it away and something needs to replace it. We give them Jesus."

"Jesus." Angela nodded. "I've been praying for her. Do you think God will give us another chance to reach Peyton?"

"We can pray He does."

"Miranda, is it hard to know God's leading in your life?"

"Now there's a question." Miranda stared at a blank TV screen. "Sometimes it's a mystery. Sometimes it's written across the sky, plain as day. Other times, it's just a sweet knowing in your heart."

"Why is life so complicated? I lived the perfect life, or so it seemed, with Todd. I lost him. My business revived. Then I lost the business." Angela exhaled. "Sorry, I'm looking backward again."

"Another trial."

"All those months, the idea of a growing business to support me took center stage. I'm confident it can happen again, but it's no longer the most important thing in my life. Surprisingly, I feel much stronger, more content. No business. Unencumbered. Undistracted."

Angela relaxed in her chair. "Those who are married ... are anxious about worldly things, how to please her husband ... the unmarried woman is anxious about the things of the Lord. A widow is undistracted. Those were the verses we studied."

Miranda nodded.

"I spent so much time and energy paying off the balloon note and now it seems it wasn't about the balloon note. Or being financially secure. There was something else I had to learn."

Angela continued. "Do you suppose there's a reason? Does He have a purpose in mind? Miranda, it's almost as if ... God has put me in this position for a reason."

Miranda adjusted her bed to sit up straight.

"I began with a superficial knowledge of God," Angela said, "learning a few rules like a child. But these last few months, I feel now I've come to know God as a person. He's with us always. We are never alone. God is more than rules. Those rules, or laws, are instructions telling us what God loves. He loves obedience."

Miranda smiled.

76

Two weeks later

A ngela put Sally on the payroll earlier than expected. Sally's design ideas proved creative and insightful.

"Angela, the teller stations make perfect niches for displaying your accessories."

Lifting her arms high, Sally angled a greeting card rack to one side. She had finally put on some weight.

"Perfect." Angela cleared a spot in the middle of the room. "Did you see the brass lighting I found in the storeroom? They agreed to rehang it for me. What a find."

"Not as much a find as our antique shopping."

Angela smiled, remembering their rental truck that toured Sally's home state of Illinois for a week. "I couldn't have done it without you. You're the one with the contacts."

"Oh yes, my aunt and uncle. They're into, well, junk." She grinned. "Their advertising, 'we buy junk, we sell antiques,' says it all."

Angela balanced a plank between two sawhorses. "Sally, where did you get this amazing talent? Especially the shop layout?"

"I majored in interior design. I just happened to find a place in floral."

"I can see one would complement the other."

"If we remove the wooden half-wall in the back, that will allow for dividers. Using the coolers as a screen, we can hide the supplies and staging area and still keep our worktable in full view. Same as the last shop." Sally handed a diagram of the back area to Angela. "What do you think?"

What could she say? It gave her everything. "The worktable size allows for three, no, four people. Shelving, room for the cooler door to swing, break table, chairs. You've even located a source for the equipment? Sally. You're too much."

A crooked smile curved Sally's mouth. "Thanks."

Sally continued to work at breakneck speed, and Angela gave her full rein just to see her ideas for displaying home furnishings.

"What about the Wisteria Tea?" Sally said.

Angela stopped and considered. "Everyone seemed to like it. I enjoyed blending it. Yes, let's handle it again."

"You're still going to call the shop Wisteria?"

"That's the plan."

"I love the whimsical sound of it."

On her drive home, Angela wrestled with the direction her future seemed to be headed. Did she really want the stress of rebuilding her business? Even though it was January, she cracked a window. The cold air stimulated her thoughts. One word emerged from them. Unencumbered. She was feeling anything but unencumbered. She pulled off the road. Had she taken the time to truly ask herself what she wanted? Or ask God what He wanted for her? She wanted her life to count. To make a difference. God had been calling, and she had thrown Him breadcrumbs of her time.

77

One month later

"Angela." Sally Griswold hobbled lopsidedly up to Angela in the lobby of Shepherd's Fold and patted her overflowing tote. "I'm moving out!"

Sally's confident smile was all the reward Angela needed. Today's Sally was a different person from the Sally who had knocked on the door of her shop in December.

"My own flower shop. I never would have dreamed it could be possible."

Angela beamed.

"I couldn't have done it without your help," Sally said. "Any of it."

Angela hugged Sally. "I'm so glad Mrs. Paulson could see your potential."

"I still can't believe she's backing me. She said she discovered we're distant relatives. I'm from her husband's family." Sally's eyes grew large. "But for her to forego my paying rent for two years? Who does that?"

Wisteria

"You'll do a great job with Wisteria." Angela gestured toward the growing noise in the hallway of Shepherd's Fold. "I'd love to chat, but I'm chief crowd herder tonight. Will you stay for the Bible study?"

Sally nodded as she and her tote dodged women and children rushing to the shelter's dining hall. "Be right back."

Angela slipped into Miranda's office. No, her office. She brushed her fingers against the nameplate: "Angela McKinley, Director." Picking up her Bible, she adjusted the wisteria plaque next to it and headed to the dining hall. Her heart swelled until it threatened to burst from her chest. She shot a look heavenward and asked God for direction for the Bible study she was about to lead.

Someone tugged on her skirt. It was Kia peeking out through overgrown bangs. She threw her arms around Angela's legs.

"Angel!"

Acknowledgments

A sincere thank you to the many who assisted and encouraged
me, with a special thank you to the following:

Beta readers:
Joanna Burke, Karen Graham, Rebekah Graham, Sue Grout,
Linda Gunderson, Miriam Neff

Coaches:
Jerry Jenkins, DiAnn Mills

Editing:
Lana Christian

Prayer Team:
Jonna Burke, Sue Grout, Linda Gunderson, Karen Ingle,
LaDonna Mourning, Teri VanWyhe, Gina Westra

Content Contributors:
Rochelle Inches, Polly Ness, David Friese,
Deputy Jen Hofschulte

Made in the USA
Monee, IL
20 July 2023

39372044R10267